ALICE C.
DESIRE TO KILL

ALICE Campbell (1887-1955) came originally from Atlanta, Georgia, where she was part of the socially prominent Ormond family. She moved to New York City at the age of nineteen and quickly became a socialist and women's suffragist. Later she moved to Paris, marrying the American-born artist and writer James Lawrence Campbell, with whom she had a son in 1914.

Just before World War One, the family left France for England, where the couple had two more children, a son and a daughter. Campbell wrote crime fiction until 1950, though many of her novels continued to have French settings. She published her first work (*Juggernaut*) in 1928. She wrote nineteen detective novels during her career.

MYSTERIES BY ALICE CAMPBELL

1. *Juggernaut* (1928)
2. *Water Weed* (1929)
3. *Spiderweb* (1930)
4. *The Click of the Gate* (1932)
5. *The Murder of Caroline Bundy* (1933)
6. *Desire to Kill* (1934)
7. *Keep Away from Water!* (1935)
8. *Death Framed in Silver* (1937)
9. *Flying Blind* (1938)
10. *A Door Closed Softly* (1939)
11. *They Hunted a Fox* (1940)
12. *No Murder of Mine* (1941)
13. *No Light Came On* (1942)
14. *Ringed with Fire* (1943)
15. *Travelling Butcher* (1944)
16. *The Cockroach Sings* (1946)
17. *Child's Play* (1947)
18. *The Bloodstained Toy* (1948)
19. *The Corpse Had Red Hair* (1950)

ALICE CAMPBELL

DESIRE TO KILL

With an introduction
by Curtis Evans

DEAN STREET PRESS

Published by Dean Street Press 2022

Copyright © 1934 Alice Campbell

Introduction copyright © 2022 Curtis Evans

All Rights Reserved

The right of Alice Campbell to be identified as the Author of the Work has been asserted by her estate in accordance with the Copyright, Designs and Patents Act 1988.

First published in 1934 by W. Collins & Sons

Cover by DSP

ISBN 978 1 915014 96 2

www.deanstreetpress.co.uk

To

Valentine Williams

ALICE IN MURDERLAND

CRIME WRITER ALICE CAMPBELL, THE OTHER "AC"

IN 1927 Alice Dorothy Ormond Campbell—a thirty-nine-year-old native of Atlanta, Georgia who for the last fifteen years had lived successively in New York, Paris and London, never once returning to the so-called Empire City of the South, published her first novel, an unstoppable crime thriller called *Juggernaut*, selling the serialization rights to the *Chicago Tribune* for $4000 ($60,000 today), a tremendous sum for a brand new author. On its publication in January 1928, both the book and its author caught the keen eye of Bessie S. Stafford, society page editor of the *Atlanta Constitution*. Back when Alice Ormond, as she was then known, lived in Atlanta, Miss Bessie breathlessly informed her readers, she had been "an ethereal blonde-like type of beauty, extremely popular, and always thought she was in love with somebody. She took high honors in school; and her gentleness of manner and breeding bespoke an aristocratic lineage. She grew to a charming womanhood—"

Let us stop Miss Bessie right there, because there is rather more to the story of Alice Campbell, the mystery genre's other "AC," who published nineteen crime novels between 1928 and 1950. Allow me to plunge boldly forward with the tale of Atlanta's great Golden Age crime writer, who as an American expatriate in England, went on to achieve fame and fortune as an atmospheric writer of murder and mystery and become one of the early members of the Detection Club.

Alice Campbell's lineage was distinguished. Alice was born in Atlanta on November 29, 1887, the youngest of the four surviving children of prominent Atlantans James Ormond IV and Florence Root. Both of Alice's grandfathers had been wealthy Atlanta merchants who settled in the city in the years before the American Civil War. Alice's uncles, John Wellborn Root and Walter Clark Root, were noted architects, while her brothers, Sidney James and Walter Emanuel Ormond, were respectively a drama critic and political writer for the *Atlanta Constitution* and an attorney and justice of the peace. Both brothers died untimely deaths before Alice had even turned thirty, as did her uncle John Wellborn Root and her father.

Alice precociously published her first piece of fiction, a fairy story, in the *Atlanta Constitution* in 1897, when she was nine years old. Four years later, the ambitious child was said to be in the final stage of completing a two-volume novel. In 1907, by which time she was nineteen, Alice relocated to New York City, chaperoned by Florence.

In New York Alice became friends with writers Inez Haynes Irwin, a prominent feminist, and Jacques Futrelle, the creator of "The Thinking Machine" detective who was soon to go down with the ship on RMS *Titanic,* and scored her first published short story in *Ladies Home Journal* in 1911. Simultaneously she threw herself pell-mell into the causes of women's suffrage and equal pay for equal work. The same year she herself became engaged, but this was soon broken off and in February 1913 Alice sailed to Paris with her mother to further her cultural education.

Three months later in Paris, on May 22, 1913, twenty-five-year-old Alice married James Lawrence Campbell, a twenty-four-year-old theatrical agent of good looks and good family from Virginia. Jamie, as he was known, had arrived in Paris a couple of years earlier, after a failed stint in New York City as an actor. In Paris he served, more successfully, as an agent for prominent New York play brokers Arch and Edgar Selwyn.

After the wedding Alice Ormond Campbell, as she now was known, remained in Paris with her husband Jamie until hostilities between France and Germany loomed the next year. At this point the couple prudently relocated to England, along with their newborn son, James Lawrence Campbell, Jr., a future artist and critic. After the war the Campbells, living in London, bought an attractive house in St. John's Wood, London, where they established a literary and theatrical salon. There Alice oversaw the raising of the couple's two sons, Lawrence and Robert, and their daughter, named Chita Florence Ormond ("Ormond" for short), while Jamie spent much of his time abroad, brokering play productions in Paris, New York and other cities.

Like Alice, Jamie harbored dreams of personal literary accomplishment; and in 1927 he published a novel entitled *Face Value,* which for a brief time became that much-prized thing by publishers, a putatively "scandalous" novel that gets Talked About. The story of a gentle orphan boy named Serge, the son an emigre Russian prostitute, who grows up in a Parisian "disorderly house," as reviews often blushingly put it, *Face Value* divided critics, but ended up on American bestseller lists. The success of his first novel led to the author being invited out to Hollywood to work as a scriptwriter, and his name appears on credits to a trio of films in 1927-28, including *French Dressing,* a "gay" divorce comedy set among sexually scatterbrained Americans in Paris. One wonders whether in Hollywood Jamie ever came across future crime writer Cornell Woolrich, who was scripting there too at the time.

Alice remained in England with the children, enjoying her own literary splash with her debut thriller *Juggernaut*, which concerned the murderous machinations of an inexorably ruthless French Riviera society doctor, opposed by a valiant young nurse. The novel racked up rave reviews and sales in the UK and US, in the latter country spurred on by its nationwide newspaper serialization, which promised readers

> . . . the open door to adventure! *Juggernaut* by Alice Campbell will sweep you out of the humdrum of everyday life into the gay, swift-moving Arabian-nights existence of the Riviera!

London's *Daily Mail* declared that the irresistible *Juggernaut* "should rank among the 'best sellers' of the year"; and, sure enough, *Juggernaut*'s English publisher, Hodder & Stoughton, boasted, several months after the novel's English publication in July 1928, that they already had run through six printings in an attempt to satisfy customer demand. In 1936 *Juggernaut* was adapted in England as a film vehicle for horror great Boris Karloff, making it the only Alice Campbell novel filmed to date. The film was remade in England under the title *The Temptress* in 1949.

Water Weed (1929) and *Spiderweb* (1930) (*Murder in Paris* in the US), the immediate successors, held up well to their predecessor's performance. Alice chose this moment to return for a fortnight to Atlanta, ostensibly to visit her sister, but doubtlessly in part to parade through her hometown as a conquering, albeit commercial, literary hero. And who was there to welcome Alice in the pages of the *Constitution* but Bessie S. Stafford, who pronounced Alice's hair still looked like spun gold while her eyes remarkably had turned an even deeper shade of blue. To Miss Bessie, Alice imparted enchanting tales of salon chats with such personages as George Bernard Shaw, Lady Asquith, H. G. Wells and (his lover) Rebecca West, the latter of whom a simpatico Alice met and conversed with frequently. Admitting that her political sympathies in England "inclined toward the conservatives," Alice yet urged "the absolute necessity of having two strong parties." English women, she had been pleased to see, evinced more informed interest in politics than their American sisters.

Alice, Miss Bessie declared, diligently devoted every afternoon to her writing, shutting her study door behind her "as a sign that she is not to be interrupted." This commitment to her craft enabled Alice to produce an additional sixteen crime novels between 1932 and 1950, beginning with *The Click of the Gate* and ending with *The Corpse Had Red Hair*.

Altogether nearly half of Alice's crime novels were standalones, in contravention of convention at this time, when series sleuths were so popular. In *The Click of the Gate* the author introduced one of her main recurring characters, intrepid Paris journalist Tommy Rostetter, who appears in three additional novels: *Desire to Kill* (1934), *Flying Blind* (1938) and *The Bloodstained Toy* (1948). In the two latter novels, Tommy appears with Alice's other major recurring character, dauntless Inspector Headcorn of Scotland Yard, who also pursues murderers and other malefactors in *Death Framed in Silver* (1937), *They Hunted a Fox* (1940), *No Murder of Mine* (1941) and *The Cockroach Sings* (1946) (*With Bated Breath* in the US).

Additional recurring characters in Alice's books are Geoffrey Macadam and Catherine West, who appear in *Spiderweb* and *No Light Came On* (1942), and Colin Ladbrooke, who appears in *Death Framed in Silver*, *A Door Closed Softly* (1939) and *They Hunted a Fox*. In the latter two books Colin with his romantic interest Alison Young and in the first and third book with Inspector Headcorn, who also appears, as mentioned, in *Flying Blind* and *The Bloodstained Toy* with Tommy Rosstetter, making Headcorn the connecting link in this universe of sleuths, although the inspector does not appear with Geoffrey Macadam and Catherine West. It is all a rather complicated state of criminal affairs; and this lack of a consistent and enduring central sleuth character in Alice's crime fiction may help explain why her work faded in the Fifties, after the author retired from writing.

Be that as it may, Alice Campbell is a figure of significance in the history of crime fiction. In a 1946 review of *The Cockroach Sings* in the London *Observer*, crime fiction critic Maurice Richardson asserted that "[s]he belongs to the atmospheric school, of which one of the outstanding exponents was the late Ethel Lina White," the author of *The Wheel Spins* (1936), famously filmed in 1938, under the title *The Lady Vanishes*, by director Alfred Hitchcock. This "atmospheric school," as Richardson termed it, had more students in the demonstrative United States than in the decorous United Kingdom, to be sure, the United States being the home of such hugely popular suspense writers as Mary Roberts Rinehart and Mignon Eberhart, to name but a couple of the most prominent examples.

Like the novels of the American Eber-Rinehart school and English authors Ethel Lina White and Marie Belloc Lowndes, the latter the author of the acknowledged landmark 1911 thriller *The Lodger*, Alice Campbell's books are not pure puzzle detective tales, but rather broader mysteries which put a premium on the storytelling imperatives of atmosphere and suspense. "She could not be unexciting if she tried," raved the *Times Literary Supplement* of Alice, stressing the author's remoteness from the so-called "Humdrum" school of detective fiction headed by British authors Freeman Wills Crofts, John Street and J. J. Connington. However, as Maurice Richardson, a great fan of Alice's crime writing, put it, "she generally binds her homework together with a reasonable plot," so the "Humdrum" fans out there need not be put off by what American detective novelist S. S. Van Dine, creator of Philo Vance, dogmatically dismissed as "literary dallying." In her novels Alice Campbell offered people bone-rattling good reads, which explains their popularity in the past and their revival today. Lines from a review of her 1941 crime novel *No Murder of Mine* by "H.V.A." in the *Hartford Courant* suggests the general nature of her work's appeal: "The excitement and mystery of this Class A shocker start on page 1 and continue right to the end of the book. You won't put it down, once you've begun it. And if you like romance mixed with your thrills, you'll find it here."

The protagonist of *No Murder of Mine* is Rowan Wilde, "an attractive young American girl studying in England." Frequently in her books Alice, like the great Anglo-American author Henry James, pits ingenuous but goodhearted Americans, male or female, up against dangerously sophisticated Europeans, drawing on autobiographical details from her and Jamie's own lives. Many of her crime novels, which often are lengthier than the norm for the period, recall, in terms of their length and content, the Victorian sensation novel, which seemingly had been in its dying throes when the author was a precocious child; yet, in their emphasis on morbid psychology and their sexual frankness, they also anticipate the modern crime novel. One can discern this tendency most dramatically, perhaps, in the engrossing *Water Weed*, concerning a sexual affair between a middle-aged Englishwoman and a young American man that has dreadful consequences, and *Desire to Kill*, about murder among a clique of decadent bohemians in Paris. In both of these mysteries the exploration of aberrant sexuality is striking. Indeed, in its depiction of sexual psychosis *Water Weed* bears rather more resemblance to, say, the crime novels of Patricia Highsmith than it does to the cozy mysteries of Patricia Wentworth. One might well term it Alice Campbell's *Deep Water*.

In this context it should be noted that in 1935 Alice Campbell authored a sexual problem play, *Two Share a Dwelling*, which the *New York*

Times described as a "grim, vivid, psychological treatment of dual personality." Although it ran for only twenty-two performances during October 8-26 at the West End's celebrated St. James' Theatre, the play had done well on its provincial tour and it received a standing ovation from the audience on opening night at the West End, primarily on account of the compelling performance of the half-Jewish German stage actress Grete Mosheim, who had fled Germany two years earlier and was making her English stage debut in the play's lead role of a schizophrenic, sexually compulsive woman. Mosheim was described as young and "blondely beautiful," bringing to mind the author herself.

Unfortunately priggish London critics were put off by the play's morbid sexual subject, which put Alice in an impossible position. One reviewer scathingly observed that "Miss Alice Campbell . . . has chosen to give her audience a study in pathology as a pleasant method of spending the evening. . . . one leaves the theatre rather wishing that playwrights would leave medical books on their shelves." Another sniffed that "it is to be hoped that the fashion of plumbing the depths of Freudian theory for dramatic fare will not spread. It is so much more easy to be interested in the doings of the sane." The play died a quick death in London and its author went back, for another fifteen years, to "plumbing the depths" in her crime fiction.

What impelled Alice Campbell, like her husband, to avidly explore human sexuality in her work? Doubtless their writing reflected the temper of modern times, but it also likely was driven by personal imperatives. The child of an unhappy marriage who at a young age had been deprived of a father figure, Alice appears to have wanted to use her crime fiction to explore the human devastation wrought by disordered lives. Sadly, evidence suggests that discord had entered the lives of Alice and Jamie by the 1930s, as they reached middle age and their children entered adulthood. In 1939, as the Second World War loomed, Alice was residing in rural southwestern England with her daughter Ormond at a cottage—the inspiration for her murder setting in *No Murder of Mine*, one guesses—near the bucolic town of Beaminster, Dorset, known for its medieval Anglican church and its charming reference in a poem by English dialect poet William Barnes:

> Sweet Be'mi'ster, that bist a-bound
> By green and woody hills all round,
> Wi'hedges, reachen up between
> A thousand vields o' zummer green.

Alice's elder son Lawrence was living, unemployed, in New York City at this time and he would enlist in the US Army when the country entered the war a couple of years later, serving as a master sergeant throughout the conflict. In December 1939, twenty-three-year-old Ormond, who seems to have herself preferred going by the name Chita, wed the prominent antiques dealer, interior decorator, home restorer and racehorse owner Ernest Thornton-Smith, who at the age of fifty-eight was fully thirty-five years older than she. Antiques would play a crucial role in Alice's 1944 wartime crime novel *Travelling Butcher*, which blogger Kate Jackson at *Cross Examining Crime* deemed "a thrilling read." The author's most comprehensive wartime novel, however, was the highly-praised *Ringed with Fire* (1943). Native Englishman S. Morgan-Powell, the dean of Canadian drama critics, in the *Montreal Star* pronounced *Ringed with Fire* one of the "best spy stories the war has produced," adding, in one of Alice's best notices:

> "Ringed with Fire" begins with mystery and exudes mystery from every chapter. Its clues are most ingeniously developed, and keep the reader guessing in all directions. For once there is a mystery which will, I think, mislead the most adroit and experienced of amateur sleuths. Some time ago there used to be a practice of sealing up the final section of mystery stores with the object of stirring up curiosity and developing the detective instinct among readers. If you sealed up the last forty-two pages of "Ringed with Fire" and then offered a prize of $250 to the person who guessed the mystery correctly, I think that money would be as safe as if you put it in victory bonds.

A few years later, on the back of the dust jacket to the American edition of Alice's *The Cockroach Sings* (1946), which Random House, her new American publisher, less queasily titled *With Bated Breath*, readers learned a little about what the author had been up to during the late war and its recent aftermath: "I got used to oil lamps. . . . and also to riding nine miles in a crowded bus once a week to do the shopping—if there was anything to buy. We thought it rather a lark then, but as a matter of fact we are still suffering from all sorts of shortages and restrictions." Jamie Campbell, on the other hand, spent his war years in Santa Barbara, California. It is unclear whether he and Alice ever lived together again.

Alice remained domiciled for the rest of her life in Dorset, although she returned to London in 1946, when she was inducted into the Detection Club. A number of her novels from this period, all of which were published in England by the Collins Crime Club, more resemble, in tone and form, classic detective fiction, such as *They Hunted a Fox* (1940). This event may have been a moment of triumph for the author, but it was also something of a last hurrah. After 1946 she published only three more crime novels, including the entertaining Tommy Rostetter-Inspector Headcorn mashup *The Bloodstained Toy*, before retiring in 1950. She lived out the remaining five years of her life quietly at her home in the coastal city of Bridport, Dorset, expiring "suddenly" on November 27, 1955, two days before her sixty-eighth birthday. Her brief death notice in the *Daily Telegraph* refers to her only as the "very dear mother of Lawrence, Chita and Robert."

Jamie Campbell had died in 1954 aged sixty-five. Earlier in the year his play *The Praying Mantis*, billed as a "naughty comedy by James Lawrence Campbell," scored hits at the Q Theatre in London and at the Dolphin Theatre in Brighton. (A very young Joan Collins played the eponymous man-eating leading role at the latter venue.) In spite of this, Jamie near the end of the year checked into a hotel in Cannes and fatally imbibed poison. The American consulate sent the report on Jamie's death to Chita in Maida Vale, London, and to Jamie's brother Colonel George Campbell in Washington, D. C., though not to Alice. This was far from the Riviera romance that the publishers of *Juggernaut* had long ago promised. Perhaps the "humdrum of everyday life" had been too much with him.

Alice Campbell own work fell into obscurity after her death, with not one of her novels being reprinted in English for more than seven decades. Happily the ongoing revival of vintage English and American mystery fiction from the twentieth century is rectifying such cases of criminal neglect. It may well be true that it "is impossible not to be thrilled by Edgar Wallace," as the great thriller writer's publishers pronounced, but let us not forget that, as Maurice Richardson put it: "We can always do with Mrs. Alice Campbell." Mystery fans will now have nineteen of them from which to choose—a veritable embarrassment of felonious riches, all from the hand of the other AC.

Curtis Evans

PROLOGUE

ON THE upper floor of a luxurious apartment, near the prow of the Ile St. Louis, a woman, stout, middle-aged and American, suddenly woke up. In the profound stillness she could just hear the waters of the Seine faintly swishing along the quais. Very late, she hazily decided—or else very early. In either case, why was her reading-lamp turned on?

As her hand brushed the smooth cover of a book, her question was answered. Of course! She had dropped asleep over a particularly abstruse work on philosophy; and when she recalled whose the work was, an unreasoning, half-guilty qualm darted through her.

Wide awake now, she glanced at her watch, to find it had run down for want of winding. Surely, she thought, it was much later than eleven-thirty, with no sound coming from the salon. Perhaps, forsooth, the party downstairs had trooped off to some shady night-haunt to prolong celebrations till daybreak. It was a usual proceeding on the part of the girl she had rashly engaged to shepherd into quieter ways. As though she, or any one else, were equal to such a task! As well try to bridle a wild mustang. . . . Still, with a certain personage in town, and likely to hear the concierge's complaint, ought she, the chaperone, to have indulged her feelings by going to bed? Possibly not; but it was hard lines for a slaving editress, in her rush time, too, to stay on deck till all hours. Not at all as though she were being paid for the job.

What was the hour? She might as well make certain—or, better still, see if that tiresome Dodo had come up.

She slid her plump feet into mules, flung a dressing-gown round her, and crept along a passage to peep, very cautiously, into another room. No one there. A faint misgiving assailed her, especially when she noticed the subdued light coming up from the crystal chandelier in the hall below. She leant over the balustrade and listened. Not a stir.

"Why should I trouble about her?" she muttered crossly. "I can't be expected to . . . ugh! Is there a draught somewhere? Perhaps I'd better go see."

Hugging her peignoir closer, she started downstairs, feeling as she neared the bottom a current of air chill and dank as the breath of a charnel-pit blow against her ankles. Why—the front door was open! What carelessness! Not actually risky, of course, for the street entrance was closed. It was the thought of that great sweep of stone steps curving down into the black void, of unseen things stealing upon one. . . .

She shut the door firmly, and turned towards the salon. Her hand was on the switch when the big clock of Notre Dame boomed a measured five. Five in the morning! And Dodo not yet in. . . .

Suddenly she grew tense, an expression of outraged incredulity overspreading her features. Was this breathing she heard? Yes, steady, rhythmic breathing, punctuated by a few frank snores. Good Heavens! Then they had not gone out at all. They were sleeping, the whole lot of them, heavily, stupidly. Dead to the world! Through a thick fog of cigarette-smoke she could just make out the blurred forms of men and women in evening attire, huddled in chairs, on sofas, some outstretched on the floor. Helpless, grotesque, not one moved at her approach. She gasped, tightened her lips, and eyed them with deep repugnance.

Now she was angry, realising the trick that had been played on her. A trick, yes—for in normal circumstances dinner guests do not succumb to slumber in this fashion, and, besides, these travelling rugs and extra cushions showed premeditation. Dodo herself had planned this escapade. That was what she was up to when, the instant she knew no curbing influence was to be on hand, she had flown to telephone her star-guest. Bullied him into complaisance.

To confirm the assumption, the gross, heavy-limbed figure sprawled across the hearth-rug was sleeping as soundly as the rest. Why hadn't she guessed? Only a fool would have been blind to what was in the air when Dodo took up with this sinister charlatan. Where, oh, where, did Agatha's child get her depraved tastes? That wretched gigolo, for instance—though there was less harm in all his sort put together than in this other, dominant male, who, according to report had wrought havoc with scores of weak sensation seekers. He was evil personified, a menace to sanity. Tommy Rostetter might shrug, but all the same . . .

Was that Tommy's sleek black head propped against a chair? Good scout, Tommy, to fill her vacant place at a moment's notice; only how was it he had fallen in with this unpleasant scheme? And the young girl, her fellow-country-woman, about whom she had felt vaguely anxious—where was she?

Failing to locate her, she concentrated on her youthful charge, who with characteristic selfishness had taken possession of the one comfortable couch. Full-blown, careless, she lay in a swirl of tumbled chiffon, dark hair clinging moistly to her forehead, right arm dangling loose with the fingertips just grazing the carpet. Lips parted—but how quietly she slept! Uncanny, this. Probably neither she nor the others could be roused. Physical disgust made the watcher draw her skirts aside to avoid contact with a black-clad body as she bent down to touch the bare arm from which she could have sworn the stored heat pulsed.

A shock greeted her. The flesh was clammy! Had the girl fainted? This was no ordinary sleep. It couldn't be. Quick, the lamp!

She knocked over a cluttered ash-tray. The next instant orange light flooded down to disclose a dark circle of wetness soaked into the damask couch, flimsy draperies sticky and crimson. Wine, it must be wine, spilled by a reckless hand. She rubbed her fingers over the spot, held them to her nostrils, then stiffened all over, throat too constricted to scream.

Wine? Good God, no! It was blood.

CHAPTER I

THOMAS Rostetter cast his eye glumly round the table and decided he had seldom encountered a collection of human creatures which pleased him less. The pervading sleekness and vapidity, varied here and there by a precociousness he found even more detestable, made him long to smite, one after another, the self-satisfied faces. Could a glimpse of the near future have been granted him, it is quite likely he would have flung down his napkin and bolted headlong into the night. As it was, less occult than hungry, he sighed with resignation and helped himself bountifully to the excellent caviare.

After all, he reflected in mollified strain, here at his elbow was an oasis in the desert of boredom—a girl refreshing to view, with crisp tulle ruffles throwing into relief the precise combination of dark-red, satin-smooth hair and apple-blossom skin which had always won his admiration. Who was she? Oh, yes, to be sure! She was the girl he had been instructed to look after. Well, he was willing enough to do it, seeing how utterly different she was from her jaded companions; but did she require his services? Serene, assured, and, despite the story he had recently heard, buoyantly gay, she was entirely engrossed in the weary Russian on her right. If she was drinking just a little too much champagne, he could hardly be expected to tap her on the shoulder and beg her to desist. Once only had he seen her before to-night. Probably he would never meet her again. Indeed, his being here at all was a matter of chance and weak-mindedness in not being able to say "No" to a woman's request.

That the woman in question was Helen Roderick, the hearty-voiced editress of *L'Étoile*, and his friend since the de Bertincourt mix-up, offered some slight excuse, for Helen was not one to take "No" when what she wanted was "Yes." He had his London article to finish? Well, and what of it? A journalist with his small regard for truth could dash off three thousand words in no time. Besides, she was in bed with a splitting headache, and must by hook or crook lay hands on a substitute to take her place at dinner. Otherwise there'd be thirteen, and the girl she was chaperoning was horribly superstitious. No, she was not at home. Her apartment was still let, and she was staying on the Ile St. Louis. Dinner was at eight. Black tie. Now hustle! The receiver banged down, cutting short his protests.

Eternally good-natured, Tommy hustled, to such purpose that half an hour later he could have been seen, shaven and scrubbed to a tingling rosiness, bare, black head gleaming with brilliantine and round blue eyes surveying the world with bland cheerfulness, rushing his two-seater round the squat towers of Notre Dame, over the bridge, and into the nostalgic calm of the farther island. It was the fag-end of September; and an evening warm, still, with the softening haze and pause of fruition which bring to mind the bloom on purple grapes. Paris's down-at-heel season; but here, between the divided waters of the Seine the air held little taint of stale petrol, while the traffic honking and fretting its way along the opposite quais seemed remote, like the echo of a former life.

Another echo, or so he had thought, was the stately, ivy-clad house before which he alighted. He knew it well, even to the mouldy green fountain plashing in the court, and the urn-filled niches along the staircase, but though he racked his brain he could not remember who amongst his old acquaintances had once lived here.

Nor could he place the elderly, Italian butler who, one flight up, stood framed in a lofty doorway, gazing respectfully upon him with lashless eyes as hard and opaque as brown marbles. Undoubtedly he had seen this man before. The grey, cropped skull and dried, ascetic features were every bit as familiar as the building itself. It was not even surprising to find himself addressed in perfect English, when he was informed that Miss Roderick would like to see him, and would he kindly step this way?

Still groping amidst elusive associations, Tommy followed his guide up a fine sweep of interior stairs to a gorgeous bedroom, where in a carved four-poster he beheld Helen Roderick snugly ensconced, wearing smart black satin pyjamas. For a second it crossed his mind she was shamming illness. That scrupulously-waved grey hair, those lips pencilled a vivid magenta, looked remarkably spruce. Then he noticed that her prominent eyes, so exactly like the eyes of a friendly bulldog, held a lurking hint of perturbation.

"Well, well!" he began blithely. "And what's your complaint?"

"Migraine," she croaked in her rich, husky voice. "And—a touch of cold feet. You see, I've had about all I can stand of Dodo's parties. They knock me up. I had to yell for help."

"Dodo?" Tommy echoed pleasantly. "And who's she?"

"English girl I'm giving an eye to—for my sins. Dorinda Quarles. You know her, of course?"

With a child-like smile Tommy replied, "By reputation. Who doesn't?" At the same time he experienced a mild astonishment.

Helen sighed. "Too bad, isn't it? So young, too, not yet twenty-one. . . . Her mother happened to be my closest friend. This was her apartment. Benedetto, who let you in, was her butler. Dodo stays here when she's in Paris, though the place actually belongs to—"

"Hold on!" cried Tommy, smiting his brow. "Lady Agatha Quarles! I knew I'd been here, though the time I speak of was fifteen years ago, before her second marriage. Let's see: Whom did she marry?"

Helen bulged at him. "Don't you know? And a celebrity, too. Why, the whole world's singing his praises. Look! Here you are."

She pushed towards him a navy-blue volume bearing the gold-lettered legend, *Beyond Relativity*. Tommy goggled at it while with a tinge of awe in her voice Helen continued, "An absolute saint, too, if ever there was one. Always patient, always devoted, although the whole three years of their life together poor Agatha was a chronic invalid. She worshipped him, naturally. Any woman would."

"Basil Jethro?" muttered her visitor, still unbelieving. "Chap who got the Sorbonne presentation this afternoon, big noise at Oxford, special chair and all the rest of it? But—Dorinda Quarles' step-father! Whew! It's like saying the Angel Gabriel and Moll Flanders!"

"S'sh! Don't talk so loud. . . . The child's not so black as she's painted. Headstrong, blatant, but she's big-hearted, generous to a fault. What I chiefly hold against her is her brutal treatment of Basil. Till she's of age he's her guardian and trustee, but beyond minding her affairs he's long since given up trying to curb her. Hopeless, you know, and so mortifying for him. How can a man of his type, living in such a rarified atmosphere that he makes you think—well, of the stars—cope with a minx who flaunts his authority, rails against him, and constantly humiliates him?"

If one credited but half the gossip current about the shameless Dorinda the situation leaped to the eye. The girl was by all accounts coarse, flamboyant, untrammeled by scruples or breeding: indiscriminate in love, and with a capacity for drink which had led her to the open boast that, like a certain gentleman of Half-Moon Street, she never breakfasted, but was sick at eleven. . . .

"I lunched with Basil a month ago," explained Helen guardedly. "At his villa in Cap Ferrat: and fool that I was I promised him to take Dodo under my wing for a bit, just while my apartment is let. I said I'd do my best with her, but never did I dream Basil would arrive in Paris and turn up at this flat on the eve of one of her parties. Yes," with a nervous glance at the door, "he's on this floor now—not stopping, thank God, only collecting some of his books to take away—but if he hangs about much longer he'll run into some of her pals. Bannister Mowbray, for example. That would just finish me! But in God's name, what can I do?"

"Bannister Mowbray!" repeated Tommy, his flax-flower blue eyes very bland. "I heard he was in town. So she's annexed him, has she?"

"She annexes every shady person within reach. Oh, I know the sort of name he's got! That's why, feeling unequal to this myself, I got hold of you. I thought you'd exert a sane, steadying influence."

"Thanks," said Tommy dryly.

"No, I mean it. The man can't do anything, of course, but the general atmosphere surrounding him . . . some of the others, too, aren't exactly my choice. There's one, though, who doesn't belong to the regular crowd. It was about her I wanted to speak to you. Remember a rather charming little American, with red hair, whom I introduced to you one day in the Champs Elysées? Dinah Blake, does those clever drawings for *L'Étoile*?"

"Um-m—yes. What about her?"

"Just look after her a bit, will you? Not that she'd ever make any kind of scene. Oh, no! But the truth of the matter is, I strongly suspect young Dodo of doing the dirty on her over a man she was going to marry. It's that good-looking Christopher Loughton, in the American Embassy. Well, directly Dinah got back from her summer holiday, she broke off with him, and—oh, it's a wretched business!"

The situation seemed to be as follows: Three weeks ago Helen returned one afternoon to find Miss Blake waiting to see her about forthcoming work, and, going into the salon, discovered her caller, the latter's fiancé, and—Dorinda Quarles.

"I saw at once that Dinah'd come on those two unexpectedly, and guessed what was going on between them. Yes, she and Dodo were acquaintances, fellow-students at Colorossi's, and they're still friendly—on the surface. Dinah's got terrific pride. She'd die sooner than let anyone suspect her reason for breaking her engagement, and to be quite fair I'm positive Dodo never thinks of herself as the cause. Utterly casual as she is, Dodo couldn't understand attaching importance to these fleeting episodes. For her Loughton's a back number, wiped out. A gigolo's got the floor, and good luck to him! But Dinah's feelings go deeper. I can swear she hasn't forgotten. If she's coming here to-night, it's just a magnificent gesture, but all the same . . ."

Not greatly interested, Tommy had picked up the Jethro book and was glancing idly at the portrait frontispiece. The face which confronted him was nobly austere, cut like a cameo, and, almost ethereal in its refinement, suggested the recluse, far removed from worldly concerns. The eyes, slightly Mongoloid in cast, had the contemplative vision which penetrated through an object to abstract principles beyond. The owner of such eyes, thought Tommy, could readily enough be associated with the fine-spun mathematical sequences contained in this treatise; but how hard it was to think of him as ministering to an ailing wife or shouldering the responsibility of an outrageous step child! Fate plays queer tricks. . . .

A door was heard to close. Helen started with nervous relief.

"There! Basil's just going." She mopped her brow with a handkerchief soaked in eau-de-cologne, and motioned him to depart "Get along down, quick, so he can see Dodo has at least one respectable man friend. Don't hate me for dragging you here. The dinner'll be good, anyhow."

Somewhat envious of her comfortable state, he prepared to obey orders; but in the passage he paused, arrested by an abusive tirade coming from the staircase and uttered in a rough contralto voice which he knew instinctively belonged to Dorinda Quarles. Whom was she addressing? Not, surely the apostle of pure reason, honoured throughout two continents; but as he caught the reply, low, restrained, and charged with fastidious shrinking, his incredulity vanished. It was the philosopher who answered, and with what patience, what perfect breeding!

"Dorinda! Please! I merely wished to know if the five hundred I've just placed to your account will be sufficient for your immediate needs. As I'm returning to Oxford to-morrow I shall not be seeing you again."

"Sufficient!" The word was snatched up and flung back with violent contempt. "Since when have you bothered two straws about my needs? Why this amazing solicitude all of a sudden? Eh, what's it all about?"

There followed a protest, still evenly courteous, which for some obscure reason seemed to lash the hearer to greater fury.

"Oh, stow it, blast you! What do I care? Only six weeks more, and after that I shan't have to come crawling to you to settle my bills. God! What a release that'll be!"

"And for me as well, Dorinda."

The unseen listener was struck by the quiet poignance of this retort, which, however, failed to impress its recipient. Instead, evidently intent on her own train of thought, she burst into a malicious laugh.

"Oho! I've got it!" she cried triumphantly. "You're upset over that question I put to you—the one you've never answered. Well, how about it? Why did she send for Macadam? Oh, I know she never saw him; but why did she send? Explain that if you can."

She seemed bent on tormenting a victim too proud to retaliate—an instance of stupid brutality which made Tommy's blood boil. Small wonder it was met by a tone of chilled exhaustion.

"All this is rather baffling. You must give me some better idea of what you mean; but need we discuss it now? It is hardly the place or the time for—"

"Time, time! You do a lot of gassing about Time, don't you? Take my advice, save it for those lovely, white-livered undergrads of yours—little tin god on a pedestal! It'll mean something to them—and it'll mean something to you, too, one of these days, if you don't keep clear of me. But if you want to go, go! I'm keeping my ammunition till I see the whites of your eyes. . . ."

With a turbulent flounce the wench was gone. As soon as the dignified step had continued its way, Tommy emerged and with some diffidence followed in its wake, so bent on prospecting to left and right that he failed to notice the suit-case set on the bottom tread till he had knocked it over. Supposing the latter to be Jethro's property—doubtless it contained the books mentioned by Helen—he picked it up to restore it to its former position; but just then the owner came from behind the stairs, hat in hand, and relieved him of it, levelling meanwhile a reserved but keen glance in his direction.

"Thank you, that is mine. I was about to take it with me."

Easy to read the meaning of that questioning scrutiny. Basil Jethro was sensitively anxious to know if this visitor, suddenly materialised from nowhere, had overheard the mortifying scene just passed. It being impossible to offer verbal reassurance, Tommy smiled detachedly and studied the other with brief, sympathetic curiosity.

What he saw was a man of perhaps fifty, taller than himself, but with the slight stoop and muscular slackness which attend the sedentary life; features of distinction if not actual beauty, above which dark hair threaded with grey receded from a high forehead. The parchment skin, creased all over in delicate lines, must normally be extremely pallid, though at the moment the cheekbones were stained a dull red, outward sign of an annoyance repressed but still rankling. The lips, fuller than might have been expected, puckered towards the centre, suggesting that their owner when a child had probably sucked his thumb. The steady, hooded eyes claimed chief attention. Neither brown nor green but some indefinable colour between the two, they resembled nothing so much as smooth stones veiled by water, and as the photograph had indicated they were Mongol in form, with all the Mongol's impassivity. A little cold, they had the look of the pure idealist; and the well-bred voice exactly matched them in character.

"Good-evening" it now murmured as the tall figure moved towards the door. Tommy had a fleeting impression of fine, nervous fingers, knotted at the joints, grasping the handle of the suit-case; of a measured but elastic step, and of an impeccably-fitting morning-coat retreating from view.

The door had hardly closed before he became aware of a hard, bold gaze fixed on him from the salon, and realised that the brazen hussy he was prepared to detest had been watching him all the time. But where before had he seen this big overblown girl with the hot brown eyes glistening like an animal's, the splashes of red like spilled Burgundy in her swarthy cheeks and the strong, sun-darkened arms emerging from apricot chiffon? What was there about the strident exuberance of her good looks, full-blooded and blowsy like fruit too-hastily matured under a tropic sun, which struck a chord in his memory?

"Where did you come from?" she demanded brusquely, then, without pausing for his reply, gave a loud laugh and extended her hand with frank, disarming cordiality. "No, don't tell me! You're Helen's friend. How jolly odd we've never met till now."

He was staring back at her with fascinated intentness.

"We have met, though," he contradicted urbanely. "In this very room, too, about fifteen years ago. Don't you remember? You were in your night-gown, very busy, cramming a complete *baba au rhum* into your mouth. I restored you to your nurse, and you bit my hand."

She uttered another careless guffaw.

"No—is that so? Sounds like me, anyhow. Greedy and vicious. Well, I still am. Have a cocktail?"

Yes, thought Tommy, watching her big, expansive gestures, she's just that now, a greedy, wanton child; but in another fifteen years, what will she be?

Nine hours later it sickened him to recall the utter impossibility of envisaging her future. Future? She had none.

CHAPTER II

SOME of the guests were known to Tommy. For the most part they represented the idle flotsam of expatriates which Paris holds in a negligent grasp, asking little about them so long as they pay their bills. Five at a side, two at each end of the table, their faces were softly lit by orange-shaded candelabra, the radiance of which centred in a warm pool round a dish of purple figs and pale green grapes and left the walls of the room, hung with the late owner's Mortlock tapestries, merged in velvet dusk. The American girl and Tommy occupied one pair of the end seats, and facing them, with the length of the board between, were their boisterous hostess and the guest of honour, Bannister Mowbray.

On the latter personage Tommy bestowed close attention, wondering to what extent he justified his forbidding reputation. Gross, pallid, clumsy, he loomed up a full size larger than any of his companions—a dark man in the middle forties, with a heavy jowl, sparse hair streaked across a pear-shaped forehead, and a flattened nose terminating in a fleshy bulb. His small, muddy eyes showed secretive boredom, his chary speech an arrogant superiority little calculated, on the face of it, to attract; and yet by all accounts he possessed singular magnetism, while he could hardly be so indifferent as he appeared, or else why was he here? Tommy shrewdly assumed that he had marked down Dorinda as a promising catch—not, be it understood, in a matrimonial sense—and that this superb aloofness of his was but the gaudy may-fly baiting his hook.

What exactly was Bannister Mowbray? Difficult to separate fact from myth. Rumour had it he came of a good Highland family, his mother a Greek; that in a remote past he had been sent down from his university for dubious practices. At all events he was known to have delved deep into mysteries the normal being eschewed, and to have founded a cult which, after being hounded from place to place, was now domiciled in Corsica. Just what went on in the circle of his initiates no outsider could definitely state, but credible report declared the man's readiness to prey on the infatuated disciples who clung to him with a strange devotion.

Would the fickle Dorinda be enrolled as one of these followers? Tommy doubted it, even though at the moment she was lavishing eager attention on her new prize, scarcely noticing the slim, dark-eyed Argentine on her left, except, now and then, to rest a careless arm on his shoulder or tweak his ear with a bearish caress. The girl was devoid of coquetry. She took what she wanted, yawned, and turned elsewhere: and yet, possibly because her frank exuberance acted on one like a heady tonic, Tommy found it hard to dislike her, easy to excuse her crude shortcomings, and—but this was after his third glass of champagne—beginning to condone her treatment of Basil Jethro, on the plea that oil and water will not mix.

He took stock of the other guests. The Argentine and a callow, noisy Italian boy called Umberto he dismissed as nonentities, together with a pink-and-white English girl, Rosemary Anson, and Rita Falkland, a languishing blond who long ago had been a star at a West-end Theatre, and was now the ex-wife of the South African diamond king, Aaron Kroll. True, the last-named was decked out in most of her jewels, including the diamond marguerite and twin ropes of pearls which had caused endless litigation, and it was amusing to see Mowbray's covetous glances at the treasures which never by any chance could be wrested from their owner's grasp save over her dead body; but apart from this, the woman, empty-headed and intent on but two passions—preserving her beauty and legal tussles over her alimony—held little interest.

Slightly more provocative was the slenderly exquisite English woman with the madonna face framed in bat's wings of glistening jet hair who was placed on Mowbray's right. She was a Mrs. Cope-Villiers, familiarly known as Dick; virginal to view, and a reputed addict to cocaine, who for years had clung tenaciously to the tired, gentle Russian painter with the string-coloured hair—his name was Misha Soukine—at present conversing with Tommy's partner.

Next door to Dick Cope-Villiers was Ronald Cleeves, second son of Lord Conisbroke, and for some time past the henchman and slave of Bannister Mowbray—a young man of radiant Saxon type and an Apollo's build, whose physical perfection was marred only by a total lack of animation. Not a muscle of his face moved; even his eyes, though they frequently rested on his idol, remained blank and expressionless, as though what lay behind them was frozen in a glacier. Or no, better still, he was like a pure Greek temple, set upon a hill, complete to the last fine moulding, and never entered by man. At intervals, after the manner of boys from the same school, he and the woman next him exchanged desultory gossip. Of the other guests he took no notice.

The woman just mentioned was the soignée, rapier-edged "Cissy" Gault, daughter of Sir Adrian Gault, steamship magnate, and she for her part was intent on cold-shouldering the eager, elderly bachelor vainly clamouring for attention on her other side. Tommy could not blame her, for in his estimation Peter Hummock, some time of South Bend, Indiana, ranked as the most pestiferous social nuisance in Paris. Peter, with his crumpled face and washed-out eyes, was inescapable. Although nominally he dealt in antiques and designed tea-gowns for middle-western compatriots, he appeared to spend his entire existence in a tireless dash from one gay function to another, impervious to snubs, detailing scandal. Scorning him utterly, Tommy let his gaze wander past to the glum and taciturn Australian poetess, Maud Daventry, who was his close neighbour in the Place du Palais Bourbon, but whom he seldom encountered except on the stairs. He had nothing against her, little alluring as was her soggy complexion, mannish dinner-jacket, and untidy mop of hair invariably flecked with cigarette-ash; but as her conversation with him so far had been limited to her Borzoi's distemper, he suspected she classed him with the swine before whom she declined to cast her intellectual pearls.

Having boxed the compass, he turned again, with relief, to study the piquant profile and delicate ear of Dinah Blake. Different, yes—a hedge-rose accidentally caught up amidst stale, hot-house blooms. Meredith's phrase about the rogue in porcelain occurred to him, and going further he could even name the make of porcelain she most resembled. Old Bow, with its reticence, hinting but not stressing—that was the correct medium to convey the moulded red hair drawn into a demure chignon, the tilted nose, the brows so faintly traced, like the feathering of oars in smooth water. Eyes? He could not see them, but he knew their colour—clear, aquamarine blue, pure as crystal, and exactly matching her tulle frock which, Victorian in its primness, sheathed her small body and billowed softly to the floor.

Alert, purposeful, the girl could have nothing in common with her present associates. He felt vaguely sorry to find her here, sorrier still to note, as he now did, the feverish texture of her gaiety. Helen was probably right about her anxiety to prove she harboured no resentment against her hostess; right, too, in believing she was wretchedly unhappy, but determined not to show it. Admiring the gallant stand she was making, he felt a sudden desire to lend his support.

The opportunity of doing so came sooner than he expected.

Momentarily silent and distrait, she was staring straight ahead of her at Dorinda, who, her apricot gown slid from her shoulder, eyes swimming darkly like pools covered in heat haze, and overripe lips curved in a smile, was sprawling blowsily forward with elbows on the table. How coarse the latter looked! Almost like a handsome octaroon. The arm touching his stiffened convulsively. Glancing sideways he saw his companion's underlip caught between her teeth, her eyes contracted with a strangely concentrated look of hatred. . . .

Tommy's ire rose, oddly enough, against Loughton, the conceited under-secretary at the American Embassy, whom he regarded as the less pardonable culprit, and whom he had already a reason for wanting to thrash. Infernal puppy! But quick, something must be done, before other eyes saw what he had seen. He addressed his partner with such precipitancy that she jumped.

"Virginia?" she repeated, gay again, and turning her clear gaze full upon him. "Yes, how did you guess it? But do I expect to go back there to live? I'm afraid not. It's a heavenly place, but how could I earn a penny amongst people who still paint natural roses on dessert-plates and adore the Monarch of the Glen? My efforts would horrify them. I should end by burning the lot—as I very nearly did this afternoon."

"What restrained you?" he inquired.

"Oh—ingrained economy, I suppose. Canvases cost money. Some day I'll scrape mine and use them again."

"The chief consolation in life," remarked Tommy lightly, "is that there's nothing to hinder one from painting a new picture on an old surface."

"A new picture?" She wrinkled her nose in scorn. "Not much. If you were an artist you'd know that scraped canvases are only good for faked-up imitations. Still, who knows? I may yet turn into one of those dreary spinsters who drag easels round the Louvre copying Old Masters. Heaps of us come to it, don't we?" she demanded of her Russian neighbour.

"Not you, I promise!"

Soukine let his tired eyes rest on her comprehendingly. Queer, thought Tommy, how the fellow always seemed subtly cognisant of mental states. That kindly, exhausted sophistication, penetrating deep, never intolerant—but possibly, in this case, he knew something the girl would not wish him to know. It was supposed that she had divulged no details concerning her ruptured love affair, but the small, tongue-wagging world these people moved in was quick to read between the lines. . . .

All went smoothly, in flippant vein, till the occurrence of the incident which, for two persons, was to be fraught with such dire consequences. If only the silver grape-scissors had done their job properly! As luck would have it, the hostess, for once alive to her guests' needs, glanced across in time to see Mrs. Cope-Villiers struggling with them, and made a long arm to the sideboard behind her.

"Try this," she cried, displaying a savage-looking dirk with a handle of white bone and brass. "I'm told it's done murder, so it ought to cut a grape-stem."

"Darling!" gasped Dick, "but how rash of you! Where did you get hold of such a divine weapon?"

"Trailed a thrilling black man round and round the Toulon quais. Did my damnedest to vamp him, but all I got was his knife."

Uproarious laughter. Peter Hummock, colour-prejudice shocked but loth to reveal it, threw out an arch remark which was lost in transit. When the fruit reached Tommy, Dinah Blake's eager hand sped past him and caught up the knife.

"I must feel it! Algerian, isn't it? I love a thing like that, all scoured and bright and deadly. Look at the point! So—so *utilitarian*."

"How about a bread-knife? That's utilitarian too."

"Not like this. Tell me," she appealed to Soukine, "if you wanted to kill someone—quickly, not bungling it—where would you aim?"

"Here." The painter gravely indicated the upper edge of her bertha. "If you'd worked in a butcher's shop, as I once did—"

"A butcher's shop!" She was stroking the blade with a sort of fascination. "But what a practical experience!"

Once again, after Soukine had taken the weapon from her, she got hold of it to play with, absently—a fact which stood forth stark and unforgettable when the rest of the dinner had become a jumbled memory, though at the moment it was her slender, capable hands which drew Tommy's attention. Resolute hands, unlikely to flinch, whether it came to making a bonfire of pictures, or—but the second idea was grotesque. He thrust it from him impatiently.

"Not three! Oh, I implore you, not three cigarettes with one match!"

It was Hummock's piping voice, dramatically protesting. With a sardonic smile the poetess tendered him her lighter.

"Superstitious, eh? Then it may interest you to learn we came near being thirteen at table to-night. What would you have done—swooned in our midst?"

"Thirteen! My dear lady! And to-night of all times, just when we're about to embark on—"

"S'sh—don't spoil it. Some of them don't—" The words were lost in a grumble as the poetess lit a black cigar and began to puff stodgily.

Some of them don't—what? It was a second later that, during a sudden lull, Tommy became aware of expectant eyes fixed on Dorinda, who, with fumbling nonchalance was unwrapping something dark, gummy and odoriferous, and cutting it up into small cubes. She called loudly for a plate, and, having arranged the unappetising lumps upon it, set it in front of Mrs. Cope-Villiers.

"Now!" she exclaimed in childish triumph. "Don't ever say you've tasted this before, because you haven't. It's a grand novelty, first appearance in Paris. They serve it at feasts in Burma—or is it Siam? I forget—but never mind, it's marvellous stuff. Try a bit."

"An Indian sweet?" Dick giggled, examining a cube doubtfully. "Looks fairly foul, like those Spanish atrocities, all honey and almonds."

"More like toffee and senna-pods," put in Rosemary Anson across the table. "But what's it taste like?"

"Musty, like old boots. Not bad, and not so good. If I'm sick, it'll be on you, Ronnie! You having some of this essence of Hindoo bazaars, or is it an old story to you?"

Thus addressed, Ronald Cleeves accepted a morsel and without a flicker of expression chewed it slowly. The adjacent guests followed suit, and in due course the plate arrived at the lower end of the table. Dinah Blake and Tommy helped themselves simultaneously; but the latter, having taken a biggish cube and decided to make two bites of it, was still sampling the first half and trying to identify the odd, medicinal flavour, when, looking up, he caught Dorinda's gaze full upon him. Mingled with the fixed brilliance of slight inebriety was an impish gleam which suggested a joke was being played and the perpetrator thereof watching avidly to note the result.

He shot a rapid glance round at the other faces, and got the impression of cats intent on a mouse-hole. Dick Cope-Villiers was smiling with secret delight, the gigolo fidgeting uncomfortably, Umberto reaching for the plate with a suspiciously greedy haste. The whole atmosphere was one Tommy mistrusted. The disagreeable tales emanating from Corsica rushed before him, and he wondered uneasily if Mowbray and the daring hussy beside him had hatched a plot the nature of which was transparent to all save the American girl and himself. Unmistakably something was going on. . . .

Bending towards his partner he whispered impulsively, "I say, suppose you give that a miss. Unless I'm wholly off the track it's—"

"It's what?" The blue eyes flashed on him in surprise. "Nothing wrong, I hope? Because if so, it's too late. I've swallowed mine."

"All of it?"

"Yes, every scrap. Why, what's up?"

A shout of laughter interrupted them. Dorinda, unable to hold in any longer, burst out with her announcement.

"Know what you've eaten? Dope! Mowbray's own, particular dope! Silly asses, didn't you guess? Oh, what a gorgeous swiz! Now we're in for it—sink or swim together, every one of us. Here till morning. Like the prospect?"

Amidst the turmoil of counterfeit excitement, Dinah gasped and put her hand to her throat. With frightened eyes and cheeks suddenly pale she clutched at Tommy's sleeve.

"Did she mean that?" she whispered. "Oh! How beastly of her! I—I—what are we to do about it? Dope! It's the first time in my life I've ever—oh, oh, I—"

Tommy, inwardly raging on his own account, squeezed her fingers reassuringly. There was nothing to be done. The stuff was eaten, all but one lump left on the plate and the unconsumed portion he still held. Surreptitiously he consigned the remaining bit to the pocket of his dinner-jacket, muttering, "Listen! Let's hear what Mowbray's got to say. . . ."

"Perfectly innocuous," Mowbray was drawling in his curiously high-pitched voice. "Nothing to get worked up about—yet."

"But later on?" demanded Hummock craftily. "Ah, you wicked man, now we're in your power it's up to you to prepare us. Are we in danger of doing anything rash?"

Rita Falkland's too-golden head nodded approval. "Quite! Are we going to have disturbing hallucinations, or just oblivion?"

A look of contempt, like the shadow of a cloud passing above, rested on Ronald Cleeves' regular features. He glanced sideways at his master, who stirred lethargically, clearing his throat to speak.

"First," he explained pedantically, "you must know that this concoction is as commonly used in the East as tobacco is with us. Wealthy citizens have their private mixtures of it, as we do with China tea. The brand is a mild one, only as it's unfamiliar to you a small quantity will suffice—"

"For what?" broke in Dorinda, cracking an almond with her teeth. "Go on, tell us. Benedetto! More brandy."

"To make you feel amazingly alive. To exaggerate your perceptions of touch, taste, and so on. Time will expand. Your senses of humour will grow acute, perhaps a little distorted."

("Hashish," was Tommy's comment. "I thought as much. . . .")

"And then," pursued their mentor, fixing his torpid gaze on a candle flame, "consciousness will dull over. Drowsiness, like a delicious cloud, will close down upon you. You'll fall asleep, and you'll dream. . . ."

"What about?"

It was Dinah who fired the question. Her face still troubled, she was leaning forward, breathing quickly.

"Exactly," agreed Rosemary Anson. "Because my dreams are generally pretty unpleasant. Like walking down the Rue de la Paix in the altogether."

"My sweet!" purred Umberto, digging an amorous chin into her bare shoulder. "Would you find that unpleasant?"

"Oh, you!" she cried, pushing him off. "I know your sort of dreams. Prophet's paradise, non-stop love-making."

"And very nice, too," declared the boy, drinking from her glass. "But let's hear the man!"

"How can I foretell the nature of your dreams?" retorted Mowbray with a shrug. "They will tend toward wish-fulfilment, of course, but the character will vary with the individual. All I can predict is that if any one of you cherishes a desire ordinarily forbidden, he may—though I can't guarantee it—taste an illusory joy of accomplishment. Have I made myself clear?"

"Now I know!" whispered Peter Hummock solemnly. "I shall dream I'm sitting on my concierge's chest, pouring molten lead down his throat!"

"Hear, hear! But that's a mass dream, that is," growled Maud Daventry, along her clamped cigar.

"Dreaming in chorus," someone amplified.

Soukine glanced at Dinah. "And what denied satisfaction do you hope to attain?" he asked softly. "This is too good a chance to miss, you know."

"Me?" The girl gave a start. Despite her worried expression, she had fallen into a reverie. "Oh, just sleep. Huge doses of it. That's my one desire, and while I wouldn't have taken this means of gratifying it, I—"

She spread her small hands apart with a gesture of resignation. Her gay mask dropped, the underlying torment of her face told Tommy she had reached the point of nerve-exhaustion. He formed the sudden resolution to get her away, take her home, as soon as it could conveniently be managed—provided she would consent. How it was he never accomplished his purpose was one of the unsolved mysteries of the evening, all he recalled being that at this juncture an absurd incident put an end to serious thought.

Noisy scuffles were going on. The bony frame of the butler was seen struggling in the combined hold of Dorinda and Umberto, who were attempting to cram the last cube of the sweetmeat between his tightly-closed lips.

"Prego, prego! Molto grazie, signorina, ma non—"

Too late. With grey head ducked and eyes watering, the old man rushed from the room, followed by a hurricane of hilarity. Benedetto, the High Priest, drugged as well! What a joke! Tommy found himself caught up in the wave of general silliness.

From now on nothing seemed extraordinary, not even the fact that Dinah, her eyes glittering through the smoke haze, should be standing beside her hostess with the latter's arm flung carelessly round her. The orgy had begun. Corks popped anew, and Dorinda, hammering on a wine-glass, called for a toast. What was the name of this superb stuff, so they could drink to it?

Imperturbable as Buddha, Bannister Mowbray smiled his secret smile upon the candle flame.

"The name?" he echoed. "Well, how about—Nirvana?"

"Nir-nirvana? Splendid!" Swaying a little, Dorinda swooped on a champagne bottle to splash its contents into the empty glasses.

"Now, then, all together—Nirvana!"

"Nirvana! Nirvana!"

The word was bandied back and forth like a shuttlecock. The room turned into a kaleidoscope of shifting colours. Pandemonium broke loose.

Lone and forgotten, the Algerian dirk lay, a shimmer of pale steel, across the debris of dismembered grapes. By a perverse trick of memory, Tommy could still recall it, when other images had receded into a hopeless blur.

CHAPTER III

WITH a shattering jolt Tommy came to.

A motor smash, evidently, for a moment ago he had been spinning over the green Killarney hills, with the sun beating down on his back and larks singing in the blue air above. But why this lurid dusk, with the full moon of a face thrust pallidly into his, and ruthless hands shaking, dragging him to unwilling feet?

"Wake up!" a voice gibbered hoarsely. "It's me—Helen! Oh, for God's sake, pull yourself together! Look! Look!"

He looked, and saw a girl sleeping heavily on a couch. Oh, yes, of course. It was Dorinda Quarles. What about her?

"Look, I tell you! Oh, can't you see?"

A veil dropped from his eyes. The whole front of the girl's flimsy bodice was glued together in sticky folds round a gaping wound in the breast. The slack lips were grey, except for one ribald patch of scarlet lip-rouge. In a stupefaction of horror he knew the truth. Dorinda, the hostess, had been stabbed to death in her sleep.

"Who did it?" Helen shook him again, hysterically. "It was someone in this room, but who? Why? You all must have taken something, that's evident. Was there—any quarrel?" she whispered between chattering teeth.

"Quarrel?" He groped back as through a thick fog. "No. On the contrary, we were all most cheery. We did eat some stuff that fellow brought. We didn't know what it was, of course; that is to say, some of us didn't. After that we danced and ragged, and then—"

His voice trailed off. He was staring dazedly at the sleepers.

Impelled by an obscure instinct, he moved towards the dining-room, but Helen clutched at him, pointing a shaking finger towards the figure on the hearth-rug.

"That beast! Did he do it?" she muttered.

"Mowbray? But why? He had nothing to gain."

Suddenly she remembered. "Tommy. The front door was open. Can that mean someone has gone away? Here, quick, let's count them. Fourteen, weren't there?" Still gripping his arm she took a sobbing inventory . . . "Ten, eleven, twelve, thirteen . . ." Her voice sank for want of breath. "One of you has gone. Which?"

His heart turned cold. "We were all here when I fell asleep. I was the last, except possibly the Mowbray chap. Stop where you are."

However, Helen clung to him so tightly he was forced to drag her with him. With one accord their eyes sought the big armchair, the back of which was turned towards the opening between the two rooms. It was empty.

"Who? Who?"

"Dinah Blake. She was just behind me."

"Dinah! Oh, my God. Then after all, she—"

"Steady on!"

He snatched a brandy decanter from the sideboard, poured out a stiff drink and forced it between her lips. Then he took a peg for himself.

"Keep calm," he whispered, fighting down a fiendish presentiment. "She's probably somewhere in one of the other rooms. We'll hunt for her."

"But the door! It was wide open!"

"Never mind that. Come, show me the way."

He led her forcibly by the hand, and together they made a rapid tour of the two floors, turning on lights as they went. Nowhere was there any sign of Dinah, though when they gazed upon the disorder of Dorinda's bedroom, with its strewn face powder and georgette undergarments flung on the floor, Tommy had the eerie sensation that unseen eyes were watching him. The cupboard he opened showed only limp gowns dangling from hangers, while the wave of heavy scent which exhaled from them turned him sick. Helen was babbling something about Dodo's maid being ill in hospital, and the cook, a daily woman, being too busy last night to put things to rights.

"What other bedrooms are there?" he demanded brusquely. "What's that door across the passage?"

"Only a storage room belonging to Basil. It's locked and he keeps the key. That's where he was last night, getting his books. Then there's my room, and Benedetto's. They're at the other end."

"We'll rouse Benedetto—if he's asleep."

She gave a sudden moan. "You tell him. I can't. He's known Dodo since she was a baby. It's too awful."

In a small cell-like chamber at the back of the apartment Tommy found the old servant lying on a narrow iron bed, his sunken eyes closed, his breathing regular. At the touch on his shoulder he stirred, muttered, and sat bolt upright, staring in a bewildered way at the two tense faces.

"Mademoiselle! Have I overslept?" he mumbled in a befuddled voice. "What—what time is it?"

"They made him take some of the drug, too," Tommy explained in a low tone. "Forced him to swallow it. No wonder he's half-doped."

Benedetto's features sharpened with comprehension.

"No, monsieur," he denied contemptuously. "I spat it up outside. But is anything wrong? What . . ."

Tommy broke the news, and, watching closely, was satisfied it came as an overpowering shock. Stunned, trembling with agitation, the butler broke into a cold sweat, but after a moment was able to answer collectedly the questions put to him. Had he heard any sound? No, none. The cook went home at ten o'clock, after which he was alone in the kitchen. When did he go to bed? At exactly half-past eleven. The clocks were striking.

"Eleven-thirty!"

Was it possible? Tommy could have sworn it must have been fully two o'clock when the pillows were brought and the company began to settle down to rest. A shadowy recollection came back to him. Just at the last, before he dropped off, he had heard a bell ringing, and, propping open his eyes, had seen a dark figure hovering in the archway to the hall.

"Did the telephone ring?" he asked. "And was it you I saw looking into the salon?"

"Yes, monsieur. Mr. Jethro rang up, wanting to speak to Miss Dorinda. When I found all of you sound asleep, the lights out, I went back and told him."

"Told him!" Helen groaned and leant against the wall. "What did he say?"

"Nothing, miss, except to leave a message."

"Oh, God!" she breathed, broken to pieces. "What shall I say to Basil about this?"

Tommy took a firm hold on her stricken form. "Come," he commanded roughly. "This is no fault of yours. Let's go, so Benedetto can dress. He'll have to make coffee for that crowd. Benedetto, keep to your kitchen. Don't disturb anything in front. The police when they get here must find everything untouched. Understand?"

"Perfectly, sir. The coffee will be ready when you ring," and the old man reached an unsteady hand for his trousers.

Seeing Helen's completely demoralised state, Tommy realised it was he who must take the helm. Instinctively he wanted to stave off as long as possible the discovery of Dinah's absence, feeling that one false step now might be fraught with irreparable consequences, though why he should so desperately long to shield this girl who was almost unknown to him was a matter he could not explain to himself. Yet immediate action was imperative. They must call a doctor, summon the police—but was there not one other thing which should be done before anything else? To him it seemed the obviously wise course, though when he mentioned his intention his companion stared in amazement.

"Telephone Dinah? But why?"

"To hear her explanation. Isn't it quite on the cards she went home before anything happened? Anyhow I'm going to do it. Yes, I know where she lives—in a flat with her cousin, a Miss Pemberton, in the Rue Val-de-Grâce. Wait, don't do anything till I've spoken to her."

Disregarding her puzzled expression he moved towards the instrument which stood on a table behind the staircase, and, having given the number, listened with a set face to the persistent ringing at the other end of the wire. Long minutes passed. There was no response. The girl was not there.

"Afraid to go back," muttered Helen in a stifled tone. "I knew it. That's our final proof."

"Nothing's proved," he declared sternly. "Absolutely nothing—yet. For that matter, don't you see what an act of lunacy it would be for her to clear off like this if she was guilty? Why, she would have been perfectly safe from suspicion if she stayed where she was. Surely you can grasp that argument."

But Helen could grasp no argument requiring mental effort. Dorinda was murdered. Dinah had vanished. What more could one ask?

"Then where is she now?" she inquired stubbornly.

"Possibly with one of her friends. The cousin's away on a visit, you know, so maybe she's not staying at the flat. You've got to keep an open mind about this. Let the police draw their own conclusions. My idea is to get them here before we wake anyone up, but you're the boss. What do you say?"

"Oh, we couldn't be so brutal! Think what it means! They didn't do it."

"You don't know that—but we'll do as you think best. Telephone the doctor—then sit down quietly on that chair and get command of yourself. I'll call you presently."

Inside the dark salon he paused, snatching at the moment of solitude to analyse his chaotic impressions of the past evening. Bit by bit he dragged the recollections from his dulled brain and fitted them together. Only a few were distinct, and it was those which troubled him.

The gramophone, he recalled, had played on and on, without cessation. For what seemed an interminable period everyone had danced, in couples, absurd, childish groups, and in some instances singly. He himself had executed a fandango on top of the piano, with nutshells for castanets. Yes, he remembered his consuming pride in the performance, greeted with riotous applause, and also that idiot of a Hummock—good old Pete he had been then—swathed in a Spanish shawl, doing ridiculous plastic poses. It had all seemed quite natural and amusing at the time. While gaiety was at its height, many normally surprising things had occurred. Even Ronald Cleeves had come alive. The Greek temple had been invaded by a band of satyrs who capered in to hold antic revelry and after a while frolicked out again, back to the forest. Singing, stamping of feet, practical jokes. And then the laughter! The poetess giving an imitation of a drunken boulevardier; Hummock running his finger over the mantelpiece lustres and solemnly declaring there was dust on them; the lad Umberto balancing a priceless Persian vase on his nose and smashing it to atoms. Oh, yes, it had been incredibly funny! A hilarious evening. Everyone happy—while it lasted. But afterwards?

He saw a blurred picture of yawning, expressionless faces, some sunk in gloom—of a few couples still trying to dance; of Dick Cope-Villiers' beautiful head, like a too-heavy flower, resting on her partner's shoulder; of Soukine, a candle on the point of guttering out, and of himself captured and held prisoner on a distant sofa by the Falkland woman, all cloying scent, dripping pearls and amorousness. How he had hated her darkened eyelids, her Narcisse Noire! He had striven to escape. He had escaped, because at that instant, hovering in the doorway like a trapped moth, Dinah had caught his eye. Since their last fox-trot together, he had lost sight of her, but here she was again, clutching at her throat, looking as though about to faint from the closeness of the room. Two strides and he had reached her side to demand what was wrong.

"Oh, stop that tune!" she had gasped. "I can't stand it any longer. I shall go mad!"

The tune? As he lifted the gramophone-needle and reversed the disc he was vaguely struck by the coincidence of the title—*Miss Virginia*. Of course, Dinah herself was Miss Virginia. This song, seductively chanted by a warm American baritone, probably held disturbing memories for her. Tunes have a way of linking themselves up with one's emotions.

> *Miss Virginia,*
> *Sweeter than the honeysuckle vine,*
> *Miss Virginia,*
> *Honey, won't you say you'll be mine?*

Anyhow, he had stopped the tune now; but the girl's face was alarmingly white. Did she want to go home? He would take her, quickly, before the cursed drug got too firm a grip on him. But as he took hold of her arm she drew back obstinately.

"No, no, you don't understand. I must go through with it—till the end. I must, I must!"

Air, then. Let him open a window. He had steered her through the maze into the darkened dining-room, unlatched a casement. Ah, that was better! A cool breeze blew in, the yellow moon shone calmly down on a little enclosed garden with tall sycamores and marble seats in the gloom below. He had asked if she was not feeling sleepy.

"Am I?" The pupils of her eyes had been black, enormous. She had drawn one hand slowly back over the polished surface of her hair with a curious, absent manner. "I don't know. I feel—queer. Look!" she had whispered with sudden loathing, and directed his attention towards the salon they had left behind. "How horrible!"

Framed in the doorway he had seen a seething tangle of slow-moving figures, unreal, tortured, like one of Gustave Doré's drawings for the *Inferno*. In the foreground Dorinda, her gown torn at the shoulder, struggled roughly free from the gigolo's arms and like a petulant child flung herself headlong on the broad couch. She yawned, stretched and lay still, overcome with drowsiness. The girl beside him was staring hard at her. But what were the words spoken in his ear, words surely never intended to be overheard?

"And she just doesn't care! That's the maddening part of it. She tramples, smashes, and never once looks round to see the mischief she's done! Why, oh, why, can't someone put a stop to it?"

At this stage Tommy mopped his brow. He would have given all he possessed to wipe that speech from his memory. He could see Dinah now as she poised beside him in the dusk, her blue-green flounces unrumpled, her eyes fixed and bright as a cat's and the strange air of purpose about her. Long after he was ready to collapse she continued wide-awake, not heeding his suggestion of finding her a comfortable place to settle down in. The yawn which finally overtook her came as an amusing surprise.

"Why, I am sleepy . . . frightfully so! How funny! And how awful it'll be, waking up in this mob! Like a railway carriage . . . but why should one mind? I don't. There, that big arm-chair's mine. Can you draw it in here where it's cool?"

He had retained sufficient wit to arrange the chair so that it faced the window, alongside the table, to fetch her cloak from the hall and tuck it round her knees. Then, finding a pillow—there was only one left from the pile the butler had brought in—he lay down a few feet away. Although he could not see her face, she was so quiet he believed she had fallen into deep slumber before the remaining lamp in the salon was switched off. It was Mowbray who performed that service, afterwards standing on the hearth-rug to wind his watch and fumble with lazy fingers at his collar-stud. Blinking stupidly at the big, burly form silhouetted against the wood-fire Tommy had thought scornfully of the man's reputed evil powers. A fig for such bunkum! Mowbray was a charlatan, out for money, nothing more. This stuff he had given them wasn't bunkum, though. It was singularly potent, to judge by the creeping inertia which drowned the senses, a tide impossible to resist. . . .

Faint snores . . . a cinder dropping in the grate . . . the persistent peal of a bell somewhere . . . then Benedetto peering into the room. That was all.

Tommy shook himself. He was awake now, the last cobwebs of sleep brushed ruthlessly from his brain by the vivid incidents he had recalled, and which, with a sudden dogged resolution, he decided not to reveal to a living soul. His mind was made up. With the matter definitely settled, he crossed the room to the nearest window, and sweeping aside the curtains flung open the casement.

The sky was streaked with faint rose. The river, battleship grey, flowed like oil between quais still inky-black. Except for chirping sparrows no life stirred on the island. He drank in deep breaths of morning air to clear his befogged head, and turning surveyed the disorder behind him.

The room was a shambles. Cigarette-stubs were ground into the Aubusson carpet together with a glittering debris of glass, torn bits of fringe and burnt matches. Champagne-corks lay about, and an enamelled vanity-case. In the middle of the floor were the two halves of a broken gramophone-record, the gilt lettering of which informed him that it represented *Miss Virginia* as sung by Percy Milsom with the Broadway Boys. The tune Dinah could not bear to hear. With a stab at his heart he looked towards the vacant chair. The black velvet cloak, too, was gone.

He studied closely the silent company, each of them apparently in a state of fatuous coma—Dick Cope-Villiers, a white rag thrown on the Louis Quinze settee, with the Anson girl's fair head pillowed on her knee and Soukine at her feet, grey-faced, sunken into himself; the actress, mouth open, aging contours in grotesque contrast to the strident gold of her coiffure; Cicely Gault, a brown witch in emerald-green just visible over the hunched shoulders of Maud Daventry's smoking-jacket. Hummock—disgusting vision—lay on his back, still enmeshed in the Spanish shawl, his flabby lips emitting a series of pig-like grunts. Cleeves, magnificent in repose, slumbered with his blond head on his arm, under the piano. And Mowbray, sprawled before the fireplace, neck bared, features grossly bestial....

Last his gaze gravitated reluctantly towards the couch, where lay the victim's body, in a welter of blood. One would have known, thought he, that the unfortunate girl had more blood in her than most. The sight of her recalled the pagan sacrifices at Stonehenge—of Brünhilde on the funeral pyre.

For a savage instant he would have liked to see flames leap up, wrap the bier in their fiery embrace and reduce the whole to ashes.

He passed noiselessly into the room beyond, where the window still stood ajar, the curtains fluttering. He made out the dark chairs merging into darker tapestry, the half-burnt candles with plastrons of run wax, the dish of grapes and figs—but where was the knife? He had known to a certainty it would not be there, but to find it gone shook him horribly. He searched about hoping to lay hands on it, and if the truth be admitted, to wipe it clean of marks; but it was nowhere in view.

He rejoined Helen and drew her with him into the salon. They must do this waking job together, taking careful note of each individual's reactions.

"Mowbray first?"

She nodded. He bent down over the prostrate form, but a gasp from Helen made him pause. Following the direction of her pointing finger he saw, half-hidden in the wood-ashes of the dead fire, a blackened, metallic object which he recognised.

"Yes," he muttered. "That's it. It's the knife we used to cut the grape-stems with. Leave it alone."

As he said this he realised, with a feeling of triumph, that after the sojourn in the fire no part of either blade or handle could possibly retain any trace of an imprint.

CHAPTER IV

WITH painful effort they roused the dreamers and confronted them with the horrible reality in their midst. Tommy derived a cruel satisfaction from the process, not sorry to see his own recent sensations duplicated; but if he had hoped to witness some betrayal of guilty knowledge, he was doomed to disappointment. As far as one could judge, the entire eleven passed through identical stages of stupefaction, shock and moral collapse, so that when all were fully awake he was not astonished to note covert glances of suspicion dart from one to another.

Dinah's absence had so far passed unnoticed. Helen had agreed to let them find it out for themselves, though just why Tommy had exacted this promise from her was hard to explain. Perhaps, knowing what these people were like, he had foreseen their avid anxiety to shift blame on to other shoulders. At any rate, their present behaviour justified his most cynical expectations. No grief here, only panic-stricken fear of inconvenience, scandal. Not one, least of all the gigolo, cared anything about the unhappy girl whose hospitality they had enjoyed. They neither loved nor hated her. Casual friends or mere acquaintances, drawn together by curiosity of the most idle sort.

With one exception—Bannister Mowbray. Last evening was nothing novel to him; but then, as Tommy had argued, what could Dorinda's death profit him? Abject, deflated, he leant now against the mantelpiece, brow clammy with sweat, tongue exploring the surface of his dry lips. Manifestly terrified, his impassivity shaken to the roots; but only, one imagined, because he was envisaging the bad hole he was in as the purveyor of a drug which had rendered murder possible.

The coffee arrived, hot and strong. While it was being drunk, Tommy slipped quietly into the hall and telephoned the local commissariat. He returned to see Rita Falkland rise with an odd look on her face, and run a swift eye over the assembled party. Suddenly she emitted an hysterical shriek.

"Thirteen! Who's missing? Is it—? Yes, of course! That red-haired American girl. What's become of her?" She seized on Helen convulsively. "Did you know she was gone?" she demanded accusingly.

Tommy intervened with firm authority.

"Sit down, please," he commanded. "Yes, we knew it. When Miss Roderick came downstairs she found the door open, so I should think at some time or other Miss Blake decided to go home."

"You think!" Miss Falkland rounded on him with furious indignation, all her *tendresse* of the previous evening forgotten. "What right had you to keep back a thing as important as that? Why, if we'd known that girl had left here . . . but it's absolutely obvious now who did it. No one else had any real reason to—"

"Don't be a fool, Rita!" muttered Cicely Gault, pulling her into her seat. "Keep your head, for God's sake."

"Well, but you all agree with me. That's certain."

Miss Falkland subsided angrily, and with revived assurance began to repair her ravaged complexion. Tommy scanned the hostile faces. Human wolves, ready to fall on the one member of the pack who showed weakness. Peter Hummock, who had been shuddering as with palsy, now wore an alert, relieved air. Ronald Cleeves exhaled a long breath and looked towards Mowbray, who with shaking fingers essayed to light a cigarette. No one spoke, but presently the ominous silence was broken by a shuffling movement near the door. Tommy wheeled, caught hold of the Argentine by the shoulders and hauled him back to his place.

"Oh, no, I think not, Mr.—I'm afraid I didn't catch your name."

"Da Costa—Ramon da Costa," supplied the gigolo with a black expression. *"Et pourquoi—"*

"Mr. da Costa, your place is here along with the rest of us. Sorry, Miss Falkland, but it's quite useless to think of leaving. The police are on their way here now, so take it easy."

"What impertinence!" raged the actress, her thin cheeks fiery red. "How can you dream of keeping us here against our wills? Why, anyone would think—"

"Listen, please!" Tommy stationed himself before the doorway with a stern glint in his eye. "Since some of you appear not to grasp the situation, perhaps I'd better make it clear. Every person present, including Miss Roderick and myself, is a potential suspect. For our own interests we've got to face the inquiry in a body. Now! Have I made that entirely plain?"

"The only thing plain to me," retorted Miss Falkland, quivering with animosity, "is that you're determined to shield that girl—that murderess. How do we know you didn't help her get away? You were pally enough with her last night."

"Oh, do be quiet!" urged Miss Gault wearily. "He's right, of course. If we go, we're only asking for trouble."

Tommy, well aware of the curious glances bestowed upon him, preserved an imperturbable air, though inwardly he was both annoyed and apprehensive. He continued to stand guard, while the women fidgeted and rolled their handkerchiefs into balls. Hummock directed at him a baleful glare, and Mowbray and Cleeves, withdrawn to a corner, conversed in low whispers. Five interminable minutes ticked by, then a thunderous pounding on the outer door set the company trembling anew.

A second later Benedetto ushered in two officers in uniform—an inspector, small, sallow and hawk-eyed, followed by a heavier-built subordinate. The couple swept the scene with incredulous eyes. Swiftly their gaze passed over the littered room and its occupants, coming to rest on the couch. The inspector's nostrils dilated.

"Mesdames—messieurs!" he rapped out sharply. "What have we here? A suicide?"

Suicide! No one had thought of this as a possible explanation. Several drew in their breath, but before any one could speak Tommy stepped forward with business-like gravity.

"That, monsieur l'inspecteur, is for you to decide. What you see is what we ourselves saw when we woke up a short time ago. Shall I tell you what we know?"

Miss Falkland and Hummock sought to interrupt, but were peremptorily silenced.

"One at a time, please. I will hear what this gentleman has to say first. Now then, monsieur?"

In fluent French Tommy gave a terse outline of events. At the mention of the drug the listener compressed his lips, but although he made no comment he was evidently in some confusion as to how to proceed in an affair which had no parallel in his experience. He took refuge in summary brusqueness.

"Yes, yes, that will do for the present. You say that one of the guests, a lady, is missing. Her name? Address? Good!" He wrote rapidly in a note-book. "Did any one see her go?"

Eager denials came with a rush. The inspector raised his hand to stem the torrent of protestations.

"The entire party, then, was under the influence of this drug. You came here for the purpose of trying its effects?"

Another negative chorus. The inspector's lip curled with disbelief, and Tommy, recalling the knowing expectancy of several faces when the drug was passed, shared the other's silent contempt. All very well to swear, as they now did, that each and all of them, Mowbray and Cleeves excepted, were taken in by the jest. To his thinking Miss Blake and he were the only innocent persons.

"And you, madame?" The inspector turned brusquely to Helen. "Did you likewise partake of this drug?"

"Certainly not!" she retorted with asperity. "I was in my room, asleep in the ordinary way. I was not well, but if I had even faintly suspected such a thing would happen—"

"Why did you come downstairs?"

"I woke up and wanted to know the time. My watch had stopped. I found the door open, and then, when I looked in here I—oh, what is that?" she broke off, trembling anew, as the sound of a bell drew attention away from her.

The inquiry was suspended while Benedetto showed in a tall, bony Englishman with a drooping moustache. The newcomer fitted a monocle into his eye and cast a disapproving glance at the debauched gathering, several of whom he appeared to recognise. Helen, relieved to find the focus shifting from herself, introduced Dr. Walter Bramson, the dead girl's physician. The inspector gave a curt bow.

"I see. Then before going further we may as well secure his opinion—but you, ladies and gentlemen—" He jerked a dictatorial thumb in their direction—"will remain seated and hold no communication with each other. Now, doctor, perhaps you will examine the body."

The physician, moving very deliberately, cleared a space on the table for his bag of instruments, and with sundry clicking noises of the tongue bent over the corpse. Soon grunts and disjointed words were heard: "Clean incision . . . left ventricle deeply penetrated . . . death almost instantaneous." In reply to a suggestion offered by the inspector he shook his head decidedly. No, self-destruction was an utter impossibility. The victim, whom he knew to be left-handed, could never have aimed a blow which slanted at this angle. Besides, an act of this sort required the full sweep of the arm. It was dealt from above, by someone standing close beside the couch.

"And the time?"

The doctor studied with distaste the clots of dark blood adhering to the wound, and before he spoke wiped his hands carefully on an immaculate handkerchief.

"Six to seven hours ago," he answered slowly. "Though we can make only a rough guess. Very little rigidity . . . room is warm. But on the whole, we're safe in assuming the murder to have been perpetrated in the neighbourhood of midnight."

Astonished eyes questioned each other. No one save Tommy had the least idea that the drug had taken its full effect at such an early hour. To be sure, Mowbray had said something about time expanding, but midnight—! Why, that was only the edge of the evening!

The physician and the officer conferred in undertones. The former elevated his brows and gazed with profound repugnance at each of the wan faces in turn.

"Have you found out what particular narcotic was used?" he inquired coldly.

"Not yet—but rest assured we shall do so," snapped the inspector with venom.

Rita could contain herself no longer.

"Doctor," she appealed hysterically, "why should innocent people like ourselves be subjected to this indignity? We all know who's responsible. Yes, I will speak!" she cried defiantly. "Ask Miss Roderick who left the room while we were asleep. Ask her about the open door."

The plea produced an unexpected result. Before Dr. Bramson could do more than stare, the inspector issued rapid orders to his assistant to secure the finger-prints from the door-knob. There would probably be several sets, but one set would belong to the absent guest.

Tommy's heart stood still. Directly afterwards, however, he realised how meaningless it would be to find Dinah's prints on the door she must certainly have opened in order to get out. If it was the knife now . . . But here he felt safe. With a grim spirit of mischief, he called the officer's attention to the knife buried in the cinders, and watched in amusement while the other stooped and gave a start.

"*Comment!* And whose is that?"

Tommy explained the ownership, and described how all the members of the party had handled the dirk, which at the end of the dinner had been left lying in the dish of fruit. Again the suspicious glances darted to and fro, with the journalist as the main target. The watchers held mute communion while the weapon was drawn forth with the fire-tongs and held out for the doctor's inspection.

"Probably the weapon used," assented the Englishman cautiously. "You'll take proper measurements, of course, but it looks likely enough. Anything to be got from it?"

"From this?" grunted the inspector with scorn. "No! Every mark has been burnt off. The handle is charred to a crisp."

He laid the knife down with disgust, and proceeded to view the carpet between the hearth and the couch. As Tommy had previously observed, not a drop of blood could be seen. The explanation of this appeared when the searcher picked up a fold of the victim's chiffon skirt and pointed triumphantly to a long, double smear.

"You see, monsieur? The blade was wiped. Wiped clean, then thrown into the fire. Careful work."

Tommy registered this fact for future consideration. It might, he felt, have a deep significance, though at present he was incapable of following any line of thought to its logical conclusion. He saw the doctor speak to Helen, who with visible reluctance approached the body, took a close survey, and shook her head.

"Her jewellery is all there," she whispered. "I fastened her gown for her last night, and I know she wore only that string of pearls, one brooch and the fire-opal ring. You're not thinking of Benedetto, are you? As you know, he's been in service here for nineteen years. Besides, there was no need to commit murder. He or any one else could have taken what they wanted without that."

The inspector now retired to the dining-room, into which, one after another, the guests were shown to be privately interrogated. Mowbray was detained for ten minutes, da Costa, cringing, green to the gills with fright, for seven, the others for shorter periods. The finger-prints of all were taken, and when the proceedings were completed the whole group, reassembled, were subjected to a final harangue.

"None of you," wound up the inspector in a menacing tone, "will be free to leave the city until permission is granted you. You will each be summoned before the *juge d'instruction* for further examination, for which you must hold yourselves in readiness." He paused, looked about and suddenly remembered his subordinate's task. "Laugier! Have you finished? What is your result?"

The other officer creaked towards him with a puzzled air.

"Can't make it out," he mumbled. "Knob, smooth brass, was polished yesterday morning, since which time at least five persons have touched it. That is to say, the deceased, this lady—" he motioned towards Helen—"a manicure woman, the deceased's father, who came here last evening, and the butler. The missing lady would bring the list up to six, but all I have got hold of is three sets of prints. Two, actually, because the third set is a duplicate of the second."

The superior officer knit his brows and suggested that some of the persons mentioned might have worn gloves. Helen, on reflection, declared that as she had been in a hurry the previous morning she had gone out carrying her gloves in her hand, while she was inclined to think Miss Quarles had done likewise. For the manicure woman and Mr. Jethro she could not answer, as she had seen neither of them leave the apartment. Tommy, as it happened, remembered noticing that Jethro's hands were bare.

"*Hein!* In that case, we should certainly have not less than five sets of prints, with several repetitions of the butler's. Laugier, show me your three."

Necks craned as he compared the specimens taken from the brass knob with the sheaf of smudges obtained from the company.

"Here we are!" he exclaimed, indicating the ones which corresponded. "They are yours, mademoiselle, and those of the servant. It is quite plain they represent the occasion when you closed the door this morning, and the time when the doctor and ourselves were admitted. But—" in a sharp tone to his assistant, "are you certain there are no others?"

"None."

Then why was it Dinah's fingers had left no mark? Here was a new problem to be thrashed out, but like the business of the knife it paled to insignificance beside the one really momentous question: where was Dinah herself?

CHAPTER V

A FLEET of taxis had borne the shattered men and women away to baths, beds and other restoratives. Tommy, whom Helen Roderick had implored to wait till she could speak to him privately, lingered on, and in so doing caught a low exchange of remarks between the two officers of the law.

"Think it's true that big Englishman has got no more of the stuff in his possession?" asked the subordinate doubtfully.

"We'll soon find out," returned the inspector with a shrug. "An hour ago two of our men were dispatched to search the studio where he's living. If there's anything there, they'll have laid hands on it."

All at once Tommy recalled what he had hitherto entirely forgotten. He fished up from his side-pocket the unconsumed portion of the sweetmeat, with lint adhering to it and presented it to the speaker.

"In case you men don't find anything, this is a sample of the drug we took. I happened to save some."

"You saved it? Why?" The black eyes narrowed with suspicion.

"Merely because I had important work to finish this morning. Drug-taking isn't a hobby of mine, and what I did eat was sufficient to plunge me into a heavy sleep. You may remember I came only at the last minute, to oblige Mademoiselle." It was impossible to say if the inspector was satisfied with the explanation. Accepting the bitten cube he continued to regard the donor very closely. He suggested, "Perhaps the lady who went away—she was your partner at dinner I think—made a similar pretence and left part of her share?"

Tommy met the challenge without a tremor. "You are wrong, monsieur," he answered composedly. "I watched her swallow the whole lump. She was much distressed when she discovered what she had eaten."

"But like the servant, she may have got rid of it directly afterwards when she went upstairs with the other ladies."

"I hardly imagine so. It's true she was out of the room for a few minutes, but I can swear positively that she showed every symptom of succumbing to the soporific effects."

"Then how do you account for her subsequent departure?" snapped the officer with a swift glance at his companion.

"I don't attempt to account for anything. I do say, however, that it will be hard to convince me she had any hand in this murder."

Although he had spoken with the utmost confidence, Tommy was far from being as certain as he pretended. At the first opportunity he put through another telephone call to Dinah's flat, and from the daily servant, just arrived, learned that the girl had not come home. Where in Heaven's name could she have gone? He replaced the receiver heavily and joined Helen, who with the aid of her address-book was supplying the inspector with the names of such English and American residents as Dinah knew intimately. To his intense relief, she did not refer to Christopher Loughton. The inspector pocketed his notes, announced briskly that his colleague would remain on guard to superintend the removal of the body to the Institut Medico-Legiste, where the complete autopsy would be performed, and that till further notice the salon and the dining-room would be placed under official seal.

"One thing more, mademoiselle. Has any one informed the victim's father of this occurrence?"

"Not yet," she stammered painfully. "There's nothing he can do, and I wanted to spare him as long as possible. For a man in his position . . ."

"Ah, yes, I understand. He is, you say, the gentleman who was received yesterday by the Ministre de l'Instruction Publique?" The little martinet's voice showed the respect a Frenchman accords to a foreigner only when the latter's worth has been recognised by France. "Well, mademoiselle, he will have to be told now, but I am willing to leave that matter to you. We shall have to interrogate him, naturally, but we shall take care not to subject him to any needless inconvenience. Meanwhile, I hope to have a report to make to you concerning the lady now under suspicion."

The instant the man was gone, Tommy whispered urgently, "Quick! Give me those addresses. I want to find that poor child myself before she falls into the clutches of the police. For her sake, it's absolutely essential."

"You think it will help?" She eyed him doubtfully. "I'll let you have the list, of course, but, oh, don't waste time on that now! I was going to beg you to break this awful news to Basil. It's my business to do it, but I simply can't!"

He hesitated. What she asked was singularly distasteful to him, besides hindering his immediate intention. Still, how could he be so brutal as to refuse? The big, usually composed woman was on the verge of collapse.

"I'll do it, on one condition," he agreed reluctantly. "You must promise to ring up all the people you mentioned and see if Dinah is with any of them. Whatever view you may take of this, it's certain she never knew what she was eating, and that, having eaten it, she was not herself. There's something deucedly queer about it all which we've got to get unravelled or she'll be in a ghastly fix. You'll do your utmost to get in touch with her?"

"Yes, yes—only go, right now, to the Hôtel Mirabeau and—"

"Pardon, mademoiselle!" It was Benedetto who interrupted her, coming forward from the back of the hall. "Mr. Jethro is not stopping this time at the Mirabeau. He told me last night he was not able to get his usual room on the court, so he put up at another place . . . the Hôtel Stanislas, Rue Berger. Miss Dorinda was to ring him up there in the morning."

"Hôtel Stanislas? Never heard of it." Helen seemed surprised. "Oh, well, I dare say Benedetto knows. I expect Basil felt anxious to get a quiet night's rest before flying over to-day. He was very tired and noise disturbs him. Hurry along, do. I know you'll manage it tactfully."

The Rue Berger was only some ten minutes away. Eager to get the disagreeable duty over as quickly as possible Tommy ran down the stairs to the court.

At the door of the loge the concierge and his wife, both drab, respectable people, were conversing with the neighbouring butcher, and from evident signs, extracting the last drop of ghoulish enjoyment out of last night's sensation. At sight of yet another guest emerging from the scene of the crime they stopped dead to stare with cold reserve at Tommy's dinner-jacket and hatless head. The butcher withdrew, and Tommy, to satisfy himself on a matter of grave importance, accosted the couple with hardy determination.

"Exactly when," he inquired, "did you close the outer doors last evening?"

The male member of the firm sought counsel behind his gold-rimmed spectacles and his wife, who hitched her triangular black shawl closer about her shoulders and displayed hostile reticence.

"Come, come," said Tommy impatiently. "There's no harm in answering a simple question like that. When did you close up?"

"At a quarter past twelve, monsieur. It was later than usual, but thinking Mademoiselle would follow her general practise of taking her guests on to some place of amusement at about midnight, we waited, rather than be waked from our first sleep. When no one came down, I shut the doors and went to bed."

"No one came down! You're sure of that?"

"Not after the doors were closed, monsieur. They'd have had to call 'cordon' in order to get out."

The statement proved conclusively that Dinah must have quitted the building prior to twelve-fifteen. If the doctor was right about Dorinda's being stabbed at some time close to midnight, the inference was terrifying. Tommy steadied himself.

"Did you hear any one pass through the court before the doors were shut?" he demanded.

"No, monsieur; but someone may have done so. For the last three-quarters of an hour we were in the kitchen, at the back. I was mending the leg of a table, hammering and so on. My wife was helping me."

"Thanks. That is all I want to know."

The two stared after him as he walked towards the street to scan the quai for a passing taxi-cab. While he paused in the entrance the woman made a suggestion to her husband, who answered in the tone of one recalling a forgotten duty. "Ah, that! All this excitement has quite put it out of my head; but as I told you before, I ran my torch all over the court last night, and couldn't find it."

"All the same, it must be there. Come along, we'll hunt now."

Together the pair went to the back of the court and began stooping and poking about in the crevices of the flagged pavement. Tommy eyed them with slight curiosity, and almost at once saw the man pounce upon some small object and hold it up with triumphant amazement.

"There, now!" he cried. "If it had been a snake, I should have been bitten. I must have been blind not to see it, lying in full view like that. Well, well! I don't suppose the poor man will trouble to ask for it now, but if he does remember it, why, here it is."

"Pauvre homme," probably referred to Basil Jethro, who apparently had lost something; but before Tommy could speculate on the subject a roving car lurched in his direction. He hailed it, and in another moment was bowling over the north bridge and into the wide Boulevard Sebastapol, which leads to the Rue Berger.

The sun shone warm upon pavements freshly-sluiced with water. Early breakfasters sipped their coffee at the small cafés along the way; an army of toilers, composed of shop-assistants and women with compact coiffures and string-bags for marketing, trudged by in an unceasing stream. At sight of so much alertness and thrift Tommy felt depressingly conscious of his own dulled faculties. The effect of the drug still weighed upon him, his head throbbed, and with every fibre of his being he shrank from the task imposed upon his good nature.

What if the man he was about to visit could not be expected to experience any great sorrow over the horrifying occurrence? He was certain to become embroiled in degrading publicity, utterly hateful to one of his type. It was impossible not to sympathise with him, but unfortunately that fact did not make the present undertaking any easier to perform.

With an effort Tommy steered his thoughts towards the philosopher's incongruous marriage to Agatha Quarles. The latter, a prominent hostess during her widowhood, had been an impulsive, emotional woman of no intellectual depth, while Jethro, lately sprung to fame, was invariably represented as the embodiment of pristine reason, remote from human passions—a sort of Mount Everest soaring high above his fellow-creatures. After all, though, were not the journalists largely responsible for that picture of him? With their senseless ardour for creating labels, they had coined a phrase now quoted on every side: The Man Without a

Hobby. Ugh! What stupidity! Reportorial jargon, about as meaningless as most tags. Jethro was a man, not a machine. Most likely he had been attracted to Lady Agatha's warmth and womanly charm. Helen, who had been in a position to know, declared him to have been the ideal husband, patient and devoted under what must have been trying circumstances.

Trying . . . but hold on! Hadn't there been some talk at the time of the wife's death, something slightly peculiar? To be sure there was! If he hadn't been slow-witted he'd have remembered it last night. Drugs—that was it—an unsubstantiated rumour of suicide, or at any rate, an overdose of veronal or some other sleeping-mixture. All the time Helen was gassing to him he had known in the back of his mind . . . but the recollection was vague. The incident happened five years ago, when he had been in Russia. However, it was easier now to understand why Helen was in such a mortal funk lest Jethro should find out about his step-daughter's prank. One member of a family was bad enough, but to have a second one tampering with drugs! No wonder Helen dreaded the meeting with the man who had trusted her to keep the head-strong girl out of harm.

The Rue Berger was a far cry from the Rue de la Paix, while the modest, typically-French hostelry before which the taxi halted seemed a decided come-down for a person accustomed to the luxurious Mirabeau. Tommy was a little surprised that a man presumably well-off—he must be that, for Lady Agatha had been a rich woman—should have selected an hotel as unpretentious as the Stanislas. The place advertised itself instantly as the port of call for respectable provincials of the middle classes. The rooms on the court were probably quiet, but the same would apply to others in more prepossessing quarters. It crossed his mind for a second that just possibly the philosopher might be wanting to economise, but the reflection did not hold his interest for long.

The cramped lobby had a lift on one side, a desk on the other, with glass doors between showing a glimpse of wicker settees and dessicated palms in tubs. The manager, a sleek, sloe-eyed Frenchman, bustled out from a private lair, eyed the visitor's untimely apparel with inquisitiveness, and on hearing Tommy's wish looked dubiously at the clock.

"It is barely eight, monsieur. M. Jethro particularly asked me not to call him before nine. Is the matter an urgent one?"

"Extremely so. I'm afraid I must insist on being shown to his room."

With scarcely-veiled curiosity the manager summoned a small chasseur and ordered him to conduct the gentleman up to Room Eighteen.

"And here, Joseph—while you're about it, you might as well carry Monsieur's suit up with you. It has been pressed and brought back. He may be requiring it."

"Not that one," thought Tommy, noticing that the garments draped over his guide's arm were light-grey summer flannels, and so ancient that he wondered why their owner had bothered to have them pressed at all, especially at this time of year. The inner pocket of the coat sagged outward so that he could see the tailor's label—Mayhew, Savile Row, London. He marvelled briefly over what seemed to him very exclusive, even extravagant tastes. Jethro might be cutting down expenses in some ways, but at all events he ordered holiday flannels from the best tailor in Mayfair, and whatever their age sent them, on the verge of a journey, to be put in condition. The circumstance struck him as paradoxical.

The lift crawled upward, hiccoughed at the second floor, and came to a wavering halt. The chasseur marched along a dark passage, turned a corner and rapped on a door, while Tommy, close behind, blundered over a pair of boots obstructing the path. These articles, he chanced to observe, were black, clumsy-toed, and conspicuously new. Resembling countless similar atrocities seen on the feet of sober, undistinguished Frenchmen, they presented a striking contrast to the ones the Englishman had left outside his door—well-cut, carefully treed, with breeding in every trim line.

The boy rapped again, and this time a cultivated but drowsy voice murmured, *"Entrez!"* Through the opened door Tommy saw a common though not exactly sordid room, darkened by chenille curtains, and in a brass bed the long mound of a recumbent body covered with a green figured quilt. The voice continued in excellent French, "Put the tray on the table—but surely it is not yet nine o'clock?"

"No, monsieur. A gentleman to see you."

"What, at this hour?"

Tommy motioned the chasseur aside and stepping into the room gently closed the door behind him.

CHAPTER VI

NO GOOD trying to soften the blow. In a few bald sentences Tommy got it over, and with a feeling of sympathy saw the remnants of sleep stripped away to reveal stark horror.

"My step-daughter . . . but . . . but . . . you must allow me a moment to take this in."

Jethro sat up, his parchment skin bedewed with sweat. Presently he drew a handkerchief from beneath the pillows, and with mechanical care wiped his forehead. His hand trembled slightly.

"Please give me all the details," he said, showing an admirable self-command, and as Tommy complied one could almost see the cool brain labouring, with method and precision, to grasp every aspect of the situation thus violently thrust upon it. Here, thought Tommy, was a man at all times dominated by reason. He was shocked, he was physically bowled over, but his mental processes were not dislocated.

The Mongoloid eyes, more than ever resembling stones under water, never wavered from the narrator's face. One could see that many things were passing behind them, not excluding the effect this decidedly lurid scandal was going to have on their owner's life. Indeed, Tommy was aware of two distinct lines of thought—one following the actual facts of the crime, the other keenly speculative, possibly for personal considerations.

"There's nothing more to be done at the moment," concluded the bearer of news. "The police have taken our statements, and are in possession of the apartment. Miss Roderick was anxious not to disturb you till it became absolutely necessary, which is why you weren't informed sooner."

"I appreciate her kindness—and yours, too."

If the courtesy of this reply sounded a little formal, it was only natural in the circumstances. The man, for all his forced composure, must be badly shaken. Tommy wondered if he had better go at once, but while he hesitated he saw the eyes opposite narrow and fix on him a penetrating scrutiny.

"We have met before, I think?"

"In the hall, last night before dinner. I am a friend of Miss Roderick's, and my name is Rostetter."

"But you knew my step-daughter, of course?"

"No . . . though actually I did see her once or twice when she was a small child. You see, I had some slight acquaintance with your late wife."

"Indeed!" There was a flicker of interest in the eyes. "That was previous to my marriage, I suppose. And your profession is—"

"Journalism. I was with Reuter for a long time, but now I'm a freelance. Incidentally, though my influence may not be great, please count on me to do my best towards suppressing any needless publicity this affair may lead to. No human power can prevent its making a stir, but—"

He was checked by a dignified gesture.

"Pray don't consider my private feelings in the matter, Mr. . . . Mr. Rostetter. I can only lament, very bitterly, my complete uselessness towards helping justice. Unfortunately my step-daughter's life was a sealed book to me. I have no knowledge of the persons you mention, and have never so much as heard of this young woman who absented herself while the rest of you slept. Am I to understand that suspicion attaches to her?"

"For no reason whatever except that she was not there." Tommy spoke with combative energy, determined not to divulge one whit of what he had learned the previous evening. "To my mind, there are several reasons for thinking her entirely innocent. Why, for one thing, should a guilty individual commit the supreme imprudence of going away when safety lay in remaining in our midst? And why should the outer door show no signs of having been touched by her?"

Jethro eyed him again, attentively, then shook his head.

"I am afraid I can't venture an opinion. Drugs—" As before when this part of the affair was mentioned a look of repugnance crossed his features—"may be responsible for many vagaries of conduct. The subject's medical history might be of importance—but there, how is it possible to theorise at this stage? You yourself," he added slowly, "saw nothing, heard no sound?"

"I was dead to the world. We all were."

It seemed to Tommy that Jethro, without voicing an opinion, had been struck by the warmth of his defence. Up till now it had scarcely occurred to him to bother about his own position, but all at once he realised that to an unbiased view he might be regarded in the same light as the other suspects. The thought made him uncomfortable, so that he was not sorry when Jethro, with a movement of rising, gave the signal for his guest's departure. Still, he felt a slight compunction about deserting a fellow-being about to face a trying ordeal, and thinking the man really looked far from well he made a tentative suggestion of accompanying him to the apartment. To his relief, however, the offer met with a decided refusal.

"No, no, I prefer to go alone. Don't let me detain you; but if you will be so kind, you might on your way out countermand my breakfast. The idea of food is rather distasteful."

During the past few seconds, Tommy had, in a purely mechanical manner and chiefly to avoid staring at his companion, let his gaze roam round the room. There was little to be seen beyond the meagre furnishings. The wardrobe, wide open, showed two suits dangling from the rod; the chest of drawers held only a pair of military brushes and a clean collar and tie, the cabin-trunk strapped in readiness for to-day's journey, stood on a stand, and on top of it was a handsome case of pie-crust coloured pig-skin, the lid thrown back to display neatly-packed personal belongings. A dressing-gown and a pair of morocco slippers made up the total; yet, taking a final survey, Tommy felt dimly conscious that there ought to be something more. What was it he had all this while been looking for? His brain must still be clouded or he would have known. Perhaps it was a freak of the imagination. At any rate, it could not possibly matter. He said good-bye and retraced his steps along the passage.

It was while waiting for the lift that he suddenly remembered he had failed to speak of his donation to the police. Jethro might be interested to know that the police were in a position to estimate the effect of the drug employed, thinking which he went quickly back to supply the information. He tapped on the door, but there was no response. Did this mean that Room Eighteen possessed a private bath and the occupant was in it? Certainly the public bath and lavatory just beside him were empty, for the doors of both stood ajar. He listened, but the only sounds came from the denizen of Seventeen, whose clumsy footwear had been taken inside. Jethro's shoes, too, had disappeared. Oh, well, it was of no importance. He descended, delivered the message about breakfast together with a word of explanation to the manager, and cutting short the latter's expressions of horrified concern hastened to his own abode in the Place du Palais Bourbon.

A hot bath and more coffee cleared the lingering mists from his brain. By ten o'clock, clad in suitable tweeds, he had finished and posted his weekly article, and on fire to learn the result of Helen's telephoning dashed back to the Ile St. Louis—now driving his own rather battered two-seater.

Just in front of him a taxi drew up, and from it Basil Jethro alighted. This must be a return visit, he thought, considering almost two hours had elapsed since their earlier meeting; but in any case he saw at once that his presence here was not welcomed. He was, indeed, slightly taken aback by the stiffness with which the philosopher remarked:

"You really need not put yourself out in any way over this regrettable catastrophe, Mr. Rostetter. Already you have been inconvenienced quite enough, and from what you yourself said to me I can hardly suppose your interest to be professional."

"On the contrary, it is purely friendly," replied Tommy, nettled by the veiled hint that his solicitude bordered on the officious. "I promised to come back as soon as possible. Miss Roderick is in a badly-shattered state."

His explanation was received by a cold bow. Without further speech the two men reached the second floor, where Jethro, as he rang the bell, murmured that he possessed a latch-key, but had had the misfortune to lose it the evening before.

"I was stupid enough to let it fall over the balustrade. I couldn't find it in the poor light, so I instructed the concierge to search for it with his electric torch."

"Then that's what I saw him pick up this morning!" exclaimed Tommy, enlightened. "It was lying near the foot of the staircase."

"This morning?" A look of annoyance on the pale, lined features gave way to intent preoccupation. "What carelessness! And yet, if it couldn't be seen at night . . . No, I admit the slight doubt in my mind is now dispelled. This crime must have been perpetrated by someone on the inside of the apartment."

"Why, had any other explanation occurred—"

Tommy left the question unfinished, for at that moment the door opened, and Helen, now dressed in black, pushed past the butler with a choking cry.

"Basil, Basil! So you've got here at last!"

At last? The Hôtel Stanislas was barely five minutes' taxi-ride from the island, and Tommy had left Jethro in the act of getting dressed. Why this long delay? However the next words gave an adequate solution.

"I had an attack of faintness after your friend left me and was forced to lie down, otherwise I'd have been here long ago. No, I am quite recovered now. It was nothing."

But Helen, her over-wrought emotions seeking relief, clung to his arm as she begged him to take a glass of brandy. Tears blinded her to the odd spasm of shrinking which Tommy noticed on the philosopher's face, a look of sensitive irritation, as though human touch at this moment were distasteful to him. He did not want sympathy, Tommy thought. He wanted to be let alone. The climax was reached when, with a burst of sobs, Helen heaped blame upon herself for what had occurred.

"My dear Helen," he said, detaching her hand with great firmness. "This is unthinkable. Can any one know better than I how impossible it was to prevent the unfortunate child from doing what she wanted to do? If this last folly of hers led to so terrible a result, it is not you who can be held responsible." He spoke in a shamed undertone, evidently unwilling for a third person to intrude upon family concerns, then with an abrupt dismissal of the topic turned to the closed doors on the left. "It was in here, wasn't it? Has the body been removed?"

Tommy detected a slight hesitation before the word "Body." Helen answered in the affirmative, adding that two inspectors were going over the salon now, looking for clues.

"Though what they hope to find, I don't know. Even the knife—did Mr. Rostetter tell you—is so badly burnt there's nothing to be got from it."

Jethro opened the doors and gazed inside. Tommy seized the opportunity to whisper eagerly: "What have you heard about—her?"

"Dinah? Nothing. No one's seen her, she simply vanished. You see how awful it looks. It couldn't be any worse."

His heart sick within him Tommy asked if she had been able to communicate with the cousin, Miss Pemberton, but Helen shook her head.

"All I can find out is that she's somewhere in Versailles; but when she does hear about this I don't suppose she'll know how to locate Dinah any more than we do. I can't conceive what's happened, unless—"

"Unless what?" he demanded sharply, still keeping his voice low.

"She may have committed suicide, you know."

"And again she may not." A steely glint had come into his eyes. "Look here—she's got a studio, hasn't she?"

"She had, but she gave it up last week. I tell you, I've thought of everything! I almost rang up the Embassy, only the Loughton man I told you about would be the last to—"

He interrupted her by a pressure on the hand. He had an uneasy fear lest the moment she was alone with Jethro she would make a clean breast of her belief concerning the cause of Dinah Blake's broken engagement, and to guard against this he whispered, chaining her attention by an effort of will. "Listen, Helen! You don't actually know for certain about that matter, now do you? You're only putting two and two together. Isn't that so?"

Helen shot him a glance of stubborn surprise. "If you're thinking of him," she replied, indicating Jethro's abstracted profile, "you needn't worry. A man with his open mind and sense of justice—"

"Never mind. The point is *you* know nothing—so bear that in mind, and remember our agreement. S'sh—the telephone! It may mean news."

He waited impatiently by Helen's side while she snatched off the receiver and spoke in a subdued and agitated voice. When she had finished she looked more perplexed than before.

"That was Christopher Loughton's sister-in-law, Pearl—his brother Hubert's wife. She sounded terribly upset, hardly able to speak, and says she's coming here now to tell me something. I can't imagine what it is, but as it's private I'll have to get rid of you two."

She gave a troubled glance at the abstracted profile in the doorway, but her difficulty was met by Jethro's coming forward with the request to write out a few telegrams at her desk. It was necessary, he said, to cancel his arrangements at Oxford, and let his housekeeper know he was detained in Paris.

"Certainly," cried Helen, relieved. "You'll find all you want in my room upstairs."

Thanking her, Jethro bowed with frigid politeness to Tommy, and waited in a slightly pointed manner till the latter had taken up his hat; but Tommy, determined to learn what Mrs. Loughton had to say, hung about till he and Helen were alone, then asked if the expected visitor was Dinah's friend.

"Oh, a very warm one! That's what bothered me about her tone just now. If it had been Christopher's mother now, I could have understood. Unbearable snob she is, mad for that precious boy of hers to make what she calls a good match. I know for a fact she was delighted when this engagement broke up. You see, Dinah's got no money at all. It's the greatest credit to her that she's been able to stick here in Paris on her earnings, but Edna Loughton would consider a girl like that a handicap to a rising diplomat's career."

When the bell rang Tommy tip-toed upstairs, and selecting the bath as a suitable retiring-spot, lit a cigarette and prepared to wait till the interview below was ended. Before many minutes had passed a measured tread approached along the passage outside, and through the half-open door he saw the author of *Beyond Relativity* wander into the dead girl's room across the way and vanish from view. Now it would be extremely awkward to be discovered here, thinking which Tommy rose, intending to slip out; but just then his eye caught a reflection in a mirror, and in spite of himself he lingered to watch what the philosopher was doing.

Little enough, apparently. With an aimless air the stooping figure had paused before the disordered dressing-table, from which it presently moved on to the writing-desk beside the window. Here it was partly hidden by the bed, but not for long. It emerged again, and Tommy dodged guiltily to avoid being seen as close at hand a key grated in a lock. Jethro had quitted Dorinda's bed-chamber and gone into the small room next door to the bath where, according to Helen, he still kept some of his belongings. For a short time he could be heard moving about and opening drawers, then he came out, relocked the door, and moved back in the direction from which he had come.

Purely to kill time, Tommy now ventured across the passage to survey, as Jethro had done, Dorinda's own room. The amber curtains had been drawn apart to let in the soft sunshine, but the same careless litter lay about, and there was nothing to show that the police had extended their activities thus far. Bottles, jars, eye-black, rouge, all remained untouched, and on the desk—yes, this must have been what held the step-father's attention—lay an engagement-block with the owner's appointments for to-day scrawled in a big, bold hand.

"Ritz, Gigi," Tommy read, and remembered that Gigi was the Argentine lover. "2.30, Claudine—3, Chanel's opening; dinner, Umberto; Théâtre Libertin, Chez Mon Oncle."

The Théâtre Libertin was a sordid playhouse in Montmartre; Chez Mon Oncle the night-club where Gigi was employed. The inspector would probably want this record, uninteresting as it appeared at cursory glance; and yet had he been here after all? Tommy bent over suddenly to inspect four tiny clean marks in the light film of dust on the walnut surface of the table. Something had been removed, though what it was he could not say. He stared at the evenly-spaced imprints, scratched his head thoughtfully, and finally returned to stand in the passage gazing hard at the locked door of the storage-room.

The ash from his cigarette tumbled in a heap to the floor. Glancing down he noticed a minute trail of some white, crystalline substance proceeding from under the door to a round, compressed pellet near his foot. Picking up a bit, he sniffed and got a strong odour of camphor which told him what the snowy stuff was—merely the fragment of a naphtha-ball, that familiar precaution against moth, which Jethro must have trodden upon and tracked out. Doubtless it had been dislodged just now from some trunk or drawer.

Irritably he turned towards the stairs, and to his intense relief caught sounds indicative of the caller's departure. A frightened American voice was uttering these words:

"I hate to say it, but I do believe that mother-in-law of mine is pleased—yes, pleased—this has happened. As though it proved her right, you understand. Isn't it too hideous?"

"I suppose it's no worse than if Dinah did commit the murder," answered Helen's deeper tones. "Oh, it's perfectly awful, the whole thing! After what you've told me—"

"But she couldn't, Helen! Even if she did, I should still feel . . . but then I know so well what a time she's had, with mother against her and all. Swear you won't mention this to the police. I wouldn't have come, only..."

The speech ended in a sob. A second later the door had closed, and Tommy was at Helen's side, demanding an explanation.

CHAPTER VII

THE bewildering story may be outlined briefly. Shortly after twelve the night before, Mr. and Mrs. Hubert Loughton were returning home when near their street door in the Rue Madame they encountered Dinah Blake, come to pay a call. Seeing that the Quarter folk drop in on their friends at odd hours, this in itself was not peculiar. Pearl Loughton, who had seen little of the girl since the latter's break with Christopher, and who rather feared Dinah was avoiding her, was relieved, delighted. At the same time, having had a private notion that Dinah in spite of pretence to the contrary was most unhappy, she was puzzled to find her in such evident high spirits.

Where had Dinah been, all dressed up in her best evening frock? Oh, just a fearfully dull party, was the flippant reply. Awful people, so boring, and the room like an oven! She had got fed up, and come away. Whose party it was she did not say, and Pearl neglected to inquire.

In the little salon upstairs they drank ginger-beer and chattered gaily. Not a word was said of Christopher, about whom Dinah from the beginning had preserved a rigid silence. It almost seemed that he was forgotten, and certainly Dinah was her former self again, lively, sparkling, and a little inconsequent. Pearl and her husband found themselves exchanging mystified glances. Both wondered if their guest had fallen in love with another man. Only that, they thought, could account for such a complete restoration of serenity; and yet serenity was hardly the right term.

"She absolutely bubbled over," Pearl had confided. "We said to each other afterwards something must have happened. We didn't know what— but somehow we weren't quite comfortable about her. It's hard to explain. You see, she had a sort of self-satisfied, secret air. As Hubert put it, it was that I-have-eaten-the-canary expression."

This, in retrospect, cast a gruesome light on what then had been merely a bit odd; but far worse was the remark she made just before she left. Pearl quoted it with shuddering reluctance:

"If you expect to get anywhere in life," Dinah had said, "you've got to cut, slash, shove aside whatever gets in your way. Kill or be killed—that's my motto. I wish I'd learned it sooner."

Pearl had laughingly accused her of reading Nietzsche, Hubert of too many cocktails; but Dinah, looking very demure in her Victorian flounces, had gone off chanting the famous ditty from "Pippa Passes," only at the line about the snail she had broken off to ask, "By the way, did you ever squash a snail?" and burst into peals of merriment. Hubert saw her home, called "Cordon," and left her about to enter the door.

"She was smiling," Helen whispered, staring as though into an abyss of horror, "with the same tantalising air—and though the door actually opened, we know now that she never set foot inside it. Where did she go? What did she mean about squashing the snail?"

Tommy shook his head. Into his brain there crept again the impression which from early morning had tormented him—the idea received last night that Dinah's clouded mind had been irresistibly drawn towards some definite goal. . . .

"Tommy, did she really eat that stuff? You must know."

"Every morsel. That's certain. As to what all this tale means, I'm as much in the dark as you. You say she seemed in full possession of her senses?"

"So Pearl believed. I can't make it out."

After a heavy silence Tommy said, "Look here, what's this about the senior Mrs. Loughton being pleased? For that matter, who told her?"

"A woman in the same building, whom I rang up. She hurried up with the news, and Mrs. Loughton promptly telephoned her daughter-in-law. And that reminds me—Pearl declares she is sure Christopher knows something which he won't give away. It was he, even more than Hubert, who vetoed giving any information to the police."

"Naturally." Tommy shrugged in scorn, then pinned her with his eye. "What makes your friend think that young blighter knows something?" he demanded.

"Oh, instinct. Why, where are you off to?" she cried as Tommy sprang up with brusque decision and crammed on his hat.

"Never mind where. Just keep quiet about this, that's all."

Why this violent prejudice against Christopher Loughton? Tommy, pacing the reception-room of the American Embassy, was forced to admit that the sentiment long ante-dated Helen's disclosure; going back, in fact, to an incident, relatively trifling, which still rankled in his memory to quite an absurd degree.

Six months ago he had come here on business, to be received by Loughton, then newly installed in his post of third secretary. Finding the chair designated for visitors' use embarrassingly remote for confidential communications, he had as a matter of course tried to hitch it nearer the official desk. Nearer? Oh, no! It was firmly screwed to the floor.

He could feel again his shock of mortification, see the distant chary smile with which the attaché in take-it-or-leave-it tones had explained that he had been obliged to have the seat anchored to prevent tiresome people from crowding up and leaning their elbows among his papers. A good enough reason, no doubt, but to Tommy it seemed a disgrace to the whole American tradition and a personal affront as well. Such exclusiveness from a tuppenny-ha'penny sprig of diplomacy, grown too big for his boots! The lines of the famous jingle rang through his angry head:

> "Hail to our city of Boston,
> The land of the bean and the cod,
> Where Lowells speak only to Cabots,
> And Cabots speak only to God."

And this, he reflected, was the supercilious blackguard who didn't want the police informed. Afraid of stirring up mud which would soil his own immaculate socks. Afraid to confess that—

"Mr. Loughton will see you, sir."

Once more the wide expanse of polished parquet, the row of immovable chairs; once more the haughty, unrecognising stare which told him he was classed with the elbowing Dicks and Harrys; but Tommy, out for blood, strode straight to the orderly desk and leant over with his chin at an aggressive angle.

"Loughton," he said abruptly, "I've just one question to put to you. Where is Dinah Blake?"

He got what he wanted. The third secretary stiffened to rigidity and flushed a dull crimson under his fair, tanned skin. His hands clenched, and he rose, tall, very erect, and furious. His eyes, which were brown and unlikely in contrast to his pale blond hair flashed a glance in which fear fought with resentment; he breathed in through constricted nostrils.

"You'll have to explain that," he muttered in a fierce tone. "In the first place, who are you? No—I remember. Your name is Rostetter. I suppose you're representing the press?"

No words can convey the contempt with which this last sentence was charged. Tommy, glaring back, made swift calculations as to the advisability of meeting the insult in the one satisfying way, and decided nothing was to be gained by it.

"You suppose wrong. I want to keep this out of the papers—if I can. I was Miss Blake's partner at that dinner last night, and I'm out to find her before the police do. That's why I came to you."

Christopher Loughton's expression altered. It was now less enraged than watchful, hunted.

"Why assume I know where Miss Blake is? I don't."

"At any rate, you have some information on the subject, and if you hold it back you're doing her irreparable harm. You must realise the construction that's being put on her continued absence, and that whatever her reasons for keeping hidden, she must come forward, in her own interests. Is that clear, or must I diagram it?"

The young attaché's face grew ashen, haggard. There were deep circles round the eyes, which Tommy interpreted as anxiety on his own account.

"If it's your own miserable reputation you're protecting," went on the accuser scathingly, "then let me tell you—"

"My interests? Good God!" the other burst out in an agony. "Haven't you the wit to grasp it's Dinah I'm thinking about? If I could explain what I saw, I wouldn't hesitate. It's the misinterpretation they'll put on it, the—the—" He checked himself, sweat breaking out on his forehead.

"Then you do know something about last night!" Tommy exclaimed in relief. "Never mind the interpretation—and I suppose I'd better apologise for the tone I adopted to get at the truth. Trust me, won't you? If you feel as I do about this business, why can't we tackle it together?"

In spite of the total change in Tommy's manner, it seemed doubtful if Loughton was going to speak. Face averted, he opened his lips twice before any sound emerged. At the third attempt he gave voice to a few disjointed statements.

"I ran into her—late last night. Purely by accident and—I lost her again. Where she went, I don't know. I wish to God I did!"

There was now not the slightest doubt as to his sincerity, or the acuteness of his suffering. Oddly enough, he no longer seemed to Tommy a self-important prig, but a good-looking, somewhat austere-featured young man who was intensely reserved and shy—probably the victim of strong repressions. If such an one fell from grace, he would fall hard, thinking which Tommy's heart perceptibly softened.

"Tell me the whole thing. When and where did this meeting take place?"

"It was about twenty minutes past one, along the upper end of the Boulevard Raspail. I'd been for a long walk, and was on my way back. All at once I saw her, coming towards me, in an evening gown, with a little black wrap about her shoulders—"

"Was she coming slowly, or—"

"Briskly—as though she were going to some definite place. I didn't stop to wonder what she was doing out in that direction. It was the first time I'd seen her for—weeks, and without thinking I caught hold of her arm and spoke her name. She didn't answer. . . ."

"What—not a word?"

"No. She looked either at me or through me, with a smile that was . . . well, impish is the only way to describe it. I took it she didn't want to—" He paused, moistening his lips. "Then when I said something she pulled away, and as I caught at her again she ran like a hare, out into the middle of the street where there was a taxi-rank. You know the width of the boulevard. I was so dumbfounded I must have lost a few seconds. Anyhow, when I followed, she had completely disappeared."

"Into one of the cabs," suggested Tommy sharply.

"No, for I searched them all. The one driver on duty was dozing, so had noticed nothing. When I realised she must have darted across the street under cover of the rank, I spent an hour hunting up and down the whole neighbourhood, then had to give up. I can't think who told you I had anything up my sleeve, but possibly you can appreciate why I held my tongue."

"It was your sister-in-law; but tell me this: what cross-street lay nearest on the opposite side?"

"I can't say its name. I could find it quite easily."

"Has she any friends thereabouts?"

"Not one that I know of."

"Was she agitated in her manner?"

"On the contrary, I tell you she was happy—smiling, and now I think of it, humming to herself."

Tommy's eyes deepened with concentration. "Humming, was she? Did you recognise the tune?"

"As a matter of fact, I did," Christopher admitted, surprised. "It was that blues they played so much about two years ago—*Miss Virginia* it's called. But what—?"

"Quick!" Tommy seized his arm. "I want you to come now and show me the spot where you lost her. It's probably a fool's errand, but we'll have a go at it."

Meeting his glance, Christopher instantly opened a cupboard and took down his hat from a peg. As he did so, the desk telephone rang.

CHAPTER VIII

IT WAS the hall-operator speaking. Tommy could catch every word: "Lady Joan Raefield, sir. Shall I put her through this time?"

"Tell her I've gone out," replied the attaché between set teeth.

The listener watched him closely. Joan Raefield, with beauty enough for two women and a quarter of a million in her own right, could have her pick of quite twenty eligibles; "this time" indicated that her choice had fallen on Christopher. That the latter was in vulgar phrase "not having any" scored a point in his favour and was, no doubt, a sore irritation to Mrs. Loughton's matchmaking designs. Tommy was yet reluctant to overlook the screwing down of chairs, or the havoc wrought with Dinah's affections, but he began to suspect that the Dorinda episode was on Christopher's side a mere slaking of thirst. At any rate, there were no visible signs of grief over the loss of this unfortunate temptress, only paralysed concern for Dinah's fate.

They quitted the building and climbed into the two-seater. Both preserved a constrained silence till they had whizzed past the Concorde and reached the left bank. Then Tommy spoke. "So you believe she recognised you?"

"I got that impression," admitted his companion uncertainly. "It happened so quickly, you know. She was there one second, and gone the next."

"Forgive the question, but should you have expected her to cut you?"

"I can't say what I expected." The attaché paused painfully, and under his breath added: "If she did do it, she had a perfect right."

Courageous admission for one over-weighted with pride. That Christopher Loughton's protective covering had even for one moment been ripped away argued great emotional stress. Tommy, never for long able to resist human suffering, had to tell himself sternly how just it was for this young man to shoulder some part of the penalty.

The Boulevard Raspail swept ahead, its broad expanse punctuated with grills, beneath which the Metro thundered. Crossing the tram-lines of Montparnasse, they sped past a few turnings. Then Christopher called, "Stop! It's here, on our left."

The narrow street into which they ventured was luridly entitled the Passage d'Enfer, and consisted of tiny villas, wedged like sardines. Each had its separate entrance, and no concierge. Several displayed *A Louer* signs.

"I suppose we'd better do a house-to-house canvass," suggested Tommy, frowning at the bizarre row. "Shall we try?"

They encountered an odd assortment of persons, among them a blear-eyed Irish sculptress who nightly imbibed port at the Rotonde café and waxed tearful over reminiscences of Rodin. She, as it happened, knew Dinah by sight, but had seen nothing of her recently, while the other inhabitants denied any knowledge of the girl. At two doors they hammered and rang without result. In short, it was rapidly borne in upon them that if Dinah sought cover in this street it was only to hurry through it to some farther destination.

They explored a wide area, questioning with no success. At last they sought a public telephone and rang up the flat in the Rue Val- de-Grâce, but all they could learn from the frightened maid was that the police had been in twice to interrogate her, and that Mademoiselle Pemberton, having rushed back from Versailles, was out sending cables to America.

At the junction of the boulevards the two men's eyes met. Each knew to a sick certainty what the other was thinking—that if Dinah was not deliberately hiding from justice, she had made away with herself.

"She was going in the opposite direction from the Seine," remarked Tommy argumentatively.

"The river's not the only way."

"Still, you mustn't overlook the fact that she seemed happy."

Christopher said nothing, but the anguish in his set features forbade the offering of further consolation. When so little was known, what could be said one way or the other?

"Shall I drive you back to the Embassy?"

"No, drop me here. I'm going to see Hallie Pemberton."

Till now the shared anxiety of their quest had constituted a bond between them, but Tommy imagined that Christopher was fast regretting his bestowal of confidence. The brown eyes searched his face with a look half-inquisitive, half-resentful, as though their owner suspected he had not been told everything.

"Wondering, I suppose, if I've fallen in love with the girl," reflected Tommy as he drove away. "But God knows that's not the case."

No, at eight-and-thirty one doesn't fall in love overnight, or even play Don Quixote with any especial fervour; yet Tommy knew that for some obscure reason he would champion Dinah's cause if she stood in the dock now, charged with a dozen crimes. Besides, did not instinct keep insisting that there was something queer about it all, that the red-haired girl with her crystal-clear gaze and her piquant stubbornness was no less a victim than the one who had been so foully butchered?

He hied him to the commissariat in the Rue Vieille du Temple, found audience with the chief, and by dint of persistent questioning elicited a few facts. Dinah, it appeared, had not quitted the city by train, though whether she had done so by car remained unsettled. She had not spent the night with any of her friends, nor at an hotel. Having given up her studio she had not taken another, for her canvases were at her apartment. In other words, her whereabouts were a total mystery, but there was no mistaking the look on the chief inspector's face. The anticipated solution was suicide.

Suicide! That meant confession of guilt, against the very thought of which Tommy had set his face. Dinah Blake was no murderess. To prove it he reviewed, bit by bit, the two inexplicable and in some respects conflicting accounts of her conduct.

First of all, what was her state of mind subsequent to her departure? The Hubert Loughtons declared her quite rational and collected, puzzling enough in all conscience, when one considered how her companions had been affected by the drug. Christopher had mentioned her "impish" smile, and the fact that she was humming *Miss Virginia*—a tune which earlier in the evening she could not bear to hear. But had she recognized her former lover? Ah, if only one could make sure on that point! To walk over a mile to her friends' dwelling and converse sensibly bore every evidence of reasoned thought, while the same might be said of her refusal to acknowledge Christopher, and her bolt for freedom. Who could say what was in her mind? And then again, how to explain that speech quoted by Pearl Loughton?

Cut, slash, shove aside, kill or be killed . . . mere verbal extravagance, provided, of course, she was unaware of what she had left behind her; but could she be thus completely ignorant? To come on foot to the Rue Madame and arrive at about ten minutes past twelve she must have left the Ile St. Louis not much later than twenty minutes before midnight. Say she wandered a bit first, making it eleven-thirty—but, no, that was impossible. At eleven-thirty Tommy had still been awake, and very soon after this Dorinda met her death. *She must have known.*

Tommy drew back, appalled. Of course she knew! Now in a flash he grasped the true significance of her words, saw in them a final gesture of bravado on the part of one determined to take her own life. How else to construe them? When Christopher met her, she was singing to keep up her courage—but had that courage borne her through or broken down at the last moment? There seemed a faint chance that she was still alive, but terrified to reveal herself.

The noon papers were out. He bought a copy, and devoured the account of last night's sensation. The bare facts, the list of guests, but little more, except, between every statement, the clear implication that the vanished girl was guilty. Here, though, was something which struck him as paradoxical. In reference to the step-father's telephone call Benedetto declared that Mr. Jethro had wished to set forward the hour of a luncheon engagement already made with Miss Quarles. Luncheon engagement? It was hard for Tommy, with the tone of that discordant conversation still ringing in his ears, to understand how Dorinda could have intended meeting Jethro the following day. Indeed, there must have been some misunderstanding on the butler's part. Certainly Jethro had said on the stairs, "As I'm not likely to see you again." Tommy's own hearing might have been at fault, but he was inclined to doubt it.

Still, this was neither here nor there. What mattered was that no specific motive for murder was mentioned, a circumstance which brought him intense relief. Motive in a case like this, where there could be no eye-witnesses, was everything.

He was tempted to hope that as Dinah herself had apparently given nothing away, neither her friends nor her enemies could bring anything against her. He was not satisfied, though. The odious Falkland woman had made violent assertions, ill-founded, perhaps, but calculated to do much mischief. Afterwards she had shared a taxi with Peter Hummock, the most notorious scandalmonger in the Quarter. Cicely Gault, too, by her very manner, had suggested she knew something about Dinah's private affairs. Would it not be a good idea to delve into this, ascertain just how far rumour had been at work?

Aimless driving had brought him near the Rue du Bac, in which street Hummock had his combined bachelor apartment and shop. He heightened speed, and five minutes later was shown by a charwoman into a room hung with Genoese velvet and smelling of incense. In a Louis Quinze bed, under a rose canopy, lay Peter, prostrate, woebegone. On his head was a wet towel, beneath which his crumpled visage showed pasty-hued with nausea and fright.

"You!" he groaned, and after a single look of loathing burrowed deep into the pink sheets. "I strictly forbade that old hag to let anyone in," he complained in muffled and aggrieved tones. "What does she mean by it?"

"Ten francs," replied Tommy cruelly, "was the price of admission. What's wrong? Feeling squeamish?"

"Squeamish! A shock like this for a man of my constitution, and you have the brutality to ask if I'm squeamish!"

"Dope's bad, you know, especially at your age. Bound to frazzle the nerves."

The pale eyes came to the surface to glare balefully. "How dare you speak of that wretched stuff! Oh, let me forget, let me forget. I'm ill, I tell you—and what's more, there's a plainclothes man watching my door. I shall most likely stay right here in this bed like a hermit, till the beastly affair is cleared up."

"A hermit-crab, I should call it—and a jolly comfortable shell, too. I saw your man outside, staring at your show-case, but I thought he was detecting faked antiques. What makes you think he's got his eye on you?"

"It's not just me, it's every single one of us that'll be spied on, followed about, as long as that Blake girl's at large. Oh, don't I know these French police methods!"

"So you feel certain Miss Blake's responsible, do you?" inquired Tommy coldly.

"How can there be any doubt of it? Didn't she worm her way into that party last night simply because she was in on the dope stunt, and saw her chance to do a murder without getting the blame? It's clear as day, when you know the facts."

"It's not at all clear to me that she expected to take dope," said Tommy between his teeth. "I'm sure she didn't. And if she did know what was planned, why do you imagine she drew definite suspicion to herself by going away?"

"She weakened, I guess. Murder's not a thing you do every day. But the whole Quarter's wise to the way she's been absolutely stalking Dodo Quarles for the past few weeks. Green-eyed over that Embassy fellow Dodo took away from her." Stalking! By a perverse chance the word conjured before Tommy's eyes a scene recently witnessed along the crowded Boul' Mich'—a brawl between two street girls over a youth, slim, slouching, with wide hat and trailing cigarette. When the victorious wench had gone off arm-in-arm with her prey, the discarded mistress followed relentlessly behind, pacing with long strides like a lean and hungry tigress. Abuse streamed from her scarlet lips, her eyes were glazed with hatred.

Onlookers drew back, stared, and threw derisive comments. Someone whispered that she had a knife in her hand. . . .

"See here, Hummock," said Tommy sternly. "You know as well as I do how little truth there is in these stories. What I'd like to find out about this one is who started it—because I happen to know it's a lie. Am I to understand Miss Blake confided in you?"

"Oh, you will rag, won't you? Why, I scarcely know her. She has the name for being awfully close-mouthed, too."

"Exactly. Well, I want to say that your remarks on the subject are extremely offensive to me. To me—get that? I warn you not to do any broadcasting."

Hummock's jaw dropped. His eyes took on a shrewd look as he protested in an injured voice. "Oh, well, how was I to guess she meant all this to you? I suppose I'm wrong then. I dare say none of these fresh young things go in for dope, and that little Cope-Villiers isn't just regularly saturated with cocaine. One hears these yarns, but—"

"That's enough," cried Tommy furiously.

"Well, if you're going to get ratty—but just see what the whole town'll be saying by to-night. That'll show you."

Kicking over a beaded stool that barred his way, Tommy made a violent exit. What he had heard disturbed him, indicating as it did the suggestions sure to be made to the judge by those frantic to shield themselves at another's expense. A surmise alone would suffice to set fire to the train of gun-powder, and if it were remotely hinted that Dinah had been a party to the drug-taking project, the presumption of her guilt would be strong indeed. No use reminding himself that such a possibility was unthinkable. Those in authority would not find it so.

He regretted now that his hasty temper had forbidden him finding out precisely what that flabby fool Hummock referred to as facts. Still, there was Mowbray, who undoubtedly knew better than anyone else just when and how the fatal joke originated. Of the man himself, scoundrel though he might be, he had no direct suspicion, but Helen had told him that Dorinda, after knowing no restraining influence would be present, had rung up her principal guest and held a conversation with him. If as Helen supposed the affair was arranged then, without previous preparation, the circumstance would tell in Dinah's favour.

"I'll hunt the fellow up now," Tommy decided. "He may not tell me, of course, but I can see if he's lying. Where the hell does he keep himself? I heard something about him and Cleeves occupying a friend's flat, but—hold on, though! The addresses are all in the newspaper."

So they were, with that of Messrs. Mowbray and Cleeves, given as 24 rue Guynemer. Without more ado he sped towards the Luxembourg Gardens.

With Hummock's speech regarding police supervision fresh in mind, he had little difficulty in placing the shabby lounger who, picking his teeth, leant against the iron railings along the garden side of the street. It occurred to him to wonder what a single sleuth would do if his two suspects came forth to go in separate directions.

"But that's his funeral, not mine," he reflected, as, crossing to Number 24, he made inquiries of the concierge.

CHAPTER IX

A SHARP-faced man-servant in a striped coat showed Tommy into what evidently was not a working studio, though the immense window admitted a flood of sunshine. The walls were roughcast, the chairs and divan cushioned and low, with a prevailing colour scheme of neutral greys. Against this background stood out one solitary painting—that of a gigantic steel spring uncurling against a green-blue sky. Books sprawled upon low glass tables, flaming gladioli soared from a square glass jar, and in and out of all this cigarette smoke trailed in festoons.

Mowbray and Ronald Cleeves, wearing dressing-gowns, sat close together, in earnest discussion over bowls of *café au lait*. At the visitor's approach they abruptly ceased talking and stared with a sort of stilled attentiveness. Mowbray did not rise, and an ungracious interval elapsed before his young companion got up, vaguely hostile in manner. Neither uttered a word of greeting, and the subtle antagonism conveyed by both roused Tommy to resentment. Feeling he had interrupted some serious conclave, he wondered if he ought to accept the seat so tardily proffered; but, keeping to his usual tactics, he did so, and inquired with cheerful blandness if his hosts had heard anything new.

"We have not been out," returned Cleeves with glacial contempt, whereupon silence was renewed.

Unpromising, but Tommy was not to be baulked by rudeness. "I was rather speculating," he said, "as to whose idea it was—originally, that is—to hold that party last night. Could you give me any notion as to how it came about?"

Telegraphic glances passed from one to the other. Cleeves folded his arms mutely, but Mowbray, fixing his small, muddy eyes on the toes of his shabby espadrilles, spoke with lethargic indifference.

"To begin with," he said slowly, "I may as well tell you the exact extent of my acquaintance with Miss Quarles. I had met her just twice before last evening—once in August, when she came ashore with a yachting party near my place in Corsica, and once the day before yesterday. Cleeves here knows her rather better, but not well. He is, in fact, a sort of relation of hers, his father and her mother being second cousins. I think that's right?" He appealed to his friend, who did not answer. "Well, then! On the Corsican occasion we talked, and she asked a great many questions, the upshot of which was that we were both to dine with her when we came to Paris. We did not see her again, however, till we met, by chance, at a big afternoon reception. The invitation was given then, and accepted."

"There were others of our party present?"

"All, I think, except yourself and the Argentine, da Costa."

"It was a simple dinner invitation, then? No general discussion of drugs?"

Mowbray shot a cold look at him. "I protest against the word 'drugs.' If such a thing was discussed, it was not in my presence."

"I see," Tommy ruminated, feeling he was not likely to get much further. Then an idea occurred to him. "Do you mind telling me who gave this reception?" he asked.

"Not at all. It was the Baroness Waldheim."

Old Sophie Waldheim! Tommy himself had been invited to that particular function, though as a matter of course he had not gone....

"And you say Miss Blake was in the group when the dinner-party was suggested?"

"Miss Blake? Ah, the American girl! I believe so. Yes, she was there."

Although both pairs of eyes were steadfastly averted, Tommy had the sensation of being watched. He could swear these two were on guard, but he could not be bothered to investigate the reason.

"By the way," he ventured brightly, "what exactly was that stuff you gave us?"

Ronald Cleeves sat still and tense, but Mowbray laughed with scornful amusement.

"Ah, that's the whole point! A small experiment of mine in the line of suggestion. The mixture you ate contained no narcotic. To be quite candid, it is an innocent compound the result of which depends on the extent to which people believe in its powers. The response last night was a marvellous demonstration of what stimulated imagination can do. I had spoken to Miss Quarles about the joke I occasionally practised on credulous people, and about seven o'clock last night she rang up to ask if I would help her try the same deception on her friends."

"Then our behaving in that fashion, tumbling fast asleep and so on, was only due to suggestion?" demanded Tommy, dumbfounded.

"Entirely so. It's too bad the police, after turning this place inside out, didn't find some of the concoction. It would have been worth something to see their disappointment."

Tommy smiled. "Never mind, you'll still get your laugh on them. As it happened, I saved a generous hunk of my portion. The police analyst is working on it now."

There was a smothered explosion.

"What! You gave some of it to the police?"

Mowbray had lumbered to his feet, jowl out-thrust, face so swollen with fury that he reminded Tommy of a Black Mamba preparing to strike. Cleeves, too, sprang up, eyes blazing, hands clenched. Every vestige of indifference had vanished. For a moment it looked as though the visitor were going to be manhandled.

"You swine! You mean to say you've made it possible—for—for—" Cleeves got thus far and broke off, breathing hard.

It was time to go, and Tommy went, but not before he had completed the unfinished sentence.

"For your friend here to be arrested for drug-purveying? Yes, that's about the size of it, I fancy. Six months, I believe, is the penalty. Thanks for telling me what I wanted to know."

So Mowbray, well aware of the drug's dangerous potentialities, had hoped to skin out of his difficulty by failing to produce a specimen! No wonder he was terrified to find his fiction unmasked. For that matter, if Dinah were located and convicted of murder, he would probably be in for something rather worse than half a year's imprisonment. . . .

If—! Tommy suddenly realised he was still ignorant of the specific thing he wished to ascertain, and asked himself which of the remaining guests could be relied on to furnish an unexpurgated version of events leading up to the party. A woman would be better than a man, for women have an eye to detail. Rita Falkland was too biased to be of any use, but what about Cicely Gault?

The latter, in emerald pyjamas and horn-rimmed spectacles, offered him whisky and soda, and gave sphinx-eyed attention to his request.

"Wait!" she commanded. "What are your sentiments regarding Dinah Blake—for, or against?"

"Dead or alive," he answered promptly, "I want to see her get a square deal."

"Shake! So do I. That's why I'm not handing the police one scrap of unnecessary information, and though I can't absolutely bank on it, I believe I'm the one person who could. Listen!" She got up and closed the door. "Now, I'll give you a few facts."

She began with an account of a stupefying *faux pas* made by the Baroness Waldheim, whose propensity for dropping bricks was too celebrated to require comment. The moment Dinah arrived at the reception-room the old idiot shouted lustily, "And why haven't you brought along that good-looking fiancé of yours? What's become of him?" To which Dinah replied with admirable coolness, "Oh, didn't you know? He's not my fiancé any longer." "What!" screamed Sophie. "So it's really true you've let that young hussy Dodo Quarles snaffle him from under your very nose? Fie, for shame! Why don't you scratch her eyes out?"

"Several of us heard," continued Miss Gault slowly. "And indeed it's certain Sophie meant the remark for Dodo herself, though Dodo, who was standing three feet away, paid no attention. It was horribly embarrassing for Dinah, but I'm going to tell you she carried the situation off like a breeze. She laughed, treating the affair like a silly joke, then joined Dodo and stuck by her the remainder of the afternoon, pretending they were far more intimate than they actually were. That showed spirit. Being present at the time, she was naturally included in the sort of wholesale invitation to dinner which Dodo extended to Mowbray, Ronnie Cleeves, and the rest of us. I believed then—and I still think I was right—she accepted purely to show she bore the girl no grudge. It was a question of pride. As to what she may have done afterwards—"

Tommy waited uncomfortably for her to go on, but she had stopped dead. He therefore inquired whether or not the subject of drugs was broached in her hearing.

"Not in so many words. Of course, we all knew about Mowbray. Who doesn't? I seem to recall Dodo dropping some pretty broad hints. She was nicely squiffed, as usual, so she wasn't exactly discreet; but Mowbray was extremely cagey. Wouldn't commit himself."

Miss Gault glanced doubtfully at her caller, drew towards her a copy of the latest extra, and pointed to the scare-lines across the page.

"Just look at that! Poor kid! Even her manner of dying was spectacular. As for the rest of us victims—"

But Tommy was not to be sidetracked.

"Is that all you've got to tell me?" he asked quietly. "You can trust me to show discretion. If there's another weak spot in her defence—"

She examined her crimson nails, hesitated, and looked at him straight in the eyes.

"There is," she replied abruptly. "I rather hate mentioning it. As I was leaving I passed the men's cloakroom. I glanced in, and saw Dodo holding on to Mowbray by the lapels and whispering to him. Trying hard, I thought, to persuade him. I caught the words 'dope' and 'telephone.' And at that very instant—"

"Go on."

"Dinah Blake came running up, looking for some one. She peered into the cloakroom, saw those two, and joined them. I left them, so I don't know anything more."

Tommy sat very still. "But you got the impression of a three-cornered conference?" he suggested after a pause.

"Well, as a matter of fact, I did; but I may be mistaken. In any case, I've said nothing about it. I don't intend to, either. . . ."

Tommy paid no more visits. Though till a late hour that evening he continued to roam restlessly about, he avoided contacts in order not to hear what he knew now was being said. From a distance he sighted gloating groups of English and American citizens, the pavement-tables of cafés thronged and buzzing with conjecture, all on one topic. What an apéritif for jaded palates! A drug-orgy—the notorious Dodo Quarles stabbed to death in a circle of intimates—a Virginia artist vanished from human ken! "There was always something about her, you know. . . ." Still more infuriating were the shrugs of sober Parisians, the contemptuous glances which meant that only idle foreigners committed these excesses.

He clung still to his belief that Dinah's presence last night had been actuated by pride; but afterwards—what? The deed must have resulted from temporary derangement induced by the drug. No other explanation was compatible with his reading of the poor girl's character. A period of elation had followed, then reaction set in. Overpowered by the knowledge of what she had done, she had taken the one way out. Very soon, now, the chapter would be closed.

Yet when two-thirds of the next day had dragged by uncertainty still prevailed. Exhausted and despairing after a fourth call at the commissariat, Tommy leant over the parapet of the Pont Neuf, just as the clocks were striking five, and gazed down, hypnotised by the lapping waters below. The river was a symbol, no more. He did not feel at all certain that somewhere along these tricky bends a blue-green frock was lodged in mud and slime. He was no longer sure of anything, except that he would never set eyes on Dinah again.

He was quite wrong. At the precise moment that he formulated this belief, the subject of his thoughts was alighting from a red taxi-cab outside her own entrance in the Rue Val-de-Grâce. Her demure chignon was scarcely ruffled, her cheeks the tint of apple blossom; but there was a stealthy haste in her movements as she darted past the concierge's lodge and raced up the stairs.

Inside the door of her flat she paused to listen. No one here. What a relief! She must get out of this ridiculous dress at once. Heavens, how she had slept! And way off there, too, though the funny part of it was she ... oo-ooh! She had not yet properly waked up, it seemed. Well, she had wanted to sleep, and she had got her wish.

Within her own room, she cast her wrap on the bed, stifled another yawn, and glanced guiltily in the mirror. Then, unfastening her frock with one hand, she spread in front of her the copy of *Le Soir* purchased on her way home. The date of issue puzzled her. Sunday, October second? Impossible, when yesterday was Friday. Still, how could a newspaper be wrong about the date? And then those crowds of people strolling about the Luxembourg....

Something else caught her attention—her name—hers, in heavy print. Was there another Dinah Blake? But what was the meaning of this second headline:

> ON RECHERCHE TOUJOURS LA JEUNE FEMME
> SOUPÇONNÉE
>
> DU MEUTRE DE MISS QUARLES.

She grasped the sheet in both hands, stiffening as she read. The type swam before her in a blur.

CHAPTER X

SOME indefinite period after this her cousin Hallie Pemberton came into the flat, passed the door of the bedroom, and saw her standing frozen in the same spot. She hardly heard the gasping cry, or felt the trembling clutch of the arms about her. Gradually, however, she became aware that the little spinster was sobbing words of frantic relief.

"Dinah—Dinah! Where have you been? Two whole days! Oh, you poor, poor child."

Hallie was gazing at her through prim pince-nez, running uncertain fingers along her rigid arms as though to make sure this was flesh and blood, not the ghost she half-suspected; but still Dinah could not speak.

Poor Hallie! Petrified with fear, crushed with shame as she fancied every eye in the Quarter fixed on her with sinister meaning, she had fled from the post-office like a criminal, trying to escape notice. At the corner dairy shop she had lowered her head, for there, haranguing the dairy woman, was Irene, their daily servant—Irene, who was lavishing on this sensation the full force of a nature starved of romance. All the tradespeople gossiped and gloated, but even they were less to be shunned than the kind friends against whom Hallie had firmly shut her door. Like Dinah, she was proud.

"Dinah! Say something! Oh, don't stare like that, dear. Tell me where you've been, what you've been do—" She choked on the final word.

The image came alive. One stiff finger pointed at the headlines spread above two columns of print.

"Look!" whispered the girl. "Do you see what I see, or am I still dreaming?"

Hallie's mouth fell open. Her glasses dropped, dangling from their tiny gold chain.

"Why, what do you mean? Dinah! Did . . . didn't you know?"

"How could I know anything? I've only just waked up. But wait—what's to-day? Saturday, isn't it?"

"Saturday!" Hallie's voice broke hysterically. "Oh, you poor thing! It's Sunday, of course. You've been gone two days."

Two days! Then it was true. . . .

Laughing weakly, Hallie sank on to the bed and pushed back her hat from her mouse-coloured, net-enclosed hair. Oh, she had tried all along to believe there was some explanation! Dinah couldn't—but what was she to think, in the face of what the papers were saying?

"But where were you?" she insisted. "I must know all about it, quick, too. Every second is vital."

"I'll tell you what I can," answered Dinah, her teeth chattering. "But it's so little, for I simply haven't an idea how . . . you see, yesterday . . . no, I mean Friday, I suppose . . . when I was lunching at the Rotonde, I . . ."

In a whisper, the breath in her body insufficient to sustain her voice, she brought forth the halting sentences. Hallie Pemberton, dumbfounded by what she heard, believed. She had never failed to believe Dinah, for

Dinah always spoke the truth, or else kept silent. Dinah couldn't lie. Only this story was so preposterous. Would any outside person credit it? Above all, would it stave off what seemed inevitable, the poor child's arrest on a charge of wilful murder?

As she coped with the terrible problem her arm was clutched in a grip of steel.

"Hallie! Look me in the eye. Does everybody think I did this? Did you think it?"

Hallie quailed under the fierceness of the question. "I . . . oh, my dear, I . . . I just tried not to think. I was afraid you weren't alive."

"Then you did believe it . . . oh, I don't blame you. And now, I suppose, they'll be coming to arrest me for murder. Is that so?"

"No, no!" Hallie winced, stung to desperate activity. "What you've just told me ought to make all the difference, only . . . oh, dear, if there was some one to advise us! That wretched inspector's sure to drop in again any minute, and unless we can think of something now, this instant . . ." She fluttered like a trapped bird, then an idea came to her. "I know! Take off your clothes, get into bed. I'm going to ring up Dr. Barnes, and . . . but there, I've forgotten something. Did that old cat downstairs see you come in?"

"The concierge? No. She was frying onions. No one saw me."

"Thank goodness for that! Now . . . but s'sh! There's that worthless Irene coming in the door. She'll have to be told you're here, but anyhow she shan't stir out again to spread any more gossip. Just wait till I've seen her."

Outside, the door closed behind her, Hallie addressed the maid in her careful American French.

"You've been a long time, Irene. Have you got the eggs? Good. Then make tea, and an omelette . . . for two. Mademoiselle has returned."

Irene's eyes bulged. The string-bag holding the eggs slipped from her grasp, but Hallie caught it.

"Mademoiselle! Ah, my God! Then she's alive, not—"

"Certainly she's alive," retorted Hallie crisply. "And very hungry. Now, quick about it!"

"Hungry!" The wily Irene sidled back along the passage. "In that case," she murmured unctuously, "I'd better descend and search a few mushrooms, a little Suisse, some fruit—"

"You'll search nothing. Into the kitchen!"—and laying firm hands on the unwilling shoulders, Hallie bundled the girl about her task.

She rang up the doctor, but he was out on a maternity case. This meant delay—but whom else could she call upon? She realised dimly that a lawyer would probably be required, but during her three years' sojourn in Paris neither she nor Dinah had ever needed legal advice. If only Christopher were not exiled from the flat! Hallie could trust Christopher, whom she still thought of with lingering regret. Dared she telephone him to come round? Dinah would be furious, but then this was a desperate case. Perhaps if she kept her voice very low Dinah need not hear. She was just picking up the receiver again when a sharp rat-tat on the knocker outside brought her quivering to her feet. The police!

"Go back!" she hissed to Irene, who, preternaturally punctual, was hastening to answer the summons. "Don't make a sound. Let them think we're out."

When the servant was gone, she remained, not daring to breathe, her eyes glued to the door. The knock was repeated, with growing insistence. It might, she thought, be the concierge with another cable from home. If she waited, the envelope would be slid under the door. Yes, look! Something white was just appearing on the mat. Not a telegram, though. A visiting-card. Whose?

Curiosity prevailed. She picked up the bit of cardboard, read a man's name which, though familiar, conveyed nothing to her, and in still greater mystification saw that the line pencilled beneath was addressed to her.

"Miss Pemberton," it ran, "please let me in. I am a friend of Miss Blake's."

Dinah's friend? Then there could be no harm in just having a peep at him. She opened the door a hand's-breadth and gazed up into a pair of blue eyes which she had never seen before, but which somehow inspired confidence. They were set in a fresh-coloured face which she knew to be English. The tweed suit was English, too. The next moment the stranger had stepped inside.

"Forgive me for intruding on you like this," he cried earnestly. "You see, I'm the man who sat next your cousin at that beastly dinner. I felt I had to talk to you about it. Are you alone?"

The urgency in his voice told her that here was some one who had shared her terrors. In a flash she knew, as one does know these things, that here at last was some one to whom she could with safety unburden herself.

"Mr. Rostetter," she whispered, drawing him into the salon. "Dinah's come home. She's in her room now. Oh, can you tell us what we ought to do?"

Tommy reeled. The whole of his gloomy horizon became suffused in rainbow tints.

"Come home? Here, tell me about it! Is she . . . is she all right?"

"Yes . . . no . . . oh, it's so peculiar, I don't know what to say. Will she be believed? That's the point. You see, till half an hour ago she hadn't the remotest conception that . . . that this murder had occurred. Her memory's a blank. Not till she saw a newspaper and read how they were searching for her—"

"Hold on! You say she doesn't remember . . . anything?"

"Not one thing since the dinner-party. You may think it's impossible. I would, if I didn't know Dinah. Listen, this is what happened."

In intense agitation she repeated Dinah's recital. Tommy's eyes remained fixed on her little, drab, middle-aged face, so frank, so sensible. Then, he thought, it was the Passage d'Enfer after all—one of those villas which had its windows shuttered. Yet what a row he had made on the knocker!

"And she can't tell you how she got here? She doesn't recall anything that happened on the way?"

"Not a thing. When she woke up this afternoon she couldn't imagine where she was. Then it came back to her, or at least she did recognise the room as the Van Valkenburgs' studio. How she got there was a mystery, but, you see, that very day at lunch she'd run into the Van Valkenburgs, who were just off to the Dolomites. When she mentioned she was looking for a place to paint in, they said she might use their studio while they were gone, and gave her the key there and then, only they begged her not to say anything about it. That was because they'd refused to lend it to several people, on account of the filthy state most of these artists leave a room in. It's their house, you know, and they like to keep things nicely."

"And the key? I suppose she had it with her?"

"Of course—in a little change-purse, inside her evening-bag. She must have walked all the way, for they haven't found any taxi-driver who drove her."

"She did walk," said Tommy. "And she paid a call on the way. I expect you've heard something about that, but have you told her?" he demanded sharply.

"Not yet, though Mrs. Hubert Laughton did—"

"Then don't. If she's forgotten that, too, the fact will help prove she's speaking the truth. The police will have to know, of course, and when they come to question her they'll soon see she's not shamming ignorance. The trouble is, though, will that be sufficient to clear her?"

"Oh, Mr. Rostetter! You think they may arrest her anyhow?"

"I don't know. It's to be hoped they'll merely examine her closely, and go ahead with the investigation, but one can't be sure."

Tommy pressed his hands against his eyes and thought hard.

Hallie watched him in tense perturbation till he looked up at her with his keen, blue gaze.

"Miss Pemberton," he said. "As I see it, there are just two things against your cousin. First, her disappearance, which may be got over now she's given a plausible story which can't be disproved; and second, a possible—mind, I only say possible—motive for the crime. It's that motive I must speak about. I beg your pardon for being so blunt, but have you any definite notion as to why Miss Blake broke off her engagement with Mr. Loughton?"

Hallie's drab cheeks flushed uncomfortably.

"Dinah never gave me her reason, Mr. Rostetter. She's very reserved in some ways. If I've heard talk—"

"Talk!" He gave an angry exclamation under his breath. "Talk is what worries me. I can see you know what's being said. With two women in the case, the police will immediately scent jealousy, and look for the man—and they won't have far to look, I'm afraid. It's a good thing your cousin hasn't noised her affairs abroad, but it won't help her much—by itself, that is. If we're to wangle her out of a desperate situation, we must—we absolutely must—find some means of discrediting rumour. Now can such a thing be done?"

"I'm sure I can't think of any way. She never quarrelled with that girl—of that I'm positive. They were only art school acquaintances, anyhow, but whatever may have happened, they were outwardly friendly. Why, the very fact that Dinah went to Miss Quarles' party—" Hallie stopped, realising her mistake.

"There's a snag there, isn't there? And nothing will prevent the judge from putting a nasty construction on her going. Let me think—let me think!" He closed his eyes again, to open them suddenly. "Miss Pemberton, I can imagine just one way of clearing up this matter. I'm sure the man in the case would consent with alacrity—but would your cousin agree, could she be persuaded, to pretend the difference between her and Mr. Loughton was made up before this party took place?"

"Dinah agree to that?" Hallie shook her head emphatically. "Never! You don't know her as I do. Besides, would any one believe it? Christopher's not been near this flat for three whole weeks."

"Too bad!" muttered Tommy despairingly. "It would have done the trick. Well, then, what about being engaged to some one else? For the time being, you know. There's an idea," he cried triumphantly. "I wouldn't suggest it if I saw any other way. Any one not too improbable will do—a lay figure, that's what we want. Come to think of it . . . see here, Miss Pemberton, what about me?"

Hallie gasped. "You? But, Mr. Rostetter, Dinah scarcely knows you. Could any one be taken in by such a fabrication?"

"I think they could. I've shown a lot of interest in her, both at the dinner and since. Roused comment, in fact. As an actual fact, I was introduced to her just about the time she sent Loughton about his business. We might even give it out that she chucked him in favour of me. By Jove, that's the stuff!" he exclaimed, enraptured with his idea. "If we can get that notion firmly rooted in the judge's mind, he won't give tuppence for any theory about revenge. There'd be nothing to revenge, would there? Oh, I can see it working. She can leave me to invent the necessary lies. It's part of my job. Can I see her? We must fix this up at once, you know, or it'll be useless."

Half-rising, Hallie regarded him as though slightly dubious of his sanity.

"You're not joking, Mr. Rostetter? You honestly believe this would save Dinah?"

"Am I likely to joke at a time like this? I believe it will save her— and I believe, too, in her complete innocence to such an extent that I'll perjure myself up to the hilt to prove it. Let her say the word—that's all."

"Dinah's stubborn, you know," murmured the little woman, moving dazedly away. "I don't suppose for a moment she'll—"

"She won't!"

It was Dinah herself who spoke. She had thrown open the salon doors, and with her dark red hair streaming over the white peignoir which swathed her and scarlet spots in her cheeks, stood confronting them with heaving breast.

"Oh, what's the good of your plotting to help me?" she cried in an agonised voice. "I killed Dorinda. I stabbed her in the heart with that Algerian knife. So now you know . . ."

CHAPTER XI

EVERY drop of blood in Tommy's veins froze. He stared fixedly at the girl's abnormally brilliant eyes, and in the few seconds which elapsed before either he or his companion could recover sufficiently to speak, his opinions boxed the entire compass to return to their starting point.

It was Hallie who first broke the silence. With a stifled wail she flung protecting arms round her cousin's taut body, whispering, "Hush, hush! Oh, Mr. Rostetter, Dinah's hysterical, that's all. I tell you, I saw her with *Le Soir* in her hands! She didn't know till then. I swear it!"

Tommy had regained his self-possession.

"All right," he said briskly, taking Dinah's icy hand and drawing her to a sofa. "Now, just sit down quietly and let us know all about it. You say you stabbed Dorinda with the Algerian knife—the one we used for the grapes. Is that the idea?"

"Yes," answered the girl with a shudder. "You must have noticed how it fascinated me. When I felt its sharp point I kept thinking how easy it would be just to stick it into any one who was sound asleep. Well, when the chance came, I did it."

"Exactly," he pattered, nodding his head. "And the knife itself? Did you take it away with you? Perhaps you've got it now?"

As he said this he drew out his own copy of *Le Soir* and quickly scanned the front page. No, the weapon was not mentioned.

"I—I can't remember," she faltered, looking a little blank.

"I must have thrown it into the river when I crossed the bridge. Yes, I feel sure that's what I did."

"I see." Very casually he took her right hand, and studied the pink, manicured nails. Though not over-clean, they showed no trace of darkening round the cuticle. "By the way," he asked, "have you had a wash since you woke up?"

"I was just going to. Why?" in dull surprise.

"Oh, nothing. Now about this knife; would it astonish you to hear that since this paper went to press the police experts have decided the murder was committed with some other quite different weapon?"

"Not that knife? But I don't understand. I thought—"

"Don't think," ordered Tommy, exultant over the success of his simple bluff. "Only you mustn't expect us to be taken in by this confession of yours. You don't really remember anything, now do you? Ah, I thought not! Well, then, if that's your story, stick to it. Don't go drawing on your imagination, please. Surely," he went on with deliberate brusqueness, "you're not fool enough to confess to a crime you can't remember?"

She turned her aquamarine eyes on him slowly.

"Hallie," she said to her bewildered cousin, "leave us alone a minute, will you?" She waited till the door closed behind Miss Pemberton, then grasping Tommy's arm spoke with terrifying conviction: "You see, I wanted to kill her. Never mind why. All through that awful meal there was murder in my heart. Now do you understand why I know I did it?" Tommy laughed light-heartedly. "My dear child, what rubbish! Every human being at one time or another feels like that about someone. Why, supposing I'd killed half the people I've wanted to kill? I'd be a second Landru. But I don't go around pretending to deeds I've merely wanted to commit." She shook her head obstinately. "What about the dreams I've had? They've gone from me now, but they were wonderful—satisfying. Why, when I woke up, did I feel that everything in life was perfect?"

"Precisely. Would you have felt that if you'd known yourself guilty of murder? What you experienced was the result of that drug. Didn't that Mowbray fellow tell us we'd dream of accomplishing some secret desire?"

"And to think that my cherished desire was—murder! Me, a murderess!" She examined her slender hands with a sort of numb horror. "I don't pretend," she said in a more reasonable tone, "that I'd have done it in my right senses. I'd have seen too clearly the consequences—and I can't say I'd really choose to have any one's death on my conscience; but all the same, I must have done it. Who else in that crowd had any reason to?"

"Ah, that's what we'd all like to know!" He pinioned her wrists in a grip that made her wince. "Look at me, Dinah! May I call you that? I want you to grasp that your safety in this matter depends almost entirely on yourself. Whatever happens, you'll be hauled up before the *juge d'instruction* and asked a lot of troublesome questions. You can tell a straight story without adding anything to it, can't you?"

"I don't see why not."

"But you need not give away your private feelings towards Dorinda. Your thoughts are your own. Now, what about that suggestion of mine which you seem to have overheard?"

"That?" She gave a little, scornful laugh. "It's good of you to want to sacrifice yourself for me, but really, you must see how useless such a pretence would be. Me, engaged to you!"

"Why that tone?" he demanded, ruffled. "Is there anything so fantastic about it? Women like you have made worse selections, let me inform you."

"I—I didn't mean that!" she stammered, reddening. "But who'll believe us?"

"Why shouldn't everyone believe us? I take it none of those people the other night were in your confidence?"

"I should say not!" she replied with slight hauteur. "I despise the whole lot of them! If ever I'd guessed that horrible trick was going to be played—"

"That's another point." He spoke very casually. "When you were talking to Dorinda and Mowbray in the Baroness Waldheim's cloakroom, was anything said on the subject of this so-called joke?"

She stared at him, puzzled. "Who told you about that? No, of course there wasn't. They stopped talking when I went in to ask if it really was the coming Friday we were asked to dinner. I went out and left them together. I don't know what they were discussing."

"But you realised, I suppose, that Mowbray's drugs had a morbid fascination for Dorinda?"

"She'd been chattering about them that afternoon, but from what she said I never imagined the stuff was something to eat, still less that she would dare hand it round at a dinner-party. Why, you must have seen how upset I was to find I'd swallowed a drug without knowing it! I've a perfect horror of such things."

He believed her.

"Good! Now let's return to the main subject. I propose to furnish you with a brief outline of what might have happened after our one and only meeting in the Champs Elysées. You recall it, don't you?" Retaining her wrists in a close hold he drove home his points with a series of squeezes. "You may remember we walked as far as the Madeleine together. Didn't we?"

"And separated."

"Wrong! We lunched together and went to see a film called 'Love's Wings.' We were much attracted to each other, you see; and after a week of daily meetings, I laid my heart at your feet and was accepted. Why, God knows; but that's your affair. Are you listening? Then I'll go on. Owing to the suddenness of it all," he continued, warming to his subject, "we agreed not to make our engagement public just yet. Your cousin knew, of course, but no one else. You didn't tell me you were going to dine with Dorinda, because you knew I disapproved of her, and you also kept quiet about having a studio lent you, for the simple reason that . . ." Here he drew up. What in Hell's name was the simple reason for this unlikely occurrence? "Oh, yes! You knew I considered you over-tired, and had made you promise me to take a complete rest from painting. There!"—in triumph. "That's the skeleton. We can pad it out later. Not bad, what?"

"How can you explain never coming here to the flat? They'll find that out from our servant."

"She sleeps out, doesn't she? Then she can't possibly know how often I was here in the evenings, and certainly she can't prove we didn't meet outside, sit in the Luxembourg Gardens, drive into the country. So long as we agree on the essential fact they won't enquire too closely into the details. The point is, have I your sanction to go ahead?"

The spell exerted over her unwilling fancy was broken. Too distraught to bear more she huddled her white peignoir about her with a shiver of desperation.

"No! No! I can't act a lie like that. They'd see in a minute there was no truth in it. Why, I know nothing about you except that you're a friend of Helen Roderick's and write for the papers. Who, what, is Thomas Rostetter?" she demanded, toying with his card.

"Tommy, to you," he murmured in a pained voice. "And I'll have you know I'm no such inconsiderable trifle as you appear to think. But why advertise my qualities if you're dead set against this idea? If you won't, you won't. However, while there's time, it's my duty to mention one thing. It's fairly certain the police have searched this entire flat. Were there any letters here from your former fiancé?"

"Not one. I burned the lot," she whispered, a hard look in her eyes.

"Good girl! And it's no use urging you to fall in with my plan?"

"Please don't ask anything so impossible. I appreciate your taking all this trouble, but—I must just fight through this by myself as best I can."

He heaved a despondent sigh. How could she guess what lay in store for her? In her present state of mind argument would do no good, and unless she consented at once, it would be too late.

A diversion was caused by the cyclonic entry of Irene with a tray. The dishevelled girl gave a dramatic start, and the thought in her mind lay open for all to read. What, the returned wanderer, suspected of murder, sitting with her hair down and her hand held in a lover's clasp? *Mon Dieu!* And it was scarcely yesterday that the other one, tall, white to the lips, had stalked down the stairs to come no more! *Sacré!* To think there were fools who called the English phlegmatic and cold! She could tell them a thing or two. . . .

"Food!" cried Tommy, one eye on the maid, the other lured by the succulence of an *omelette garnie*. "Do you think there's enough for three?"

"It doesn't matter. I can't eat anything."

"After two days' fast? Nonsense, my dear girl! And as I shan't eat unless you do and you are the cause of my recent starvation, you can't in common decency refuse."

For the first time a faint interest stirred in her eyes.

"I'll try, then—though I can't quite see why my disappearance should have put you off your feed."

"Nor I," he agreed frankly. "Weakness of intellect, Birdie, I cried—but there it is. Come in, Miss Pemberton!" He jumped up to pull forward a chair. "We've said our say, and the decision is No. It's a sad blow to my pride. May I comfort myself with a cup of tea?"

Though he continued to prattle, fear gripped him hard. He saw Dinah exposed to every shaft of suspicion, discredited, without defence. Something must be done to bring her to reason. When her nerves had calmed down a bit, he would tackle her again; but alas! the opportunity was denied him. The omelette was hardly finished before a thunderous knock brought the three of them to their feet in consternation.

"The inspector!" cried Hallie, trembling like a leaf. "Oh, what are we to say to him?"

"The truth—no more, no less," ordered Tommy grimly. "Here, take this,"—and he thrust a cigarette into Dinah's hand and pushed her back among the sofa-cushions. "Now! Let him in."

He was in the act of tendering his lighter when the inspector entered, stopped dead on the threshold, and darted a nonplussed glance at the little group. Tommy looked up in glad welcome.

"Oh, it's you!" he exclaimed. "We thought you'd turn up before long. Yes, as you see, here's the young lady you're looking for, safe and sound, though a bit under the weather from that drug. In fact, we've sent for the doctor; but I dare say she's quite equal to being interviewed. Aren't you, Dinah?"

The officer eyed Tommy with sharp distrust. He appeared to suspect that some trick was being played upon him.

"You, monsieur, are the gentleman who was with this lady at the dinner on Friday evening, and afterwards furnished us with the specimen of the drug?"

"Right on both counts. I was fortunate enough to arrive here immediately after her return, and—"

"Please!"

It was Dinah who spoke, her manner cool and collected. Shaking back her long red hair, she addressed the inspector in clear, incisive French.

"Monsieur, in case you are wondering a little at Mr. Rostetter's solicitude on my account, I'd better explain that he is my fiancé. He and I are engaged to be married."

CHAPTER XII

BY HEAVEN, she had done it after all! Spellbound with admiration Tommy saw his original estimate of her justified. The girl was game to the core.

But would the fiction pass muster? Had gossiping tongues already conspired to cast doubt on it? There was a harrowing pause, then Tommy saw the inspector nod to himself, as though the explanation accounted for many things hitherto puzzling.

"H'm—ah! Your fiancé, is he? Very well, let me hear what you have to say."

Pale, but in perfect command of herself Dinah re-told her story of lapsed memory, emphasising nothing, letting the bare statement speak for itself. How much the inspector believed was impossible to tell. His black eyes remained inscrutable, his manner increased in wariness, but he offered no comment and took notes assiduously. At the end he put a single question.

"You cannot say how you got to the Passage d'Enfer, mademoiselle?"

"You mean did I walk or ride? I haven't an idea of anything from the early evening on Friday until this afternoon, when I woke to find myself lying on a couch-bed in a studio that was vaguely familiar. Still we ought to be able to tell by the money in my purse, oughtn't we? I know I had just one fifty-franc note when I arrived at the dinner, and I spent six francs for my taxi home just now, and twenty-five centimes for a paper. That would leave me forty-three francs seventy-five. Hallie—would you mind fetching my evening-bag?"

The bag was handed to the inspector, who drew forth a change-purse containing the exact amount Dinah had named.

"This seems to indicate that you went on foot, mademoiselle. And these?" He held up a steel-ring with two keys attached.

"The large one belongs to this flat, the small to the villa in the Passage. I must have used that, I suppose, to get in—but I don't recall it."

The inspector pocketed the second key, took down the Van Valkenburgs' address in the Tyrol, and rose to go.

"You will be sent for, mademoiselle, probably tomorrow morning, to appear before the *juge d'instruction*," he tersely informed the girl. "It is not for me to say whether or not you will be put under arrest, but at all events a guard will be placed in the court below and your movements watched. An officer will come to fetch you to the Palace of Justice."

That was all; but Tommy, following the inspector outside communicated the circumstances of Dinah's two encounters on Friday night, supplying the addresses of the Hubert Loughtons and Christopher. Seeing the black eyes narrow with suspicion, he hastened to add that he had not wished to mention these things before his fiancée, as she evidently had no recollection of them.

"In her present state of bewilderment, monsieur, it seemed most unwise to introduce more confusion into her mind; but if the judge knows, he will be in a position to test her, won't he?"

The shrug which greeted this was not exactly reassuring.

"We should have been informed before. Am I to understand that this second gentleman you refer to is well known to mademoiselle?"

"Mr. Loughton? Oh, yes! Strictly between ourselves, I fancy he had till recently some hope of marrying her. I mention this merely to show you that she could not have failed to recognise him if she had been in her normal senses. I rather expected some history of automatic action," he lied with engaging frankness. "But, of course, in my total ignorance concerning this studio I was as baffled as the rest of you. Mademoiselle is an indefatigable worker at her art. I suppose some unconscious desire to get on with her painting drew her to the Passage d'Enfer."

"Humph! Perhaps. But all the same this holding back of important evidence does not place you or these others in a very favourable light. The judge may consider it a conspiracy to defeat justice."

"A conspiracy of loyal friends," agreed Tommy with a fatuous smile. "May you and I, when our turn comes, meet with a like devotion."

"Your turn, at least, will come sooner than you think," retorted the inspector with a malevolent gleam of humour. "Don't forget there are twelve persons not out of the woods yet, and you are one of them."

He turned brusquely and his heels clicked down the staircase.

Though far from requiring this reminder that he was not as Caesar's wife, Tommy could not repress a feeling of satisfaction over the success, thus far, of his ruse. That last shot on the inspector's part did not frighten him, for the reason that every action of his for the past two days went to confirm the hastily-invented fiction of an engagement to Dinah. He could not say if he had been closely followed; most likely he had; but his particular sleuth would have nothing damaging to report, and a good deal that was indicative of a distracted lover's behaviour. The Chief of the Commissariat would stroke his beard and murmur: "Now I know why that Englishman kept bombarding me with questions." Peter Hummock, if he mentioned their conversation, would say how he had twigged at once some tender relationship. In short, Tommy could not have done much better if he had all along had this scheme in mind.

But Helen! What about her? She knew too much, far too much. Still, she was a good sort, and could be dealt with.

As for Dinah herself—what a thoroughbred, taking that hurdle like a breeze, not turning a hair! Just let her keep this up, and she might yet race, unscathed, past a multitude of dangers.

As he quite expected, she was a bit done-up now with the strain of the interview, her frightened eyes seeking his for support.

"That man didn't half believe me," she said with conviction. "What I'm wondering is why don't they arrest me right away?"

"The French have a different method," he explained. "But don't imagine you're free. Everything you or your cousin do will be watched. Telephone calls will be listened in on. Even the servant may be followed when she does her marketing. Does she understand English, by the way?"

"Irene? Not a word."

"I was afraid she might have been eavesdropping. Take her into your confidence a bit, say you've been secretly engaged to me and it's only just being made public. She'll love the idea of intrigue, and if you handle her properly she'll prove a useful ally. So will your doctor. Let him think you've been too excited and happy to sleep. See my point? It'll help explain why you slept for two days after taking that stuff. No doubt that is the true explanation, except the happiness part." He avoided her eyes and went on quickly, "You will be wanting a lawyer. I'll find a reliable man and bring him along."

"A lawyer? When I'm not under arrest?"

"Yes, since 1905 no suspected person can be examined before a judge without the presence of legal counsel. Naturally we shan't let your *avocat* in on our deep machinations—and let me warn you now not to let any one suspect this isn't a valid engagement. You understand, don't you?" he said with the utmost gravity. "I mean that having launched on this deception the worst thing possible would be to have the fraud shown up."

"I suppose it would look as though I were guilty and knew it," she answered uncertainly.

"It would—but don't be alarmed. There's no need to be found out, so long as you don't go giving away gratuitous information. Now, let's settle a few details and get the whole thing water-tight. We must find out a little more about each other, mustn't we?"

He had hit on the best means of diverting her attention from the horror surrounding her. Their heads were still close together over a plan Tommy had hastily roughed out when Hallie Pemberton ventured timidly in with a bottle and three glasses.

"Mr. Rostetter," she said waveringly. "I don't know who you are, but no words can express how grateful I am to you. Don't you think a little sherry might steady our nerves?"

Another game one, reflected Tommy, looking down into the Virginia spinster's face with its plain features so firmly set against heroics. He smiled and accepted the proffered refreshment, raising the glass to his lips.

"To our engagement," he pronounced solemnly. "May it meet with a speedy dissolution. Unflattering," he added ruminatingly, "but practical—what?"

Dinah's eyes lit with a faint spark of appreciation. "May you soon be rid of the encumbrance," she murmured as she drained her own glass.

"What a girl!" he thought, and again on his way downstairs: "What a girl! There's spirit for you. I knew she was like that."

He was in a curious frame of mind. In the seventh heaven of relief, he was in almost greater confusion than before Dinah's return. Many problems loomed before him, not the least of which was how best to apprise certain individuals of the facts, true and false, which he wanted them to accept. In the Café du Dôme he called for writing materials, and composed a series of notes, to be delivered at once by hand. The first was to Mrs. Hubert Loughton, warning her of the inspector's approaching visit. The second was to Helen and required several fresh starts. Finally completed it read as follows:

"Dear Helen,

"Heaven be praised, Dinah's turned up, with her mind a complete blank for forty-eight hours. Poor child, she had no notion whatever that Dorinda Quarles had been murdered. As you'll soon know all that part of it, I'll confine myself to news of a different nature. Perhaps it won't be news to you. You women are so infernally clever! Anyhow, here it is: Dinah and I are going to be married. We hadn't expected to let it be known just yet, but circumstances alter cases, and in view of the rather trying time ahead of my little girl it may be as well to let people see how impossible it was for her to have harboured any ill-will towards your unhappy friend.

"Yours in haste,—

"Tommy."

"P.S.—I'm not forgetting my debt to you for bringing us together. Bless you!"

The third note came easier and afforded its author malicious entertainment. When it was finished, Tommy jammed on his hat and turned himself into a messenger-boy. What the recipients of his disclosure chose to think did not concern him. Enough that they had been informed.

Thus far excitement had swept him along, but now reaction set in. He dwelt again on that hysterical confession of Dinah's, and turned cold over the possibility of its being repeated. No one knew better than he what the French cat-and-mouse method of procedure can be like with its refinement of torture. Endowed with unlimited powers, the *juge d'instruction* can employ any device which pleases him, and while he busies himself with tricks and snares his agents prowl and ferret out new evidence. Day after day the victim is played upon, often cajoled into thinking himself safe, and then just as he begins to breathe freely, snick, snack!—the trap is sprung. Would Dinah be equal to the test? Above all—ghastly thought!—what would she do when brought face to face with Dorinda's corpse?

CHAPTER XIII

Christopher Loughton let himself into the handsome modern apartment in the Rue d'Assas where he lived with his mother. On the table in the hall lay a note addressed to him in an unfamiliar hand. He picked it up dully and took it into the salon to read.

As usual these days he had stayed out late in the hope of avoiding the members of his family, but although it was nearing midnight here the lot of them were—Hubert, Pearl, a younger brother David—detained from Harvard because of a polo accident—and, of course, his mother. That the quartette were discussing the topic of consuming interest manifested itself by the sudden hush which greeted his appearance.

"Chris! Why weren't you here for dinner?" demanded the elder Mrs. Loughton with disapproval. "What on earth has kept you all this time?"

Since Christopher had been old enough to go out without a nurse she had never failed to ask this question; but lately his replies had grown decidedly unsatisfactory.

"Work," muttered the young man laconically, and moving to the empty fireplace stood with his back to the company.

The hush continued. Pearl, a fragile but determined-looking blonde, glanced at her brother-in-law with troubled eyes. Hubert, square, sober-faced with owlish spectacles, cleared his throat awkwardly. David, lounging with superb indifference, fluttered the pages of *The Film Weekly*, and Mrs. Loughton, who never lounged because of her stays, sat up still straighter with her faint brows raised in annoyance. She was a massive and imposing woman, admirably dressed in grey lace with borders of smoked fox. The pearls on her bosom were real, her iron-grey hair was moulded in hard undulations from which not a shred escaped, and her skin had the parched look which comes from a life-time spent in over-heated rooms. At the sides of her nose were the permanent depressions made by a pince-nez. Even her breathing was imperious.

"Did you get your letter?" she inquired, purely to force some verbal response from her son; but Christopher seemed not to hear her. His back, flat and uncompromising, made it impossible to see what he was doing. She tapped an impatient foot. Really, the boy was getting hopelessly out of hand!

Actually, Christopher was reading Tommy Rostetter's note. Its double communication stared him in the face bewildering, incredible, and after his first reaction of overwhelming thankfulness at the thought of Dinah's safety he struggled in the clutch of wild, black rage. Alive, unharmed—but going to be married to another man! Could this absurdity be true? Monstrous, unthinkable—and that suave chap Rostetter, of all people! He crumpled the sheet in his hand and stood perfectly still.

From early years he had schooled himself to hide his feelings. Even now his features moved not a muscle, for he guessed instinctively his mother was craning her neck to see his reflection in the glass; but the turmoil within him made all previous storms seem mild. Presently, when the talk behind him recommenced, he smoothed out the sheet of notepaper and stealthily examined it again. There must, he felt, be some trick about this. He refused to believe that the hope he had clung to in secret all during these weeks of misery could at one stroke be demolished. Yet here it was, a plain, unequivocal statement; ending with these words:

" . . . I owe you an apology for misleading you as to the extent of my acquaintance with Miss Blake. I imagine, though, that my announcement will not be wholly displeasing to you, since it means she has someone to stand by her in the emergency just arisen. I should like to make one suggestion, the wisdom of which you will appreciate. If by chance you have kept any of Dinah's letters, it would be advisable to burn them without delay. If the police get hold of them, they might lead to false conclusions."

The cheek of it! He, Christopher Loughton, calmly ordered to destroy Dinah's correspondence, and by a muckraking journalist whom, till yesterday, he had never dreamed of in connection with the girl! A joke, surely ... but no, it could not be that. Rostetter would never dare to pretend a thing of this kind without Dinah's acquiescence. Had she taken the fellow out of bravado, wounded pride? So soon, too. It was unbelievable that she could love him.

And yet again, why was it unbelievable? Christopher had been painfully aware of a slight rift in August, when Dinah went off as the guest of Virginia relations to Venice. Something had gone wrong ever since the Rome post fell through, and another long postponement of their marriage seemed inevitable. It was his fault, for not standing up to his mother. He had dimly felt that Dinah, though she said little, had in her heart despised him for want of resolution. Nothing like that in her character, so she couldn't understand it in others. How well he recalled all his early admiration of her, plucky little thing that she was, asking favours of no one, and always managing to look so immaculate, so smart in her little makeshifts of clothes! Why, she'd have married him long ago and lived on his meagre salary, doing her own work. Of course, she despised him. No doubt it was that knowledge in the back of his mind which had allowed him to commit his brief, brutish stupidity. God knows he had flogged himself with scorn and remorse till every inch of his soul was raw—damned, unutterable swine that he was!

Yes, he made no excuses for his conduct, then or now. No good saying how the close sultry days had weighed him down with dejected lassitude, how every letter from the Lido rang in his ears like ice tinkling in a glass, taunting him with the sense of his own inferiority. He had felt, to be sure, that nothing he did mattered, and a sort of drunk recklessness took hold of him when Dorinda, full-blooded, conscienceless, flattering appeal to his masculinity, swooped down upon him. The strange part was he had never cared for the girl. Or was it strange? No, that accounted for it. It had seemed no disloyalty to indulge an appetite with one who never in any sense could be Dinah's equal. If Dinah had not come home unexpectedly the incident, over within a week, would have been buried and forgotten. As it was, it burst like a bomb, wrecking two lives.

Two? He was wrong, it appeared. Dinah's life hadn't been wrecked. Probably she'd been looking for an excuse to end a tie grown irksome to her. He ought to thank God, since now the paralysing doubt in his mind would be dispelled. She could have nurtured no bitter hatred against Dorinda, which meant she could speedily prove her innocence. Indeed, dispassionately viewed, there was no cogent reason to assume she had taken this Rostetter out of pique. The man was clever in a way, and for all one knew might be attractive to women. Above everything, he had decision. Yes, Dinah knew what she was about in exchanging a cracked egg for a good one. . . .

He was still standing stiff and motionless when his mother's voice, purposely raised, penetrated through to him.

"Oh, well, you may say what you like, but I always knew she was flighty. Those so-called Southern aristocrats, they're a law unto themselves, unprincipled, hot-headed and—"

She stopped, her cold eyes slightly bulging. Christopher had turned to fix on her so terrifying a glare that iron woman though she was she quailed inwardly. For an instant she saw an abyss at her feet. One more remark in that strain, and Christopher, her adored one, sole member of her family who lived up to her ambitions, might walk out of her apartment and never come back. Even now, as he left the room, she had a nervous feeling about him. The spacious, brilliantly-lighted salon, so American in spite of its French furnishings, held an ominous silence. It was the daughter-in-law who spoke first, chiding, admonitory.

"Mother! You must be careful! Did you see his face? I tell you, Chris still loves Dinah—and, oh, she may be dead!"

"He won't love her if she's tried for murder," retorted Mrs. Loughton, bold enough now. "And she most certainly will be tried, if she's caught."

"How can you say such things?" cried Pearl, reddening with anger. "You don't know the truth of this. No one does."

David chipped in, smoothing back his gleaming mane of hair with a nonchalant hand: "Why all this bilge about a little thing like murder?" he drawled. "Why, murder's done every day. Who cares a hoot if she did stick a knife into a worthless bitch—?"

"David!"

"Well, what was she, then? You tell me a nice name for her. Oh, I know her mother had a title, but that doesn't alter facts. Dinah, now, is a darned fine girl, streets ahead of old Chris, if you ask me. I'll say she had guts. The one trouble is, Chris isn't worth it."

"David! Really!" His mother's lips tightened. "If those are the morals they teach you at Harvard I'm sure I don't know what your father would have said. What America is coming to!"

"And if you're going to put on that radio, I'm going," announced Pearl springing to her feet. "Hubert! Get my things."

"Oh, what the hell? Got to liven things up somehow," muttered David, languidly turning knobs.

Pearl was angrily adjusting a little sable about her neck and her husband balancing constrainedly back and forth on his well-shod feet when a male voice from the cabinet spoke with poignant clarity.

"Miss Blaise, la jeune Americaine que l'on recherche depuis deux jours, a reparu cet après-midi vers cinq heures. Les circonstances sont assez curieuses. Elle déclare avoir passé son temps a dormir, dans une villa dont les propriétaires sont ses amis, Monsieur et Madame Van Valkenburg, artistes-peintres . . ."

"Mother!" sobbed Pearl, clutching at the lace-clad arm. "Do you hear that? She's back! She was asleep, that's all. It was the drug, after all. Oh, now will you believe me?"

Mrs. Loughton, grey-faced and shaken, breathed in through compressed nostrils.

"I'll believe nothing," she declared between set teeth. "Nothing whatever, till a jury says she's innocent."

On the homeward walk, in the shadow of the Luxembourg wall, Pearl said to her husband, "Darling, whatever the explanation of this is, you may take it from me it's mother who's to blame."

It was *lèse-majesté* to criticise Mrs. Loughton. Pearl was prepared for Hubert's pause and the elaborate astonishment of his reply.

"Mother! Why, how do you make that out?"

"You know quite well what I mean. If mother'd made it possible for Chris and Dinah to marry, instead of setting her face against it, none of this would have happened. Chris ought to have had more spunk, of course. No grown man ought to be kept on leading-strings as he's been—and as you were, too, before I got hold of you, poor dear. Oh, I admit the insurance business isn't diplomacy, you haven't a long climb ahead with a grand position to keep up; but mother could have helped financially, and it was her business to do it, seeing it was she who forced Chris into this career. The trouble was Dinah didn't suit her book. Dinah's never paid suitable homage to her and she can't forgive her for it. Now, if Chris showed an interest in Joan Raefield, for instance, you'd see how handsomely she'd come across."

Though secretly endorsing every word of this, Hubert felt bound to make a mild protest. "Mother's ambition can't excuse Chris's own behaviour," he muttered dogmatically.

"Oh, that!" cried his wife impatiently. "Chris was foolish, of course, and he's been cursing himself ever since. I expect he was feeling down on his luck, ashamed—and when men get like that these things happen. But it never touched his real self. Dinah's his anchor in life and—"

"But this murder? You're talking as if you believed she did it after all."

"Am I? Oh, dear! I don't know what I believe! As I've said all along, if she did, it was because she wasn't responsible. She . . . look, Hubert! There's Chris, now. I didn't hear him go out. Chris, wait! I want to speak to you."

The tall figure dodging with lowered head behind a kiosk faltered uncertainly. Pearl caught up with him, breathless.

"Chris, Dinah's found! We heard it on the radio. Did you know?"

He looked at her with guilty, strained eyes.

"I knew—before you did. That note I had . . ."

"You knew and didn't tell us?" she almost shrieked. "Oh, Chris, how could you? What was the note?"

"An English chap named Rostetter," he mumbled. "You may as well know, I suppose. Dinah's engaged to him."

"Engaged! What nonsense is this? Chris, come back!"

But the figure had fled, leaving her gasping with shock. She caught hold of her husband and shook him.

"Hubert! Did you hear what he said, about Dinah's being engaged to some Englishman we never heard of?"

"Rostetter?" Hubert blinked through his spectacles. "But I know him. Darned able chap. Gave us the tip that saved the company millions of francs over that arson case. See here," he exclaimed, a light breaking over his plodding features, "was this what Dinah had up her sleeve the other night? She was pleased about something, remember."

Pearl gave scant attention. A light twice as vivid in her eyes, she whispered hysterically, "But Hube—don't you see the—the difference this will make about establishing her innocence?"

"Difference? I don't quite follow."

"Oh, you are dense! Why if this is true, then she didn't, she simply couldn't have wished Dorinda any harm. The prosecution won't have a leg to stand on. Oh, it's too marvellous! I—I—" She burst into tears of relief.

Their meeting with Christopher was lucky. How else, ignorant of the note awaiting them, could they have faced the inspector, seated in their front hall, with exactly the aplomb best calculated to serve their friend's interests? Even the dense Hubert came, quite unconsciously, up to the scratch.

"We understand, now, inspector, why she was in such good spirits. Quite exceptional, you know. It was this engagement of hers. I said to my wife at the time, 'I believe there's a man in it.'"

"Was that your opinion too, madame?" demanded the officer turning sharply to Pearl.

"Yes—though I didn't know what man."

"Was she rational in her manner?"

"Oh, absolutely—and yet, just a tiny bit vague. Mysterious."

"Humph! And her appearance?"

"Never seen her look better," replied Hubert with conviction. "Bright colour, eyes—" He looked toward his wife.

"Honey, do you remember her eyes? How big and black the pupils were?"

"The pupils were dilated?" The inspector exclaimed under his breath as he made a quick note in his book. "So you noticed them, did you?"

When he had gone Pearl said slowly, "Why do you suppose he wrote down what you said about her eyes?" Then, not waiting for an answer, "Oh, Hubert, are they going to charge her?"

"Can't say. If there's no one else they can blame for it, they might bring a case."

They glanced at each other in troubled silence, knowing only too well how unlikely it was to prove anything against the other guests.

"Well," cried Pearl with resolution, "they won't get out of me what she said about cutting and slashing. I shouldn't have told Helen—but I dare say she can be trusted to keep quiet. In any case, Dinah was—odd. You know that as well as I do."

"She was—but the trouble is, will that fact argue for her—or against?"

It seemed, indeed, the crux of the whole matter. At that very moment, Tommy, the deceiver, was turning and twisting the problem and at every fresh movement feeling the barbed end of it pierce deeper into his consciousness.

CHAPTER XIV

SOMEWHAT earlier than these events, Tommy sat in the Café de Paris with a sandwich, a bock, and a bit of torn envelope beside him. On the last-named property he bestowed continuous and frowning attention, as though the lines scribbled on it summed up all that was most vital at the present moment—as indeed they did.

He had not been idle. Having secured the services of the *avocat* accredited by the American Consulate—a swarthy Frenchman called Maître le Gros—he had taken him to the flat in the Rue Val-de-Grâce to confer with Dinah. He had paid hurried calls on Cicely Gault, Misha Soukine and one or two others to acquaint them with his false situation as Dinah's affianced; and last, because he could think of no better broadcasting instrument for his news, he had sought the Baroness Waldheim, to find that lady out. Never mind, he would catch her in the morning, and meanwhile, weary with rushing to and fro, he paused to thrash out matters to his own satisfaction—if that could be done, which he was beginning to doubt.

The torn envelope contained his problem, set down in the form of three questions:

One. Is Dinah telling the whole truth?

Two. Will she be believed?

Three. Could she have committed the crime without conscious knowledge of it?

To the first he had scrawled an underscored Yes! To the second, Perhaps. Will depend largely on medical opinion regarding the effects of this particular drug. To the third, God Knows!

He might have added a fourth: was he a fool to meddle instead of letting the case stand on its own merits? He had not exaggerated the danger when he warned Dinah against being found out, and it was this skirting of quicksands which frightened him. Still he could think of no one in a position to give the show away except possibly Helen, who was not a malevolent woman. A little indiscreet sometimes; her part in the de Bertincourt affair proved that; but in the present instance she had been cautioned to hold her tongue. Anyhow, he had committed himself now, and there was nothing to do but play the hand and take all the tricks he could. After all, he could see no other way of clearing Dinah out of a beastly mess.

It was Question Three which unnerved him. How could it be solved, ever, unless some unexpected evidence came to light? All he could say was that thus far no clue pointed to Dinah exclusively. Take for example, the defaced knife and the unrevealing door-knob—could either be construed as proof against the girl?

He thought not. The action involved in throwing the knife into the fire might have been that of a calculating person anxious to remove finger-prints, or equally it might have been purely automatic, without conscious thought, the sole argument against the latter being Dinah's apparently sensible behaviour half an hour afterwards in the Rue Madame. A jury was not likely to split hairs over what must remain a matter for conjecture; but the door-knob presented something more tangible to grapple with.

Opening a door, he argued, may be instinctive, mechanical. Sleep-walkers frequently did it; but wiping off finger-prints from a metal surface surely indicates much greater awareness to danger than casting knives into fireplaces. Besides, in Dinah's case, what purpose could it serve? She went out—that was enough. Why trouble to rub the knob carefully with a moistened handkerchief, which is what she must have done, to obtain a useless result? The action was incredible in either a sane or a sub-normal state. She would never have done it—and yet it had been done. Which was absurd.

He puzzled over this paradox for several minutes, then brought his fist down hard on the table. Of course! Doddering imbecile that he was, the door was already open, the knob previously or subsequently polished clean by someone else. To pass through an open door without bothering to close it fitted in perfectly with what he conceived Dinah's mental condition to have been, and turned her departure into an incident unrelated to the chief event. Nor was this all. The elimination of finger-marks became just what it was supposed to be—the deliberate ruse of one bent on escaping detection.

A thrill shot through him. Now, now he was getting at something! Whoever cleaned off the knob was Dorinda's assassin. Did that mean it was one of the company, who, shamming sleep in the earlier stages, stabbed the girl, decided in a panic to clear out, and then thought better of it? The wise return might have been prompted by seeing Dinah wander out, unwittingly self-branded as the suspicious person. Only which of them could it have been? Tommy went over the list again, considering each individual in turn. Then he shook his head. In the past two days he had made countless inquiries into private histories, and had found nothing whatever to suggest a motive. No, it was far simpler to postulate an unknown—X—entering from outside and making a getaway all within the three-quarters of an hour after the company was asleep and before the street-doors were closed. It could have happened. The concierge on his own admission spent that interval hammering in the kitchen, so need have heard no sound. The only difficulty was, how could X get into the apartment without a key?

The first answer occurring to him was that X was let in by an accomplice on the inside—Benedetto, perhaps. For a second Tommy cast a doubtful eye on the old butler, then a blinding recollection flashed on him. Who said there was no key to be had? Why, there was Jethro's lost key, lying all night in the court for anybody to pick up.

Someone, he decided, must have prowled in from the quai and discovered it. It was evident to him now that Jethro himself had thought of this as a possibility, and rejected it because the key was found in the morning—but that meant merely that it had been put back again. A professional thief—an Apache perhaps—would most certainly have taken precautions against identification, particularly if his finger-prints were on record; and it was not hard to imagine a reason for his failing to bring off a burglary. Suppose while he stared about in stupefaction at the bizarre sight of men and women all heavily slumbering, one of the latter had frightened him by a sudden movement. Dorinda herself it would be, as he went to take the pearls from her neck. What more natural than to plunge a knife into her breast and then bolt off without possessing himself of the spoils? If it had been Dinah, now, as it well might have been!

He considered this theory and shook his head. All very plausible in a way, but far-fetched to picture a marauder stepping over three prostrate forms to get a knife he could hardly have seen in the darkness. How could he know the knife was there, or that other persons would not rouse? Also, Rita Falkland was nearer the door, and her pearls were more tempting than the victim's. Too bungling a job. It did not suggest that X was a man who got his living by this sort of thing.

Still, the latch-key offered possibilities. Did the police, wondered the reasoner, know about it? Eager to find out, he paid his bill and within a quarter of an hour was imparting his information to the level-eyed *chef de commissaire*. He was nettled to see the other stroke his magnificent beard and smile in a pitying fashion.

"Monsieur, we were told of this incident at once, by the gentleman himself. M. Jethro wished the matter to be thoroughly investigated, but we have fair reason to assume the key was not touched during the night."

The bubble of his conceit pricked, Tommy clumped down the stairs to the street. He might have known Jethro would not neglect a duty like that, even though to himself it appeared unimportant. And yet Tommy could not feel satisfied over this key business. Hadn't he heard the concierge swear to having gone over the spot where the object lay with an electric torch and still not seen it? He wavered a moment, then drove resolutely over the bridge to the island to delve more deeply into the matter.

The concierge blinked at him a little dubiously, but was willing enough to fetch his torch and stand below while Tommy ran up two flights of stairs to drop his own latch-key over the balustrade. The key fell with a tinkle, bounded several yards, and came to rest in full view near the fountain. Three times the experiment was repeated, and on each occasion the man in the court retrieved it within two seconds.

"Just as I thought," muttered Tommy. "No place for the thing to get hidden in." He glanced sharply at his assistant's gold-rimmed spectacles. "Are those the glasses you wore on Friday night?" he asked.

"Yes, monsieur, they are my only pair."

"Then why do you suppose you couldn't see the key then?"

"Well, monsieur—I didn't hear it fall, of course. That may have something to do with it; but really I can't account for it, as I said to my wife."

He couldn't find it because it wasn't there, reflected Tommy, but all he said was: "See here, just when did you make the search?"

"At the time Monsieur spoke to me about it . . . soon after eight."

If true this seemed to veto the possibility of the key having been used prior to the first search; but the concierge might be lying. The fellow looked honest, but quite likely he had neglected the matter till a much later hour coincident with the borrowing of the key. Though what a cool villain X must have been to put the thing back again where he had found it! Such a person would hardly have skinned off like that without helping himself to something worth taking.

Brisk steps sounded on the stairs behind. Tommy turned and in the dim light discerned his old friend, the inspector, come from the flat above. In spite of some coldness on the officer's part Tommy followed him into the street to question him about the truth of the concierge's statement. All he could obtain was a shrug and the equivocal answer: "How can one be sure of anything, monsieur, where there are no witnesses? The man declares he looked for the key at eight o'clock, his wife bears him out, and that's that."

"There's something else I'd like to speak about," said Tommy after realising how futile it was to argue further. "Has that drug been analysed yet?"

"Yes, monsieur, we have the report. The test shows a compound of two ingredients, both of Eastern origin—hashish and datura."

Datura? The name, vaguely familiar, meant nothing, though it would be a simple matter to learn all about it from a medical volume Tommy had at home.

"Bad?" he asked.

"It begins to look," replied the inspector enigmatically, "as though this case were likely to have far-reaching consequences. Drug-trafficking in high circles as well as low—a wholesale round-up."

"Beginning with M. Mowbray?"

"Something like that, perhaps," and with a satisfied air the speaker made off into the night.

Tommy hastened home, fired by the inspector's ominous tone to read up on the subject of Oriental narcotics, but his intention was balked. Entering his small flat, he found the lights ablaze, and indignantly anticipating a police-raid flung open the sitting-room door to behold a strange sight.

"Holy Moses!" he cried in disgust. "What are you doing here?"

CHAPTER XV

IN THE saddle-bagged arm-chairs two young sunburned, very English striplings were lizard-lounging, with their legs out-stretched to a fulsome fire, and newspapers spread in front of them. The one addressed, snub-nosed and rusty-haired, raised a pair of blue eyes remarkably like Tommy's own, and setting down a generous whisky-and-soda rose with genial cordiality.

"Well, well!" he said in a hospitable manner. "I said you'd be turning up before long. Didn't I, Filly?"

It was, in fact, Tommy's nephew Rankin Rostetter, a hare-brained youth who at an utter waste of parental money was idling his way through a university. Tommy could recall few occasions when he had been glad to see Rank. This time he was outraged.

"I'm damned!" he exclaimed rudely. "Why the hell aren't you back at Oxford?"

"Only a day or so late," declared his visitor pleasantly. "Doctor's certif. to prove I've had Pink Eye. Fact is, we're ambling towards Calais now."

"Don't let me keep you."

"Not at all, not at all. We shan't push on much farther to-night—and I couldn't dream of passing through Paris without condoling with you and so on over this rotten mess you've got into. Devoured every word of the accounts, and felt it my duty to get the truth straight from the horse's mouth. Is this doping a new thing of yours, or—?"

"I don't care to discuss it," growled the uncle stiffly.

"No?" in a soothing tone. "Well, well, I quite understand. All the same, meet Bilfilian."

Rank waved a royal hand towards the companion who lurked diffidently behind him. This was a sallow, meagrely-proportioned young man with a nervous secretiveness in his preternaturally large eyes and slinky black hair trained long at the sides. Tommy found him unpleasing, like something turned up under a stone, but seeing him unprovided with a refreshment curtly asked why Rank had not offered him a drink.

"Bilfilian," said the nephew with weighty sententiousness, "doesn't imbibe. What's more," he added, "he's just going to cut along to the garage you patronise to see if our magneto's okay. You won't mind, will you, if I just jot these little repairs down to your account? I can settle up when I return you that last fiver I borrowed at the beginning of vac. Or was it six quid?"

"Seven," corrected Tommy tersely. "Perhaps you'd better go with him."

"No, no, he can wait for me," replied Rank easily, watching the slimy one, too dry-mouthed for speech, sidle towards the door. "The car won't be ready. In fact," as the door closed, "I sent him away because I wanted to jaw a bit. About him, you know." He took a long drink from his glass. "Queer cove, Bilfilian. Wouldn't think to look at him that he'd got a past that's a spot lurid? He has, though. Trying to bury it now. Booked for the Church, grandfather who's a bishop footing the bills. Makes him cautious, you see. But the way he's gloating over this murder racket! Full to the brim of tales about your pal Bannister Mowbray and his Corsican Crew. Says they practice the Black Mass with human sacrifices when they can get them, and have got the habit. He's not sure whether it was Mowbray or Cleeves who ran amuck and knifed the hostess. . . ."

"If that's what you've stayed behind to gas about, you may as well cut it short," interrupted the exasperated Tommy.

"But anyhow he declares the missing girl witnessed the slaughter, went off her nut, and chucked herself over the nearest bridge. You don't cotton to that idea?" inquired the youth earnestly, as his uncle opened indignant lips only to close them again. "Well, let it pass. I must say what thrills me to the core is to find Our Chief Exponent of Mathematical Monism, the Ace-High Choice of the Watmough Foundation, allied with said victim. That relationship's been kept remarkably quiet. Not a murmur of it up our way."

"What about it?"

"Oh, nothing—though it would seem a bit of a coincidence if the lad who's just left us was relating a *bona fide* experience a short time ago—which he categorically denies, of course. Mind, I said at the time it sounded fishy. Didn't seem to square with the known facts; but just the same . . ."

"What on earth are you maundering about?" snapped his uncle with renewed irritation.

"Bilfilian—obviously," Rank retorted with reproachful hauteur. "Re topic of Distinguished Parent. You see,"—here the speaker emphasised his remarks with digs of his pipe-stem in his uncle's stomach—"it happened like this: Fil and I were discussing Mathematical Monism's periodic disappearances. The Man Without a Hobby he's called; but I contended that no man's without some kind of a hobby, if it's only counting lamp-posts—that when a chap who never looks at a woman or a horse or a cricket-bat or goes to symphony concerts but drives his brain overtime night and day—I repeat, when a chap like this makes a regular practice of bunking off without leaving any address, you may rest assured there's something behind it."

"How do you know he doesn't leave an address?"

Tommy's eyes strayed longingly towards the faded covers of *Medical Jurisprudence*, which he itched to take from its shelf. He felt small interest in Jethro's disappearances, and less in the guest who theorised about them.

"These things get round," Rank informed him loftily. "There's the usual interpretation of seeking solitude—as if he didn't get plenty of that in Oxford! No intimate friends, colleagues falling over themselves for an invitation to dinner—just a walking brain, and a dashed cold-blooded one at that, if you ask me. Well, as I was saying, Bilfilian was nicely squiffed. He'd got a chill, and I'd poured him full of Black and White, as a result of which he let loose some of his fruity reminiscences. Seems that last Easter Hols, when he was spending a week in this city on the cash his aunt had given him to visit Chartres Cathedral, he went the rounds with one of those cut-throats who pilot you through the Maze of Vice. You know, five hundred francs to squint through a shutter. Well, at one of these places, he strayed off to do a bit of prospecting on his own. He climbed some stairs, walked in a door that wasn't properly closed and saw—whom do you think?"

"What, Basil Jethro?" cried Tommy, feeling that Rank's air of mystery was the final straw. "Utter drivel. Tell that to the Boy Scouts."

"Quite," agreed his nephew imperturbably. "I told you I didn't altogether credit the yarn. Yet at the time I mention Bilfilian was solemnly positive about it. Said he couldn't have been mistaken."

Though the matter did not seem worthy of pursuit, Tommy asked sarcastically, "What happened? I suppose Jethro spoke to your friend and inquired the right time."

"Wrong," retorted Rank cunningly. "His eyes had a sort of filmed look, and he didn't recognise Filly at all. It was Fil who got the wind up and made a bolt for it. Not quite the ring of truth, I admit," he continued with great fairness. "First and foremost, Fil was probably too blind to identify his own grandfather in gaiters. The only queer point is, why does he deny it now? Why has he apparently not the dimmest recollection of the conversation we had? He gets quite heated over it, pooh-poohs the whole idea. Is it all bunkum? Or is this a sort of Freudian memory, locked in the unconscious, and liberated only when he's drunk? Which?"

"Take your choice," said Tommy. "I don't want to hear any more about it."

"I'm afraid I haven't interested you in my little problem," said Rank regretfully. "It's puzzled me a lot, though, especially since this business has cropped up. I've kept saying to myself, 'Important philosopher . . . secret life . . . daughter done in . . .'"

"Step-daughter," muttered his bored uncle.

"Have it your own way. No, I fear there's nothing in it. A pity, somehow."

Rank rose, drained the final drop of his whisky and stood swaying tentatively from one leg to the other. There was a pregnant pause, then Tommy blurted out, "See here, you limpet—is it another loan you're after?"

Rank immediately brightened. "Now you mention it, funds are rather short," he replied with alacrity. "What with doctor's bills—" Here he coughed. "Telegrams and . . . Oh, many thanks!" He accepted the note thrust angrily in his direction and slid it carefully into a pocket-book. "I'll add this on to the six—no, seven quid. Well, bung-o. Hope you square out of this all right."

But when Tommy thought he was gone he shoved his snub-nosed visage round the edge of the door to deliver a last titbit of information.

"I say—Fil declared he was wearing a magnificent dressing-gown. Just thought I'd speak of it."

Tommy heaved an irritated sigh. He was totally unimpressed, as always, by his nephew's highly-coloured narratives, and glad he had not imparted the news of his own engagement, since Rank's patronizing felicitations would have added insult to annoyance. Far away in Oxford, the boy's wagging tongue could not help the deception, and anyhow by tomorrow morning the announcement would be in the papers. Reaching the coveted volume, he turned to the section headed "Indian Drugs" and read absorbedly.

The sub-title, "Insanity in India," sent a qualm through him. He could not discover that drugging was held as more than a contributory cause of mental disturbances, but according to this dementia did occur in certain cases where a mixture of hashish and datura was employed. He gave close attention to the details concerning both these drugs.

Hashish, as he already knew, was another name for Indian hemp, used variously for smoking, drinking and eating. What Mowbray supplied was evidently the sweet-meat called *majun*—concocted of *ganja*—the dried flowering tops of the female hemp-plant—and *bhang* (hemp-leaves), with a basis of milk, sugar and spices. *Majun*, it seemed, was very popular at certain Indian feasts, being falsely accredited with aphrodisiac properties. It gave strength and free course to the animal nature, producing intoxication shown by laughter, singing and other emotional expressions. Hallucinations might occur, these being governed by the nature of subjects towards which thoughts were most often directed. As Mowbray had said, to the sensualist the effects were sensual, while the ascetic found his powers of contemplation increased.

The clause which troubled him most was: "These being governed by the nature of subjects towards which thoughts were most often directed." However even more alarming was the following passage quoted from the *Journal of Mental Science* of 1894:

> "Abuse of hemp-drugs, *especially when adulterated with datura*, will produce even in healthy persons a very violent intoxication simulating mania, or may lead to a morose melancholy condition, or to dementia. These conditions are generally of short duration and the patient ultimately recovers."

Datura, the seeds of which were used and resembled chillies, he found to be a plant growing practically wild in India and Malay. Taken in sufficient quantities it produced giddiness, staggering as in ordinary drunkenness and great dryness of the throat, followed by deep sleep or coma, sometimes within a quarter of an hour, the time varying in accordance with the amount consumed. *A noticeable peculiarity was the dilatation of the pupils.*

Tommy stared hard at these last words. How well he remembered the enormous size of Dinah's pupils! He could see again, too, the gesture of clutching at her throat, as though she were stifling. If he had had any lingering doubts as to the girl's being genuinely drugged it would now be dispelled; but the trouble lay in that fatal phrase, "violent intoxication simulating mania." In spite of all his arguments, in spite of the contrary evidence of the door-knob, it came over him overwhelmingly that Dinah could have committed murder and afterwards retained not the slightest recollection of it. He knew to a certainty that she had gone about for weeks in mental torment aggravated by repression, her unconsciousness surcharged with the primitive craving for revenge which her reasoning self forbade. Under the influence of a drug as dangerous as this *majun*, who could say what forces might have been liberated?

He could bear no more. Banging to the covers of *Medical Jurisprudence*, he hurled the book across the room.

CHAPTER XVI

AT TEN next morning Tommy was ushered into the apartment of the Baroness Waldheim, in the Avenue Kleber.

He had slept badly, and could not yet rid himself of the dream which awoke him—a horrible nightmare in which Dinah, under examination, repeated her statement of guilt. She had made the declaration once. Did that mean that for all her blank memory she retained some intuitive knowledge of events? If so, she might under pressure throw up the sponge, or, though she escaped actual trial, remain in her own eyes a criminal. He had to fight down his lurking fear, and keep his mind fixed on bolstering up the lie which was to save her. It was he who had persuaded her to this step, consequently it was up to him to get his story accepted as solid fact.

A gold-laced footman led him through palatial corridors to a boudoir which in equal parts resembled an aviary and a padded cell. Cushions sprawled on an inch-thick carpet, the walls were covered in Empire brocade inter-wadded, and against this background a snow-white cockatoo, several gaudy macaws and a whole colony of green love-birds preened themselves, splashed water, and scattered seed. A pair of little yapping griffons rushed belligerently forth, adding shrill barks to a clamour already that of a zoo; and Sophie Waldheim, herself not unlike some grotesque parrakeet, screamed curses at them in French, German, and Hungarian.

Sophie, keg-shaped and swathed in a peach-coloured negligee, lay on a gilded chaise-longue, her Titian wig imprisoned in a net cap to guard its waves. Fresh from the ministrations of her maid, her wizened face was a mask of fresco, out of which red-brown eyes darted glances of burning curiosity.

She held wide her short arms and folded Tommy in a stifling embrace.

"My adored one!" she shouted. "So you've come to tell old Sophie the real facts of this desperate affair. *Ach, Gott*—that poor, hot-headed Dorinda, butchered under your very nose! And the sweet little Virginia girl, so charming, so dignified. Still waters—*n'est-ce-pas?* Think of it, my dear boy! Both of them, here in my salon, only the afternoon before! When I picture it, I cannot close my eyes for horror."

"And I, darling," said Tommy blandly, "had intended to come here with Dinah, only I had work to finish. We meant you to be the first to hear our news, but when Dinah found you surrounded—"

"Comment! What news?" The Baroness pinioned the griffons by their collars, and bored her visitor with a look. "You and she? You mean to say you know this Dinah?"

"But, my dear lady, haven't you read the morning papers?" cried Tommy, his blue eyes wide with astonishment. "But I forgot, the announcement's only mentioned in one of them. Why, Dinah Blake and I are going to be married. It's an old story now, only not yet official."

"Married! You are going to marry this . . . this . . ." Sophie sank back, overcome, and fanned herself with a scented handkerchief.

"Tonnerre de Dieu!" she muttered, evidently thinking of her own *faux pas*. "I can't cope with such shocks. I had no notion of this, *comprends-tu*? None whatever. How was one to guess? And . . . and . . ." She battled hard with her emotions and finally blurted out, "And Dorinda? Did she know about it?"

"I imagine so," he returned, his smile utterly fatuous. "Who was it who said that neither the presence nor the absence of love can be concealed? La Rochefoucauld, I fancy. He made most of the famous wisecracks."

"*Diable!* So both those young hussies were laughing in their sleeves!" mused the lady, darting little curious glances at her visitor's face. "I was under the impression, you know, that it was that young man in the American Embassy."

"Loughton? Oh, that episode petered out some time ago. Decent chap, of course, but—" He gave a tolerant shrug.

"However, what about congratulations?"

Sophie surged towards him. "My pet, my own! I do wish you happiness, *de tout mon coeur*! More, I approve your choice. The child has good blood in her veins. Any one can see that. Blood tells. Blood . . ." The word brought back to her the present situation. "But how shall you deal with this devilish business? To be sure, what you have told me alters it completely, but . . ."

"Why, what does it alter?" inquired Tommy innocently.

Sophie stirred uneasily. "Oh, all these vile insinuations in the press," she stammered. "Even now the poor infant has come home again, they are hinting . . . it's quite true, *mon cher*, that she recalls nothing?"

"Nothing whatever. If you like, I'll give you the full account," volunteered Tommy obligingly, and with a confidential air he set forth the circumstances he wished to make public.

The Baroness drank in his words, nodding eagerly from time to time.

"Ah, that does not astonish me!" she exclaimed when the narrative was done. "Why, I myself once entertained the Rumanian minister an entire evening, after foolishly taking some veronal. Afterwards the man declared I scintillated with brilliance. Scintillated . . . but *zut*! I did not remember he was even there. So, you see, there is nothing so peculiar about it. . . . Who, though, perpetrated this slaughter? Not . . ." here she shuddered, "not that fascinating fiend, Mowbray?"

"I accuse no one," answered Tommy with a shake of his head. "However, as the party seems to have been arranged here in your apartment, perhaps you noticed something. Did you?"

"I? But no. They were all most friendly. It's true when I looked in on the group in the library I caught some mention of a drug. Dorinda, poor girl, had taken rather too many cocktails, so her voice was uncontrolled. Never shall I forget the mortified expression on her step-father's face when I drew him away from the door and—"

Tommy's muscles stiffened.

"What!" he cried, thinking there must be some mistake in his hearing. "Was Basil Jethro here too?"

The Baroness, he realised, was a dauntless lion-hunter, but somehow it had never occurred to him she would be able to lure a non-social man like Jethro to one of her crushes. It was odd, too, that not one of his informants had mentioned the philosopher's presence. Sophie, however, was nodding complacently.

"To be sure Jethro was here. A feather in my cap, *hein*? I'd met him at my bank, invited him then and there, and when I saw him about to decline—you know how hard he is to entrap!—I told him Dorinda would be coming."

"You mean you offered that as an inducement?"

Incredible that even Sophie Waldheim could be so stupid! Yet was it not harder still to believe that Jethro, knowing he would run into his step-daughter, had put in an appearance? Perhaps, thought Tommy, he was wrong about all this. After all, judging from the telephone message the man left for Dorinda, he had been expecting her to lunch....

"I wanted him, you see," retorted the Baroness shrewdly. "And just because he wasn't supposed to get on well with the poor girl I thought he'd give gossip the lie by not refusing to meet her. And I was right, evidently; but I regretted afterwards playing the trick on him when I saw how shocked and humiliated he was to find Dodo behaving boisterously and making a set for that sinister fellow, Mowbray. Yes, he took one look and slipped away. Ah, well, one makes these mistakes."

Tommy sat very still, his hostess's chatter now become a mere part of the twitterings and screechings of her varied menagerie. He felt he must escape from this bedlam to think, to sift, to piece together again his bits of puzzle. Kissing both the hands extended to detain him, he made his adieux. As he reached the hall, he heard Sophie scream for her car to be ordered, and knew his purpose to be accomplished. Inside two hours influential Paris would be buzzing over Dinah and himself, and the first step taken towards hoodwinking justice.

As he whizzed down the Champs Elysées amidst a swirl of golden leaves, he sought to marshal his rushing fancies into coherent order. Why had Jethro turned up at the Baroness' reception? Was it true that secret vanity urged him to prove himself superior to petty annoyances, or did he really wish to extend an olive-branch to the girl who flaunted and abused him? If the latter, his intention had certainly come to naught; but it did seem to bear out the evidence of the luncheon engagement. Come to think of it, though, Tommy did not feel satisfied about that affair of the telephone. According to Benedetto's statement, Jethro wanted to put forward an appointment already made; yet had not Jethro said in Tommy's own hearing: "As I shall not be seeing you again?" Here was a contradiction impossible to explain.

And another thing—why, when the philosopher learned that his step-daughter was asleep at eleven-thirty—she who was giving a dinner party, and usually saw the day break—had he made no comment? Helen had asked the butler, who must surely have noticed if his late master had shown surprise. One would assume Jethro was not surprised.

"Suppose," muttered the reasoner, "he happened into the cloakroom while Dorinda was holding her secret conclave with Mowbray? If he had caught the drift of her remarks—a sentence might have sufficed—he would have been prepared on the following evening to find her asleep at an early hour. And, hold on! Wasn't he in the room across the hall from hers when she rang Mowbray up at seven o'clock to confirm her plan? There's an extension in her room. I saw it. He might easily have heard her talking then, too."

Conjecture was running away with him. He pulled himself up, realising there was no way of proving either of these suppositions, while against both he had to set the probability that Jethro was not the sort of man to pry into another's affairs. Hard to imagine him as eavesdropping....

"Still, I don't like the look of it. Why did he spin that yarn about feeling faint the other morning? He must have been totally unconscious not to hear me knock. Besides which—great suffering cats! What about the latch-key?"

In a blinding flash he saw a whole new construction to be put on this seemingly simple matter. On whose word rested the assumption that the key had been dropped? Jethro's—his alone. But for his admission no one need have known, and whatever the case, it was inexplicable for the concierge not to have found it till morning. Suppose the key was never lost at all, but had remained in its owner's pocket to be deposited in the court at a later hour? No valid proof that this exact thing had not happened.

"Yet, Basil Jethro! Why, the idea's mad."

Utterly mad. Why should a man universally esteemed and set on a pedestal lie about the loss of his key? Unthinkable unless ... yes, there was no burking it now—unless in excessive caution he had pretended to be without a key to make it quite plain he was unable to enter the apartment.

The supposition was so stupefying that Tommy reeled before it. Assuming it true, what superb acumen it showed, what masterly cunning! Not, to be sure, the deception about the key itself. That was perhaps stupid; but the idea of slaying a victim while she slept surrounded by other sleepers! It was sheer genius, nothing less—even though the reason behind such a crime might not on the surface of things appear. Certainly neither police nor public faintly dreamed of attaching blame to the scholar who, behaving with great dignity and restraint, had proposed voluntarily to absent himself from his duties to assist justice in so far as he was able. Yet, setting aside all question of motive, was such an act within physical bounds of possibility? Very likely not. If Jethro went out on the evening of the murder every moment of his time would have been accounted for by now, as a pure matter of routine. However, Tommy experienced a burning desire to find out for himself what had happened.

He drove straight to the Stanislas, mentally revolving on the cause which had brought about this particular choice of an hotel. Economy? He shook his head. Hardly, for a mere matter of a few nights. Quiet? There were many better places with this advantage. Proximity to the Ile St. Louis? Ah, that was the question. The Rue Berger was certainly much closer to the island than the Rue de la Paix, where Jethro usually stayed—ten or twelve minutes on foot, five by taxi. An old haunt, or a new one? That must be determined.

Entering the lobby, he bade the manager an affable good-morning, and inquired if M. Jethro was still there. No, was the reply, M. Jethro had an hour ago settled his account and departed. Tommy pretended disappointment, mused a bit, then put another question.

"I wonder if you can tell me whether or not M. Jethro received a telephone message I directed to be sent to him on—what evening was it now? Friday, of course, at about eleven-thirty. I know it was Friday, because that was the evening the unfortunate event occurred."

"Yes, yes, monsieur, it was Friday—but there was no telephone-call for M. Jethro as late as that. I myself should have taken it, for I was here on duty the entire evening. In any case, it would have to be written down and delivered in the morning, since M. Jethro wished not to be disturbed."

"I remember your telling me something of the kind," said Tommy with a dissatisfied air. "But when did he give you those instructions?"

"About the time you mention . . . eleven-thirty. However, to make sure, I'll ask the waiter. Jacques!" he called to an attendant who was passing. "When was it last Friday evening that the English gentleman gave you his suit to be pressed?"

The waiter scratched his head. "It was twenty minutes past eleven, monsieur. He asked the time and set his watch, just before turning out the light. He was already in bed."

"I thought so," said the manager. "And just afterwards he made a call on his own, then rang me to say I was not to put any one through to him."

"Oh! So he didn't go out, then?" persisted Tommy, stupidly.

"Certainly not, monsieur," with suave patience. "I would have seen him, because I didn't stir from this desk till one o'clock."

"It's the only exit, I suppose?"

"The only public one. He didn't," suggested the manager in a jocose manner, "go through the back way, did he, Jacques?"

"No, monsieur," grinned the waiter. "He'd have fallen over Adolphe and me and all the rest of us in the kitchen. We were all there."

Muttering that there was evidently some mistake about it, Tommy withdrew. For a second he had wondered a little at what struck him as a time-honoured ruse, that of asking the correct time; but he dismissed the idea impatiently. The manager was in the lobby till one o'clock, and the street doors of Dorinda's house were closed at a quarter past twelve. In short, Jethro had remained in his room during the whole critical period, therefore was exonerated of all suspicion.

"I'm thankful, at any rate, that he's gone and not likely to learn about these idiotic questions of mine," he reflected with an ignominious feeling of having behaved foolishly. "If he caught me nosing about like this . . . but there, no harm's done. We're just where we were, that's all."

Just where they were. . . .

At the flat in the Rue Val-de-Grâce Miss Pemberton met him with nervous apprehension written on her small, worn face. "The lawyer's here," she whispered. "They're sending for Dinah at two o'clock. Oh, dear! I'm terribly frightened."

When he interrupted the conference in the little salon, Dinah came forward, pale but with no visible sign of her distraught condition beyond a look of fear in her eyes. He thought how courageous she was to dress herself so carefully, and how trim and upright her slim figure appeared in its dark-blue frock with snowy collar and cuffs. Suddenly recalling his role of affianced lover, he kissed her warmly.

"Oh, there you are, darling," he cried, and turning, extended his hand to le Gros.

Splendid girl! Her momentary gasp was noticed by no one but himself. She'll go through with it, he assured himself, thinking the smile she gave him supremely touching.

CHAPTER XVII

Le Gros, a corpulent, curly-haired Frenchman with a bluff manner and an American accent, withdrew to speak to the cousin, leaving the lovers together.

"Were you able to sleep?" Tommy instantly inquired. "Some. I couldn't bring myself to take the sedative the doctor left for me—but then I'm a day ahead with sleep, anyhow," she added with a flash of humour.

He steered the talk away from herself, and because he still could not rid his mind of a certain preoccupation, drew her out on the subject of Dorinda's relations with Basil Jethro. Had the girl talked much about her affairs? It seemed that she had.

"I never knew her really well," explained Dinah, coming out of a sort of trance. "But she did run on a lot, at Colorossi's, at places where we lunched, anywhere—especially after a couple of cocktails. She'd hated her step-father always, so she couldn't say anything good about him. I'm afraid I didn't take her at all seriously."

"What did she say?"

"Oh, utter nonsense, not worth repeating. Her word wasn't to be trusted, you know—though please don't think I'm abusing her. I think her aversion in this case was purely infantile, due to jealousy when her mother married again. She'd have resented any one in Mr. Jethro's position, and the idea that he was her guardian and trustee till she came of age was insupportable to her."

"I fancied that was the trouble," mused Tommy, recalling the scrap of heated conversation he had overheard on the night of the dinner. "But could she have had any cause for complaint?"

"I'm positive she hadn't. If she was always head over heels in debt, it was through her own wild extravagance. Jethro gave her far more money than was good for her, but she was never satisfied, called him a stingy miser, accused him of using her income for himself, and—oh, much worse than that. In a few weeks from now everything would have been turned over to her to manage, so then she'd have seen how preposterous her suspicions were. I don't suppose he'll ever know the tales she was spreading."

And yet, Jethro may already have guessed. What was the precise taunt Dorinda had hurled in his teeth? Something about . . . oh, yes, now he remembered! It took the form of a question. "Why did she send for—" What was the name? A Scotch one. MacArthur? MacDougall? No . . . it was Macadam. "Why did she send for Macadam?" There could be little doubt as to the person indicated by the pronoun "she." Dorinda had meant her mother. And Macadam—Tommy knew but one Macadam in Paris.

"Did she by chance ever mention the English solicitor here—a man called Macadam?" he ventured casually.

"Why—how did you guess that?" cried Dinah, astonished. "She did speak of him often. He was her mother's legal adviser."

"Had she anything in particular to say about him?"

"Not about him, but—well, here it is, for what it's worth. In July, just before she went off on a yachting party, she took me back to the apartment for lunch, and while we were in her bedroom she showed me an old letter she'd found sticking between the pages of a book. That is, it was only the beginning of a letter, addressed by her mother to her when she was at school, and broken off with a blot of ink. It was undated, but Dodo declared it must have been written five years ago, just before her mother died."

"Why did she think that?"

"Because the book, with the pages inked where the sheet was shut up in it, was a first edition of one of Aldous Huxley's, published in 1927. Not bad of Dodo to notice that, was it? Anyhow, she was fearfully excited over her discovery. You know, don't you, that certain people thought Lady Agatha committed suicide?"

"Either that or an accidental overdose. Did Dorinda think it was suicide?" asked Tommy with interest.

"She was never certain, and when she came across this letter she jumped to a horrible conclusion. She'd got it firmly fixed in her head that . . . oh, I hardly like to say it! . . . that Jethro gave her mother the overdose. Wasn't it grotesque?"

"And where does Macadam come into it?" said Tommy, eyeing the smoke from his cigarette.

"That was the whole point. The letter began, 'Darling Do—my head hurts so badly I can hardly hold a pen. I only wanted to tell you that things have reached a crisis. I've sent for Macadam and . . .' That's where the blot came. Dodo believed her mother had stopped suddenly and stuck the paper out of sight to keep Jethro from seeing it; but that he found out her intention about the lawyer anyhow, and took steps to prevent the interview."

"What were her mother's intentions? Had she another ingenious theory about that?"

"She didn't know. She thought it might have meant a divorce, or another will to be drawn up. As it was, Jethro got a lot of money."

"But had Lady Agatha quarrelled with her husband?"

"I tell you, Dorinda simply knew nothing at all. She was at home very little, and never saw her parents on anything but good terms, in spite of which she'd worked up a whole history out of her imagination—refined persecution, that sort of thing. Said she was sure her mother was miserable and frightened, but lacked the courage to make a stand."

Tommy pondered these statements, half-inclined to share Dinah's view of them. He was about to abandon the topic when a sudden recollection made him put another question.

"Do you think the police may have found this letter?"

"I shouldn't wonder—though I doubt if they could make much of it. Dorinda had it in a lacquered box on her writing-table. She told me she meant to hold it over Jethro if he tried what she called any monkey business over her property. As though he would!"

Tommy had seen no such box; but with a thrill he did recall the four clean marks on the walnut surface of the table where some object had formerly rested. He glanced at his watch and rose, promising to drop in later in the day to hear how she had fared.

"Now, have you got your statement quite clearly in mind?" he asked, holding her hand firmly in his. "No stupid notions about upsetting our little game?"

"You may depend on me." She met his eyes bravely, then added in a low voice, "I owe it to you not to let you down."

"Think of yourself, not me. And in case you've got any silly idea about favours on my part, let me tell you I'm getting a terrific kick out of posing as your fiancé. Why, I'm advertising it all over the town."

That last remark of hers, however, left him vaguely uneasy. Could it be she was conscious of some glimmer of returning memory which threatened shipwreck to their plans? What preyed on her was, he suspected, less the approaching ordeal at the Palais de Justice than her own rooted self-distrust. He had called her bluff yesterday when she made that fanatical confession of guilt, but he had not annihilated the doubt which lay behind it.

From a street vendor outside he purchased an armful of crimson roses and sent them up by the concierge, then drove quickly to the Ile St. Louis. As he had hoped, Benedetto was alone in the apartment, though both Helen and Basil Jethro would be in any minute for lunch. The latter was taking up his abode here now, as Miss Roderick was about to return to her own home.

"I'm sorry I can't show you into the salon, sir," apologised the butler. "We're not allowed to use it till they've held the reconstruction of the crime—though when that's to be they haven't told us."

So they meant to stage that ghastly farce, thought Tommy with annoyance and chagrin. He might have guessed the French police, with their passion for the dramatic, would never miss a chance like this. Well, at any rate, they'd put it off till they'd made an arrest. . . .

The moment Benedetto had retired, Tommy ran softly upstairs to Dorinda's bedroom, now restored to order. His pulses leaped as he saw, on the writing-table, the very box Dinah had described, a small lacquered casket once a tea-caddy, standing on tiny claw feet. Yes, it was back in its place. But who had borrowed it, the inspector, or some one else? In the bathroom mirror he had seen Jethro pause before the table, looking down thoughtfully. Had he touched anything? Ah, that was the question! Tommy had not been able to see whether he had anything in his hand when he withdrew to the locked room across the passage, though it was certain enough the box was not here three minutes later. Was it possible, moreover, for Jethro to have surmised the existence of a letter? He might never have known what prompted Dorinda's question, and then on the other hand....

Anyhow, there was no letter here now, not even a scrap of paper ... only half a dozen business-cards belonging to coiffeurs, furriers and the like, and some valueless jewellery. Then it occurred to Tommy that the box might on Saturday have been locked. He wished he had asked Dinah about that, for if this were the case it would provide an excuse for removing it to break it open at leisure. The lock certainly did not function, and round it were two minute scratches, seemingly fresh, though it was difficult to say how recently they had been made. The inspector himself might have used a pen-knife to prise the box open, but perhaps Benedetto could shed some light on the matter.

The butler came to the door of his red-tiled kitchen, a box of sardines in one hand, an *hors d'oeuvre* dish in the other.

"When did the police examine Miss Dorinda's room, sir? Not till nearly midday, if I remember rightly. I was with them when they looked about in there, much earlier than that, but they didn't disturb anything. The second time they made a thorough business of it—took away a lot of letters, a bunch of keys, and I don't know what else."

From this answer Tommy felt fairly satisfied that Lady Agatha's fragmentary letter was already missing when the full investigation was made. Of course, the servant might be mistaken in his facts, and it would not do to question him to the point of making him suspicious. Also Jethro was not the only person in the flat on Saturday morning. Both Benedetto and Helen must be considered; but would either of these have had any reason for wanting an almost meaningless bit of paper destroyed? No, in spite of the clinching evidence that Jethro could not have quitted his hotel on Friday evening, Tommy was convinced in his own mind as to what had happened about the lacquered box. Not that it proved anything against Jethro, except that the latter was aware of Dorinda's indiscreet assertions, and unwilling—naturally enough!—for a document, innocent in itself, to be misinterpreted by strangers. Any one in his position would have taken this common-sense precaution.

Tommy reached the hall just as Helen and Jethro came in together. Helen was talking in low, earnest tones, her companion according her indifferent attention; but seeing Tommy she ceased abruptly, and when the philosopher had bowed somewhat distantly and gone upstairs, she spoke with not quite her usual warmth of manner.

"Well! It's about time you explained yourself," she declared with asperity, settling her black turban. "I want to know what this nonsense of yours means. Have you gone absolutely potty?"

"Over Dinah," he returned naively. "Yes, I expect potty adequately describes my condition. But why, may I ask, this absence of congratulations? Are you huffed because I didn't tell you sooner?"

Her prominent eyes bulged at him with an outraged expression.

"Huffed! Tommy Rostetter, have you the unutterable gall to expect me—me—to believe in this engagement of yours?"

"Why not?" he retorted, injured. "If Dinah believes in it . . ."

"Look here," she blazed at him. "You may fool some people, but I know for a fact you never set eyes on that girl from the moment I introduced you to her till last Friday evening. Don't try those tricks on me, please! Now, come clean. Why are you doing it?"

Tommy was silent for a few seconds. Then he sighed, and made a gesture of giving up.

"You're right, my dear Helen, it's a four-flush. I'm doing it to protect Dinah—but you surely guessed that?"

She looked at him hard. "In that case, it's because you know she's guilty. You've fallen in love with her, and you're perjuring yourself to get her out of trouble."

"No, my dear. Both those statements are false. I'm not in love, and I believe from the very depths of my being that Dinah has no more guilt on her soul than I have—or you. I can't ask you to understand my motives. I don't understand them myself—but I'm not going to see Dinah suffer simply because certain appearances are against her. Some of those appearances can be altered. Her being engaged to me throws a different construction on the whole affair. I would do exactly the same for you."

"You wouldn't need to."

"Oh, yeah?" He was growing huffed on his own account. "Well, don't be so infernally sure about it. Come to think of it, is your position so unassailable? You had a better opportunity than any of us to stab that poor girl. I don't know what becomes of her money now she's out of the way, but suppose her step-father gets it? Suppose it's suggested that all these years you've been scheming to marry Basil Jethro? Had you thought of that?"

"Tommy! How dare you!"

She gazed at him in horror, and—there was no doubt of it—trepidation. He felt sorry he had been so brutal, but her frozen silence made him wonder if, with one of his speculations at least, he had come near the mark. When she recovered her speech it was to murmur indignantly that Basil would never marry again, that she herself wanted no man, and that if she admired this one more than any living person . . .

"Yes, darling, I know it's only hero worship—but now let's get down to brass tacks. No one knows the truth about this situation but you. Got that? In other words, Dinah's fate is in your keeping. One careless admission about Dorinda's being the cause of the split between Dinah and Loughton, and—well, you nay be signing a death-warrant, that's all. So, if you want to act decently over this, you'll give the child her chance to pull through. You'll do that, won't you?" He looked her squarely in the eyes. "You'll be a good pal and not open your lips to any one—not even to Jethro."

For an anxious second he feared she might already have given away some hint, but though she turned from him consciously her assurance was definite enough. She got out her vanity-mirror and dabbed powder on her nose.

"Of course I won't tell. Why should I want to injure the child? You needn't worry about Basil, though—that is to say, if I had said anything to him. He's not the man to stir up mischief, or . . ."

"Well, anyhow, don't tell him. It's better not."

They stopped, for Benedetto was just entering with a little card table which he began to lay for lunch. Helen indicated a suit-case Jethro had deposited beside the stairs and gave orders for it to be unpacked and when empty put into the storage room.

"You'll leave the key in the door," she said to the butler. "Mr. Jethro wishes everything to be open, in case the inspector wants to go over the apartment again."

"Certainly, miss."

Tommy noticed that the bag in question was the pale, pigskin one marked with initials which he had seen during his visit to Jethro on Saturday morning. He stared at it absently.

"By the way," he said, "I suppose you knew Jethro went to the Waldheim reception where Dorinda and Mowbray and the rest of them were?"

"He mentioned it, but it seems he slipped away without meeting any one. He hates affairs of that kind. I don't believe he even caught sight of Dodo, or Mowbray either. Will you have a drink before you go?"

"No, thanks. Now I can rely on you to be extremely careful about that other matter?"

"Oh, certainly—but I do think you're being foolish to meddle."

"That's my risk."

Half-way down the outer stairs he halted and swore aloud.

"Of course!" he muttered. "Ass that I am, that's what I kept looking for in that beastly hotel room! The other suitcase—dark, shabby, the one he took away the books in. I didn't see it—in fact, it was not there. Now, what the blazes did he do with the thing?"

CHAPTER XVIII

IT WAS the merest trifle to make a mystery over, and indeed almost at once several explanations occurred to Tommy. One was that Jethro, in view of his coming departure, had deposited the bag in the manager's office; another that he had left it somewhere en route, perhaps at the home of a friend. And yet, now the question had come up, a nebulous idea, forgotten till this moment, took definite form in the reasoner's mind.

It will be recalled that Tommy knocked the suit-case over and picked it up again to restore it to its owner. Now, if Helen had not specifically mentioned books, he would have thought no more about the matter, but with books registered in his brain he had been just a little surprised at the soft thud with which the case fell, and the impression he received, of a light shifting contents. Books are solid things. A bag even partly filled with volumes would weigh heavy in the hand, whereas this one suggested something quite different—clothing, not tightly packed, or a loose travelling-rug.

"It wasn't books anyhow," he mused with a frown. "Come to think of it, what about that naphtha ball he tracked out of the storage room? You don't pack up books with camphor, unless they happen to be shoved in with a lot of woolens." His thoughts recurred to the ancient suit of flannels the philosopher had taken such pains to have pressed. Was that what he had carried away? If so, it made matters still more inexplicable, though here again he had really nothing to go on. Besides, Helen might have been mistaken . . . but no, she wasn't, because Jethro in his statement to the press had said definitely he had called at the apartment just before dinner time to fetch a few reference books he had left there. If he was fetching clothes, why call it books? For that matter, why particularise at all?

The circumstance seemed to indicate a small, pointless untruth, hard to reconcile with a man of Jethro's known character. One felt that if it were an untruth, there must be some good reason underlying it. Had Jethro erred by too scrupulous attention to detail? Accidentally erred, of course, for in the expected order of events there would have been no one able to contradict his word. That he was doubted now was due to Helen's dropping out of the party and getting Tommy to fill her place. This single alteration in the scheme of things had brought an observant eye to bear on a series of fortuitous happenings which otherwise would have escaped comment. And what absurdly trivial items they were—irreconcilable facts about a latch-key, a man's failure to respond to a knock on his door, four clean marks on a dusty table, the weight of a suitcase!

"Oh, there can be nothing in it," reflected Tommy as he partook of *oeufs sur le plat* at a humble café along the quai. "Why, if I breathed a word of this I'd be ridiculed, howled down. Bring a charge against a scholar of international renown on evidence no better than this? I mustn't forget I'm not in a hell of a strong position myself. If I started slinging mud the Sûreté might clap me into jail, and that wouldn't do Dinah much good, would it? And yet, I'd like to settle this doubt somehow or other. Were there books in that bag? And, in any case, where's the bag now?"

He glanced to the right along the island. Only a short distance away, on the Ile de la Cité, lay the grim Palace of Justice where at this very minute Dinah was being subjected to a sort of refined third degree. She would be called again tomorrow, the next day, the day after that. Oh, there was no doubt what was in store for her! The judge would devise diabolical snares.

Chance favoured the idea forming in his mind. As he left the café he saw Helen Roderick and Jethro emerge a hundred yards to the left, stand talking for a moment, and set off in two separate taxi-cabs. In another two minutes Tommy was back inside the apartment spinning the classic yarn about mislaid gloves. No, he didn't want Benedetto to look for them. He knew where they were, in the bath-room, where he had been to wash his hands.

Would the key be in the door? It was. He stepped into the small, stuffy room reserved for Jethro's stored belongings, and ran a rapid glance round. Trunks, hat-boxes, the new pig-skin case, an old roll-top desk, book-shelves filled to overflow with dusty volumes—but that was all. No sign of the shabby, dark bag. The mystery—which was probably no mystery at all—deepened.

What he did see, however, was the trail of crushed naphtha balls, leading to a battered leather trunk in the corner. The trunk being unlocked, he raised the lid and turned over a jumble of antiquated evening clothes, woollen underwear and old cardigans; but there was not a book to be seen, nor did any volume appear to have been taken from the crowded shelves alongside. The desk was similarly unrevealing, with only some receipted bills from five years back and a few pages of abandoned memoranda in the philosopher's handwriting. One of these, torn from a note-book, he slipped into his pocket, having an inquisitive wish to study its characteristics. Handwriting interested him. This ever-widening margin was said to indicate extravagance; the small, rapidly flowing letters with their uneven alignment pointed to the scientific mind, and the clogged e's and o's—but here his knowledge failed him. He would have to consult an authoritative work.

As he drove homeward, he knew he could not rest till he had pursued his inquiry about the suit-case to the Hôtel Stanislas; but here he scented a difficulty. Already he had risked rousing suspicion of himself by his persistent questions. If he hoped to obtain full information it would be necessary to establish some sort of footing with the manager and staff, and how accomplish this except by becoming a guest? If the police were keeping him under supervision, as one might assume they were, a change of address would be asking for trouble. Still, when he reached the quiet Place du Palais Bourbon there was no one in sight who suggested a sleuth. Resolving to chance it, though realising how foolish he would feel if his investigations came to naught, he collected a few belongings in a bag and quickly repaired to the Rue Berger.

The manager eyed him rather dubiously, but friendly relations were soon cemented when he learned the newcomer's intentions.

"All I want is a quiet room I can occupy for a night or so, while my flat is undergoing repairs," explained Tommy with his most ingenuous manner. "I'll use it or not, according to how badly I'm incommoded at home. This place is suitable because it's near; and also my friend Mr. Jethro advised me to try it, as you had made him extremely comfortable."

"That was very kind of him," answered the manager, highly gratified. "The room he had is still vacant if you would care to have it," and he selected several keys from the rack.

On the way to the lift Tommy made a show of sudden recollection.

"Oh, by the way," he remarked, "Mr. Jethro wanted me to inquire whether or not he had left a piece of his luggage behind. It was a dark-brown leather suit-case, the one he brought in with him the evening before the unfortunate affair, and he can't recall what he did with it. Did he give it to you to keep down here?"

"A suit-case, monsieur?" The man looked surprised. "No, Mr. Jethro left nothing of the sort in my care. I don't even remember his . . . and yet, let me think . . . it was Friday evening, was it not? Then he may have had a suit-case with him. I really can't say, because I didn't see him come in. Yes, that's true, the first intimation I had of his return was when he rang the office to have his dinner taken up. He ate his dinner in bed that evening. I hardly believe anything of his was left behind, but we'll ask the attendant who took down his trunk."

Tommy murmured that the suit-case was probably left in a taxi-cab, and, dismissing the subject, bestowed complete attention on the choice of rooms. Number Eighteen took his fancy. So this was Mr. Jethro's, was it? He had forgotten. Yes, it would suit him very well. And might he have a whisky and soda? He gave this order to cut short the flow of questions about the murder, for the manager, agog with curiosity, showed a tendency to dawdle and gossip. Then, alone in his temporary quarters, he set about deciding certain matters which from the beginning had puzzled him.

First he examined the room to see if there was any place in which the suit-case could have been hidden. He clearly recalled the long empty space under the bed, the vacant interior of the wardrobe, and the general look of bareness wherever his eye had strayed. The various drawers were not large enough to conceal so bulky an object. No, beyond the slightest doubt, on Saturday morning the thing was not here. Could it have been stowed in an adjoining room?

Here again the answer was in the negative. There was no private bath or cupboard, and the communicating doors on each side were locked and their keys removed. At one stroke he had deepened not only this particular mystery, but another one as well, for now he knew that the former occupant could not have retired into any adjacent apartment at the moment when his own knock sounded from without. All along he had felt uncertain about Jethro's failure to respond. Did he really faint, that is, lose consciousness to the extent of not hearing a rap on the door? If so, he must have succumbed within two minutes, yet difficult as this was to accept, it was the only available explanation of his silence. It was impossible for him to have gone into the public bath or lavatory across the passage. Both those doors stood open at the time.

Muttering discontentedly, Tommy turned his attention to a third matter, namely, the question of getting out of the hotel unobserved. Throwing wide the casement window, he saw a sheer drop of thirty feet to the court below, without fire-escape, ledge, or any sort of foothold to aid descent. Nor was this the sole obstacle to egress, for even if one managed to reach the ground one would be forced to re-enter the building itself in order to get to the street. Two doors gave on the court—one leading to the lounge and lobby, the other, by evident signs, connected with the kitchen premises. The manager had made it clear that till one o'clock Friday night no one could have passed out without being seen by him, while the waiter's jocular assurance showed how unlikely it was for an exit to have been made through the rear. Still, this second possibility must be gone into with more thoroughness—and as the waiter, Jacques, now appeared with the whisky and soda, the opportunity was at hand.

"Plenty to do here, I suppose," remarked Tommy genially. "Shouldn't wonder if you waiters were up till all hours, eh?"

Jacques, an undersized, humorous-eyed individual, shrugged as he polished a tumbler on a napkin.

"You may well say so, monsieur," he answered readily. "Midnight and after, as a rule, before we get off to bed. Understaffed—that's the trouble. Run off our legs we are."

"The hotel seems fairly large. Goes back to the street behind, doesn't it?"

"No, monsieur, only to an alley which leads through."

"I see. Do the guests ever go out that way?"

"Never, monsieur." Jacques looked at him in slight surprise. "They'd have to pass through the kitchen."

Tommy took a thoughtful sip of his whisky and mentioned Jethro's lost bag, but Jacques declared positively he had seen nothing of that description.

"Only a cabin-trunk, and a light, beige case, marked with initials, monsieur. I carried them down myself."

A few minutes later, on his way to the lift, Tommy spied a small housemaid's cupboard next to the lavatory. Here, he thought, was one conceivable spot where the bag could have been put overnight, and there was a distinct chance that Jethro himself conveyed it down in the morning. He descended, scrawled his name as illegibly as possible in the register, and reverted to the former topic.

"No, the waiter declares there was not a second suit-case," he informed the manager. "So I should think it most probable Mr. Jethro took it away in person. Did you happen to notice if he was carrying anything when he went out Saturday morning? A little before ten it would have been."

"To tell the truth, monsieur, I did not see him go. I can't imagine why, either, because I was watching for him rather especially, after what you told me. Ten o'clock? In any event it was much earlier than that, for feeling worried about his not requiring breakfast, I took the trouble to send upstairs to make sure he wanted nothing. That was very soon after you left, monsieur—say a quarter of an hour—and his room was empty, so you see he had already dressed and gone." Tommy felt a shock of amazement. What, no attack of faintness? Gone inside a quarter of an hour? Here, at all events, was an instance of out-and-out lying—a deliberate falsification to account plausibly for the long delay in reaching the Ile St. Louis. Not likely to be found out, either, since it was by the merest ironical chance his arrival coincided with Tommy's. But what had the prevaricator done, where had he gone in the interval that he did not wish to tell the truth about it? It was easy enough to say that the most impeccable men invent excuses to cover up private concerns, less easy to think this particular man would trouble to that extent without cogent reason.

Suddenly he asked another question.

"I dare say you often have Mr. Jethro staying with you?"

"On the contrary, this was his first visit, monsieur. Some one in the south recommended us."

More than ever did Tommy incline to his recent belief that the philosopher had some definite cause for selecting the Stanislas. That cause mattered little if, having come here, he had remained shut in his room the whole of Friday night, but linked with the other peculiar circumstances it arrested the attention. For a few seconds he toyed with the idea of Jethro's having employed an accomplice to do the actual killing, but this theory seemed absurdly untenable, indicating as it did an entire disregard of the first principles of caution. No man with so much at stake would risk being blackmailed for the rest of life. If he wished his step-daughter out of the way, he would execute the removal with his own hand or not at all. Revealed facts seemed to show that the latter alternative was the right one.

Jethro must be innocent. For the second time that day Tommy arrived at this conclusion, but having just discovered the man in a lie he could no longer regard him as a pure, unspotted soul. He decided to desert Opportunity and concentrate on Motive. The scrap of paper taken from

Dorinda's room did not, to his thinking, represent a sufficient reason for committing murder, but there might be a better reason not far to seek. From Helen's manner he had surmised that the philosopher stood to benefit by his step-daughter's decease. It would not do to ask Helen point-blank what she knew about the terms of Lady Agatha's will, nor could she tell him certain other details he was curious to learn. What about approaching the firm of solicitors who had handled Lady Agatha's affairs. He had some acquaintance with both the Macadams, father and son.

"That's an idea!" he reflected with sudden hope. "No doubt they drew up the will. Old Macadam is a clam, I shan't get much out of him, but Geoffrey Macadam's entirely human. Anyhow, I'll have a go at it."

On the way to the Rue Auber he dropped in at the dignified Hôtel Mirabeau and asked the reception clerk if Mr. Basil Jethro had been staying there?

"No, monsieur," he was told. "As a rule Mr. Jethro does take a room with us, but this time we have seen nothing of him."

Tommy expressed astonishment.

"But surely he inquired for a room and went away because there was not one vacant on the court?"

The clerk shook his head. "We've had several vacancies on the court this week and last. I assure you he has not been in."

Another lie! In short, the Stanislas was a definite first choice. Cutting down expenditures? Half the hotels in Paris were reducing their prices this season, to lure people into them. No, there must be more to it than that. . . .

At this point Tommy's thoughts flickered back to the tale spun by his scatter-brained nephew, Rank Rostetter. He viewed it from every angle, and, as before, cast it into the discards. It might or might not be true, but in either case what could it prove? Nothing helpful to him in his present quandary. He sighed deeply, and drove towards the Opéra.

CHAPTER XIX

Geoffrey MacAdam pushed a box of cigarettes towards his guest and tried to conceal his curiosity. "Too bad my father's not in France just now," he said regretfully. "Though I doubt if he could give you much help. We didn't draw up Lady Agatha's will, you see; only handled her investments and so on during the latter years. She lived partly in Paris and partly in London—a flat in Bedford Square, I think. You could quite easily get hold of a copy of her will from Somerset House."

"If I go to London, I'll be committing contempt of court," replied Tommy. "And it wouldn't do to compromise myself at the present moment, on my fiancée's account."

Geoffrey's grey eyes tactfully avoided the speaker. "Can't you get some one over there to look up the matter, or don't you like taking any one into your confidence?" he suggested. "That's just the difficulty. It's a ticklish business, isn't it?"

"Very ticklish." There was an awkward silence, then the young lawyer spoke again with slight hesitation. "I want to tell you how glad and . . . well, relieved, my wife and I were when we heard about your engagement. Surprised, too. That is to say, Catherine knows Dinah Blake quite well, is decidedly fond of her, in fact, but neither she nor I realised there was anything of that sort . . ."

"Between us?" Tommy met his gaze with great frankness. "That's natural enough. I never met her till fairly recently." He went on to add details, with that smooth dovetailing of fact and fiction which made him the perfect liar. Geoffrey listened, nodding with sympathetic interest. There was no valid reason to disbelieve what he heard, and indeed he did not question it.

"It's a queer case," he remarked. "But it's a jolly comforting thing to know Dinah's got you to look after her. It's no joke for a young girl, virtually alone in Paris, to find herself up against the French courts."

"Quite," agreed Tommy. "And you'll readily appreciate how important it is, from her point of view, to get completely clear, not simply be let off for lack of evidence. It would kill her to imagine there was the faintest shadow of doubt hanging over her. It's for that reason I'm sticking my oar into all sorts of unlikely places. You don't know anything, do you, which might shed light on that matter I mentioned?"

"I'm afraid I don't . . . but wait! I'll just call in Howard. He's an old clerk of ours, rather a remarkable fellow for pigeon-holing information about our clients. You can speak to him quite openly. He's the soul of discretion."

It was plain that the grey, gaunt Englishman who presently appeared had read his newspaper very thoroughly. His sunken eyes sharpened with intelligence when he caught the visitor's name, and as the explanation proceeded grew reminiscent. He did not, however, offer much assistance, having no knowledge of how Lady Agatha's property was left. He believed Lady Agatha, who was the second daughter of the Earl of Campden, was left very well off by her first husband, Mr. Jonathan Quarles, part-owner of the big Quarles colliery and chemical works in Yorkshire, but as her second marriage took place in London, and her will was drawn up in that city soon afterwards, he had never had occasion to learn its terms.

"One moment," interrupted Tommy, struck by the clerk's intimacy with family history. "Just what relation was she to Lord Conisbroke?" He was thinking of Ronald Cleeves, who, according to Mowbray, was some connection of Dorinda's.

"I can tell you exactly, sir. Lady Campden, her mother, was second cousin of the former Earl of Conisbroke. If it's young Mr. Cleeves you're thinking of, he and the murdered lady were very distantly related. Also, as Lord Campden was so impoverished he had to sell his Berkshire estate, I feel quite sure Lady Agatha's money had nothing to do with her own family. There could be, you see, no entail which would affect even a near cousin, still less a fifth or sixth one."

"Had you heard," put in Geoffrey Macadam, "that Mr. Basil Jethro was appointed guardian to his step-daughter?"

"I had not, Mr. Geoffrey—but I should think it most probable. With her daughter well under age, Lady Agatha would have had to appoint trustees, and as she was undoubtedly much attached to her second husband—some might say infatuated—she would almost certainly name him as one of them."

"Could Mr. Jethro be occupying the position of sole trustee?" inquired Tommy hopefully.

The old man looked scandalised. "Certainly not, Mr. Rostetter," he answered reprovingly. "Such a thing would be unheard of; in fact, under the new act, impossible. A good thing, too—not that I'm suggesting anything against a man of Mr. Jethro's character. I only mean the old law put too much power into people's hands. An unscrupulous person could take advantage of it to abuse trust funds."

"Precisely when did this new act come into force?" asked Tommy thoughtfully.

"Let me see . . . 1925, wasn't it?" Geoffrey hazarded with a glance at Howard.

"1926," corrected the clerk firmly. "I see what's in your mind, Mr. Rostetter. You'll say this particular will was drawn up before that date. Well, so it was . . . but even so I feel satisfied no solicitor would have allowed his client to appoint only one trustee. Lady Agatha couldn't have got her way if she'd wanted to—headstrong though she was," he added under his breath.

"So Lady Agatha was not always responsible, I take it?"

"Go ahead, Howard," said Geoffrey with a smile at the clerk's hesitation. "We won't give you away."

"Well, sir, if I may speak my mind plainly, I've seldom seen a woman more impulsive and capricious. Very emotional, and rash, though of a most generous disposition. First and last, Mr. Macadam had a lot of bother with her, humouring her whims and trying to curb her wrong decisions—but then it's the solicitor and the family doctor that see the worst of people, I always say."

Tommy reflected that just possibly Dorinda's mother had been more foolish than any one knew over the matter of trustees. He was wondering how to bring out his next question without giving it suspicious importance, when Geoffrey solved his problem by asking if there was not something more he wished to inquire about.

"Oh, yes," replied Tommy, casually. "It concerned an appointment Lady Agatha made with Mr. Macadam just before she died. Have you any recollection of the circumstance?"

"She did make an appointment, by letter," answered Howard slowly. "She wanted Mr. Macadam to come to her apartment the following afternoon—but he arrived too late by half an hour. She was dead from an overdose of morphia, as you probably know." The clerk paused, then went on thoughtfully. "That fact to our minds explained a good deal, especially when we learned that for some time past she'd been taking drugs to relieve the pain she'd been suffering. I think it quite certain she had not been herself for more than a year."

This stressing of the irrational in the poor woman's conduct did not further Tommy's tentative theory. A victim of morphia is apt to live in a distorted world, fancying wrongs where none exist. Still, in pursuance of his point, he asked if Howard had any notion what the appointment was about.

"Not the slightest, sir. Mr. Macadam never knew."

"You didn't hear, I suppose, any hint of her wanting a divorce?"

"Divorce?" echoed Howard, astonished. "Oh, most decidedly not! That is to say, she was married to Mr. Jethro only three years at the outside, and she showed every sign of being devoted to him—and he to her." He uttered the last words with cautious conviction. "Even at her worst times, he appeared to exert a calming influence over her. I should call him a man of great understanding and forbearance."

"Thank you, Howard," said Geoffrey. "I don't think you can tell us any more." Then when the clerk had withdrawn he continued: "Howard's quite right about Lady Agatha's neurasthenic condition and her husband's manner of dealing with it. I have just remembered an occasion, towards the last, when she came in unexpectedly, and was shut in my father's office for quite a long time. She was very hysterical, though what it was all about I can't say. My father afterwards declared she was talking simply rubbish. Anyhow, in the middle of it, Jethro turned up, quieted her instantly, and took her away. He was gentleness itself, but she must have been fond of him, for she was like wax in his hands. I'm sure the whole trouble came from her getting in the grip of drugs. She had the sort of highly nervous temperament which is absolutely wrecked by that kind of thing."

"Was Bramson her physician?" asked Tommy, rising to go.

"He was. My father found him arriving at the same time as himself the day of her death."

Within a quarter of an hour Tommy was ringing the bell at a smart modern residence out beyond the Étoile. He felt he had made no progress at all towards establishing a motive, but realising how long it would be before he could learn any facts from the senior Macadam he had resolved to sound Dr. Bramson on the subject of Lady Agatha's drug-habit. If the woman was normal when she sent for her legal adviser, it suggested one thing: if her judgment was deranged by morphia, the conclusion drawn would be quite different. In either case he could understand Jethro's wanting to destroy evidence as to her intentions, but that understanding did not content him. There was much more he was eager to find out, and knowing how hard it is to entice confidences out of professional men, he had his plan ready.

When Bramson entered the reception-room, his manner assured and abrupt as befitted the foremost English practitioner in Paris, Tommy began at once to pour out the history of Dinah's disappearance and return.

"I've been looking up the stuff we took," he explained, a worried frown on his brow. "It turns out to be a combination of hashish and datura—but I can't discover anything dependable about its properties. You see what I'm getting at, don't you? My fiancée's position is bound to be influenced by medical opinion. I know it was impossible for her to have committed a crime, no matter what state she was in; but others may not share my belief—as to her lost memory, I mean. Could you, if called upon, give an authoritative statement?"

"As to the effects of this combination?" Bramson eyed him steadily, pulled at his old-fashioned moustache and cleared his throat—to gain time, Tommy thought. "I'm afraid, Mr. Rostetter, my knowledge of eastern narcotics is too slight to make my opinion of much value. It's a special subject, you see. No doubt there are medical men in Paris who have studied it more deeply than I have—though, like me, it is fairly certain they would say the results would vary both with the individual concerned and the circumstances of administration. One can't be dogmatic about it—which, in the present case, is at once an advantage and a disadvantage," he declared pointedly.

Tommy looked downcast. He sat silent for a moment, then, as though struck by an irrelevant idea, remarked: "A bit tragic for Mr. Jethro, isn't it? I mean, to have a second member of his family meet death through drugs."

Bramson eyed him in cold amazement. "Through drugs?" he repeated in a mystified tone. "Ah, you're referring to his wife's unfortunate end. An entirely different story."

"Oh, quite! I knew her, you know. I suspected, as did many of her friends, that she'd contracted a drug-habit, but what no one could understand was how she managed to get hold of the . . . what was it? Morphia?"

The random shot told. Bramson drew in his breath and appeared to debate with himself whether or not to allow this statement to pass without comment. When he spoke again it was with extreme caution.

"Lady Agatha suffered from a chronic mastoid, wrongly diagnosed before she became my patient," he said carefully. "The pain she endured was so great that I was obliged at times to inject morphia; but I need hardly assure you I never once permitted her to have morphia at her own disposal, nor did I realise she was using it steadily . . ." He hesitated. "Well, as a matter of fact, it was her husband who first brought it to my attention. He came to me privately, much alarmed over the suspicious symptoms she was showing—erratic vagueness, unreliability and even downright untruthfulness. The last is a familiar characteristic of the morphia-addict."

Tommy murmured something about an uncle of his who had been thus affected, telling lies in the most distressing fashion.

"Yes, yes, quite so. With Lady Agatha it became so noticeable that her word could not be depended on at all. Mr. Jethro concluded she had some secret way of obtaining morphia, but as he was unable to discover the source of her supply he very properly sought my advice. There was some talk of getting her into a private sanatorium for treatment, provided we could gain her consent, but before any steps were taken she took the fatal overdose. It was not the first accident of the kind in my experience."

"And what about the morphia?"

"You mean where it came from? We never knew, though we found a bottle of it together with a hypodermic syringe locked in her jewel-case. She must have been giving herself injections of increasing strength for some time. It was the butler who found her, collapsed on the sofa in her bedroom and at once rang me up. Mr. Jethro was out and did not know of her death for an hour or so."

After prolonging the conversation a little the searcher after truth took his leave, abashed, and, to be honest, sorely disappointed. The letter Dorinda had cherished now revealed itself as another instance of "rubbish," the creation of a brain distorted by drugs; the man involved emerged without a stain on his character, proved to have been the first to notice his wife's condition and zealously anxious to remedy it. Probably each of the trivial fabrications—if fabrications they were—on which Tommy was placing so much stress would be explained away if their author were given the chance to speak. Viewed in cold blood, what did they amount to?

"It's childish, from start to finish," muttered Tommy, getting back into his car. "It's this insane desire to save Dinah from harm that's leading me off on such an idiotic goose-chase. I might be better employed."

He put in two hours at what he termed "snooping about"—otherwise collecting all the available information regarding the members of the dinner-party. The results were nil. No one present on Friday night showed the least sign of bearing the victim a grudge or of having to gain by her death. None of them had ever suffered from mental derangement. A deadlock again—and still, though he cursed his stupidity for bothering about it, he had been able to devise no solution regarding the missing suit-case.

When his watch told him he might expect to find Dinah back at home, he turned his face in the direction of her flat, on the staircase of which he met Le Gros just coming away.

CHAPTER XX

AT SIGHT of the lawyer's beaming expression a load fell from Tommy's mind.

"But she is splendid, your little friend! Such poise, such a cool head! I tell you, I have seen big, strong men go to pieces when they are shown the corpse, but she—how do you say?—never turns a hair. The judge is

Gramont, too. You know what a terror he is with his traps and bullying, but not once did he make her contradict herself. She has all my admiration."

"You think the worst may be over?"

Le Gros's effervescence subsided somewhat. "Well, not yet," he replied cautiously. "With no one else under definite suspicion, it may mean a long siege. To-morrow Gramont will try the word-test on her, with the instrument for registering heart-action—perhaps other things. Still, if nothing new crops up, we need not be afraid."

Tommy's first glimpse of Dinah was less reassuring than the counsel's verdict. She was seated bolt upright on the sofa, face white and drawn, eyes blankly staring at the opposite wall. When she saw him she sprang up with a smile, but her hand was icy.

"Well, I'm still at large," she announced lightly. "Sit down, I'll tell you all about it. You smoke a pipe, don't you? Then light up and be comfortable." She ran on in this strain till her cousin, after an anxious glance, had slipped away. "Do you wonder how I knew you smoked a pipe? Just instinct. Pipe-smoking's considered a rather noble attribute, isn't it? Inspires confidence—like keeping bees. I know, too, that you like your tea strong, with three lumps of sugar. Oh, I'm learning a lot about you—almost as much as though we were really engaged."

"We are engaged," he declared firmly. "Did the judge show any doubt on the subject?"

"Not a bit. Funny, wasn't it? And I do believe he'll end by accepting my lost memory—against his inclinations, of course. No, it wasn't half so bad as I expected, except for one thing—and that, thank God, won't happen again."

Quite suddenly her steadiness deserted her. She pressed one hand over her eyes with a spasm of pain.

"Oh!" she whispered, shuddering. "You wouldn't believe they'd do such a thing! They had her propped up in a chair, dressed in the same evening-gown, with the poor hair all waved, and—yes, actually rouge on the cheeks!" She began to laugh hysterically, tears running through her fingers.

"Don't!" he commanded almost brusquely. "It's over now, and after all, horrible as it was, what could it mean when you had nothing to do with it? Tell me this: was something said about your other engagement?"

"The judge hasn't heard about it—yet. Some of his questions, though, were very bewildering. I got the feeling he knew more about me than I know about myself. It raises rather frightening possibilities."

"What do you mean?" he demanded, relieved to find her still ignorant of her two midnight encounters.

"Why, that for a short time I may have gone quite out of my mind. Temporary insanity, you know. None of my people have gone insane, but I may have done it, mayn't I?"

"My darling child, what rot!"

"It isn't rot. With a great gap in one's consciousness how can one say what may have happened? I just don't know. *Not knowing* . . . maybe I shall go on like this for months—for the rest of my life."

The reasoned conviction of her tone alarmed him more than any frantic outburst, the beastly part being that no argument of his could give her the inner certainty she craved. Hiding his own uneasiness, he sought to divert her by tactful questioning.

"What did you tell the judge about your last impressions of Friday night?" he asked.

"Oh, about feeling giddy, my throat absolutely parched. That I seemed to remember standing by an open window, getting better, but yawning a lot. I said I had a dim idea you were with me. Were you?"

He resolved not to help her out. "Was that all?" he inquired.

"Not quite. At the very end I suddenly thought, very vaguely, about something I'd meant to do and hadn't done, that is go to see Pearl Loughton, so she wouldn't imagine I was avoiding her. I didn't tell that part of it," she explained hastily. "I just said Pearl was a great friend of mine whom I'd neglected because I'd been seeing so much of you. That was clever of me, wasn't it?"

"Sharp girl!"

With exultation Tommy saw the Loughton visit in the light of simple wish-fulfilment, subconsciously carried out. Probably the other incident fell into the same category. He threw out a delicate feeler.

"By the way, while your cousin was in Versailles, did you spend much time alone in this flat?"

"No! I'd come to hate the very sight of it!" She cast a look of repugnance round the pleasant room. "So much had happened here—but I'd rather not talk about that. I wandered about all day hunting for a studio. When the Van Valkenburgs lent me theirs I was glad, because it meant I had somewhere else to go."

"Then when you went there Friday night you were undoubtedly following your instinctive longing for new surroundings. You might drop a modified hint of this tomorrow. Say you were anxious to finish a picture, and had the thought of it on your mind."

She looked at him with alert intelligence, grasping his idea. Her colour had revived a little, and when he gave her wise advice about the tests likely to be applied at the next examination she took in all he said.

"Le Gros has already prepared me," she assured him. "When the judge goes over the list of words the second time I am to be careful not to change my answers, or else it will look suspicious. I don't suppose I can control my heart-action, though. What if he brings up something disturbing?"

"He won't," replied Tommy, "for the simple reason that he doesn't know anything disturbing." He said this with secret satisfaction, reflecting that most of what was damaging was locked in his own breast.

"Oh, your roses!" she cried suddenly. "Look! Aren't they lovely? And I had forgotten to thank you!"

Had the crimson blooms purchased from a cart grown larger, handsomer, overnight? There seemed twice as many, filling two big jars. It crossed his mind that someone other than himself had been sending red roses, but he made no comment and presently said good-bye.

Hallie Pemberton followed him outside the flat door.

"How does she strike you?" she murmured apprehensively, and before he could answer hurried on: "She hasn't said a word to me about that idea of—of her guilt, but, oh, I can see it in her eyes! Poor child, she's in torment. Can't we possibly get rid of her obsession?"

"Yes, if we find the real murderer," he reluctantly informed her. "At the moment I can't think of any other way."

"And if we don't? It's three days now, and not a syllable in the papers to give us any hope. Every account she reads strengthens her fear."

"Do you think she'll break down before the judge?"

"Oh, you can trust her not to do that now she's given you her word. Dinah's fragile to look at and very sweet, but she's got a will of steel. It's her own doubt that's worrying me." He comforted her as best he could, and with a troubled heart descended the stairs.

In the dusk of the court a police sergeant was pacing up and down. He stopped, gave Tommy a piercing glance and watched him out. On the pavement outside a second restless figure was hanging about. Recognising the well-knit shoulders and fine profile shadowed by a felt hat-brim, Tommy strode resolutely forward, caught the loiterer by the arm and pulled him roughly towards the corner.

"Don't you realize there's a policeman in there on the *qui vive* to report everything he sees?" he whispered roughly. "You must be mad to behave like this. Are you trying to make trouble for Dinah?"

Christopher Loughton's brown eyes burned with shame. "I didn't think. I've got to know what's happening to her."

"You won't find out by dogging her doorstep. Here, get into my car. I'll tell you anything you want to know."

Tommy felt touched by the docility with which the young man fell in with his suggestion, even though the situation had its ridiculous side. That Loughton, good-looking, sought-after, should without question accept him as a preferred rival argued a nature less conceited than one would have expected.

"I ought to tell you," the discarded lover remarked awkwardly, "that I've been dropping in to see Hallie Pemberton. Without Dinah's knowledge, naturally. Have I done wrong?"

"No, no—it's only your behaviour just now that might be misconstrued. You looked as though you were hoping she'd throw a note out of the window."

Or a rose, he wanted to add, thinking that the mystery of the superior blossoms was explained, but that if Dinah had guessed the truth she would quite probably have chucked out the entire lot. He saw his companion wince sensitively. After a strained silence a battle seemed to have been won, the result of which appeared in broken, halting sentences.

"I'm glad I ran into you, Rostetter. I've been wanting to offer you my best wishes. I'm thankful, too, Dinah's got you to stand by her—particularly,"—here the speaker's voice dropped with mortification—"since I'm not permitted to do a damned thing."

With a side-glance at the haggard features Tommy felt an overwhelming desire to lay bare his deception. He opened his lips impulsively, then closed them again. No, the success of the plot depended on everyone's believing in it. Already there was one potentially weak spot—Helen Roderick. There must not be another.

"It's decent of you to say that," he replied kindly. "But don't worry. The only thing against Dinah is a lamentable coincidence."

"Then why are the police concentrating on her to this extent?" demanded Christopher, as though still harrowed by inward doubt.

"Merely because of circumstances. They'll soon see—in fact, they must already see—the entire absence of any motive," said Tommy with an assumption of easy confidence.

Christopher appeared to weigh the statement, perhaps torn between an egotistical unwillingness to credit it and the obvious desirability of giving it full value.

"If it's not confoundedly impertinent," he ventured presently, "just when did you and she—that is . . ."

"Become engaged?" Tommy smiled complacently. "Oh, almost at once. Astonishing, but true. It's about three weeks now."

Christopher grew very white beneath his tan. After another silence he put a yet more diffident query.

"She's told you, I suppose, about throwing me over?"

"Certainly—but, my dear Loughton, don't imagine she's said anything harsh about it."

"She had every right to be harsh," muttered the young man, his face turned away. "Especially when I couldn't make her see—or rather she couldn't be expected to understand—how my behaving like a swine never in the slightest degree affected my real—" His throat seemed to dry up. "Anyhow," he finished stoically, "if she's found a better man, she deserves it, that's all."

"Good God!" cried Tommy, to whom all this was acutely painful. "Why not wash the whole thing out? Besides,"—astutely—"mightn't the real cause of the break go back behind the incident you refer to? Hasn't it occurred to you that Dinah felt herself drifting away but lacked courage to tell you?"

He perceived the cruel injury this inflicted, and was sorry; but his respect for the man at his side rose high when he heard the self-controlled answer:

"You may be right—but there again I've only myself to blame."

"Not at all," protested Tommy generously. "But perhaps, if any awkward questions are raised, it might be a good plan to assume the separation came before Dinah went to Venice. You get my meaning, don't you?"

Their eyes met and for a second Tommy feared he had betrayed too much. Apparently, however, Christopher got the significance intended and nothing beyond.

"To avoid misunderstandings, it would be a good plan. I'll agree to it if she will. After all, there's not a soul to contradict us—living or dead," he added under his breath.

"Quite sure of that? You don't think the third party could have said anything?"

"I feel certain she never knew. Dinah wouldn't have told her, and I . . . never saw her again."

Tommy nodded to himself, as rounding the corner into his own square, he suggested a drink in his flat. Christopher declined, but as they alighted Tommy saw him taking note of the address. At the same instant he saw something else—a motionless, nondescript figure stationed in the shadow of the Chambre des Deputes opposite with observant eyes fixed on him and his companion. In a flash he divined that here at last was the guard instructed to watch his movements.

"Perhaps I've no right to ask it," said the American jerkily, "but will you keep me informed about—well, about her?"

"To be sure I will, Loughton. Drop in and see me whenever you like."

They shook hands hard, and with the forlorn appearance of not caring where he went Christopher walked towards the quai.

"Poor devil!" mused the deceiver, gazing after him. "Poor devil! Still, I dare say this will do him a world of good."

With this philosophical reflection, he glanced ruefully at the lounger across the square, wondering whether it were worth the risk to return to the Hôtel Stanislas. His room was there waiting for him—Jethro's room—but was there any secret to be learned from it? After to-day's investigations he was dejectedly certain there was not. Even Lady Agatha's will seemed of no importance since the Macadam clerk was so positive on the matter of trustees, and first and foremost if Jethro's escape from the hotel was a complete impossibility why pursue the man further?

Mounting slowly to his flat he asked himself if Dinah's feeling about her guilt might not be a sure indication of the truth. Not that this would alter his attitude towards her, for what she did during her brief dementia could not be held against her normal character; but what she had said about eternally "not knowing" turned him cold with dismay. Why, this was the sort of obsession which drives its victims into asylums! What on earth was to be done about it?

Three days later he was still asking the same question, even when, after prolonged examination, the judge had not shaken her story. The engagement to Christopher had been discovered and relentlessly probed without damage to her case. Tommy himself had been called to the Palais de Justice and made to sweat under Gramont's questioning, but beyond a futile effort to prove it was Dinah's portion of the drug which remained uneaten and not his own nothing of moment developed. Public interest in the girl noticeably slackened. Dismissal was regarded as a matter of time; and yet when Tommy met his pretended love, he read in her sea-blue eyes the self-same torment, unabated. Though at any instant she might be free to come and go as she liked, he knew she would look upon herself as a marked woman, set apart from her kind. For all his arguments about wiped door-knobs and similar trivialities, he was powerless to help her.

Then on the third day events occurred which set Paris vibrating anew. A dead Englishman was dragged up out of the Seine, and immediately after a second Englishman was snatched in a semi-lifeless condition from a gas-filled room. Two intended suicides—one of them successful. Was the key to the Quarles murder found at last?

The drowned man was Bannister Mowbray; the conscious one, nominally under arrest but for the time being allowed to remain in the British Nursing Home, was Ronald Cleeves, younger son of Lord Conisbroke.

CHAPTER XXI

WHILE the newsboys were still hoarsely shouting their newest sensation, Tommy, by a bold use of his press-card, obtained permission to view Mowbray's corpse, as it lay stretched upon a slab in the Palais de Justice mortuary. The heavy body was clad in coarse, yellow homespun now sodden with water and streaked with river-slime.

"Anything in the pockets?" he whispered to a brother journalist who, under an inspector's watchful eye, was busily taking notes.

"Nothing that matters—so we're told," muttered the reporter, a young representative of *The Morning Mail*. "They're devilish close-mouthed, though. Won't give a thing away. Nasty bash on the head he's got. What's your idea of it?"

Tommy scrutinised the purplish bruise on the temple nearest him. It showed a rough-edged cut from which at some time blood had oozed. Beckoning to the inspector he asked a question. The man shruggingly gave the opinion that in the downward plunge from a bridge the head had caught one of the stone piers.

"Not the cause of death, you think?"

"No. He may have been stunned by it, but drowning's responsible. The internal organs have been removed and examined. There's no sign of drug or poison. Lungs filled with water."

Suicide, then. Was this final act a confession of guilt? No doubt the unthinking public would seize on it as such. With this evidence before one, it was easy to say that with Dinah about to be released Mowbray saw the net closing round him; that certain in his own mind of his ultimate end he took this way out. As for Cleeves' share in things—well, to understand that would demand a fuller knowledge of the tie between master and man than was at all likely to be disclosed. Both had chosen to remove themselves. Did it mean both were concerned in Dorinda's murder? If that were so, then which incited which? And above all, why?

It was the "why" which wrecked all conclusions. Neither Mowbray nor Cleeves stood to gain by Dorinda's decease, and Tommy for one simply could not conceive of their inviting danger without ample inducement. His unreasoning elation ebbed away. His first thought had been that now, without doubt, Dinah would be freed from suspicion, but when he had collected his wits he saw no more sense in believing these men murderers than he had done before. On Friday night had he not watched Mowbray measuring Dorinda as a potential aid to his bank-account, an aid which could function only while the girl was alive? His impressions could not have gone so utterly awry, nor could he imagine the mere terror of arrest under *la loi contre les stupifiants* was sufficient to lead to this desperate step. He might be wrong, though, and if he was, then he, Tommy, was answerable for the sacrifice.

"It's a baddish knock he got," was the disconcerted reflection in his mind as he moved away. "Might have been the pier, and again . . ."

But once more, why? He had no theory to offer.

As swiftly as the traffic would allow, he hastened to the British Nursing Home. Here he was informed that while Ronald Cleeves had regained consciousness he was far too ill to answer questions. The sister in charge, her tones stilled with horror but retaining the owner's inborn homage for the ruling classes, said that the police were in constant attendance, waiting to pounce on the patient for a statement.

"But they'll wait a long time," she declared grimly. "If I'm any judge, that boy won't talk. He'll recover, but it's not because he wants to. He's in for a complete nerve-collapse."

"Mental?" suggested Tommy hopefully, struck by something peculiar in the woman's manner.

"Well, not that exactly. Still, though you mightn't think it from his looks, he's a neurotic subject if ever I saw one. But then he would be a bit queer, wouldn't he, to kill himself over a man like that?"

If this was what had happened, Tommy agreed; but his ideas were entirely at sea. He would have said that the blank-eyed, statuesque Cleeves was the last person to succumb to emotional surrender, but appearances are deceitful. The youth had undoubtedly indulged in drugs, was moreover quite evidently devoted to and enthralled by the magnetic Mowbray. He shook his head and drove to the apartment lately occupied by the two Englishmen.

Here he was in time to witness the departure of two inspectors. Letting them get well away, he climbed to the studio, and found the manservant shaken with excitement but able, on the receipt of a large tip, to give him a clear account.

Since last Saturday, it seemed, the English messieurs had remained indoors except when sent for to appear before the *juge d'instruction*. After these examinations they talked a great deal, in undertones, both very moody and depressed. However, during the past few days the elder one had changed. He went out several times alone, to be gone about an hour, and in the intervals smoked a great many cigarettes and was extremely silent. One could imagine there was something going on in his mind which he kept to himself, but that was merely the servant's idea. Last night, towards ten o'clock, Monsieur Mowbray made a suggestion, as the result of which a taxi was called and the two set off together. Only one returned—Monsieur Cleeves, at a little past midnight. The servant heard him come in, but did not know the other gentleman was absent till he took in the morning coffee and saw the bed in the latter's room undisturbed.

"Did Monsieur Cleeves seem anxious?" inquired Tommy.

"I thought he was by the way he kept going to look out of the window; but he said nothing and about noon he sent me out on an errand to buy a bottle of gin and some siphons."

"And then?"

"It took me some little time to get what I wanted. When I got back, there were two officers hammering at the door and the instant I let them in with my key we smelled gas. He was in the kitchen, monsieur, lying before the gas-oven. I was sure he was dead, for his face was the colour of plaster, and he neither stirred nor groaned. It's my belief he'd heard about his friend over the telephone and rushed at once to take his own life."

"But if no one else was here, how do you know he was rung up?"

"Because the woman across the hall heard the telephone ring and stop almost immediately, showing it had been answered. The gentlemen were very great friends," added the man significantly. "I should say the young one was completely under the old one's influence. He looked on the old one as a sort of god."

"Beelzebub," reflected Tommy, wondering if Cleeves had known Mowbray was a criminal and been determined to shield him. "And you can't tell me anything in the way of conversation which passed between them?" he asked aloud.

"I don't understand English, monsieur. I feel certain they were often discussing the murder on the Ile St. Louis. I think, too, the matter of money must have worried them, for," lowering his voice, "it's quite undeniable neither of them had a sou. Since they came here, my wages have not been paid, and they owed so much to the butcher, the baker, the wine-merchants, that there was great trouble getting credit. When my own master comes back he will find bills all over the quarter besides the gas, electric, and maybe the rent."

"As bad as that, was it?" exclaimed Tommy with kindling eye.

"Ah, very bad, monsieur. I believe the young one kept expecting some remittance, because whenever an English letter came he tore it open, took a quick look inside and flung it into the fire. One could see he was furious."

"Any letters lying about?"

"No, the police searched, but could find nothing."

Tommy left the apartment, feeling that there was much to think over but that his were not the brains to do the thinking. Stimulating enough to learn the depleted state of the Englishmen's exchequer, but could that condition have led to double suicide? More vital point, did it impinge on the murder itself? Though he continued to nose and pry, no enlightenment on either question was vouchsafed him.

To the two American women immured in the Val-de-Grâce flat, the tidings brought breath-taking astonishment. Hallie Pemberton trembled so violently that her glasses tumbled from her neat nose.

"Those men!" she gasped, turning dull red with triumph. "Oh, I knew they must have had some hand in it! Think, Dinah, think what this will mean to us!"

"Will it?" The girl's eyes as they scanned the news-page grew mystified, dubious. "I'm not so sure. . . . Why should any one suppose they did it? They didn't hate her; they weren't afraid of her, they couldn't get anything by her death. And," she ended with hesitation, "they weren't insane."

"How do you know? One may have been. Anyhow, this proves they were terrified of arrest. Oh, if only Tommy—I mean Mr. Rostetter—would come and tell us about it!"

Dinah shared her cousin's wish. She had come to depend on her make-believe lover, to draw strength from the presence of one who to her represented a sort of combined father and brother. From Virginia cables came daily offering advice, help, but there was only Tommy to whom she could say what she liked without fear of being misunderstood, only Tommy who would never condemn, who could treat her darkest moods with a whimsical common-sense which had somehow enabled her to preserve her balance. Without him what folly might she not have committed? There were moments when it required all her force of will to keep from rushing down into the court, casting herself upon the sergeant who walked up and down and crying, "Arrest me! I'm guilty!" It was the thought of Tommy's straight-seeing, cheerful blue eyes which steadied her. She had only to listen to him saying, "Don't be a fool!"

As soon as he arrived, Hallie bombarded him with questions, but it was plain he had little to offer in the way of elucidation. He listened abstractedly to her theory about Mowbray's terror of arrest, agreed tentatively, and gave the half-hearted opinion that Cleeves had tried to follow his friend's example out of abysmal despondence.

"It's leaked out, now, that he did hear the news over the telephone. A reporter rang him up. Yes, his part seems fairly simple—and may be simpler still, if only he'll talk. Or again it may not," he muttered, his brow deeply furrowed.

"But it will help Dinah, won't it?" urged Hallie with desperate appeal.

He patted her shoulder sympathetically. "Whether it does or not," he answered, "she's well on the way to being released. What's just happened certainly can't make matters worse for her. One must wait and see the interpretation put upon it."

He paused, struck by something enigmatic in Dinah's expression. He saw, too, that the girl was showing signs of exhaustion from the long strain she had undergone. The thought came to him, how much more of this will she be able to stand?

"What's bothering you?" he asked gently when she followed him to the door. "No, don't tell me it's nothing. What's on your mind?"

"You are lynx-eyed!" She tried to laugh. "Well, then, it's this: Mowbray may have seen he was going to be held partly responsible, because he gave us the drug. Maybe he knew I did it."

"You didn't do it! How could he—"

"How can you be sure he wasn't awake?" she asked quietly. "He's used to drugs, they might take slow effect on him. He would sham ignorance, because it was to his interests that none of us should be charged with murder; but if he foresaw I was going to be arrested—don't you understand how he would be placed?"

He chid her for stupidity, but in his heart he knew her reasoning to be sound. Mowbray had been left free solely that his movements might be watched. Sooner or later he would have been clapped into jail, and perhaps—who could say?—the charge against him would have been far more grave than simple violation of the drug-act. That he might actually have witnessed the stabbing was an idea it would be hard to erase now Dinah had introduced it.

"At any rate, get this into that stubborn head of yours: the judge hasn't got an inkling of any such event. You're safe—safe as houses."

"And if I am," she retorted, still with the queer gleam in her eyes, "whom have I got to thank for it?"

That evening, at a café much frequented by members of the press, Tommy ran into the *Morning Mail* reporter he had encountered at the mortuary. The youth, very callow, very romantic, was in a wild rage over the fact that a juicy story of his own finding had been turned down by his editor.

"Won't look at it," he raved. "And, man to man, it's just because the Big Chief's tied up with the Conisbroke crowd over an advertising deal. Call this freedom! Conisbroke's flown over to sit with all his weight on us. He and that cursed sister at the nursing-home. . . ."

Tommy ordered another round of gin and bitters. "What's the lowdown?" he inquired.

"Why, Conisbroke had cut off the funds. Issued an ultimatum—no more cash to Ronnie till Mowbray was off the wicket. See what that meant, with Ronnie staking his friend for the past year? Oh, it's a peach of a yarn! I'd got all the details—"

"Details? But how do they affect the Quarles case?"

"How do they affect it? My aunt! Ever get the close-up on that Corsican joint?"

Tommy murmured that he had heard tales.

"I should jolly well think so! The Black Mass—goats slaughtered on an altar—devotees frantic with hashish and heroin—an Irish countess . . ." He whispered a name. "Yes, it's true, went clean off her bean six months ago. Family hushed it up, but the peasants are complaining. What more do you want?"

"But the motive?"

"Motive my hat! Why, plain, unadulterated lust of killing. Run amuck through dope. From goats to humans is an easy step. The blighter was drunk on blood, and the point is young Cleeves *knew*. Oh, there's no doubt he knew what could happen, what in this particular case did happen—and he kept his mouth shut. Listen!" The fledgling's voice sank impressively. "What about this devil-worshipping society right here on the outskirts of Paris? Highest in the land. What about all these unidentified corpses that crop up in the Seine with their throats slit? Human sacrifices, chucked out when they've served their purpose. It's an old story."

Old, indeed! Since his own cub-reporter days Tommy had heard them, and was now too experienced a bird to be salted with such fantasies. Still, he listened while the poor old Marquis de Sade was hoisted from his grave, learned as for the first time about the wizards of the Rue de Vaugirard, and the hundred infants butchered for Madame de Montespan in the effort to fan a monarch's dying fancy. Young minds gloried in the stuff. How exactly did this coincide with the rigmarole his nephew Rank had relayed to him the other evening! A pity he could not apply it to the present case.

Others, it seemed, had a less squeamish palate, and the older American confrère who joined them to fix shrewd eyes on Tommy's face expounded a new variant of the theme. According to him, Cleeves and Mowbray had quarrelled. Cleeves struck a blow which toppled the other over the parapet of a bridge.

"Notice that gash on his head?" asked the theorist, shifting a chewed cigar. "Think that was caused by hitting a pier? I don't!"

Nor was it caused by bare knuckles, thought Tommy, while it was still less probable for Cleeves to have gone about equipped with brass protectors. He mildly interjected what was now known fact—namely, that although the two friends had gone off in the same cab, it was Cleeves alone whom the pursuing sleuth found shortly afterwards, entering a café.

"Don't forget they lost Cleeves, too, after that, so what's to prove the pair didn't join up later on? Your uncle's telling you: that boy's scared stiff. It's my belief he did the stabbing over here on the island, and that Mowbray rounded on him for hush-money. In fact, I'm just cabling a swell little story along those lines—aristocratic family run to seed and abnormal tendencies, you know. Okay stuff for my syndicate. Oh, it'll go down, it'll go down!" The speaker's rimmed spectacles turned like searchlights on Tommy. "Say, son, you'd like to think that was so, wouldn't you?" he drawled pleasantly. "Save you a lot of headache, *n'est ce pas*?"

Like! With his whole soul Tommy longed to embrace this or any other improbable yarn which could ensure Dinah's immediate release. Unfortunately the one explanation calculated to carry weight was that sponsored by the Sûreté. He had got it from a reliable source, and here it was:

Mowbray's death—it was accepted as suicide—had but an indirect bearing on the Ile St. Louis affair. The man saw his extensive drug activities about to be exposed, himself hemmed in on all sides. Deportation from Corsica was imminent, which accounted for his presence in Paris. His associates, frightened, had deserted him, all but Cleeves, who now could no longer offer him support. He was without money, suffering, moreover, from incipient Bright's disease. The game was finished. *Voilà!*

And Dinah? It was clear that her position remained the same when, after a day's cessation, the examinations began again. It seemed that Gramont, a bulldog for tenacity, was reluctant to admit himself beaten. He would hold on yet a little longer, wear her down, prod her until she cried out, or if she still withstood him, let her go—with an irremovable stain on her character.

CHAPTER XXII

BEFORE a red fire of boulets, Tommy sucked hard at his pipe and glanced abstractedly at the front page of *L'Ami du Peuple*, outspread on his knee. He knew every word on the three statements it contained, none of which supplied him with fresh matter. Indeed, it was the very absence of enlightening comment which made him study them with a probing eye, trying unsuccessfully to decide what, if anything, lay behind their curt, reserved phrases.

First came the meagre admissions finally drawn from the prostrate Cleeves, who, defending his dead friend from every criminal implication, swore emphatically he knew of no real reason why the latter should have taken his life. Yes, he had helped Mowbray to escape from the taxicab the two of them occupied, the spot chosen being close to the Concorde Metro Station. Mowbray had declared he had an appointment and did not wish to be spied upon by the police, but what the appointment was he did not say, and Cleeves had not asked. He, Cleeves, had not tried to elude pursuit. He had strolled about the Grands Boulevards, stopped for a while at a café, and returned home to find Mowbray still out. That was all, except that he denied all knowledge of how Mowbray obtained his drugs. The subject had never interested him.

The Earl of Conisbroke was even more laconic. He declared his belief that the foregoing statement was true in every detail, that his son's record at the University had been above reproach, and that it was Ronald's deep love of the classics which had drawn him into close friendship with Bannister Mowbray, whose scholastic achievements were well known. He was told that Mowbray and Ronald had been engaged in writing a speculative treatise on the Delphic Mysteries, and it was the disappointment caused by the ruin of this joint-labour coupled with personal grief for the loss of one he deeply admired which had precipitated the unfortunate young man's attempt at suicide. As soon as permission was granted, Lord Conisbroke proposed to take his son for a long cruise. Ronald's nerves had received a double shock, from which it would take time to recover.

The third interview was with Basil Jethro. It was dignified, frank and absolutely non-committal. The philosopher had no theories to offer. He deeply regretted his inability to assist the police, but hampered as he was by total ignorance concerning the private relations of his late step-daughter he was reluctantly obliged to stand aside and, though he put it less vulgarly, keep his finger out of the pie.

Words, words! Was the man's gigantic brain-power lavished entirely on the abstract? That afternoon Tommy had seen Jethro for a few minutes at Helen Roderick's apartment, and had watched him give courteous but slightly bored attention to their hostess's shuddering recital of the Mowbray rumours. His manner throughout suggested a wearied longing to detach himself from this ugly inquiry and resume his neglected studies.

"My dear Helen," he had remarked patiently, "how can I hazard any opinion when I know so little? If this Mowbray is guilty of murder, it begins to look as though he had carried his secret into the grave. It is a pity we cannot know for sure, and write *finis* to the chapter. Great as my respect for the Sûreté Générale has always been, I cannot feel that in the present instance that organisation has acquitted itself with any distinction."

Vague, general, like the declarations contained in the printed interview; and yet Tommy could not forget that the author had shown himself both definite and practical when inventing a fallacious excuse to cover up a long lapse of time; in specifying, unnecessarily, the contents of a bag, and accounting—again falsely—for his failure to put up at his usual hotel. In short, he had gone out of his way—or so Tommy believed—to create an impression which certainly did not tally with truth.

"Why should he do these things?" muttered Tommy irritably. "He doesn't look the sort of man who lies for the love of lying. Has he got some queer quirk of vanity in his make-up which would explain all these evasions? There must be some reason. If it's not the one I first suspected, then what is it?"

He reached for the heavy volume of *Who's Who*, which he had previously consulted to little purpose, and turned again to the entry dealing with Basil Jethro. The only items which interested him were first the fact that the philosopher had received his early education on the continent, his father being employed in the British Consular service; and second that his rise to fame had been sudden, even spectacular. Until eight years ago he had been a plodding, obscure schoolmaster, contributing occasional articles to scientific reviews, but causing no stir in the world. Then he had brought out his primary thesis, by reason of which he had at once been hailed as a revolutioniser of thought. From there onward, Europe and America had followed with reverence the successive treatises which by logical steps had culminated in the celebrated *Beyond Relativity*, "in which philosophy was stripped of emotionalism and reduced to the mathematical lines of pure truth."

Truth! Was there a hidden irony contained in the word? And was there a still greater irony to be found in the fact that the thinker's first triumph closely succeeded his marriage to an emotional, illogical woman, in every way his mental inferior?

Tommy's pipe had gone out. He restoked it carefully, and, his eyes filled with speculation, put his hand almost automatically into his waistcoat pocket to withdraw a scrap of paper. It was the memorandum he had taken from Jethro's storage-room. He pored moodily over the irregular alignment, the widening margin and the pools of ink which had collected in the looped letters. Presently he rose and prying amongst the books of the shelves selected a small hand-book. The plates contained in this he proceeded to compare painstakingly with the specimen on his knee. At the end of his study he frowned, stared into the red heart of the fire, rumpled his hair, and still wearing an air of irritable dissatisfaction drew a sheet of paper towards him and steadying it on the back of *Who's Who* began to compose a letter.

The door-bell pealed. With some annoyance he flung open the outer door, and then, his expression altering, cried: "Come in, come in!" with hospitable welcome.

Christopher Loughton accepted the invitation with a hesitant air, and entering the room stood looking vaguely at the big saddle-bagged chair till Tommy settled his indecision by forcing him into it. Even then he showed no inclination to speak. Tommy, producing bottles and glasses from a cupboard, was the first to break the somewhat awkward silence.

"Well," he remarked encouragingly, "rather a lot of water has flowed under the bridge since we last saw each other, eh, what?"

"Water . . . and a body," returned Christopher, running a brown muscular hand over his hair with a troubled gesture. "What's your notion about this Mowbray business?" he blurted out suddenly.

"What's yours?" countered Tommy, busily squirting soda.

"I don't know. People are saying—"

"Tell me not in mournful numbers what they're saying. I've heard them saying it. Unfortunately, it hasn't altered the main course of events."

Christopher met his host's eyes squarely.

"You mean they're still interrogating Dinah. I know. It's utterly damnable. Why do they do it?"

"I suppose because they don't consider that either Mowbray or Cleeves had sufficient reason to murder Dorinda. Still, they can't prove that Dinah had, either; so the siege must be nearly ended."

"Are you satisfied?" demanded the younger man slowly. Again their eyes met. Tommy shrugged, pushed the cigarettes towards Christopher and lit one for himself.

"No," he said at last, "I'm not. You see, Loughton, as you probably know as well as I do, Dinah's afflicted with a sensitive conscience. This equivocal state of things has made her morbid about herself. Between ourselves, she won't ever be happy till she's entirely assured of her innocence, technical as well as moral." He chose his words with care. "And there, unfortunately, lies the difficulty. If the police don't make an arrest, what's to remove her doubt?"

As on a former occasion he feared he had said too much, but once more Christopher got the meaning intended and no more.

"I understand," he said with a nod. "She would be like that. But are you sure there's no evidence whatever to point in another direction?"

"From the official viewpoint, none. From my own . . ." Here Tommy sipped his whisky, held an inward debate, and resumed with a slightly shame-faced air. "I may as well tell you that for days there's been a sort of idea knocking round in my head. It's extravagant, ill-founded; probably at the first test it will collapse. Still, if you'll promise to keep mum about it, I'll hand it over for what it's worth."

Christopher's sombre brown eyes remained glued to his rival's face while the tale of contradictions and discrepancies was unfolded. His lips parted but uttered no sounds till, at the first pause, the words: "Basil Jethro! Good God!" burst from him in a tone of blank incredulity. Plainly no thought of the kind had brushed even the outer edges of his brain.

"Stuns you, does it?" remarked Tommy calmly. "Well, I don't wonder. Your reception of the notion confirms what I knew before—that it will be absolute idiocy to bring an accusation like this, least of all, against a public idol, without producing something tangible in the way of proof. I've already tried to get this proof and failed. For that matter, it seems certain the Sûreté has checked up on the man's movements and dismissed him with a clean sheet. Only I kept asking myself would they have dismissed him so readily if they'd known what I know?"

Christopher regarded him searchingly. After a moment he asked further details about the letter, the very existence of which seemed unknown to the police.

"Do you imagine it represented a menace to Jethro's reputation?"

"Hardly. Dinah, who saw it, declares it was undated and gave no definite information. The doctor tells me authoritatively that Agatha Jethro was a confirmed morphia addict, whose word on any subject would be considered unreliable—also that her husband realised her condition, and was the first to report it. Dorinda, attaching exaggerated importance to her find, certainly had some idea of using it as a threat, but as to Jethro's motive for murder, I'm afraid we shall have to look elsewhere than towards this almost meaningless and now non-existent scrap of paper. Personally I have a hankering to examine into that trusteeship. In spite of being annihilated by Macadam's clerk, I still feel there's just a chance of Jethro's being sole trustee, in which case—well, anything is possible."

"Would any woman have been so foolish, even before 1926, as to put all that power into one man's hands?" objected Christopher sceptically.

"Women in love have been just that foolish. Agatha Jethro might have done it. If she did, it would go far towards explaining Dorinda's stored resentment towards her step-father, as well as the hints she dropped. Supposing he had managed to dip into her investments, wouldn't the imminence of her coming of age have presented a terrifying prospect?"

"Actually she was nearly twenty-one," said the American slowly. "Her birthday was in November. Why not get hold of this will and see what the position is?"

"Why don't I get hold of it? Because, my dear man, that will's in Somerset House, London, and I'm anchored here, unable to leave this cursed city without being jugged for contempt of court! I suppose I could get some Fleet Street pal of mine to look it up for me, but I don't know one of that gang I can trust not to make a story out of it. This mustn't be broadcasted, you understand. We're nosing about with nothing but a hunch to guide us. It's a delicate business, and I . . . well, I wouldn't be helping Dinah much if I landed myself in quod."

As he scratched his head in exasperation, Christopher leant forward with kindling eyes.

"I'll go," he declared quickly. "Give me your instructions and I'll carry them out."

"You?" Tommy stared, visibly delighted. "Great stuff! Put it there." They shook hands on the deal. "But," the speaker's face clouded, "will your chief give you leave to go?"

"Leave be damned. If it's denied me, I'll chuck my appointment."

The quiet announcement caused Tommy to stare again with deepening appreciation. He felt he was making discoveries.

"By Jove," he exclaimed, clapping his guest on the shoulder. "Why didn't I let you in on this sooner? Not that you believe in it. I don't expect you to . . . and the fact is, it may be just pure bunkum. Never mind, we'll team up and go for it. Listen!"

He hitched his chair close. How odd it seemed that, all enmity forgotten, these two men should be hatching schemes together, schemes whose sole purpose was to free the mind of a girl who, when all was said and done, would belong to neither of them! Not that Christopher realised that fact. As far as he knew, he alone was the loser—an erroneous belief which made his present attitude all the more praiseworthy in his fellow altruist's eyes.

"First," began Tommy in a low voice, "find out the precise terms of the will . . . who benefits, under what conditions. Next, clear up the matter of trusteeship. Third, investigate Jethro's private finances. I know," he agreed, answering his companion's raised eyebrows, "that part won't be easy. In fact, if there's crooked business afoot, it will undoubtedly be covered so deep it will take the C.I.D. to dig it up. But get a line on the man's mode of life. Pry into the flat in Bedford Square, talk to the servants or the caretaker—and when you've got all you can from the London end, press on to Oxford. Oxford . . ."

Tommy glanced toward the note he had begun to write before Christopher's arrival interrupted him. He rubbed his nose, and his manner subtly altered.

"It so happens I was just dashing off a line to a make-weight nephew of mine at Magdalen," he went on musingly. "I'll tell him to pilot you round and assist in any dirty work which may crop up. He'll esteem it a privilege," opined the uncle, recalling the nauseous telegram of congratulation he had lately received from Rank, who, while showering good wishes on him, had suppressed any reference to the payment of debts. "And the dirtier the job, the more he'll take to it. You understand you may have to bluff, lie, even burgle. Any objection?"

"None . . . though I can't flatter myself I've your aptitude for that sort of thing."

Tommy let the dubious compliment pass.

"Another thing," he continued thoughtfully. "While you're in Oxford, I want you to get hold of a slimy little blighter who blew in with my nephew a few nights ago. Name of Pillion, or Hellion, or—well, it doesn't matter, the lad will put you on to him. Point is, he's supposed to be sitting tight over some alleged recollection connected with Jethro, which, if it proves authentic—as I'm fairly certain it won't—might possibly lead to something useful. Never mind how wild the story sounds. Get it if you can, and give me the details. We can't afford, you and I, to scorn anything, however remote or unpromising, which may shed light on the hidden places. When can you start?"

"By the early morning 'plane. That will mean I ought to be back here Tuesday afternoon."

"Good work! Now, get this straight. Your job's Motive; mine's Opportunity. One's no good without the other, so while you're snooping about across the channel, I mean to fasten on like a leech to the Hôtel Stanislas and not leave it till I've sucked it dry. I don't see the least chance of smashing Jethro's alibi, but I have yet to tackle the question of his having had an accomplice. Anyhow, though I've drawn blanks so far, I'm going to begin all over again this very evening, and see what comes of it."

When the two had separated, Tommy gazed fixedly at the leather chair where his visitor had sat. What wanton tricks Life played! Here, thought he, was a decent chap, furthermore Dinah's choice, and all because of a single mis-step, or rather the bad luck of being found out, he was chucked overboard, denied all hope of reinstatement. Nor was it the least good trying to patch matters up between them. The girl's heart had simply closed up, like a sensitive plant roughly handled. It would take a long time to reopen, and when it did it would be for some other man, not Christopher....

Some other man....

Tommy saw in his mind's eye a small, proud head with satin-smooth red hair moulded round it, two clear eyes like aquamarines, a peach-blossom cheek his fingers itched to caress. Little, lovely, in distress....

He gave the leather chair an angry punch.

"It won't be me, at any rate," he muttered, annoyed with himself. "And a jolly good thing, too. To hell with this drivelling, when there's work to be done! Now how the blazes am I going to sidetrack that sleuth across the way?"

Switching off the lights, he peered cautiously through the curtains towards the spot where, in the gloom, a casual figure patrolled the silent square. Yes, there against the dim façade opposite, glowed the fixed red star of a cigarette, pulsating steadily as the smoker faced his direction. After ten minutes it wandered near, paused, and with a brisker air set off as though on its homeward way.

Now was the moment to slip out. Tommy did so, glancing surreptitiously around. When he had satisfied himself that no guardian was in sight, he took a rapid though devious course to the Hôtel Stanislas.

CHAPTER XXIII

ALTHOUGH there seemed not the slightest reason why he should be followed, Tommy had the unaccountable feeling that some one was dogging his footsteps all the way to the Rue Berger. Every few yards he turned to scan the pavement behind him, and at each loitering wayfarer directed a searching glance. It was with relief that he reached the haven of the hotel lobby, but here the manager's cool, reserved greeting racked his nerves afresh. Had anything happened to rouse suspicion of him, or was the man merely nonplussed over his engaging a room and then failing to take possession of it? If the latter, it could soon be put right, but as the manager at this moment was summoned to the telephone, Tommy went through into the lounge, ordered a bock, and after a disinterested glance at two black-bearded commercial travellers who were volubly debating the subject of disarmament, settled himself to grapple with his own problem.

It was hard to collect his thoughts. Ever and again the bruise on Mowbray's pear-shaped forehead came before him, linked with the American reporter's theory about blackmail, and Lord Conisbroke's lofty reference to the joint research into the Delphic Mysteries. Was it possible there had been a violent altercation between the two friends? What had become of Cleeves after the police lost him? Had he tried to kill himself through grief, or through fear? Whatever the case, there seemed little likelihood of shaking his story. Again, it was an affair of no eye-witnesses, which left all conjectures without a leg to stand on, Tommy's private one as well as the others; but as the purely hypothetical idea which had arisen this evening demanded exactly the same support as the previous abandoned one—in fact, was part and parcel of it—the only thing to be done was, to quote his words to Christopher, "begin at the beginning." In short, one must delve once more into the question of how Basil Jethro could have effected an exit from these premises at a stated time.

Tommy had been obliged to accept the main door, leading to the Rue Berger, as the one which must have been used, the trouble being that he was likewise obliged to see the difficulty, nay, the impossibility, of Jethro's crossing the small lobby without the manager's noticing him. Most positively had the man declared his constant presence at the desk all Friday evening up till one o'clock, and even if the statement were not strictly accurate, if, for example, he had retired into the office behind the desk for a moment or so, he would still have heard Jethro's step and looked to see who was passing. Logic asserted one of two alternative conclusions: either Jethro did not go out, or else he accomplished the puzzling feat of doing so unobserved. At first inspection the latter seemed an absurdity; but, stop! Had not the philosopher achieved the exact thing on two admitted occasions?

No doubt about it, he had—once at his entrance Friday evening before dinner, and again next morning when he quitted the hotel. The first occasion was natural enough, but the second was less understandable, for then the manager, morbidly interested in his bereaved guest, had been watching out for him. How odd that Tommy should have overlooked this circumstance! He told himself that if a thing can be done once—and here it was apparently done twice—it can be done a third and fourth time. One must simply examine the trick, if trick it was, and discover the mechanism of it. Just possibly it was accidental, of course; but having seen the manager's curious turn of mind and his acute interest in a guest who was not only vastly superior to the general run of Stanislas patrons but also a central figure in a murder sensation, Tommy was inclined to think that the latter must have worn a cloak of invisibility to escape unobserved.

What, he asked, does the professional magician do to prevent the audience seeing him produce the Egyptian queen from the concealed trap-door? Why, he fires a pistol into the wings, or he has an assistant create a commotion up-stage to draw attention from his own movements. Unfortunately for the argument Jethro could not have fired a pistol, nor was it conceivable he had an assistant working with him. More, the ruse employed would have had to do service four separate times—two exits, two entrances—each under differing conditions. If one accepted the known invisible transits as deliberately contrived, the same reason why they were unremarked must apply to the remaining pair, *i.e.*, the sortie and return during the evening. Now how could a man walk by in full view and yet be believed to lie in his bed two floors above? The only answer Tommy could think of was that he adopted some plausible disguise.

Why, obviously—it was the answer! How on earth had he overlooked it? Merely because he had paid insufficient attention to what had been told him. Now, however, he saw a possible means of accounting for Jethro's unnoticed presence in the lobby on the admitted as well as the theoretic occasions. Indeed, all four occasions were essential to the scheme; the two central ones for the preservation of the alibi, the first and last in order to introduce the individual impersonated into the hotel and to get him out again when he was no longer required. It was a perfect explanation—if it worked.

But whom could Jethro have pretended to be? In a small place like this any stranger would be instantly remarked if not challenged, therefore the entity chosen must be provided with a good excuse for passing in and out, and, since he must spend the night in the hotel, he could not be any one supposed to sleep outside. Yet it was fatuous to think of imitating one of the hotel attendants, or for that matter any one of previously familiar appearance. The person therefore must be (1) staying in the hotel; (2) created on purpose to meet the emergency. In short, an imaginary guest.

A guest, yes . . . but that was not enough. It must be a guest who arrived on Friday and left early Saturday morning, incidentally—and this was the crux—sallying forth during the evening for an interval long enough to get to the Ile St. Louis and back. If by a lucky chance such a man could be found, a man of the philosopher's height and build—

At this point in the argument one of the commercial travellers dropped his cigar, and in searching for it thrust his legs out in front of him. Mechanically Tommy's eyes gravitated toward the pair of badly-cut, typically-French boots protruding in his direction.

Boots! Like a blow in the face the memory struck him. What about those black, clumsy, brand-new boots in the passage outside the closed door of Number Seventeen, boots which, when he tapped the second time on Eighteen, had been taken inside?

Holy Moses, he'd got it! He sprang up, upsetting his bock, and made swift strides towards the lobby; but as he pushed open the glass doors he recalled the manager's manner a few minutes ago, and quickly devised a method of dealing with it. The pose of casual sojourner would have to be dropped, and an excuse invented for his erratic behaviour. Well, excuses came easy to him. Ten seconds' pause, and he had one, ready-made, calculated to fill all the requirements.

The manager was in his office, chatting with a small, sharp-faced man in a checked waistcoat and spats. While allowing him to finish, Tommy opened the register, and studied the entries for the date in question—Friday, a week ago. There were four:

Gaston Delarmes et femme, Bordeaux.

Mlle. Berthe Lenoyer, Brussels.

Gustave Leysac, Lyons.

Dr. Emil Karl Klauber, Prague.

At each signature Tommy looked closely, comparing it with the well-known writing of Basil Jethro on the preceding page. All differed substantially from the Englishman's—M. Delarmes being angular and spidery, Mlle. Lenoyer's round and open, Leysac's the niggardly effort of an ill-educated person, and Dr. Klauber's upright, semi-script, with large capitals which had caused the pen to sputter. Yet if the theory were correct, one of these signatures—

"Monsieur?"

The manager, now free, came forward to fix his sloe eyes on Tommy, drawing in his breath in a tentative manner. Tommy picked up the register, walked calmly behind the desk and into the office, and closed the door.

"I have an explanation and an apology to offer you, monsieur," he said in a low, frank tone. "When I took one of your rooms the other day, I misled you as to my reason, but now—" hesitating, he resolved by one bold stroke to discover why the man's attitude had grown suspicious and at the same time to introduce his newly-concocted fiction. "Might I inquire," he continued, "if during the last few days you have received a visit from the police?"

The manager's eyes narrowed. Evidently Tommy had hit the mark.

"The police have been to me, monsieur, to ask a few purely formal questions. The inspector was quite satisfied with my answers, only I could not help recalling your own inquiries regarding this same gentleman, and wondering if—"

"Why, what gentleman are you referring to?" interrupted Tommy, innocently astonished.

"But naturally, Monsieur Jethro."

"Monsieur Jethro!" Tommy's brow cleared. "I imagined you meant quite another person, and could not understand how you could possibly have read my mind. It's not Mr. Jethro I'm interested in—oh, no, not at all—but another person whose name I can't find in your register. And yet I could have sworn I saw this man that morning, Friday week it was, in the passage upstairs. That's why I engaged a room, but afterwards I discovered the man had left. In fact—but I had better explain my position."

Speaking in a confidential manner, Tommy proceeded to outline an invented situation. As a representative of the British Press, he had been asked to keep an eye out for a certain individual who by forged credentials had defrauded a London stockbroker's firm of a large sum of money. He had been sent a photograph of this man and a list of the hotels in which he was likely to stop. The Hôtel Stanislas was one of these, and by sheer coincidence, having come here to acquaint Mr. Jethro of the murder, he had run into the very man he was hoping to find.

"As least I believed it was he. I can't be absolutely sure, for I hadn't the photograph on me at the time. And I haven't it now," he added regretfully. "Indeed, I'm rather afraid I've lost it. Still, I'm informed he may come back here again, also that he was probably using one of several aliases. So now you see why I've turned up once more, and why I need your assistance. If the Paris police have not asked you about him, it only proves how careful he has been. However, if it was my man, he spent only one night under your roof—the night of the Friday I mention. Can you tell me anything about these three arrivals I see put down for Friday, September 30th? We'll rule out the lady, of course."

So saying, Tommy laid the open book under his companion's eye, well-pleased to find his jerry-built story holding up under the strain. The manager had grown friendly again, and with every sign of wishing to help bent over the entries.

"M. Delarmes," he read. "He's a regular client—comes here with his wife about this time every year. A wine-importer from the south, short, excessively stout, and lame. No? I thought not. Well, then M. Leysac—but that was M. Leysac whom you saw talking to me just now. You could scarcely have meant him?"

"No," replied Tommy. "It was not M. Leysac. But how about the German? What is he like, and, more important, is he still with you?"

"Dr. Klauber? A Czecho-Slovak, monsieur, a professor, I believe, from the German University of Prague. Tall, middle-aged, studious-looking, a little eccentric in dress, but the last person I should ever suspect of anything crooked. He spent one night, on his return from England, and has gone back to Prague."

"So he's gone!" mused Tommy, his satisfaction over this circumstance marred by the manager's appearance of knowing Klauber well. "But is he, too, an old client?"

"Not old, monsieur, but he has been here before. About a month ago he stayed with us two days. This time he intended to make it a week, but a letter he found on his arrival made him change his plans. He left early Saturday morning."

"Was this letter an English one?" asked Tommy, feeling there was little use to pursue the inquiry, since Klauber had been here before and, if he received mail, must almost surely be a genuine person.

"No, monsieur, I happened to notice it was posted at Marseilles. It came fully twenty-four hours before he got here." Marseilles! This was slightly better. Jethro, as he reached Paris from Cap Ferrat on Wednesday, must have passed through Marseilles Tuesday evening. A letter posted in that city would have arrived in Paris—no, that would be too early. Unless, to be sure, he gave it to a station porter to post and the porter delayed doing so. . . .

"Klauber doesn't look exactly promising," Tommy declared doubtfully. "However, can you tell me the precise times of his arrival and departure? They are important."

"He came straight from the Gare du Nord, reaching here at about eight-thirty in the evening—or perhaps slightly later. I remember, because I asked if he wanted dinner, but he told me he had already eaten. He left next morning, without taking any breakfast, at about a quarter to nine. He said he would get coffee at the station."

These hours accorded perfectly with Tommy's idea, but without a satisfactory answer to his next question they went for nothing. Did Klauber remain in the hotel the entire evening?

"Let me think," replied the manager, cogitating. "No, he went to his room to write letters, and quite late—towards eleven-thirty or thereabouts—he went out to catch the last post from the Bourse."

A thrill shot through Tommy. How often he had risked life and limb to catch that last post! Hiding his excitement, he inquired how long the professor was gone, and if he had taken a taxi.

"The Bourse is only a step from here, as you know," answered the manager. "And as Dr. Klauber never takes taxis, I feel certain he walked. Yes, even when he left us each time he went on foot to pick up a 'bus, carrying his own bag. I should say this time he was out about three-quarters of an hour. I was here when he came in, and seeing me he asked to have his account made up in readiness for the morning."

Better and better—for if Jethro had a dark deed to perform he would have avoided taxis, besides which he could easily have walked to the island and back in the stated time. Only Tommy could not rid himself of the notion that Klauber was real. How typical he seemed of the methodical, serious-minded German pedant, travelling with a definite purpose, economising at every turn! The previous visit and the letter posted at Marseilles might both form parts of a well-organised plan, but there was no doubt they helped to build up a solid, four-square personality.

"Did Klauber receive any other letters while he was here?"

The manager replied that while there was only this one this time, he thought at the former visit there were several. Whether they came before or during the professor's sojourn he could not recall, nor could he say anything definite about them, though he rather believed they bore French stamps.

Everything now depended on the final throw. Could the manager give an accurate description of Dr. Klauber's appearance?

"He is a fairly tall man, monsieur, a good deal taller than you or I, but he has a slight stoop. I never saw him without his hat, but his hair at the sides is grey, and he has a somewhat full face with a grizzled beard trimmed to a point. He gives one the impression of being heavily built, but that may have been due to his wearing a thick, bulky overcoat."

"He wore a thick overcoat a month ago, when the weather was warm?" demanded Tommy keenly.

"The whole time he was in Paris we had heavy rain. There was really more excuse for the coat then than last week—though he had just crossed the channel, of course, and I imagine he had wrapped up warmly on account of his abscessed face."

"Abscess!" repeated Tommy reminiscently. "Yes, the man I saw had a sort of . . . a sort of . . ."

"Surgical dressing on his cheek? *Mon Dieu*, then it may—it must have been the same! Did he also wear thick-lensed spectacles?" asked the manager, electrified.

"He did," confirmed Tommy, thinking that this news about spectacles was good hearing. "My idea is he was disguised. Would you recognise him without the hat, overcoat, spectacles?"

"I think I should, on account of his accent—for although he speaks fluent French, it is that kind of guttural speech Germans always use. He has, too, a slight impediment. I imagine it's from a badly-fitting dental plate. It's quite distinctive."

Dental plate? More likely a strip of plaster placed across the upper gums—and "plumpers" inserted in the cheeks to give them a fuller contour. With these devices, well known to the character actor, and the addition of a beard, disfiguring lenses, and a great wad of cotton-wool stuck on with adhesive tape, the man could have made himself unrecognisable. His admirable tailoring would have been concealed by the clumsy great-coat—and then the shoes—but that could wait for a moment. The matter of luggage had to be considered.

"No trunk, I suppose? Any labels on his bag, and what was the bag itself like?"

"Quite an ordinary one, dark brown leather, if I remember rightly. I did not see any labels. No, he had no trunk."

If the said bag was identifiable with the one Tommy had striven hard to locate, then it was simple enough to define its contents when it left the hotel. Jethro's own hat would have been inside it, a pair of his shoes, possibly a collar and tie.

"Could you say whether this bag was heavy or light?"

"No, monsieur, and I don't believe any of the attendants could tell you that either."

The manager smiled significantly, as though familiar with the type of client who is anxious to avoid giving tips, but to Tommy the reply meant that Jethro had not wished any one to notice how little his bag had in it.

"One last point," said the theorist thoughtfully. "What room did the professor occupy on his second visit?"

The manager, unable to recall, rang for a waiter. Jacques appeared, scratched his head over the question, then brightened.

"What, the old German, monsieur? He wanted a room on the court. There was only one vacant just then. It was on the second floor, Number Seventeen."

CHAPTER XXIV

TOMMY tingled from head to foot with excitement. How marvellously it all fitted in! What a simple matter for Jethro to choose a room with a vacancy next it into which, disguised as a German, he could slip! He could then go out if and when he liked, running no danger at this end except that of being recognised by the manager. Every one would be ready to swear he had not left his room.

"What steps do I intend to take?" Tommy came to from his triumphant dream. "At the immediate moment, this—but, by the way, did the man leave you his address?"

"I have it written down here, monsieur. You see? Just the Deutsche Universität, Prague. What are you looking for?"

"A telegram form. Ah, thanks!" Tommy scribbled rapidly, handing the result to his companion to read. "I am wiring at once to a friend of mine in the Reuter Agency at Prague," he explained truthfully, "asking for particulars. If no Karl Emil Klauber exists, then the details you have given me must be handed over to the police, here and in London. By tomorrow some time we shall know what to think."

"The operator will dispatch this at once, monsieur—but I cannot help believing you have been misled by a resemblance. Dr. Klauber—well, I consider myself a fairly good judge of people, and he did not seem to me an imposter."

The manager, at any rate, had been thoroughly taken in, but Tommy had expected as much. After all, when a guest has come back for a second time to an hotel, the staff begins to take a proprietary interest in him.

"If the fellow's cornered," said Tommy, rising, "I suppose you won't object to identifying him? I can assure you the brokers' firm I mentioned will gladly compensate you for your help."

He said this merely to remove any doubt of his sincerity from the other's mind, but really it was not necessary. The manager, not unmoved by the hint of remuneration, answered that he would come forward whenever he was required. Tommy bade him good-night, and started towards the lift.

The small chasseur sprang up, rubbing drowsy eyes. On the way up Tommy asked him whose job it was to attend to the boots. The boy replied that as a rule he cleaned them.

"Ah! Then perhaps you can tell me whether you noticed anything about those of the German gentleman who was here for one night last week, in Room Seventeen?"

The chasseur regarded him thoughtfully. "The German gentleman, monsieur? His boots were quite new, not dirty at all. I only had to give them a wipe over."

"Do you know if he wore those same ones when he was here a month ago?"

The small face looked blank for a moment, then lit with recollection.

"He did, monsieur. They were just out of the shop then, the soles hardly marked. He can't have worn them much in the meantime."

Filled with contentment, Tommy handed his informant a tip and walked towards his room. A late arrival had just taken Seventeen, from the door of which a tired chambermaid was now issuing. Tommy spoke to her, asking whether she could give him any information about the late occupant of the room, but it seemed she had caught but one glimpse of him—not, as might have been supposed, when she went to turn down his bed, for although the light was on and papers strewn about on the table, the gentleman had slipped out for a moment.

"But I met him here, in the passage, next morning when he was going away. He said good-bye, and gave me ten francs."

The woman, too, had apparently noticed nothing unusual; but the matter just mentioned struck Tommy as highly significant. Now that a service tax is included in the bill, few but English and American travellers distribute additional tips. That a man too careful about expenditures to indulge in taxis or even a hotel breakfast, carrying his own bag to save a couple of francs, should have bestowed needless generosity on a chambermaid looked decidedly queer; but if this man were inwardly trembling lest he be spotted as some one different, his natural instinct would be to put his hand in his pocket, thereby changing possible doubt to goodwill.

So far all was excellent—so excellent, indeed, that the reasoner had to remind himself that his conclusions rested wholly on surmise. Jethro might be proved to have had no motive for crime. Dr. Klauber was, perhaps, a genuine person. At all events action must be deferred till a satisfactory report had come from Prague, but there was no harm in arranging the set of supposed facts into logical sequence. Lighting his pipe, Tommy evolved the following order:

Jethro, resolved on murder, established himself at the Stanislas a full month ago in the shape of some one as unlike his own person as he could convincingly manage. Quite possibly he meant to achieve his ultimate purpose at this earlier date, but to make certain on this point one would have to know whether he was absent from Cap Ferrat just then, and also if Dorinda had arrived in Paris. If some accident supervened to prevent the initial attempt, nothing was lost, and the position strengthened by Klauber's being accepted as a familiar figure.

Why was this hotel chosen? Because it was about the only one within walking distance of the Ile St. Louis which was thoroughly respectable. Since it was important to keep out of taxi-cabs, the distance to the island must be considered; and as in addition the bag must, for safety's sake, be carried by himself, the individual portrayed must be the sort of man who would walk and handle his own luggage without causing comment—another reason for not putting up at an expensive place.

Now as to the actual disguise. Jethro would probably use what he already had—outer garments, long since abandoned—rather than risk purchasing new ones which might be traced. Shoes alone were a difficult problem. His own, however ancient, would have stamped him at once as English, therefore he had to buy a pair of characteristic, cheap continental boots. This would explain why the ones worn by Klauber were still new after a whole month. They had been kept exclusively for the right occasion, doubtless in company with the overcoat and hat, locked up in the trunk Tommy had ransacked. The owner had to go to his step-daughter's apartment to collect them.

Whatever form the plan originally took, it seemed fairly certain it was altered after the Baroness' reception, to which Jethro probably went to erase any impression of unfriendliness towards his proposed victim. Seeing Dorinda slightly intoxicated, he naturally did not approach her, but the scrap of conversation he paused to overhear must have suggested a golden opportunity. How doubly safe would he feel if the girl were found dead in a circle of defenceless people! It would be necessary to assure himself the drug had taken effect before venturing into the apartment, but was not this exactly what he did do by telephoning at eleven-thirty? Also he would not have dared enter the building after the outer doors were closed, in case his voice, when he called "Cordon," should be recognised by the concierge. Everything depended on chance, but chance favoured him.

Having secured his disguise—under the pretence of collecting books— he must have repaired to some public cloak-room to transform himself into the German professor. First, though, as an extra precaution, he devised his fiction about the latchkey, so that it could afterwards be thought he was without means of getting into the apartment. That the key would not be found till morning mattered hardly at all, since the concierge would always believe he had merely overlooked it. A fairly ingenious idea, this, but it had one fault: it was too elaborate. The common pitfall of amateurs, reflected Tommy complacently. Rather than leave a small tear, they must mend it with too many stitches.

But to continue: dressed as Klauber—this time adding the cotton-wool dressing, since he would now have to pass the severer test of being juxtaposed to his genuine self—Jethro returned to register as Klauber and obtained Room Seventeen, previously ascertained to be the one vacant bedroom on the court. Quickly divesting himself of his outer accessories and laying out papers to give his abode an occupied look, he slipped into Eighteen, donned pyjamas, and when in bed ordered his dinner. In his own person he had not been seen to come in, but no one was likely to remark on that fact now he was here.

By going to bed he had shown the management his intention of settling down for the night, but as the hour of the adventure drew near he took pains to buttress up the false belief. Ringing for Jacques, and giving as an excuse the flannel suit to be pressed, he inquired the correct time. A quarter-past eleven. Good! The waiter when questioned would remember that—and now it remained only to put on his Klauber outfit and when dressed ring up the apartment. The call served a dual purpose. It informed him it was safe to set out, and it demonstrated his expectation of lunching next day with his step-daughter. Again the pretence of amicable relations. Last of all, he told the manager not to disturb him in case any one rang, as he was about to retire to rest.

As Klauber, bound for the post-office, he sallied forth, reaching the apartment in, let us say, twelve minutes' time. The doors being open, it was easy enough to dodge past the lodge without making a noise. He must, however, have experienced some breathless moments when he stood in the midst of the slumbering company upstairs. What if one of them woke? It must have been while he surveyed the dormant figures that he caught sight of the Algerian dirk and decided to substitute it for whatever weapon he had provided. Chance again played into his hand, for was it not better to use what was there and leave it as evidence against some member of the party? That he threw the knife into the fire when he had used it proved he did the deed bare-handed, and the same argument applied to the door-knob so scrupulously cleaned to remove his imprints.

Here Tommy came to a halt. Where did Dinah enter the scene? Did the murderer see her go out? If so, he must have remained hidden from her, or there would have been two crimes instead of one. Either she left just before Jethro's arrival, or else she passed him in so evident a somnambulistic condition that he let her go unharmed, perhaps realising in her movements a stroke of luck for him. However obscured events were at this point, Jethro's subsequent actions were not difficult to construe. The assassin went as he came, deposited his Klauber garments in Seventeen, and returned to Eighteen to wait till morning. Immediately after receiving the notification of Dorinda's death, he hurried back to the room next door, and was in there changing his clothes when Tommy knocked and obtained no reply. He effected his exit from the hotel as Klauber, carrying away his customary hat and shoes in the bag which constituted the German's luggage, and went by foot or by 'bus to some place, most likely a railway station, to change back again into his own attire. If the cloakroom used on this occasion was far away, the long delay in getting to the scene of the crime was readily explained. All that remained of Dr. Klauber was now stowed away in the suit-case. The Professor, having served his purpose, was no more.

The reconstructed history had some noticeable flaws in it. For instance, even though Dorinda was known to be asleep, how could Jethro be sure her companions would all have succumbed? The risk run seemed so enormous that for a moment Tommy began to wonder if Benedetto, honest though he seemed, might not be an accomplice. However, he rejected the idea, partly because he himself had witnessed the old servant's shock on hearing the news, more since he could not conceive of Jethro's taking any one into his confidence.

But again, what would Jethro have done if caught wearing his disguise? The question raised a curious point. In strange clothing and a beard, he would have been lost; as himself he had a perfect right to enter the apartment if he wished. On these obvious assumptions, Tommy decided that Jethro must have removed certain suspicious features of his disguise on the landing outside, to be resumed at his departure. Not a good solution, but the best he could manufacture with his present incomplete knowledge. After all, why worry over such fine details? If one could establish the fact that the English philosopher and the Czecho-Slovak were one and the same person, the rest could take care of itself.

Tommy was now so thrilled with his anticipated victory that the mere denial of Klauber's existence failed to content him. What a *coup* it would be, journalistically speaking, if he could lay hands on the incriminating suit-case! Reason told him it might be done. It was not easy to destroy a leather bag and varied contents in the short time at the murderer's disposal, wherefore it would have to be stored in some convenient spot till such a period as its owner should deem himself sufficiently safe from observation to deal with it. Once more a railway station seemed the most probable hiding-place. A bag could remain there undisturbed for days, weeks, and as this particular bag was not a source of danger unless the police came to know about the dual identity game, it was not at all likely that any one should give it a second thought.

"It's there, in one of half a dozen left-luggage offices, waiting to be claimed," reflected Tommy with growing confidence. "With any sort of luck, I can find it. That's my to-morrow's job."

CHAPTER XXV

AT A phenomenally early hour, Tommy went back to his flat, pleased to note that his guardian angel had not yet come on duty. Secure in his belief that Klauber was a myth he sang in his bath, beamed on his reflection while shaving, and when his charwoman turned up, ate a second breakfast with deep enjoyment. When Christopher rang him on the telephone to say he was just about to leave le Bourget flying-field he had to sit tight on his enthusiasm so as not to give too much away.

"Oh, it's coming along, it's coming along," he announced radiantly. "Since last night I'm beginning to see a loophole in the wall. No, I mustn't give you any definite information just now. It's possible I may be too optimistic. Do your damnedest and report to me as soon as you can. Meanwhile, make your mind easy about Dinah, I'll look after her."

Not till he had replaced the receiver did he realise how, absent-mindedly, he had stepped outside his role of triumphant lover. It sounded a bit odd, that last assurance, but what did it matter when at almost any moment now the deception would be ended? He stifled a sigh. A pity, in a way, he couldn't go on playing this engagement game a little longer. He had not felt so ridiculously young for years. He wondered if Dinah would soften towards Christopher when she knew he had entered the lists in her service. He dared not mention the young man's name lest he give offence, yet it seemed unfair for her to remain ignorant of so genuine a devotion—wrong, too, to allow her to go on suffering when a word from him might lessen her load of care. Ought he to drop her a hint about his new discovery? He half decided to do so, but with his hand on its way to the telephone he caught sight of a book lying open at his elbow. It was Basil Jethro's *Beyond Relativity*. He picked it up and began to read, and as the clear, incisive sentences penetrated into his brain the whole theory he had concocted last night floated before him filmy as smoke, ready to be blown away by the first puff of wind.

What! The author of this a cold-blooded butcher? In spite of every deduction, it seemed sheer impossibility to unite the idea with the known aspects of the philosopher's character. There must be some gross error of judgment, or else in the midst of elation one could not pause like this, feeling the bloodless unreality of it all. No, in case of a mistake, better not lead the poor child on with false hopes. Wait, wait till the answer to his telegram arrived. Then and not till then could the facts be disclosed with impunity.

"It won't be long now," he assured himself, shoving the disconcerting volume out of sight. "And I've got work enough to keep me occupied till the wire comes. What-ho, for the suit-case!"

Alas, for his ardent expectations! Those who have tried to identify lost umbrellas or bags will not need to be told the sort of fate in store for him. At every one of the great and small railway terminuses he beheld brown leather cases by the score, whole platoons of them ranged on shelves, packed, jammed, jumbled, and in nearly every instance bearing a close resemblance to the one he sought. Long and hesitating scrutiny, painful comparison of the likely specimens, elimination of the undesirables, and at last the decisive announcement to the official in charge:

"That top one, monsieur—yes, the dark, stained one at the left-hand corner. I left it here on Saturday morning, over a week ago, and I have had the misfortune to lose the claim ticket—but if you'll be good enough to get it down and open it, I'll give you a description of the contents to prove it's mine."

Pleas and arguments on one side, shrugging objections on the other; the display of a note, and in the end the bag would be hauled upon the counter while the alleged owner rattled off his tale of an old, heavy overcoat, a felt hat, a pair of new black boots. (He suppressed the smaller accessories, since these, he imagined, could have been thrown down a drain.) Next would come the tussle with the assortment of keys brought with him, the attendant's eye growing more and more contemptuous; or, if the lock yielded, he would lean forward, heart in mouth; to discover some article like pink underclothing, a fringed shawl, or an infant's diaper.

The entire day was spent in fruitless search. From the Gare de Lyon to the Gare du Nord, from the Gare du Nord to the Gare St. Lazare he went, patient, persistent, and in the end despairing. He still clung to his belief that Jethro's property was among one of these maddening collections of luggage, but as far as his recovering it was concerned it might as well have been in the Roman catacombs. Only the police, empowered to order a wholesale ransacking, could bring it to light, and until he had the authoritative denial of the German professor's existence he was debarred from setting that machinery in motion. His dream of an individual "scoop" vanished into mist.

From the various cloakroom officials he met with little better success. At the Gare de l'Est he did learn of a tall gentleman, foreign in appearance, who on Saturday—or perhaps it was Monday—took possession of the private wash-place and remained in there for a considerable time. However, this gentleman certainly had no great wad of cotton-wool fastened to his cheek, and as for the beard and spectacles—well, nine days was a long while to remember, *n'est ce pas*? It was—too long, by far. After a dozen queries at as many different sources of information, Tommy gave up in disgust.

But success, luckily, did not depend on these theatrical bits of evidence. The Reuter telegram was the thing. That would set the authorities buzzing, that would stir them up—but why the devil didn't it come? Had Strauss left Prague? Home again, a stale roll in one hand and a lump of Camembert in the other, Tommy roamed ceaselessly to the window, scanning the square below for blue-coated messenger-boys.

At last! He rushed to the landing to meet the concierge lumbering upstairs, snatched the envelope from her hand and tore it open. A glance at the contents, and swept from stem to stern by blank fury, he cursed without stopping for a minute and a half.

To think that scarcely any doubt of his theory had entered his mind since its first inception, yet here it was blown to atoms by four lines of terse fact:

> *Dr. Emil Karl Klauber holds chair bio-chemistry Deutsche Universität age fifty-three tall powerful build grey clipped beard thick glasses typical continental scholar old school just returned France England.*

Snick, snack! The kaleidoscope shifted, and the fragments composing the pattern slid automatically into a different arrangement. Klauber was real—not the English philosopher in great-coat and spectacles—and by inevitable sequence, Jethro was not a murderer. Tommy might as well fetch his pyjamas and tooth-brush from the Hôtel Stanislas and dismiss the matter for good and all.

No words can convey the utter abyss of disappointment into which he was plunged. One cold comfort only was left him—the reflection that his cocksureness had not led him to some fatal commitment. He could bear being looked upon as a moral leper, but the derision of his colleagues would have shrivelled his very soul. He could hear them now: "Rostetter? Oh, yes—he's the poor shrimp who wanted to brand Basil Jethro—Basil Jethro, mark you!—as a Jack-the-Ripper. Priceless notion, what?" A lifetime of discreet deeds would not have wiped out the shame.

But Dinah! Ah, there was the heart-breaking part of this! With the chase narrowed down to one girl and that girl able to plead nothing better than a lost memory, what hope was there of doing more than wresting her, still doubting, from the arms of the law? Tommy himself began to waver again, not in his allegiance, but in his beliefs. What good to keep repeating the dogmatic assertion that if she had driven the dirk-blade in up to the hilt her nails would have retained some traces of blood? Since she had found her way to widely-separated places, talked sensibly, opened a strange door with a key, who could say she was incapable of washing her hands? He must do his utmost to convince her she was guiltless. Unfortunately he knew quite well no assurance of his could quell her constant fear.

"Your account, monsieur? Certainly, it will be ready when you come down. Joseph, the lift!"

The little chasseur threw wide the iron gate. Sunk in gloom, Tommy stepped inside; and then a delay occurred, caused by the cage getting jammed and having to descend below the floor level to right itself. In that brief interval of time a tall man came in at the street entrance and with measured tread crossed to the desk. Though Tommy was screened, he could see clearly the slightly stooping shoulders, the pale, cameo profile turned towards him. His heart skipped a beat. It was Basil Jethro.

What was he doing here? Not once had it entered Tommy's mind he would return—but then if the man was innocent of wrong-doing, why should he not go where he pleased? At any rate, here he was, asking in a cool, well-pitched voice, whether, in the agitation of his departure, he had forgotten to leave his address. The manager, obliging and wreathed in smiles, replied that although no letters had come, he would not, in any case, have been at a loss.

"You see, monsieur," the latter explained, "the gentleman who brought the sad news to you last week has been stopping with us. He would have known how to find you. And that reminds me—did you recover the suitcase he was inquiring about?"

Inside the dislocated cage Tommy groaned, "Merciful God—that's torn it!" He was seized by the desire to find the deepest hole in Paris and crawl into it; but in the self-same breath, as it were, he was straining his ears to catch the philosopher's reply. The lift, however, checkmated him. With matchless perversity it chose this exact moment to give a volcanic shudder and lurch skyward, the grinding of its mechanism drowning every other sound. To-day was evidently marked for ill-luck.

"Caught with the goods!" muttered Tommy, as, hot with shame, he flung his belongings together. "Now he'll be wondering what the hell I'm up to—and he won't have to wonder long. He'll know. The point is, what'll he do about it?"

When after a suitable interval he ventured down again, the lobby was clear, and so, strangely enough, was the manager's brow. While he was designing a careless inquiry which would elicit the truth, the information he sought came forth unsolicited.

"Mr. Jethro came in just now," remarked the man brightly as he juggled with change. "I took the opportunity to ask if he had found his suit-case . . . and three francs makes twenty-five. Thank you, monsieur. . . . He said he had been mistaken about losing it—left it somewhere in a fit of absent-mindedness. So that's all right."

Tommy, transfixed, turned the amazing answer over and over. It did not suggest the spontaneous rejoinder of one taken by surprise and justifiably annoyed at interference in his affairs; and yet, he argued, Jethro was not exactly a spontaneous man. He had a quick brain, and great self-control. He must have grasped the situation in a twinkling and devised the sort of reply calculated to nip curiosity in the bud. This almost certainly would be the explanation, but all the same a germ of doubt stirred among the dead ashes in Tommy's mind. He lit a cigarette, took a few meditative puffs, and returned to the topic of the German guest.

"I'm afraid I was quite wrong about your Dr. Klauber," he said. "Here's the wire I got from Prague, and, as you see, there's no pretence about this professor business. For that matter, the man I took him for is certainly English, and a German accent in speaking French is not easy to imitate. That should have warned me. I suppose his clothing looked German, too?"

"Well—I could not say for sure. There was nothing very distinctive about the hat or the overcoat. The latter was good but old—might have come from almost anywhere. I imagine it was kept mainly for travelling, because it had creases in it, as though it had been packed away, and it had a decided smell of camphor."

Camphor! It was coincidence, nothing more. Countless winter garments are stored with naphtha balls. That the garment in question was over-heavy for the time of year formed no argument, either, since it is often more convenient to wear a large coat than to pack it. Only, would an odour of camphor resist the damp channel breezes and remain strong enough to be noticed? The idea that Jethro might have chosen to impersonate a real man seemed wholly fantastic. It would be waste of time to pursue this will-o'-the-wisp further—and yet . . .

Proof! Tommy felt he must get hold of incontrovertible proof, or else he might for ever blame himself for giving up the chase a moment too soon. The wording of Strauss' telegram left it uncertain if France or England had been visited first. To wire again for fuller details might suffice, and again it might not. Was there nothing here at hand which could put the matter beyond a doubt? His eye fell on the register, and at once he knew the answer. Hand-writing!

He cursed himself for not having thought of this long ago, knowing as he did how impossible it is to fake hand-writing so as to deceive an expert. If Klauber was Jethro, this signature of his would reveal to the trained eye insuppressible evidences uniting it with the small, uneven characters it so little resembled. He could hardly ask to borrow the register, and, besides, a single signature might not prove sufficient. There were, however, the alien registration slips, filled in by every foreigner on arrival. He asked if these had been collected for the past ten days, and to his great relief was told they were here, in a drawer.

"The police are not very regular about coming for them, monsieur. Sometimes a fortnight goes by—and again they may want them to-morrow, in which case it might be awkward for me if one is missing."

Tommy explained that he would require this particular slip for one night only. That would not be risking much, would it? The manager gave his consent, and in another minute Tommy was running through the pile of forms from which he selected Klauber's. The name alone was in block letters, the other entries in writing which corresponded with that in the register. Tommy still had the page of Jethro's notes in his pocket, and, moreover, knew the correct man to give a verdict on the two specimens. If they were executed by the same hand, this person would know. Once before this year Tommy had had occasion to consult him over the matter of a forged cheque. Bank officials themselves had been taken in, but the expert's word had brought the forger to justice.

Then there was another detail which offered illumination. Would it do any harm to test this slip of paper for fingerprints?

"No harm, monsieur—and no good, either. I remember noticing the doctor wrote with his gloves on."

"With his gloves on?" echoed Tommy, suspiciously.

"Yes, but many people do that. It's quite a common practice."

So it was, on the continent. Tommy had seen fellow-travellers, in the hottest weather, sitting up all day with gloves on their hands, filling out embarkation cards and performing other actions without troubling to remove what must have been a hampering discomfort. Yet at the thought that here, just possibly, was a fresh instance of caution, he recaptured a modicum of his lost enthusiasm. Jethro's fine, slender hands might have been recognised—and certainly they would have left marks to be traced, if the authorities ever got on the right track.

Seeing by the clock that it was almost seven-thirty, he dashed post-haste to the Rue de l'Echelle, toiled up four flights of dusty stairs and hammered on a door. No response—the expert had gone home, and though Tommy put in the best part of an hour trying to locate him, he saw, at last, he would have to postpone his test till the morning. Bad luck again! Still he had little hope anything would come of this final, despairing attempt. He was going on with it from a sense of duty, no more, and after a day of failures and disappointments he was feeling spent with fatigue. He paused long enough at a restaurant to partake of a thick steak and a cup of black coffee, then drove to Dinah's flat. Hallie Pemberton met him, and a single glance at her face told him things were not going so well.

"Oh, please talk to Dinah!" urged the little woman agitatedly. "She declares she's just physically worn out—they were at it five solid hours to-day—but I believe there's something more than that. Maybe she'll tell you."

With fear at his heart, he went into the little bedroom where the girl lay, staring up at the ceiling, her hair in two heavy braids resting along her shoulders. When he sat down beside her and took her cold hands in his, she made a brave effort to reassure him.

"I'm all right, really. It's just this cat-and-mouse business that goes on and on. I thought they'd finished trying to worm things out of me, things I don't even know myself—but this afternoon I had that beastly instrument attached to me again while the judge kept bringing out objects to show me."

"Go on," Tommy prompted. "What sorts of objects?"

"Everything under the sun. A ring Dodo wore, a sketch she did at Colorossi's, a handkerchief with her scent on it, an old photograph of . . . Chris. No, that didn't upset me, but something else did. It was—" She broke off, voiceless.

"Don't be afraid. Let's have it."

"A—a gramophone record—broken in two."

CHAPTER XXVI

He had forgotten that cursed record. To find it cropping up now after so long a time was disconcerting, to say the least. He searched her eyes closely, secretly terrified lest the sight of the broken disc had brought back some submerged horror; but he answered with perfect casualness.

"I know the one you mean. It was lying on the floor next morning. But why should it upset you?"

"Because," she whispered, her small face ashen under the shaded lamp, "it was . . . our tune. All last year we called it that. I was 'Miss

Virginia' of course. Gramont knows what it means to me . . . though how he's found out I simply can't imagine."

"Gramont knows nothing," declared Tommy emphatically. "It's the actual record he's interested in, not the tune. Why, I'll prove it to you! He thinks perhaps it was you who trod on it when you left the room, and that, provided you were in your senses, you'd have been frightened at making a noise. This is merely a try-on to see if it rouses any emotions. If it had been the music itself, he'd have arranged to have a hidden gramophone suddenly begin playing it."

Her tension began to relax.

"How clever you are!" she sighed with relief. "But all the same it did rouse emotions. Fearful ones. What will he think about the needle jumping about on the chart?"

"Gramont's sharp enough to know that you're in a state where the least thing will cause agitation. On principle, where a man is under suspicion, his motto is *cherchez la femme*. With a woman, it's *cherchez l'homme*—but searching and finding are two different things. You've nothing to worry about. You're engaged to me."

"Oh!" she cried. "When you're here, how comfortable it all seems! It's when I'm alone, or with Hallie, that I can't forget how I hated that poor girl. The thought of it is with me, even in my dreams. Last night I . . . I saw myself standing over her with the knife in my hand."

"Dinah," he said, and never in his entire existence had so much tenderness gone into his voice. "What a little egotist you are! That knife never was in your hand after we left the table. Do you think you were the only person who hated Dorinda Quarles?"

"Maybe not . . . but don't try to fool me over certain things. You pretended it wasn't that particular knife that was used, but I know now it was. My hands, too. You looked to see if there was blood round the nails, but I may have washed them at the villa. I seem to have done a good many actions I can't remember, so why not . . . murder?"

It startled him to find how closely her own train of thought had followed his. If he had seen her this morning, he would have been able to combat these fears, but now . . .

"Caught!" he groaned. "So you call me a prize liar, I suppose?"

"No . . . an angelic one. Oh, Tommy, Tommy, how good you've been! What can I ever do to repay you?"

"Stick to your guns—that's all. It'll soon be over now."

"I'll do it," she promised, resolute again. "I didn't mean to let you see what a funk I was in," and sitting up suddenly she put her arms round his neck and kissed him.

Tommy reeled. Every nerve in his body responded to the touch of her fresh lips, the faint fragrance of her skin. Abashed as a school-boy, he gazed hard for one sober, almost frightening moment into her clear, green-blue eyes. Then seeing what was in them, he smiled, himself again, and patted her gently.

The danger was past. Notwithstanding a brief, wild pang of regret for what could not be, he told himself how thankful he would be to-morrow to find himself still unattached. How young she looked, with her two braids hanging down and the fluffy blue borders of her little bed-jacket folded across her small breasts!

"Now, go to sleep," he counselled soothingly. "And mind, no more bad dreams. Don't forget I'm here to look after you, and that it's the happiest job I've had for a long time."

"I won't forget," she murmured, smiling into his eyes. "Good-night—Tommy."

The guard in the court below returned his salutation incuriously. Tommy borrowed a light from him, and whistling the tune of *Miss Virginia* in meditative fashion, rounded the corner into the dingy Rue St. Jacques, where he had left his car.

He was bending over the raised bonnet when a step along the pavement passed, hesitated and returned. A shadow fell across his line of vision, and with the feeling that someone was about to address him, he looked up to see, close behind him in the dusk, the tall figure of Basil Jethro. A shock ran through him. The hooded, impersonal gaze fixed on him roused an inward sense of guilt. Now I'm for it, thought he, foreseeing that the matter divulged by the hotel manager—confound his blabbing tongue—was about to be hauled out on the carpet. Yet even as this certainty flashed on him he recognised that here was the final proof of the man's innocence, come to meet him.

"Mr. Rostetter," said the composed, judicial voice, "this encounter is most opportune, since it has spared me the necessity, otherwise unavoidable, of seeking you out. I need hardly tell you that a conversation between you and me will serve your interests as well as mine. As neither of us will wish to be overheard, perhaps you will allow me to get into your car for a few minutes? We can then secure a reasonable privacy."

Acutely mortified, Tommy found himself reverting, willy-nilly, to his original estimate of the philosopher—if, as he now began to doubt, he had ever genuinely departed from it. He had come very near doing this man a gross injury. It would be churlish now to refuse so justifiable a request. With an inarticulate murmur he slid into the driver's seat, held open the door, and braced himself for what was to come. Jethro got in and with a chary gesture bade him drive wherever he liked.

"Towards the Opéra, if you are not pressed for time. If you see the wisdom of the suggestion I am going to make—and I believe you will see it—we shall then be heading in the right direction. However, that must be entirely subject to your wish."

Right direction for what? Curiosity, barbed with a tiny point of doubt, darted through Tommy, but the question in his mind vanished as he glanced to the right. His companion's attitude betrayed utter weariness somehow galvanised into activity by a supreme effort of will. The austere features, more pallid than ever, were set as though to perform an irksome duty, the hands, gripping a pair of doe-skin gloves, rested motionless but a little tense on the knees. No, there could be nothing to dread except inevitable humiliation—bad enough, in all conscience!

When they had shot round into the traffic of the Boulevard St. Michel, Jethro spoke, quietly and with a sort of forced determination.

"I'm afraid it is a lamentable weakness of mine," he said, "to dislike giving explanations for my private conduct. However, it would be sheer stupidity not to realise that now and then I must do so, or else lay myself open to grave misinterpretation. Such an occasion has just arisen. I am told that you have been making inquiries about the bag I removed from my step-daughter's apartment, and while I am amazed that a mystery should have been made out of that trifle, I cannot fail to guess what is in your mind. There is no need, I think, to put the thing into words. Incidentally, I was hard pressed to conceal my natural astonishment from the manager of my little hotel, but in case the affair is not yet ended I can see but one course to pursue—confront you openly and clear up your misconception once and for all."

Tommy could think of nothing to say. All along he had known there might be some simple, ordinary explanation for what had puzzled him. Now he was to hear it, and the knowledge made him feel ignominiously like a third-form boy caught plotting behind a master's back. Every inch of his skin burned, red-hot, as the voice at his side continued.

"Please don't imagine I blame or criticise you, Mr. Rostetter. In your fiancée's interest you had a perfect right to query each individual connected in any way with this unfortunate affair. For this reason I cannot expect you to be content with mere denials on my part. Obviously, if I were what you suppose, I would not hesitate to lie to save my skin. You can, however, verify the facts I am about to give you. Indeed, I should like to insist on your doing so, out of fairness to me. I think I am justified in asking that much."

It was perhaps not so much caution as a tattered remnant of vanity which adjured the listener to keep his wits about him. Not very pleasant to be shown up by the object of his recent suspicions. To preserve a semblance of dignity one must be on the alert, eye cocked, ears strained to catch any flaws in the coming statement. It must not be said that Thomas Rostetter had been hypnotised by smooth phrases.

"The bag in question," went on the philosopher in the same uneventful accents, "contained a large canvas 'roll-up'—useful to supplement a traveller's luggage—wrapped round three books—a thesaurus, and two specialised dictionaries. These books, together with the roll-up, I had promised to lend to a colleague who is engaged in translating my latest work. He is an invalid, not at all well off. I am turning over to him my villa at Cap Ferrat for the winter months. You may quite possibly be ignorant of his name. He is an academician called Renouff, a contributor to *Le Gaulois*, and the author of various metaphysical treatises."

It was nettling to one already feeling small to have this slur cast on his knowledge.

"Hippolyte Renouff?" said Tommy shortly. "But of course—he is a man of considerable repute. I have met him personally a number of times."

"I am glad to hear it, for in that case you will the more readily believe him when he assures you the bag, with the contents I have described, was left by me at his apartment soon after I quitted the Ile St. Louis. You will now understand why it never entered the hotel; but I repeat, I cannot expect you to accept my bare word for it. What I propose is that we go together, now, to M. Renouff's home and obtain his confirmation. I should like you to see the bag itself and the books."

"You want me to go with you to M. Renouff's place?" exclaimed Tommy, taken aback by the unexpected suggestion.

"I can devise no better arrangement, on account of my friend's state of health. He is at present confined to his room, with an attack of rheumatoid arthritis."

Tommy was well aware that the old writer was suffering from the complaint just mentioned. Only a few days ago there had been a reference to his condition in one of the papers; but this was not the only embarrassing thought in his mind. He had heard the weight and "feel" of the suit-case plausibly accounted for, as well as its non-appearance in the owner's room. Klauber was Klauber, not a part doubled by an Englishman with something to hide. With his main articles of faith destroyed, what of the romantic hypothesis remained save *a smell of camphor*? And what of his pet theory regarding Mowbray's death? Gone—exploded. Cleeves in the nursing-home was speaking the truth.

Suddenly he revolted violently from the situation about to be thrust upon him.

"There's no need to trouble M. Renouff," he muttered. "I'll take your word for this—and I'd like to assure you that whatever notions I may have had I've kept quiet about them. Where can I set you down?"

But Jethro shook his head firmly.

"We must not stop at half-measures, Mr. Rostetter. Painful as this promises to be, for both of us, have we a right to shirk it? How can I be guaranteed that at some future time your doubt will not crop up again? I beg you to view the matter from my stand-point and accede to my request."

The man was right. Once Tommy had set eyes on the suit-case and heard Renouff's confirmatory evidence, he would be convinced, but not before. For Dinah's sake he must act sensibly—and yet, how was it Jethro guessed that the bag formed the corner-stone of his belief? How much had that fool of a manager revealed? His thought must have communicated itself to his companion, for out of the gloom the veiled eyes turned on him a look of keen divination.

"I don't pretend to know what your idea was, Mr. Rostetter. I am not even interested in its precise nature. Still, I can scarcely fail to realise you would not have expended time and energy on finding my bag if you had not supposed it to contain incriminating evidence against me. What other reason could you have for troubling about it?"

Tommy shrugged, his objection answered, the last doubt fading like breath from a mirror.

"Where does M. Renouff live?" he inquired. "Somewhere to the north, isn't it?"

"Yes, in an apartment he has occupied for thirty years, and which, though the locality has changed in character, he seldom quits except for his annual journey south. If you will go towards the Trinité, I will direct you."

Tommy swung the car past the dark bulk of the Opéra into the Rue de la Chaussée d'Antin. Amid honking confusion and the coruscation of lights he thought bitterly of his wasted days, his smug confidence in his own acumen, of Christopher Loughton dispatched on a fool's errand.

As a detective he was a good hack-journalist, no more. Every moment now was wormwood and gall. Let him hurry through with it and wipe the slate clean. Thank Heaven for one thing—Dinah, at least, was safe from actual harm.

Soon they were mounting a narrow street, from which they diverged into a wider, well-lit one running east and west. On one hand was the Théâtre of the Grand Guignol; on the other the Société des Auteurs. Then came the Place Pigalle, centre of lurid night-life, and a second later more busy, teeming thoroughfares with little dark turnings leading out of them. Chestnut vendors hawked their wares. Painted girls chattered in groups, old women in shawls shuffled to and fro on their down-trodden slippers. Somewhere a hurdy-gurdy ground out a debased version of *Miss Virginia*. Did Gramont guess the reason for Dinah's emotion? The man was sharp, devilishly so. . . .

"This is our street," said Jethro quietly. "The house we want is the one just beyond the first lamp-post."

CHAPTER XXVII

THE passenger 'plane heading for le Bourget, skimmed high above pale brown fields. Christopher looked impatiently at his watch, hoped Tommy would be waiting to meet him, and for the hundredth time reviewed the findings of the past thirty hours. Success or failure? For the life of him he could not say which.

With no real faith in his friend's "hunch," he had snatched at the project eagerly because by no other means could he display activity on Dinah's behalf. At least, he was doing something for the girl who no longer belonged to him, however worthless his efforts might prove, and it slightly eased the weight on his soul to reflect that he had risked his career, chanced being locked up in jail, and been grateful for the privilege. As to the results—but just what were these results?

First, the terms of Lady Agatha Jethro's will had staggered him with their direct implication of a motive for crime, not because there had been any opportunity for funds to be misused, Jethro having shared the trusteeship with the family solicitor. No, it was the disposition of the property itself, which in the event of Dorinda's decease before the age of twenty-one passed entire into the step-father's hands. One-third to him—two-thirds to her, and the whole to the one who survived, *until the daughter attained legal management of her portion*. In other words, if

Dorinda had lived till November tenth, Jethro would have had to content himself with his original third, whereas now, by the simple fact of her dying before the approaching birthday, he had automatically fallen heir to the complete fortune.

Motive enough—but had Jethro contrived the decease by which he stood to benefit? Figuring interest at five per cent., Christopher reckoned the philosopher's annual income, exclusive of tax, at something like five thousand pounds—nor was he taking into account book royalties or the salary drawn from scholastic labours. Surely sufficient for the man's requirements, although with three residences, a car, chauffeur, clubs and so on to keep up, it was quite possible the owner lived up to the hilt. On the other hand Christopher could find no sign of financial embarrassment, nor even any cutting down in expenditure. As Tommy had foreseen, the difficulties in the path of probing the true situation were insurmountable unless one had an amplitude of time; but all the same Christopher doubted that a man could be in dangerously low waters without betraying some indication of the fact.

He sought an interview with the co-trustee, a Mr. James Kirby-Grant, of the Inner Temple, and sensing antagonism at a glance boldly declared himself as representing the American Embassy acting for Miss Blake. Having gained a respectful if grudging ear, he obtained information on certain points, though made to feel that inquiries of any kind regarding Basil Jethro were a species of high treason. Two months ago, it appeared, the two trustees had met, preparatory to relinquishing their charge of Miss Quarles' property. All was in perfect order. The investments were the same originally sanctioned by the courts, and while there had been in some cases depreciation owing to the recent slump, careful husbandry over the period of five years and reinvestment of unspent income made up the deficiency. Miss Quarles if she had lived would have found herself exceedingly well-off, and, as for her absurd allegations—Mr. Kirby-Grant had heard talk on the subject—why, there was not, could not, be a word of truth in them.

Mr. Jethro's private finances? Ah, the lawyer knew nothing about them. He believed, though he was not sure, that Mr. Jethro handled his affairs in person. Mr. Jethro was, as the world could confirm, held in the very highest respect. There was every reason to consider him a model of circumspection.

"I fail to see the drift of your questions, Mr. Loughton," declared the solicitor caustically. "Or rather, I refuse to see, but I can assure you confidently that your energies are being wasted."

By means of a bribe and an invented story about having heard the place was to let, Christopher managed to insinuate himself into the Bedford Square flat. The caretaker, though allowing him to poke about at will, scornfully repudiated the idea of Jethro's giving up the spacious Regency rooms which he had kept on since his wife's death, but seldom occupied.

"Now he's up at Oxford, he don't come here much, but what's that to a gentleman like 'im, that's for ever buying things and sending 'em home? A museum, that's all this plyce is. Look at that now—" She pointed to a bulky crate which blocked the hall. "More belongings—china, or whatnot. Have to wait till he comes to unpack it—though when that'll be 'eaven alone knows." She gave a lugubrious sigh, by way of reference to the débâcle in Paris.

Christopher glanced at the lettering on the crate. It came from a famous art-dealer in Paris. Already he had caught sight of an El Greco head which must have cost several thousand pounds, a Cézanne, a Gauguin, and a Van Gogh, several fine Chinese glass-paintings, and other evidences of money lavished apparently without stint. Extravagance, but no proof. Taking advantage of a brief freedom from observation, he pried into the unlocked drawers in various cabinets and tables, but found nothing relevant to his quest. All he gained was the impression that Jethro was in no wise economising, on the contrary continuing to indulge tastes both exclusive and expensive. Would a man in difficulties keep on an unnecessary abode merely to house treasures he rarely enjoyed? It seemed reasonable to assume that all this would have gone as soon as pressure had arisen.

He took an afternoon train to Oxford. On the station platform he was met by the youthful Rostetter, whose ardent welcome was heavily underlaid by excitement evoked by Tommy's telegram.

"Poor old duffer!" mused the undergrad in a fatherly way. "Fancy his booting me out the other night without spilling one word about this girl of his. I wondered why he was so close-mouthed—but you, being a pal and so on, must know the lass—what?"

Fortunately for Christopher, grown hot under the collar, the host did not wait for a reply, but babbled on rapidly about the plan he had mapped out to comply with his uncle's instructions.

"First, I propose a visit to Jethro's house, which is just off the High. We'll give it a quick once-over—but I say, what's this you're telling me about the priceless will? I want to warn you, massed opinion in these parts will be dead against any slur on old Monism's honour. Why, between you and me, I never believed that yarn my friend Bilfilian gurgled in his cups, though I admit it's queer the way the little blighter shut up after his one allusion to the affair. Anyhow, I've laid in a couple of bottles to tempt him when he drops round this evening. Maybe we'll loosen his tongue, particularly if you can vie with him in the shady reminiscence line; but I'm much afraid our local ice-berg has no vices, patent or hidden. Here we are. Now leave it all to me."

They brought up before a compact Georgian house with clipped bay-trees in front and a shining brass knocker on which young Rostetter hammered lustily. To the staid female who opened the door he addressed himself with portentous gravity.

"My friend," he said, "is a visitor from Harvard University, and would like to inspect the portrait of Mr. Jethro, as well as the study where he works. He is collecting material for his thesis—The Influence of Pythagorean Mathematical Ontology on Subsequent Philosophical Theories, with especial reference,"—here the speaker coughed—"to Plato, Descartes, Leibnitz and Russell. Can you let us in for a squint?"

The Oxford housekeeper takes such things in her stride. The woman nodded without surprise and stood aside, merely remarking: "Indeed, sir! Well, I'm quite used to showing the house to visitors when the master's away. Only last week there was a German gentleman here wanting to see the portrait, which you'll find here in the library—and a fine likeness it is, sir, if I may say so."

She stood in the doorway while the two men prowled about examining the painting let into a panel over the fireplace, studying the leather-bound books which lined the walls, and gazing with pretended awe at a large imposing mahogany writing-table. In furtherance of the agreed arrangement, Christopher made furtive signals to his companion to draw the housekeeper off and give him a chance to explore, but to his annoyance Rank remained blandly unobservant. Ten minutes of useless pottering, and they were politely shown out again with nothing accomplished.

"I saw your wig-wagging," declared the Magdalen student sagely. "But believe me, old man, that woman has eyes in the back of her head. Don't worry. While you were chatting away with her, I unlatched the side window. Now do you see the idea? When the servants are in bed, we'll ransack the house from top to bottom."

The prospect of housebreaking gave Christopher's law-abiding instincts a distinct shock, but his accomplice in crime seemed astounded that a good American should balk at what film-study proved to be a recognised activity in the Land of the Free. After all, reflected Christopher, there was a pressing necessity for going through Jethro's private papers. If Rank Rostetter could risk being sent down, surely he need not be squeamish.

The strange exhilaration which took hold of him reached its height some hours later when he clambered with bated breath over a casement sill and stood listening for the non-existent dog. In his pocket was a torch and an ingenious assortment of lock-picking tools collected by the amateur cracksman at his side; but here, as in the London flat, all lay open to view. Soon he was examining neat files of receipted bills, covering every conceivable outlay from the Oxford butcher's account to the purchase at Christie's of an early palimpsest manuscript. Some of the figures ran high, while there was considerable evidence of careless expense, but what did that argue? All was cleared off. Except for the telephone account, just delivered, there was no indebtedness of any kind.

"Looks okay," whispered Rank, replacing the stack of papers. "Though his pass-book might tell an interesting story. Wish we could find out if he's got an overdraft. And the dates—notice how nearly all of them centre about the end of summer term? Doesn't it strike you there's something decidedly wholesale about the way all this is settled up?"

"Hush! We'll discuss it later."

On the way out, Rank directed the torch full upon the lifelike features over the mantel—lips slightly puckered, but compressed; eyes covered by a glistening film through which, as behind a gauze transparency, they gazed forth in retired condemnation. So might a recluse look upon the world which for him held no interest. A Thibetan monk in his cell . . . only a Thibetan monk would not collect *objets d'art* at fantastic prices.

"Let's be shifting," muttered the youth with a slight wriggle of discomfiture. "That look makes me all goosey. Here, what's this? Letters by the late post? Shall we take them along?"

He picked up a pile of envelopes from the door-mat. In the warm security of his own rooms he and Christopher steamed them open over a tea-kettle. Some were circulars. The others—

"Here, look at these!" Christopher held out two identical sheets of engraved paper, the heading of which was that of a stockbroker in London. The first represented the sale-certificate of a block of industrial shares, the second was a communication from the broker himself expressing regret that his client had deemed it advisable to part with holdings at the present inevitable sacrifice. "He dropped a colossal amount on them," continued Christopher with a frown. "I wonder why he's disposed of them now?"

Rank met his glance significantly. In both their minds hovered the same thought. If Jethro did this, it must mean he needed cash—needed it badly. Was there any connecting link between the mad unloading of stock, not the first move of the kind to judge by the broker's tone, and the sweeping clearance of debt? While Rank slipped out to drop the letter back through the philosopher's door, Christopher sat wrapped in puzzled cogitation, but little came of it, and still less with the sallow, large-eyed stripling whom the host brought in with him on his return.

For Bilfilian, candidate for the Church, proved a complete and utter washout. Christopher looked back with disgust on hours of weary boredom spent in unavailing attempts to lure the one-time wastrel into a repetition of his famous confidence. Prim and sedate, though with glinting eyes, the youngster drank in all the wild tales concocted for his seduction, never offering a syllable of his own. Bullied at last into admitting sundry excursions into unsavoury haunts, he denied recollection of anything save the resultant headaches.

"But, blast you!" stormed Rank in desperation. "If the place I mean was so celebrated, you must at least remember what it was called. That's all Loughton wants to know—how to find it."

"Sorry," murmured Bilfilian apologetically. "The whole episode's a blur, you know. Wasn't myself. No, I won't have any more whisky, thanks all the same. Stomach won't stand it. And anyhow, I don't know what you're getting at. Did I say I saw someone I knew there? If so, it's all wiped out."

In Christopher's waistcoat pocket was a pencilled precis of the will, together with a copy of the broker's letter. These and the sudden clearance of indebtedness were the sum total of what he had to offer Rostetter. There seemed to him a remote chance of Jethro's having committed murder, but granted it was so, how could one establish the fact? But for the tone of elation detected in Rostetter's voice over the telephone yesterday he would be ready to class all suspicion of Jethro with the Bilfilian myth. Rostetter must be the judge.

Le Bourget. Like a homing pigeon the 'plane swooped to the precise section of the wind-swept field allotted for its reception. Christopher sprang from the step, eagerly scanned the faces about him and felt a keen disappointment. His friend was not there. Emerging from the customs, he bought an evening paper from a clamouring newsboy, glanced at the front page, and felt a ton weight crash down upon him.

Dinah was arrested for murder.

CHAPTER XXVIII

THE first wild idea which raced through Christopher's brain was that he had been allowed to get out of the country secure in the belief that no immediate danger threatened in order that this blow should be struck unawares. It was like some ghastly trick. What was meant by "Fresh evidence," "facts deliberately suppressed," "conspiracy to defeat justice?"

Then he saw. Dinah and Rostetter were not, never had, in any genuine sense, been engaged to each other. The arrangement between them was a counterfeit one, designed simply to throw dust in the eyes of the law. It had succeeded, too—till some hitch occurred, though what that hitch was did not at once leap to view.

For an instant unreasoning relief swept over him, but as he grasped the full import of the situation he cursed his stupid egotism. This was no occasion for jubilation. Dinah's entire immunity had lain in her position as Rostetter's affianced bride. With that position shown up as false, it became speedily apparent that the girl's deception could have sprung from but one cause—anxiety to cover up an incentive to crime. Till now Dinah had been accredited, publicly at least, with no motive, but here, staring him in the face, was categorical proof that a motive had existed. Half a column of print set forth his own relations with Dorinda Quarles, the episode stripped of every softening circumstance. Added to this was an unexpurgated account of Dinah's visit to his sister-in-law's apartment, giving those damaging speeches of hers which had been so carefully excluded from the judge's knowledge. Throughout the whole page Jealousy stalked—Salome at the feast. The English journalist was named as *complice*, with obscurely unpleasant suggestions as to his purpose in thus defending one who but for his intervention would days ago have been locked in a prison cell.

Impossible to tell who had supplied this damning information. A line at the bottom furnished the sole reference to the subject: *Early this morning a deposition was made to the authorities by someone in complete possession of the facts, which the prisoner had now admitted, without, however, deviating from her statement of lost memory.* Who had done this vile thing? For that matter, who could have done it? Stunned and bewildered Christopher could think of no immediate answer. Only Rostetter could enlighten him. He must seek Rostetter at once, and learn the truth of the situation.

Within the half-hour he was hammering furiously upon the journalist's door, getting no reply. Downstairs the wrinkled concierge, with a queer look on her face, informed him that M. Rostetter had not come home at all the previous night, but that she had not the remotest idea as to his whereabouts. The police, she added meaningly, had been inquiring for him at intervals during the day.

Recalling his friend's stated intention of sticking close to the hotel which had been Jethro's temporary abode, Christopher dashed to a telephone to ring up and inquire if M. Rostetter still occupied the room engaged by him a few days ago. A waiter answered. No, M. Rostetter had gone, since yesterday evening at about seven o'clock, since which time nothing had been seen of him. The manager might be able to furnish further details, but unfortunately that functionary was out.

A pall of foreboding descended on the listener. He hurried with all speed to the Rue Val-de-Grâce, to find Hallie Pemberton in agitated conference with the fat consulate lawyer, Maître le Gros. Pushing past the maid he was just in time to hear the little woman's despairing protest:

"No, no, what you say it absolutely grotesque! I tell you, Mr. Rostetter isn't like that. How could we be mistaken in him? All through these terrible days he's been so kind to us, a pillar of strength, a—"

"Pillar of strength! Bah! A liar, a mountebank—that's more like it." Le Gros's oily features were flushed and swollen with rage. "He's foisted this trick on me—me. Don't you understand what that means? He's made me look a fool, or worse, a scoundrel like himself."

The speaker wheeled, saw Christopher, and underwent a swift alteration of manner. He sucked in his breath, his little blood-suffused eyes retreating to pin-points of suspicion.

"Ah-h-h," he breathed slowly. "So you're here. Mr. Loughton is here. Perhaps he can tell us what's become of Mr. Rostetter? I dare say he knows, since it's pretty evident this whole business was cooked up between the two of them. Eh—how about it?" he demanded insultingly.

Hardly able to believe his ears, Christopher returned the man's stare with cold fury. He had never liked le Gros, for all the latter's usual suave good nature. At present he found him insufferable.

"I don't pretend to understand you," he retorted tensely. "I hurried here to ask the same question you're putting to me. I've just come back from London. I haven't seen Mr. Rostetter—and you may as well explain what you mean by that bullying tone."

"Mean? I'll tell you what I mean." With his face close to Christopher's the lawyer brought out the angry announcement. "An hour ago Rostetter's car was hauled up out of the river, close to Vincennes. It had been run in over the parapet—but there's no sign of a body. Make what you choose out of it."

Christopher grew white. Instinctively he turned to Hallie, who nodded brokenly.

"But, oh, Chris," she whispered with positive conviction in her voice, "he wouldn't go off like that and leave poor Dinah in the lurch. Nothing can persuade me M. le Gros's idea is the right one."

"And just what is your idea?" demanded the young man meeting the irate lawyer with hostility. "I'm curious to know."

"The police, every soul concerned, thinks as I do," returned le Gros with a surly air. "Simply that he made off to avoid arrest. There's a warrant out for him since this morning. They're looking for the body, but they don't expect to find it. He wants us to think it's suicide, but there's little doubt he's lying low watching his chance to slip out of France. This lady's faith is rather touching," he added with a sneer, "when you consider how he's landed her cousin in the soup. If I'd been handed the true facts at the start, I could have got my client off without any difficulty."

"Could you?" Christopher flashed back with bitter sarcasm. "I should doubt it."

Directly he had spoken he regretted his incautiousness. The other viewed him with narrowed eyes as he took in the involuntary admission.

"Ah, you say that, do you? Well, you ought to know. All the same, she'd have had a chance—which is more than she's got now, let me tell you. Once she's been caught in a lie, how can we expect any jury to swallow her statement about remembering nothing? She's got the whole world down on her. Gramont is out for blood. He's holding the reconstruction of the crime this very evening—striking while the iron's hot—and she'll have no Rostetter to back her up. I'd stop it, if I could. I know something of these reconstructions. As likely as not, they'll wring a full confession out of her—*et voilà!*" He gave a vast shrug.

Christopher's heart contracted with terror. Steadying himself as best he could he attacked what seemed to him the crucial point in the whole matter. Who, he inquired, had supplied the information which had precipitated Dinah's arrest?

"I can't tell you that," muttered le Gros shortly. "No one knows who did it. One of those witnesses, probably. One wonders now why it didn't happen before."

After a pause Christopher declared his intention of seeing Dinah at once. Could the lawyer arrange it for him?

"If Gramont hasn't put his foot down on interviews—he's got the power to do it—and provided you think it advisable," replied the Frenchman indifferently. "I'm willing to go along to the prison with you. Personally, I don't believe it a wise thing."

"That's my affair. You'll find my taxi in the street. Wait in it till I join you," said Christopher curtly.

He waited till the avocat had withdrawn his sulky presence, then gripping Hallie's hands in his bade her tell him exactly what had happened. She complied, and as the breathless sentences came from her Christopher saw that his own surmise was correct. Rostetter with his customary quickness had seen Dinah's extreme peril, and out of pure, disinterested generosity constituted himself her shield against suspicion. That he was being cruelly misjudged now was only to be expected. Le Gros, coarse-fibred, upset in his professional vanity, was ready to snatch at any theory except the simple and obvious one.

"You mustn't pay any attention to what M. le Gros says," urged Hallie earnestly. "Why, he was swearing a moment ago that Tommy knows the child is guilty—that he was protecting her because he hoped to get something by it. His first notion, of course, was that Tommy had fallen in love with her."

"Do you agree with him there?" demanded Christopher quickly.

"I . . . I can't tell. It wouldn't be at all unnatural, would it?" she answered naively. "But if it's so, he's shown no sign of it to me."

Christopher nodded to himself. Whatever the case, Rostetter had acted like a true sportsman. His admiration for the journalist became tinged with awe.

"He's a good chap," he murmured constrainedly, and in answer to her expression of surprise went on hurriedly: "Oh, yes, I know him, and I feel as you do about his behaviour. He's not the sort of man who would cut and run. As for this disappearance business, I don't like the look of it. When did you last see him?"

"At nine o'clock last night. I don't believe anyone's set eyes on him since he left this flat."

"Did he mention any suspicions he had about—well, any one connected with this murder?"

"No, nothing at all."

It was clear that at no time had Hallie been taken into Rostetter's confidence, a fact entirely understandable, since Rostetter was anxious to avoid raising false hopes. He had merely paid his usual call, and finding Dinah unnerved over her latest session with the judge had assured her she not only had nothing to fear but that within a day or so the inquiry regarding her would surely be abandoned. No hint of preparation for the bolt which was so soon to fall. It seemed evident he had not expected it. The officers had arrived, two of them, early this morning, with a warrant. Hallie had flown to telephone Rostetter, but could obtain no reply.

"Something awful's happened to him. I know it, I know it."

Christopher shared her opinion, but made no comment. "What," he said, "did that swine of a lawyer mean by accusing me of being mixed up in the plot?"

"Oh, why waste time on anything so unutterably stupid?" she wailed. "I tell you, I didn't listen to him. Go, go! And when you've seen Dinah, come back and let me know how she is."

She pushed him to the door.

On the drive to the St. Lazare prison the lawyer showed himself sullen, uncommunicative. Finally, after pressure, he vouchsafed a statement which drew forth an indignant exclamation.

"That's an infamous lie! Miss Blake knew nothing whatever about the plan to take dope."

"You'll think differently when you hear the new evidence. Gramont is convinced she egged the whole thing on, banked on the rest of the crowd being put to sleep, but that she herself took only enough to ginger her up to the crime—maybe none at all. Rostetter was aware of this, because it was her portion he put in his pocket. Since he decided to stand between her and justice, it's assumed he expected to gain by it. I'll say no more."

On the point of demanding an explanation, Christopher restrained himself. Of what importance were Gramont's beliefs, or le Gros's either? Both men were hopelessly prejudiced. Still, with bitter sarcasm, he put another question: How did the judge account for Miss Blake's quitting the apartment?

"Sheer panic, over the prospect of remaining with the corpse. Lost her head, which is pretty clearly shown by the things she said at your brother's apartment. Later on she pulled herself together and worked out a fairly plausible story. With Rostetter's help, it served the purpose—for a time."

The theory sounded horribly convincing. A jury could easily be induced to accept it, whatever flaws it might contain. One of these flaws, a glaring one, came before Christopher now. What, he asked, did the judge make of the door-knob so carefully wiped free of marks? Was that compatible with his idea?

The man at his side fidgeted moodily before replying. "At that stage, and under the given circumstances, she might have taken the precaution without realising the utter futility of it. Gramont himself doesn't imagine she was acting in a normal way. It's our one remaining hope," he muttered speaking to himself. "Though even that hope may be annihilated after to-night. I'm still her counsel. I must put up the best fight I can. All I say is that your Rostetter pal has just about dished her chances."

Christopher restrained himself with difficulty. "How can you be so sure," he said slowly, "that someone hasn't dished Rostetter?"

The Frenchman grunted and surveyed him with pitying scorn.

"So that's your notion, is it? I dare say he's been feeding you some fancy tales. Well, take my advice and wash them all out." He made a sweeping gesture with the stump of his cigarette. "Speaking for myself, I wouldn't give two sous for any statement Rostetter made."

Christopher shut his lips tightly and preserved silence till the taxi halted outside the prison gates. He had, however, made up his mind on one point. Dinah's defence should not be left in the hands of one who so evidently believed her guilty.

Inside the grey, forbidding walls of the St. Lazare, a tiresome wrangle took place between the avocat and the governor. Christopher, impatiently waiting, was able to catch only the rumble of voices and what appeared to be a conversation over the telephone. At last, as he began to fear his request would not be granted, the two men emerged, and in brusque tones he was informed that he might have five minutes with the prisoner. A warder conducted him to a dingy room with barred windows. Here he waited again until presently Dinah, in company with a hard-faced wardress, entered. The eager cry on her lips died instantly to a gasp of acute disappointment as she saw who her visitor was.

"So it's you," she whispered in a deadened voice. "I thought . . ."

No need for her to finish the sentence. In a flash of bitter enlightenment Christopher guessed what had happened. She had been allowed to think it was Rostetter come to see her. Probably the two attendants had been instructed to take note of her reactions.

His own newly revived hope died miserably. She wanted Rostetter, not him. In the face of the cruel rebuff he could formulate no speech, and stood looking at her blank eyes and pale cheeks in mute agony. In the end it was she who broke the silence.

"Where is he?" she demanded in a low voice. "What's happened that he hasn't been here?"

She had heard nothing, then—and it was he who would have to tell her. He did so in a few hesitating words, repeating what le Gros had said about the car and the search for Rostetter. In the eyes which never left his face he saw first incredulity then complete horror. For a second her knees gave beneath her weight. He put out his arm to catch her, but the warder interposed, placing a chair. She refused to sit down, steadying herself by holding on to the back.

"Why? Why?" Her voice was barely audible. "I don't understand."

"No one understands. I spoke to him yesterday morning, just as I was leaving for England. There was nothing wrong then. He wanted me to make some investigations. I made them—as well as I could. When I got back I found you arrested and him—gone."

"Gone!" It was the one part of his information which appeared to register on her brain. After a moment, however, she seemed to take in the rest and find it strange. "He told you to go to England? But you . . . he . . ." She gave it up. "Oh, what does it matter? If he's gone, nothing matters." Her tone was one of utter despair.

"Dinah!" he whispered, trying hard to capture her attention. "Hallie told me how Rostetter stepped in to save you. It's the first I'd heard of it. I believed, like everyone else, you were really engaged to him. I suppose that beast of a judge bullied you into admitting the truth?"

"There was nothing to admit. He knew it all. I'd kept up the pretence mainly because I'd promised I would. It wasn't fair not to play the game once I'd started, but now—oh, what does it all mean?" she broke off in hopeless bewilderment.

"Listen," he went on, with a glance at the watchful couple standing a few yards away. "You may not know it, but Rostetter suspected someone. Just because of that, it means everything to find out who gave this evidence against you. Think—think hard. Who could it have been?"

"I don't know. I didn't imagine any one hated me like that," she returned with weary indifference. "Yet evidently someone does."

"Helen Roderick?" he suggested. "Had you thought about her?"

"Helen?" she echoed in surprise. "Oh, no, I can't believe she would go out of her way to injure me, whatever she might think. It's not like her."

"Still she was the one person who had the information at her disposal. She may have given it to someone else who—"

"C'est fini, monsieur," announced the warder, pointing to the clock on the wall, and at the same moment the woman attendant took a firm hold on Dinah's arm to lead her away.

Christopher snatched wildly at the few remaining seconds to urge Dinah to keep cool, not to worry. He would be back to-morrow, and as often as they would permit him to come. He would move heaven and earth to—

She turned and stopped him with a glance which passed straight through his body as though he had not been there.

"There's nothing I want you to do," she said mechanically. "Except one thing. Find Tommy for me. Find him. That's all I ask."

The door closed. Christopher heard the big key grate in the lock.

CHAPTER XXIX

HE SAW it now. What a fool he must have been not to have guessed it before! Dinah loved Rostetter. It was Rostetter she wanted. No presence other than his could bring her solace or stiffen her resolution to fight. As for her former lover, why, he no longer existed. That last unseeing look of hers had made the fact devastatingly plain. Christopher Loughton was merely a member of the vast, undifferentiated crowd which had ceased to hold interest.

It may be chalked up to the latter's credit that after the first crushing shock he swallowed the pill stoically, accepting its bitterness as his just due. Mortification, acute disappointment, he thrust aside, as it were to clear the decks for action. He had been given his orders to find the man she loved. Well, he would find him—if such a thing were possible. With a mighty effort he strove to reduce the chaos in his brain to some sort of orderly arrangement, for confused as he was he could form not the faintest conception as to how to set about his task.

First of all, did he believe there was one syllable of truth in le Gros's villainous insinuations? Emphatically, no! The Englishman's deception had been an honourable one, the pure unselfishness of which could inspire nothing but gratitude and respect. That it could be followed by a treacherous and cowardly withdrawal simply because its author's plans had been defeated was an idea to be indignantly spurned. But if this were not the case, what alternative solution remained? Christopher could see but one. Somehow the unhappy journalist had become a menace, for which reason steps had been taken to suppress him. Was it Basil Jethro who had got hold of him, at the same time, to consolidate his own safety, directing a definite charge against Dinah? If one could but answer that question the whole thing would be simplicity itself.

The trouble lay in the fact that Christopher possessed no reliable knowledge except his own discovery at Somerset House—and this might easily prove valueless. Nevertheless, over the telephone yesterday morning, Rostetter had shown an unmistakable elation. He had spoken of "a loop-hole in the wall." What could that mean if not during the previous night spent at the little hotel he had come upon some weak spot in Jethro's alibi? He had without doubt been hot on a trail. What he had done for the next twelve hours was wrapped in mystery, but at nine in the evening he had quitted Dinah's flat in excellent spirits, therefore, if Hallie Pemberton's impression was correct, in no way alarmed as to the situation. He had not mentioned what he intended doing after that, and no one had seen him. However, an hour or so before calling upon Dinah and her cousin, he had fetched away his bag from the hotel. Just possibly the Stanislas manager might be able to shed a ray of light on what at present was total darkness.

Seizing a taxi, Christopher dashed towards the Rue Berger, and within a quarter of an hour was accosting a fat, elderly man seated on a high stool behind the Stanislas desk. This person, it developed, was not the manager, but the concierge. The manager was unfortunately not in the building, though expected back at any moment. Did Monsieur require anything?

Christopher fumed with impatience. Ought he to hang about waiting for the manager to turn up? It might be wasting valuable time, though how that time could be better employed was difficult to say. He vaguely noticed the concierge's bleared eyes fixed upon him with intent interest, but was too much engrossed in his own problem to dwell upon the fact till a waiter, suspending a whispered conference with a nondescript appendage to the establishment, came forward to address him with hesitating curiosity.

"Pardon, monsieur, but were you particularly anxious to see M. Jolivet himself?"

"M. Jolivet? Who's he? Oh, the manager! Yes, most decidedly. As he's not here—well, there's just a chance you may be able to tell me what I want to know."

The waiter's slight air of evasiveness vanished at Christopher's first question. Yes, came the ready reply, the English gentleman dropped in last evening, packed up his clothing, and having settled his account drove away in his own car. What time was this? Roughly, about seven-thirty. He was an agreeable gentleman, they were sorry to see him leave. On Sunday evening he had got quite friendly with the manager in the latter's office.

"What were they discussing, monsieur? As it happens, I can tell you that, because M. Jolivet called me in to refresh his memory on a certain detail. Your friend wanted to know which room a German guest of ours had occupied on the one night he spent here, over a week ago."

"A German guest! You mean an English guest, don't you?" cried Christopher, amazed into indiscretion.

"No, monsieur, a German. Here, I will show you who he was," and whipping back two pages of the register the speaker pointed a grubby finger at an entry indited in a bold, sputtering hand.

"Emil Karl Klauber!" repeated Christopher in an incredulous tone. "Coming from London, country of domicile Czecho-Slovakia, date of arrival—" he jumped and stared hard. It was September 30th—the day on which the murder had occurred. . . .

"Monsieur!" said a new voice close behind him. Turning, he beheld the sallow-faced young man with whom the waiter had been whispering a moment before.

"Well?" he exclaimed. "And who are you?"

"The telegraph operator, monsieur. I caught what you were saying, and thought you might care to know that your friend, M. Rostetter, sent a telegram late Sunday night to Prague, making inquiries about this Klauber. I have the message on file. Shall I let you see it?"

With growing astonishment Christopher scanned the slip of paper put into his hand. It was certainly written by Rostetter, but the name of Strauss, to which person it was addressed, meant nothing, while the series of interrogations regarding a professor called Klauber presented little clue to the author's actual design. Out of the whole cryptogram only one impressive item emerged—the date. In reply to random questions the two members of the staff gave a description of the German, together with the information that the latter had made a short stay at the hotel on his way to England, some weeks ago, but from all accounts he appeared to be a studious, retiring individual, in no way calculated to excite interest. Just possibly Rostetter was not concerned about him at all, but was merely using him as a screen to cover up his real purpose. The manager alone might hold the key to the riddle, but the manager—blast him!— had chosen this crucial moment to absent himself.

Christopher glanced annoyedly at the clock, then suddenly waking to a sense of duty towards his host of last night, he scribbled a telegram apprising Rank Rostetter of his uncle's disappearance and instructed the operator to send it off at once. The sallow-faced man's eyes sharpened at sight of the message. His lips parted to speak, but seeing that Christopher had moved restlessly toward the street entrance he withdrew to his instrument.

The waiter, meanwhile, followed the visitor at a respectful distance. Christopher, having held a debate with himself, turned on him with another query, pitched in a lower voice.

"A short time ago," he said, "you had another Englishman here, who like me was a friend of M. Rostetter's. You know the one I'm referring to?"

"The gentleman whose daughter was murdered? Yes, monsieur."

"Have you seen him since he left? I was wondering if he and M. Rostetter—" Christopher hesitated—"well, if they happened to meet, that's all."

"The other Englishman did step in for a moment yesterday evening," answered the waiter promptly. "He had a few words with the manager, but it was while M. Rostetter was upstairs in his room. He was gone by the time M. Rostetter descended."

Christopher gave a violent start. "Do you know what he was saying to the manager?" he demanded tensely.

"Yes, monsieur, for when I was carrying out M. Rostetter's luggage I heard M. Jolivet repeating it, evidently thinking M. Rostetter would like to know. I was interested, too, on my own account. That's why I listened—but the matter's hardly worth mentioning."

"All the same, I'd rather like to hear what was said," declared Christopher, fingering a fifty-franc note.

"It was about a piece of luggage, a suit-case, which the other gentleman had lost, and which M. Rostetter had been asked to inquire about. It was not very pleasant for the staff to be suspected of tampering with the guests' property, so I was relieved to hear M. Jolivet telling your friend that the suit-case had been found."

"Found! M. Jethro told the manager it had been found, and the manager repeated the information to M. Rostetter?"

"That is it exactly, monsieur. Ah, many thanks! Is there anything more I can—"

But Christopher was already leaping into his taxi and shouting a furious order. It seemed to him he had just learned the very thing which provided him a clue. Before he had had time to reason matters out he had alighted at the local commissariat, where, bursting into the private room of the *chef de commissaire*, he began with wild haste to pour out his story. Almost at once he was halted with a formal request for his name, nationality and occupation. He gave them, annoyed to see a look of alert intelligence pass between the chief and a lethargic secretary seated at a table close by. The two men accorded him close attention which he dimly fancied bore little relation to the disclosure he was about to make, but disregarding their manner, he plunged anew into a recital of recent events, only to be stopped again by a summary gesture.

"Yes, yes, monsieur," interjected the chief, fondling a magnificent chestnut beard. "I understand your anxiety to locate this M. Rostetter—but am I to understand you are hinting at foul play? Please be more explicit."

As Basil Jethro's name fell from Christopher's lips incredulous scorn crossed the listener's features. Dead silence followed the culminating incident, to be broken at last by the bearded official's remarking with lofty tolerance:

"Monsieur, will it astonish you to learn that the gentleman to whom you refer has been subjected to the most careful supervision? That his alibi has been investigated with great thoroughness, his private life inquired into, his movements scrutinised? I appreciate your wish to implicate some one other than the young woman now under arrest, seeing that her trial will involve you in embarrassing difficulties, but—"

"What," cried Christopher hotly, "have my private feelings got to do with the facts I'm giving you?"

"I imagine your feelings tend to bias your judgment. Try, monsieur, to take a calm view of the situation. This missing journalist has, according to you, been agitating himself with inquiries about a transient guest of the hotel, a German who chanced to arrive on the date of the murder. Do you know why he was interested in this person? Can you trace a connection between the latter and Mr. Jethro? Ah, I thought not. Then how can you expect us to act in the matter?"

Painfully aware that his tale did not hang together, Christopher reconnoitred.

"Leave the German out of it," he said. "Or at least until you have heard what the hotel manager has to say. What I am certain about is this: on Sunday night Mr. Rostetter went to the hotel to investigate Mr. Jethro's alibi. Early next morning he gave me to understand he was on the verge of an important discovery, and since then Mr. Jethro found out what he had been doing. Putting two and two together—"

"If you get a greater number than four," interrupted the chief with irritating amusement, "you must not expect me to approve your result. However, if you can tell me just why Mr. Rostetter's suspicions became aroused in the first place, I shall be glad to listen."

With as much assurance as he could command, Christopher enumerated all Tommy had said on the subject. The conjectures about the latch-key, the assumed but unproven destruction of the letter, and the philosopher's manifold divergencies from the truth sounded even to his own ears pathetically flimsy, while the mention of the absent suit-case provoked a marked impatience on the part of the chief.

"Suit-case, monsieur?" he repeated in surprise. "Till now we have heard nothing about such an article. Is it not strange that neither the concierge, who spoke to M. Jethro as he left the house, nor any other eye-witness, least of all Mr. Rostetter, has troubled to say anything about it?"

Christopher stared back at the calm face opposite. Was it going to be categorically denied that a suit-case had been removed from the apartment? Apparently so.

"The concierge may have failed to notice it," he said tersely. "And as far as I know no one else had occasion to see it except Miss Quarles, who is dead, and Mr. Rostetter, who, when he was originally questioned, had no reason for considering it important. But Mr. Rostetter himself told me—"

"Mr. Rostetter told you!" broke in the chief. "And just how much value do you attach to Mr. Rostetter's statements?"

The low chuckle which came from the secretary lashed Christopher to a pitch of fury. He flushed scarlet, but made a strong effort to master his temper.

"Perhaps you think the waiter's lying, too. Besides, why argue, when Mr. Jethro's own avowed excuse for visiting his step-daughter's apartment that evening was his desire to fetch away some books? Did you imagine he carried them off in his hand?"

"Why not? Although I am perfectly willing to inquire. Make a note of that, Bonville," he instructed the secretary with dry facetiousness. "Let us ask Mr. Jethro what books he took away, and if he carried them by hand or in a bag."

Christopher saw that he had strayed into a vicious circle. Jethro, if guilty, would not hesitate to deny the whole story. The one person capable of refuting him was Rostetter, and Rostetter was gone. . . .

"See here!" he cried with exasperated vehemence. "What possible object could Mr. Rostetter have in inventing the bag simply to fool me? In God's name why should he want me to go to England, if he didn't believe he had something positive in the way of evidence?"

As he uttered the words, Christopher remembered that his friend at that stage possessed no real evidence, only a "hunch." If evidence existed, it came from some later discovery; but, goaded to desperation by the shrewd glance exchanged by the two men, he flung down his remaining trump-card.

"Do you happen to know that Mr. Jethro has inherited the whole of his step-daughter's property? Yes, every penny. If she'd lived six weeks longer, he wouldn't have got anything. I got hold of that information from the dead wife's will, filed at Somerset House. Now, what about it?"

"If you had come to us," remarked the chief, wiping another smile from his lips, "we could have saved you both trouble and expense. Mr. Jethro himself, with commendable promptness, furnished us with full particulars regarding his inheritance."

"What!" cried Christopher, stunned. "You knew this all along and it meant nothing to you?"

"Certainly it meant nothing, though in different circumstances it might have meant a great deal. As to the will itself, there is no remarkable feature about it. You appear to overlook the fact that if Mr. Jethro had died first, the young lady would have received his portion of the estate."

"Then you regard his alibi as unbreakable?" said Christopher after a heavy pause.

"The police are satisfied that he could not have left the Hôtel Stanislas between certain hours. In other words, he had no opportunity for committing the crime, and therefore no reason for interfering with Mr. Rostetter. I may add that during the course of this affair Mr. Rostetter is not the first to evade trial, and while the reason for his absconding may not be quite so apparent as—"

"Apparent!" exploded Christopher, bringing his fist down on the table with a bang. "It's unthinkable! It's fantastic! A man of his reputation turn tail and run like a hare? You people can say what you like about a fellow like Mowbray. I can't contradict you. But if you find Rostetter's body in the Seine, do you suppose those who know him will call his death suicide?"

"Suicide? It is your word, not ours." The speaker waxed suddenly stern. "We are looking for a live man—and we shall find him, never fear—if that is any satisfaction to you. Let me repeat, this rigmarole of yours is not worth the time I have wasted on it. If you hope to gain an audience again, you will have to produce something better than fictitious suitcases and hypothetical surmises. Good-evening, monsieur—and in your misplaced zeal take care you do not incur a libel action."

Christopher, hardly able now to restrain himself from smiting the infuriating chief in the face, strode from the room, banging the door behind him; but when he had descended half the flight of stairs his anger gave way to curiosity. He began to wonder at something indefinable in the manner of the two supercilious officials, something reminding him of le Gros's attitude towards him. On the chance that he was being discussed, he crept back, flattened himself against the wall and listened, to be speedily rewarded by hearing the secretary remark in the admiring tone of the salaried sycophant:

"You were sharp, monsieur, to guess what was up between those fellows. What put you on to their game?"

"I smelled a rat as soon as we were told they'd suddenly become so intimate," replied the chief with immense complacence. "And the minute the English rogue bolted I said to myself: 'Georges, my boy, you're right. The journalist has pocketed a substantial bribe for posing as the young woman's lover, and keeping the American's name clear of scandal.' It's easy enough to see why our friend who's just gone is frightened out of his wits. He knows to a certainty he'll be kicked out of his job. The Americans are very straitlaced about certain things."

"So one hears . . . but how do you explain this business about suitcases and Germans?" mused the secretary.

"All part of Rostetter's ingenious scheme to get the Loughton chap safely away while he cut off with the cash. I expect he was afraid of him . . . though we may find there's more behind it. Possibly an attempt to blackmail M. Jethro. Ah, Rostetter's a keen-witted scoundrel. Look at his forethought in handing over to our men the stuff the girl had dropped in his pocket and pretending it was his own. But for that it would have been difficult to disprove the purveyor's statement about its being harmless, which would have put the accused in the position of deliberate assassin right from the start. Gramont himself was taken in . . . but the old fox is on the scent now. Remember how he forced a confession out of the Chauvet woman? Well, take my word for it, tonight we shall see the same thing over again. As likely as not we shall have the prisoner admitting she was never drugged at all."

"Not drugged?" echoed the secretary gloatingly.

"*Diable*—no! She was drunk on champagne . . ."

CHAPTER XXX

A HUNDRED yards from the commissariat yawned the doors of a sordid little café. Christopher fell headlong into them, commanded a double *fine*, and tossed the fiery stuff off at one gulp.

Drunk on champagne. . . .

The words reverberated in his ears like a nauseating refrain. They prevented him from thinking clearly, but not from understanding the innuendoes which till now had puzzled him, or from realising how from now onward Dinah, her absent defender and himself would be disbelieved on all counts. He might swear himself blue in the face, but would a jury of practical-minded Frenchmen accept Rostetter's disinterested motives? Blackmail, too. . . . How easy to say these vile things when the man was not here to explain his actions! The whole world had grown distorted. As for his own precious career—good God! The insanity of thinking he cared two pins what happened to it! A cargo of hypocrisy, that was all it represented—a cumbersome cargo which had wrecked three lives. Chuck it overboard, and good riddance—only it was too late to profit by that now. . . .

The Chauvet case. . . . With terrifying distinctness he recalled the coldly impervious woman who had kept up her successful bluff until she was introduced to the scene of her latest brutal crime, and then broken down and given full details. The picture of that spectacular collapse would not have disturbed him but for one thing: he knew from Rostetter how Dinah, incapable of remembering what she had done, was hounded by doubts of her own innocence. Indeed that very fact must have accounted for Rostetter's intervention. Rostetter had known wherein the girl's real danger lay—known that if confronted by damning evidence of motive or subjected to emotional strain, she might commit some fatal indiscretion. She was in the state of mind now where she might easily burst out with an hysterical confession of guilt. If such a thing happened to-night, who was there to say her declaration had no value?

The glass he was clutching smashed in his tightened grip. He flung down a note on the sticky counter, wiped his cut palm across his forehead, and strode blindly out.

Rostetter would have found means to prevent this outrage. Rostetter had found means, only somehow—but hold on, there must surely be a connection between the wanton disclosure of information and the journalist's failure to come forward. Christopher's beliefs in certain directions were wavering. Cold water had been thrown on his attempt to link up Jethro with the disappearance, but if the smug official at the commissariat had shown stupidity over one aspect of the affair, might he not be equally unseeing in other quarters? A connection did exist. Let him think. What was the sole incontrovertible fact which he seemed to have grasped an hour ago, only now he had lost it?

Ah, here it was: the injurious truth must have emanated, directly or indirectly, from Helen Roderick, simply because she was the only outside person who knew it. In her own sessions with the judge she could not have revealed anything, or the arrest would have taken place over a week ago, therefore the betrayal must have come from some one taken into her confidence—and who could that some one be if not Jethro? The man was her admired friend, to whom, no doubt, she felt an allegiance strong enough to make her disregard the promise given to Rostetter. She would probably not even dream that Jethro, hitherto so impartial, would use the weapon she had put into his hands. Perhaps she did not realise it was a weapon; certainly she could not have imagined he needed one. Jethro, for obvious reasons, would have uttered his denouncements under seal of secrecy, and that was why his name had not appeared. He had known Dinah would be driven to admit the innocent fraud she had practised, and he had taken care that her accomplice should not be alive to stand by her. . . .

Was he going too fast? The original premises might be wrong. But no, they couldn't be wrong. He could not make the police see what he saw, but the figure lurking behind this curtain of lies was Basil Jethro and no other—the impeccable scholar, ace-high in public esteem, impossible to see without his halo of honour. He was the one to be tackled, for if he had taken desperate measures to ensure his own safety he must be afraid. Suppose he could be cornered, trapped behind locked doors, terrorised into revealing a weak spot in his armour? As matters now stood it seemed the one chance of staying the relentless machinery by which Dinah was so soon to be crushed. What was the immediate good of hunting for a man the police had not been able to locate? It might take days. The crisis was imminent.

Since eleven that morning Christopher had eaten nothing. The cheap brandy, coursing through an empty interior, did strange things to his habitual restraints, dislocated his vision, and laid bare the savage which years of training had covered over. His one craving now was to seize, strangle and subdue the hypocrite responsible for all this ghastly travesty of justice. Why waste another precious second in arguing the matter out? The slightly blurred hands of his watch told him it was seven o'clock. Just time to accomplish his purpose. He would probably fail, but even a footling venture was better than this supine inaction. . . .

The doors of the Jethro apartment opened cautiously.

Benedetto, barring the entrance, started a little at the visitor's wild dishevelment, at the streak of red running athwart a flushed and begrimed cheek. He cast a glance over his shoulder towards the salon from which came rough, excited voices arguing in French, and with some asperity declared that the master was not at home.

"Very well. I'll wait for him."

"No good doing that, sir. He's gone out to dinner and to fetch Miss Roderick back with him. They are arranging for the reconstruction now. It's to begin at eight, and Mr. Jethro won't be back much before then. Besides, the police have given very strict orders not to allow any one in except the persons concerned."

"Do you know where he is dining?"

"No, sir. I don't."

Christopher swore under his breath. The man was protected on all sides. No hope of getting him alone before to-morrow, and to-morrow might be too late. . . .

"See here, Benedetto—I want you to answer me one question: Did Mr. Jethro stay here in the apartment last evening?"

"No, he went out during the afternoon and did not come in again till about midnight. I believe he was dining with a friend."

So Jethro had spent a long interval away from home. Rostetter was last seen at nine o'clock. . . .

At Helen's apartment across the river he learned that Mademoiselle and the English gentleman had set forth together to some restaurant about ten minutes ago—maybe to the Coq d'Or, for Mademoiselle often dined there, but the maid could not be sure. Christopher sped to the Coq d'Or and thence to various restaurants on both sides of the Seine, but nowhere did he catch a glimpse of the couple he sought. He did see many acquaintances, and these in every instance eyed him with marked embarrassment. Under normal circumstances he would have felt enraged, but now he hardly stopped to notice the prevailing attitude towards him. For the first time in his life the old grooves were broken. He had completely forgotten himself.

Eight o'clock. He gave up searching. But what to do now? Suddenly he remembered that he had not troubled to question Rostetter's concierge very closely.

Better go back to the Place du Palais Bourbon and see what could be gleaned.

The withered hag who peered out at him from her stuffy living-room had little to add to her former statement. She did say, however, that all day yesterday M. Rostetter had been eagerly awaiting a telegram, which had arrived late in the afternoon, just before his final departure.

"A telegram?"

"Yes, monsieur, and a moment ago another one came. I'm going to give it to the inspector when he comes back presently. He's told me to hold all communications, but the last post brought nothing except some circulars."

Christopher's eyes rested covetously upon the bluish envelope sticking up against the plates on the dresser. How could he lay hands on it? His fingers strayed toward his pocket, but at that instant luck showed him a simpler method of obtaining his wish. In the kitchen at the back something boiled over with a great sizzling. The woman rushed to the rescue, and with one swoop Christopher snatched up the telegram and bolted.

Under the nearest street-lamp he examined his booty. The message, which came from Prague and was signed Strauss, was composed of the following lines:

Klauber visited France first then England returned Prague via Flushing and Cologne spent September fifth to fourteenth Paris Hôtel des Saints Pères.

Klauber again! Then Rostetter was really interested in this German. The present answer seemed to have been the result not of the inquiries wired from the Stanislas, but of some supplementary telegram, sent after the first reply arrived. What could this persistent investigation mean if not that Rostetter suspected Klauber of having a hidden association with Jethro? Yet if Klauber was in Paris only from the fifth to the fourteenth of last month, how could he be an active accomplice to the murder?

One thing was plain. Strauss, whoever he was, must have obtained this information from Klauber himself, and Klauber, if concerned in a murder, would certainly falsify any damaging facts. Still, it could be established whether or not he had stayed at the Hôtel des Saints Pères during the period mentioned. Christopher decided at once to check up on this statement, and, directing his taxi-driver to the Rue des Saints Pères, reached within a few minutes, the ancient, rambling building which formed the hotel premises.

He pored over the register. Yes, here was the signature he recognised as Klauber's. More, the dates were right—September fifth the time of arrival, and according to the woman clerk behind the desk Dr. Klauber, who had put up at the Saints Pères several years ago, had on this occasion left for England on the fourteenth. What sort of man was he? Oh, fifty odd, tall, stooping, with thick glasses and a grizzled beard. Very quiet and studious—a professor of some kind. He spoke good French, but with a guttural accent. The description tallied perfectly with the one furnished at the other hotel. Further, there could be small doubt of the man's having gone direct to England, because two days after his departure the clerk had received a postcard from him, giving his next forwarding address as the Deutsche Universität, Prague. The card was still here. She produced it—a picture showing the Bodleian Library, the postmark Oxford.

So Klauber had been to Oxford? All at once it flashed on Christopher that Jethro's housekeeper had spoken of a German who came to look at the master's portrait. That visitor might have been Klauber. Sent by Jethro on some errand? Christopher looked at the date on the card. It was September twenty-eighth—two days prior to the murder. Again, the handwriting was unmistakably the same as that seen in the two registers. But Klauber had not gone straight through Harwich-Flushing and Cologne to Prague. He had come again to Paris, to a different quarter, for a single night—and that night was the thirtieth!

Illumination flooded the dark places. Jethro and Klauber were allies, conspiring together to reap a rich reward. Two staid professors, one ordering his actions so that no breath of suspicion could touch him, the other, apparently a total stranger, secretly primed with the information necessary to slaying a victim never previously seen—whose death, provided he were not caught red-handed, could by no conceivable turn of events be laid at his door. Ships passing in the night, without visible exchange of signals; and yet that some signal had been observed if not properly construed seemed certain, for otherwise how could Rostetter have alighted on the clue which prompted the telegrams to Prague?

Staring intently at the register, Christopher for the first time noticed the town Klauber had written down as his last stopping-place before coming here on September fifth—Montpellier. Why, Montpellier was in the south, not far distant from Cap Ferrat, where Jethro had his summer home! He put a few more questions to the clerk, who, it seemed, had talked with Dr. Klauber and recalled his mentioning a series of visits all along the Riviera coast—Monte Carlo, Nice Cannes, all at close range to Cap Ferrat.

Christopher had heard enough. Plunging back into his taxi, he started once more to the commissariat, confident that at last he could make the irritating chief sit up and take notice. Midway the journey, however, a glance at his watch threw him into renewed panic. Hours might be spent in wrangling over this fresh theory of his, and while he strove to shift the chief's solid barrier of incredulity, that other business on the island was moving relentlessly forward. What could he do to stop it? Force his way in, create a disturbance? It would be better than nothing. He would be thrown out, but not before he had hurled his bombshell into their midst.

He leant out of the cab. "The Ile St. Louis again," he ordered, and sat on the edge of the seat ready to spring out.

A score of clocks clanged the hour of nine. The island lay wrapped in premature silence, with the dark Seine lapping past the quais. From the windows surrounded in ivy not a ray of light showed.

The concierge stepped forth officiously to turn him back.

"Useless to ascend, monsieur. There are sergeants on the landing, guarding the door. They won't let you in."

Christopher brushed past him, and with a heavy step mounted the stairs. The faint strains of a gramophone fell upon his ears, and as he recognised what it was playing his heart was wrenched with excruciating pain.

CHAPTER XXXI

THE orange-shaded candelabra poured their mellow light upon snowy napery and engraved crystal. In the centre of the board was a dish heaped high with fruit—the only food provided for the Barmecide's feast, if one excepted a plate of biscuits set ready on the serving-table. No wine was to be served. Benedetto put the chairs in their places, and stood aside, awaiting commands.

In a corner of the room the inspector and the *juge d'instruction* were holding a whispered conference. They had just received a statement signed by two eminent physicians to the effect that Ronald Cleeves was quite unfit to be present. Already three police supernumeraries had been commandeered to replace those of the fourteen who were missing—the victim, Mowbray, and Rostetter. Now another gap must be filled—but by whom? The inspector, following a message telephoned from the neighbouring commissariat, was disinclined to borrow either of the two sergeants now stationed outside the entrance.

"I warn you, monsieur," he said in a low voice, "if that American fellow gets in, we shall have trouble with him. He's tried once to—"

"Have it your own way," broke in the judge testily. "I'll find some one, only let's get on with it."

He signalled to the butler, and withdrew towards the window curtains, his swarthy face and powerful shoulders melting into obscurity. His companion joined him, and the two, with concentrated gaze and nostrils dilating with suppressed excitement, watched the guests file into the dining-room. All wore the same clothes as on the original occasion. All looked conscious and uncomfortable, a little like convicts under guard, but on each face was written a certain degree of relief. Peter Hummock had recovered some of his usual perkiness, while Ramon da Costa, no longer cowed and furtive, showed a distinct tendency to swagger. This was understandable, for the gigolo, having emerged without a stain on his character, had in the past ten days seen his drawing value enormously enhanced. Ladies rich and mighty bombarded him for private lessons; already he had two rival night clubs outbidding each other for his services.

A voice whispered that they were bringing the prisoner in.

Dead silence, as Dinah appeared, her eyes staring straight before her out of a white face framed in mahogany red hair, the flounces of her green tulle frock billowing about her small figure. Behind her hovered a wardress while from the archway to the hall a group of privileged onlookers, chief among them Helen Roderick and Basil Jethro, watched with stilled attention. She advanced in the space cleared for her, the centre of morbid interest, but not for long. The inspector, in the manner of a film director shepherding a crowd of walk-ons, assigned the others their places, and steered her to one of the end chairs.

"Mesdames, messieurs, be seated, please!" rapped the inspector's voice with business-like abruptness.

As the order was obeyed, the vacancy beside the prisoner became apparent. A murmur ran round. Thirteen again. One or two seemed to think there was some fatality about it. The three sergeants who were deputising for the hostess, Bannister Mowbray and Cleeves, glanced curiously at their superior officer, who was whispering to some one in the other room. Presently a tall figure detached himself from the distant group, came forward, and with a matter-of-fact air slipped unobtrusively into Rostetter's seat. It was Basil Jethro.

The presence of the philosopher in their midst had a curiously steadying effect on those emotionally inclined, who all at once saw the utter childishness of this effort to re-create the past. What could be gained by the careful copying of externals when the inner, psychological content of the former situation was gone beyond recall? No one here was in the same mood as before. All but one of the persons who mattered were absent. Incidentally, how incongruous it seemed for a man of Jethro's logical stamp to be drawn into the theatricalities he must with his whole nature despise!

Out of the shadows the judge's voice instructed them to converse naturally, choosing, if possible, the topics discussed on the evening of September 30th. The nine free persons sat dubious, tongue-tied, till

Cicely Gault's derisive laugh drew shocked attention towards her, but broke the paralysing spell. Sporadic chatter flared up, died down, now and then leaving vast deserts of silence. The trio of substitutes stared at their empty wine glasses and twiddled their thumbs, taking no part. Against the curtains the pair of lynx-eyed Frenchmen studied the faces sharply. Gramont held a watch in his hand, and from time to time referred to a notebook.

Dinah heard nothing. From early morning she had passed through a succession of such crushing experiences that her brain had almost ceased to function. The deep-lying horror within her had little to do with the fact that those surrounding her believed her guilty of murder. They did not count. What did matter was that she who all her life had seen human beings separated, shut as it were into water-tight compartments, no longer knew which compartment she belonged in. Things had happened to her which in her worst nightmare she would not have thought possible. To be locked in a prison cell was something which would not, because it simply could not, occur . . . yet it had occurred. She would be tried before a jury and a full court-room, and even then, whatever the verdict, she would still know no more than she knew at this moment.

Was she a murderess? With Tommy to lean upon she had managed to shut her ears to this persistent question, but now that support was taken from her—how, why was another stupefying puzzle which increased her mental confusion—she wondered why she did not rise up, declare she had stabbed Dorinda in a fit of jealous rage, and have done with the mockery. As they were sure to get her in the end, it would save a great deal of trouble, but she lacked energy to take any active step. She was like a rock sunk at the bottom of a stream, waiting for some current strong enough to dislodge it. Meanwhile she must continue to endure. . . .

Who was this seated beside her? Oh, yes—Basil Jethro. She had never seen him, nor did she feel the slightest curiosity to glance in his direction. She had almost forgotten how, ages ago, Tommy Rostetter had made her repeat the grotesque nonsense Dodo had babbled against her hated stepfather. Tommy had probably done that to distract her thoughts from herself. He had always been like that, diverting her, actually making her laugh and take a sane view of things. Only maybe that view wasn't sane. . . . The car found in the river! Did that mean Tommy was drowned too, like that horrible Mowbray man? But why? Why?

A dish of fruit prodded her arm. She roused to see, directly under her eyes, a long, bone-handled dirk—a new knife which caused her no emotion.

"Mademoiselle," said a voice at her elbow, "the witnesses state that you examined this knife very closely. Show us exactly what you did."

She picked up the dirk and turned it about dully in her hands. From the right a man's slender hand reached out and took it from her. She heard as from afar off Soukine's gentle voice murmuring, "Be careful, it is very sharp." No one, least of all herself, realised that this was not what the painter had said on the former occasion, nor did she notice the flat disappointment of the guests as they sat back in their chairs. She sank again into a blurred reverie.

Biscuits? What were they for?

"If I were you, I would not take any of this. It may have a bad effect on you."

She had not heard the whispered promptings from behind which had led to this formal, parrot-like repetition. She did, however, start at the sound of a man's totally unfamiliar voice, and turn to gaze straight into the eyes of her left-hand neighbour, Basil Jethro. A gasp of astonishment escaped her.

"So it was you I saw!" she exclaimed, as though speaking her thoughts aloud. "I passed by you as I went out the door." Why this electric tension, eyes, eyes protruding at her out of tense faces? The judge had drawn near to bend down and examine her expression. She caught Jethro's politely puzzled interrogation of "I beg your pardon?" followed by a suggestion thrown over his shoulder, "Perhaps it might be as well to ask the lady what she means."

"Mademoiselle," hissed the judge sharply. "When did you see this gentleman? What door was it? Where?"

"At the Baroness Waldheim's reception," she answered simply. "I looked up and saw him standing by the cloakroom door. I didn't know who he was then."

A woman giggled. The atmosphere, an instant ago charged with breathless expectancy, broke up into stirrings and comprehensive nods. Gramont gave a brusque grunt, and pointed to the plate of biscuits placed in front of the prisoner.

"That," he said, "represents the drug. Take one. Pretend it is your allotted portion. Now! What did you do with it? Don't fumble, answer quickly. Did you eat it, or—" His eyes bored into her. *"Did you drop it into your companion's pocket?"*

The idea that she had eaten none of the drug but concealed it had been so driven into her brain that morning that now she almost believed what this bully had told her was fact. She wavered, on the brink of falling in with the suggestion—and then something odd happened. Out of the air beside her she heard a voice—Tommy's voice—saying quite distinctly, "Dinah, don't be a fool!" It was queer. She had not known she was psychic. Possibly she was a little unbalanced, which all along had been her haunting fear. Anyhow, within her she felt faint stirrings of her old spirit.

"I ate it," she replied, and helped herself to a round, dry biscuit.

"All of it?"

"Yes, all. Why do you want me to tell a lie about it?"

"Well, well, assume you did eat it. In that case, you were sick after you left the table. That is so, *hein*?"

"No, it isn't so."

She had reached the point where recollection ceased. Presently, with the wardress in close attendance, she was herded upstairs to Dorinda Quarles' bedroom, where she was surrounded by the other women. Surrounded, yet alone. No one spoke to her, though curious glances rested on her and moved away. Some one brushed against her and without turning spoke words, apparently in another direction, yet pitched in such a way as to penetrate her consciousness.

"Keep it up," said the voice, an English one. "No, don't worry—that female's got her eye on you, but she can't understand what I'm saying. We aren't all of us down on you. Get that? You've had a rotten deal, but you can beat them yet, if you don't weaken."

Cicely Gault? She was nonchalantly manipulating her lipstick before the mirror, but it was she who had spoken. Cissy Gault, whom she scarcely knew, but who possessed about as odd a reputation as any woman in Paris. What did she mean? That among these people a few believed her innocent, or that, disbelieving, they still did not condemn her? With Cissy one could not say—yet Dinah was moved at the thought of anyone's championing her cause. She realised now that Soukine, another black sheep, had shown in mute ways he did not belong to the enemies' camp. Tolerance—but among the unmoral. Or no, Tommy had a conscience and code like her own. The very lies he had told were pure white ones. . . . Dear Tommy!

Suddenly, with the rustle of women's dresses in her ears and the lights beating down on her, an idea wholly terrible struck her full force. Tommy, too, felt certain she had committed this crime. He had gone away because he had tried to save her and failed. Of course he had known she was guilty. Of course, of course! Why hadn't she seen through it before?

He had been awake and watched her as she took up the knife and drove it into Dorinda's breast. That was why he dared not come forward now. He was afraid he would do her more harm than good.

The last prop splintered. Why fight any longer, if this were so? Yet she continued to stand upright and motionless, every hair in place, her eyes fixed with a glassy stare.

"Keep him out, send him away! If he makes trouble, why take him in charge . . ."

Who was to be kept out? Dinah, descending the stairs, got a dull impression of some disturbance going on amongst the sergeants, whom the inspector was haranguing in angry tones; but it meant nothing to her. A reporter, probably, bent on getting into the apartment. The salon already was slightly foggy with cigarette smoke. The gramophone was playing *Miss Virginia*. A new record, bought for the occasion. She had broken the other one—or so Gramont told her. The tune left her strangely indifferent. Had it once hurt her? How long ago it must have been! She sighed wearily, ready to sink with exhaustion. . . .

"Mademoiselle, come with me."

Gramont clutched her bare arm and dragged her into the dining-room, where it was nearly dark. Time had ceased to exist. She only knew that for endless hours she had been repeating monotonously, "I can't say. I don't remember."

She felt herself pushed and pulled about like a mechanical doll. Gramont consulted a little book, frowned, gauged distances, swore under his breath and moved her again. Now he was satisfied. The window was open, the cool damp breeze blowing in. Was that big arm-chair intended for her to sit in? Apparently so. She sat down facing the table. A cloak— her cloak, which had done service for three years and which she would never wear again—lay over her knees.

"There! Is that the position, mademoiselle?"

"I don't know. Is it?"

"Where was your friend, M. Rostetter?"

Rostettaire. It sounded so silly, the way he said it.

"I don't know. Wherever he said he was."

The judge gave a furious snort and turned away.

Directly in front of her was the dish of grapes. On it lay the new knife. How close it was! She could stretch out her hand and grasp it. She shuddered, thinking that this was what she must have done, and averting her eyes gazed with faint wonderment at the altered salon. Was this how it had looked, one flame-tinted lamp shining down on figures sprawled anyhow? About ten feet away she saw something which made her want to laugh hysterically. It was the thickset sergeant who had taken Dorinda's place, lying now full length on the big divan, with his clumsy boots sticking up and one arm dangling downward.

Over her shoulder Gramont spoke with slow venom.

"So, the knife displeases you, does it? Never mind, you must look at it. Keep looking at it, till I tell you to stop."

Very well, she didn't mind. She fixed her eyes on the steel, till the sight of it seemed to hypnotise her. It swam in a dark haze. She yawned. Minutes passed. In another moment she would be dropping asleep.

The lights were all extinguished now, though flames from the hearth in the other room cast great shadows on the wall opposite. The voice in her ear brought her to herself with a jerk.

"Mademoiselle! Look back. Tell me what you see."

She was on her feet, shrieking. In full view, where only a few moments ago she had seen the uniformed sergeant, lay the body of Dorinda Quarles—yes, in her apricot dress, with damp hair clinging to her forehead, and in her bared breast a crimson gaping wound! She had seen her—seen Dorinda herself. It could mean but one thing. She had gone quite mad.

Screams, words incoherently mingled, and then a crumpled heap of green flounces on the floor. It was over.

"Mesdames, messieurs, this room must be cleared. At once! Go home. I have no further need of you. Lights, please. Everyone out. I want only the wardress and the doctor."

The judge's tone was satisfied, excited. With widespread arms he bundled the curious company out the doors, spied the owner of the apartment, and signalled to him with triumph.

"Don't distress yourself, monsieur. Try to calm the lady who is with you. We have got what we were after—not a confession in so many words, but that will come later."

He buttonholed Jethro, whispered in his ear, and shook him warmly by the hand. Then he closed the doors.

Helen Roderick was sobbing, her broad face convulsed with emotion.

"Oh, what was it? What did they do? Did she see something?" she gasped, clutching Jethro's arm.

"A wax figure," he replied quietly. "Yes, it was a horrible trick to play. I had no idea myself. The French use these methods and occasionally they get results." He detached himself from her hold and consulted his watch. "I am going to take you home," he announced. "Don't be alarmed, she is in safe hands, and besides they will not allow us to go in there. This is your coat, I think?"

"No, no, Basil. You must not stir out. This has been as terrible a shock to you as to me. Benedetto will get me a taxi."

"Certainly I intend to go with you. Come, it is late."

He helped her on with her fur coat and escorted her down the stairs to the street.

CHAPTER XXXII

For the second time that evening Christopher leant over the *chef de commissaire*'s desk.

"You still won't listen to me?" he asked grimly. "Very well, then, read this telegram which I discovered at Rostetter's flat. You can't read English? I'll translate it for you."

He did so, quickly adding his own interpretation.

"The man Klauber, whoever he may be, stayed in this city at the Hôtel des Saints Pères from September fifth to fourteenth. He then left for England with the stated intention of returning from there to Prague; but on the night of the 30th he was back here again, at the Hôtel Stanislas. I can prove it. Now, do you continue to doubt Rostetter's interest in him?"

"There may two Klaubers," suggested the chief with a sphinx-like expression.

"Not with the same appearance and handwriting. Look at the registers, send one of your men to examine them—only for God's sake be quick about it."

"Supposing this German did return to Paris. What then?"

"What then? Isn't it perfectly plain he was acting with Jethro? Listen: Klauber came here the first time from Montpellier and declared he had stopped all along the coast. Jethro has a villa at Cap Ferrat. The two knew each other, I tell you. Surely out of all this you can collect evidence enough to—"

"Evidence! Come, monsieur, you are offering me your hasty conclusions and calling them evidence. That Klauber paid visits in the south of France does not mean he visited Mr. Jethro. If he came back to Paris there is still nothing to show that there was anything between him and the other gentleman. Can you produce a single witness who saw them together?"

"If they were in league to commit murder they would have taken care not to be seen talking."

"They would hardly have stayed under the same roof."

"You don't know that. There may have been a reason . . . stop, I've got it! They had to communicate at the last minute, after Jethro rang up to make certain his proposed victim was asleep. What more do you want?"

"Ingenious. But," said the chief with raised brows, "have you ascertained what Klauber did between certain hours? Because if he failed to go out, then his alibi is in every respect as good as Mr. Jethro's."

Christopher saw that a point had been scored against him. He had not bothered to inquire into Klauber's movements.

"The manager was the only person who could have told me about that," he replied. "And he was not there—but he'll have got back by now, surely. The question can be easily settled. Will you send someone back to the hotel with me to obtain the necessary information? It's not much to ask." The chief deliberated, rang a bell, and gave an order, as the result of which Christopher was presently on his way to the Stanislas, in company with an officer.

He was half-sorry he had restrained himself from committing assault and battery on the guards who had refused him admission to the Jethro apartment. Perhaps, however, he had acted wisely, for little good as he was accomplishing while at liberty, he would have been considerably less useful if arrested and clapped into a cell. Still the pent volcano within him must sooner or later break out. He did not know how much longer he could go on laboriously, step by step, with the maddening gramophone purring its honeyed notes in his ears and the thought of Dinah tearing at his vitals . . .

"Not in yet? In God's name, what has become of this manager of yours?"

Then it came out, and the indefinable atmosphere of tension Christopher had noticed became plain. M. Jolivet had been gone since last night. He was summoned away by telephone at about nine-thirty, since when nothing had been seen or heard of him. The concierge had not wished to make the matter public just yet, for now and then M. Jolivet remained out at night without announcing his intentions in advance. Still the chasseur had been despatched to the apartment of a sister in the Rue d'Amsterdam, also to a young woman in whom M. Jolivet was interested, and in neither quarter had there been any news. The chief hospitals had been rung up. The manager was at none of them.

"He's gone, too!" cried Christopher, struck by the possible significance of this second disappearance. "Half an hour from the time Rostetter was last seen. Don't you get the connection? If the man knew what—"

"Not so fast, monsieur," interrupted the inspector in a calm tone. "I'll institute an inquiry, of course, but as a general rule these affairs don't amount to much. First let us make sure of one thing. Do any of you," he addressed the concierge and the waiter, "know what that German guest, Klauber, did on the night he spent here? Did he go out?"

No one present could say. The manager alone could answer the question, because only he was in the lobby for the entire evening. The chasseur did not recall bringing the German down in the lift or taking him up again, though the lift was often worked by the guests themselves, so that constituted no proof one way or the other.

"Well, then! Which if any of you heard what was said over the telephone when the manager was summoned away?"

All assembled shook their heads. The waiter, however, had noticed that M. Jolivet seemed pleased and excited when he called through into the lounge to say he would be back in an hour or so.

"A rendezvous with a lady," remarked the inspector with a nod. "Too much to drink and there you have it. Since we're here, though, we may as well question the entire staff about this German's movements. Fetch them all in."

Another waiter and two chambermaids appeared. From one of them it was learned that the German had occupied Room Number Seventeen, next door to Eighteen, in which, successively, the two English gentlemen had slept.

"You hear that?" exclaimed Christopher to his companion. "It bears out my theory." He turned to the woman who had spoken and asked: "Did the second Englishman—yes, the one with the black hair—say anything to you about either the German or the other Englishman?"

"Not about the other Englishman, monsieur. He did mention the German who had been in Seventeen, but as I had seen this gentleman only once, as he was leaving, I couldn't say much."

Christopher felt a touch on his elbow. Looking down he beheld the bright-eyed chasseur who had pushed his way through the group.

"What is it?"

"Only this, monsieur. Going up in the lift, the second Englishman— the black-haired one—asked me whether I had noticed the German's boots. I told him they seemed quite new, and that they were the same pair he'd worn when he was here before. By the look of the soles I thought he could not have used them except while he was here."

"Oh!" exclaimed Christopher blankly. "And what did my friend say to that?"

"Nothing, monsieur. He didn't seem surprised."

The inspector looked at Christopher, who was obliged to admit he had heard nothing on the subject of boots.

"But then I didn't know about the German at all till this evening. Evidently Rostetter found out about him on Sunday night—but since he was here once before, suppose we see the date of the first visit."

They pored over the register till, some distance back, they came upon the familiar writing. Christopher gave a start.

"He arrived on September third. Miss Quarles motored up from the south on the same day to see her dentist. I know, because on the fourth I met her at a cocktail party."

The identical cocktail party which had started the mischief. Christopher felt hateful memories rush over him as he went on rapidly: "I should think that visit represented an unsuccessful attempt to murder her. On the fifth the fellow crossed over to the Saints Pères. Now why did he do that?"

"Why, indeed?" echoed the inspector with a shrug. "However, I'll jot down details about the boots and other clothing, to compare with what the Saints Pères people have to tell us. I'll also institute a search for this manager, who quite possibly could give us the connecting links." He turned to the concierge. "Have you still got the registration form Klauber filled in?"

The concierge replied in the affirmative, but after searching through a pile of slips looked up with a startled expression.

"It is not here, monsieur."

"Not here?" For the first time the inspector showed alert concern, as though at last scenting evil doings. "Here, let me look."

The registration forms dated back for more than a fortnight. Only Klauber's was missing, and no one present could throw any light on the circumstance.

It was eleven o'clock before the inspector and Christopher gave up waiting for Jolivet's return, the former to pursue his inquiries at the other hotel, the latter to gravitate back to watch the darkened windows of Jethro's apartment. The gramophone continued to play, so the thing was still going on. Not a chance of catching his man alone till the police had vacated the premises, which might not be for another hour or so.

Sweat stood out on Christopher's forehead. Tearing his eyes away he stared down fascinatedly at the oily river, wondering, as once before Tommy had wondered, what secrets it held, and if in the passage of time yet another battered corpse would come to the surface. Somehow he thought not. Rostetter was certainly done away with, but that his body would be discovered in circumstances exactly similar to those of Bannister Mowbray's alleged suicide seemed unlikely. A second affair of the kind might not be accorded so ready an explanation. It would look queer ... and queerness was the one thing to be avoided. Far better complete mystery as to what had happened. Nothing proved. From a murderer's point of view it was the one safe expedient.

Yet bodies are deuced hard to get rid of. . . .

Wasting time again! Idling here, with a brain empty as a powder-horn, while awful things were happening, that poor trapped child up there being rushed to her doom. . . .

Hallie Pemberton . . . the thought of her pricked his conscience. He might, since he was being utterly useless, dash over to her for a moment, Job's comforter though he was, with nothing better to offer than suspicions unproved, perhaps impossible to prove. He would go and come back here, to watch and wait. . . .

Hallie peered fearfully out at him, drew him with tense hands into the warm circle of lamplight.

"Have you got news of Tommy?"

"No, no news." He stood gazing fixedly at one of Dinah's canvases, a fine, bold painting of the view from her old studio window. "I saw her for a few minutes. I had to tell her about his car. I suppose it was less cruel than letting her go on wondering . . ." His voice trailed to silence. He moistened his lips and took a sudden decision to let the little woman share in his half-knowledge. "Hallie, I believe—though I may be wrong—I know who gave them away. It was Basil Jethro."

She gasped, staring at him in bewilderment.

"Oh, no, Chris! Not him! Why he's my one hope now. A man of his character wouldn't permit any injustice. I've pinned my faith to his sense of fairness, his . . . his refusal to interfere in any way. Unless he knew Dinah was guilty, to get her arrested would be such a mean, petty action. I see, you're thinking he found out through Miss Roderick. Isn't it far more likely Miss Roderick herself?"

"No, because I'm convinced she had no reason for making a disclosure of that kind. On the other hand Jethro . . . hold on, there's the telephone."

"It's the lawyer," cried Hallie, beginning to tremble as she sprang towards the instrument. "He promised to ring up the very first minute he knew about this reconstruction—the result, I mean. . . . Hello!"

Christopher heard the deep rumble of le Gros's voice. Stiffened all over he saw Hallie's face go grey and old. The receiver dropped from her hand, a single moan escaped her as she fell back against the wall.

"Quick! What does he say? Is it finished?"

"Dinah . . . she's fainted. . . . Oh, Chris, Chris, they say there's no doubt that it's all come back to her. That she's . . . guilty."

She gave way completely, her thin little body convulsed by dry sobs.

CHAPTER XXXIII

VERY cautiously Christopher let himself into his mother's apartment. There was something here he wanted, or else he would have given the place a wide berth. The lights were out. That must mean the two resident members of his family had gone to bed. A good thing. With noiseless strides he moved towards his own room, turned the electric switch, and for a second blinked stupidly at a mirrored reflection he failed to recognise.

Bloodshot eyes, hair limp with sweat, a hard mouth. No wonder he gave the impression of being drunk. He was drunk—though not on brandy. He poured out water, drank it, and without stopping to wipe the smear of blood from his face slid his hand into a table-drawer. His fingers closed on the thing he sought. He drew it forth, slipped it into his side-pocket and stole back along the thickly-carpeted passage.

Fate stepped in. As he neared the outer door, lights flooded on and his brother Dave, in elegant pyjamas, blocked the way. From under a tousled blond thatch grey eyes widened with gloating astonishment.

"Sacred codfish! Where have you sprung from? Just you wait till the old girl fastens her talons on you. I've been through it—six solid hours of hysterics, and—but I suppose you know you've ruined yourself and us too, dragged the good old name through the mud and so on. If you'll take my tip you'll—"

"Get out of my way, you blasted fool."

"What, not off again? Here, wait a minute! Give us the dope on the trip to England, the midnight prowling, the—gosh, that's torn it."

Close at hand a shrill clamour had broken out from the telephone. Christopher on the point of bolting suddenly realised that perhaps the summons was for him. He clamped the receiver to his ear.

"Who? Speak slowly. I can't . . . yes, this is Loughton, but who are you?"

"Rank Rostetter," came the breathless gasp. "I got your wire. I'm out at le Bourget—just landed. Have you located him yet?"

Rank Rostetter? How was it possible? There were no night 'planes . . .

"No sign of him. I'm afraid he's done for."

"Done for—! I guessed it." There was a choked sob.

"Then do you think that . . . that some sort of trap's been laid to get him out of the way?"

"I can't think anything else—though I haven't yet got any support for my belief. No real support. I'm going now for—the person we were talking about. I may fail, but . . ."

"Wait! Wait till I tell you. Filly's blurted the whole thing out. The business was true. He swears it. That's why we're here."

Filly? Who was he? Oh, yes, the unpleasant little squirt who had not played up last night. Had he remembered at last?

"Hell! He'd never forgotten. In a sweat for fear the bishop would hear about his goings-on, that's all. It was a private burrow he got into. Private. See? Those disappearances—double life, secret vice, oh, anything you choose to call it. The point is, it may mean a hole to stow someone in till he can be got rid of. Maybe Tommy's there now. Or his body. . . . Will you come with us to look? Got a gun? Mine's in hock. Quick, there's not a second to lose!"

"Where is this place?"

"Montmartre. Fil can't give the exact address, but says he can lead us to it. Will you meet us at that church, what's its name—at the foot of the hill?"

"Notre Dame de Lorette? . . . Twenty minutes. I'll be there."

"Christopher!"

He had not seen the figure clad in mauve brocade and swansdown who had been standing behind him, eyes bulging in the effort to contain her fury. Now that fury burst its bounds.

"No, Christopher! You're not going out again. Not another step do you take in this sordid, disgraceful affair. I forbid you—do you hear? I absolutely forbid you to go." The speaker thrust her imposing person between him and the door. "You've brought trouble enough on us, what with your intrigues, your . . . your . . . I warn you once and for all, if you defy me now, I'll—"

"Let me go, mother!"

There was an undignified struggle. Christopher tore himself bodily from the detaining hands, banging the door behind him. His feet were heard clattering down the stairs. Mrs. Loughton was left to vent her baffled rage on a youth, who mildly amused, lit a cigarette and hummed a Broadway hit.

Notre Dame de Lorette—dark, dank, neglected. Vaulting from his taxi Christopher looked at his watch, and paced the pavement in jerky strides. Within his brain a voice hammered cynically: "Dead or alive, we shan't find him. Something to do—that's all." Yet a second voice kept urging him to hurry, hurry, or it would be too late.

Just supposing Jethro had got Rostetter's corpse secreted somewhere? He would have to dispose of it quickly, and would from reasons of caution seize the first free moment to attend to the matter. Well, he was free now. In an hour, maybe less, the final traces of his crimes might be wiped away, the slate left clean. If Rostetter never reappeared to bear witness against him, what would all these riddles about a German professor amount to? Nothing whatever. Every suspicious circumstance would be explained, the past covered over, while the law wreaked vengeance on the girl who had no defence.

Past midnight. Would those men never come?

Round a corner slithered a car. The door burst open, and the rusty red head of Rank Rostetter thrust itself wildly out. Blue eyes, hauntingly like Tommy's glared with fanatical brightness.

"Get in, get in!" shouted their owner hoarsely.

Christopher stumbled over the legs of Bilfilian and a pleasantly-ugly Englishman who held a flying helmet on his knees. Rank hurled an order to the driver, who set off up the slope towards the main thoroughfare of Montmartre.

"We've got to descend the Rue des Martyrs," explained the leader of the expedition, husky with excitement. "It's a turning out of there, but Fil won't know it from this direction. Loughton, meet Coppinger, the sportsman who flew us over. The only member of the Aviation Club who'd risk it. Some flight. Fil's been sick as a cat, but we've gingered him up with brandy. Want another nip, you son of a prairie-dog? You've got to look sharp, you know."

Bilfilian, green to the gills, shook his head and gulped. Rank continued a graphic account of the adventure from the moment Christopher's telegram had arrived. The recipients had been basking before a study fire, Bilfilian immersed in the pages of *St. Irenaus on the Heresies*.

"When I read your message, I grabbed *Irenaus*—it's a fairly hefty tome—and was going to smash it over Fil's bean. Somehow it seemed the one thing to do. But he dodged and started to stammer. Hadn't we been pulling his leg last night? Was it possible we were serious about old Jethro? Serious . . . I ask you!" Rank choked at the recollection. "Anyhow, out it came—slightly different version from the original one. God help him if it's not the right one! Seems that while he was in this fruity haunt he heard a rumour about rooms overhead which the proprietress sometimes let to favoured clients—only you had to be handy with the pass-word as well as the cash. Fil got the idea these rooms didn't belong to her, that she took advantage of the tenant's absence to haul in extra money. That was your notion, wasn't it?" demanded Rank prodding his friend in the ribs.

"Couldn't be hers," murmured the sufferer with closed eyes. "If you'd seen what they were like—"

"Wait—I'll tell it. The reason for all this is there's a squint-hole drilled through the flooring. Got that? Pompous citizens with reputations to preserve like to go there and look on at the show below without being seen. Sort of screened theatre box. Well, young Fil's putrid eye-balls nearly fell out of his head when he thought about it. Wanted to see if it was so. He watched his chance, pattered upstairs, and—now, you blighter, carry on."

"The door wasn't quite closed," bleated the hero in a dying voice. "Inside a sort of atmosphere . . . exotic . . . curtains. I don't quite know what, because I only had a glimpse. But there was a big couch with a man in a dressing-gown lying on it. He sat up and stared with a glazed kind of look. He didn't recognise me, but I knew him—or thought I did. The light was low, and I'd been imbibing a little. I got out like a shot. Wouldn't do, you know. Afterwards I thought I'd better keep quiet on the subject. Not safe to prattle about."

The aviator chucked his cigarette through the window with a scornful gesture.

"Tripe!" he snorted. "Granting it was Jethro, what does it prove except that he's a favoured client? Ten to one the old harpy has an arrangement with the tenant and splits the proceeds with him. She couldn't do that if the tenant was Jethro. Besides would he go there if the place was likely to be entered by strangers?"

"If he's only there now and again, how can he tell what goes on in his absence?" objected Rank stubbornly.

Christopher was inclined to share Coppinger's view, but he said nothing, there being but one way of settling the argument: Go and find out.

The vast Place de Clichy burst upon them, brilliant with electric signs, clanging with noise. The amusements of Montmartre were in full swing. On every side resplendent commissionaires stood on the pavements to lure pleasure-seekers into the rapacious maws behind them. Spangle, glitter, then sudden gloom again as the car, slowing down, crept at a snail's pace along the narrow Rue des Martyrs.

"Now, you cuttle-fish!" Rank cried. "Look lively. Which is the turning?"

Bilfilian swayed sideways to peer with goggling eyes out the window. Each time the car stopped he shook his head but at length, when the tense watchers had begun to fear he could not identify the street, he gave the command to turn to the left.

"Sure, are you? Don't lead us wrong."

"Yes, the Rue de la Tour d'Auvergne. Keep going till you see a lamp-post and a figure of St. Anthony over a door. There—that's the house."

"Is that St. Anthony? I'll take your word for it. Come along."

The four men surged out to penetrate a cobbled court enclosed on all sides, lit by a dim, iron-caged gas-lamp, and smelling of drains. Several doors led into the various buildings. At the most distant one Bilfilian pointed a wavering finger.

"That's it. You ask for Madame Hoche. Am I to come too?"

"Come? It's your job to introduce us, you poor nut."

The chauffeur, catching the name of Hoche, shrugged with philosophical contempt, and diving into the recesses of his clothing for a Maryland settled down for a long wait.

A concierge challenged them, but on learning their objective retired to his loge, leaving them to proceed towards the building at the back. The walls of this rose stark and black to a squat Mansard roof on a higher level than those of its neighbours. The stairway inside was badly-lit, the dingy wallpaper veined to imitate marble.

"One minute," whispered Rank. "What money can we raise between us? Fil and I hadn't time to make a raid, so all we can muster is a couple of quid. You chaps any better off?"

They turned out their pockets. Coppinger, fortunately, had cashed a cheque that morning, while Christopher had several hundred francs and a handful of English silver. The total ought to suffice. It was agreed that Christopher should act as spokesman, Fil being apt to turn sick,

Rank, though reading for modern languages not yet prepared to do much in the conversational line, and Coppinger boasting to two formulas: *"Combien?"* and *"Qu'est-ce que c'est que ça?"*—both useful enough, but not extensive for argument.

As they neared the third landing a door swung softly open to emit garish light, music and a stench of patchouli.

"You are looking for Madame Hoche, gentlemen?" purred a loathsome voice. "Come in, come in. You are vairy welcome."

They saw before them a thickset, corpulent person in a tight dress-coat with diamond-studs blazing from his shirt-front.

His greasy, dark skin and the jet eyes narrowed to crescents by an habitual smirk suggested Egyptian origin, or maybe Armenian. He had fat, hairless hands which filled one with repulsion, and a prominent gold tooth.

As they trooped into a lobby hung with crimson looped curtains, a tinkle of sequins sounded, and a middle-aged woman with densely black hair and cushioned neck and arms plastered dead white tripped forth to greet them. Her teeth gleamed in a smile at once arch and commercial, her eyes, heavily encircled with mascara, swept the four faces and came to rest on Bilfilian with shrewd inquiry.

"Messieurs . . . vous désirez?"

Christopher gave the prearranged explanation. Madame Hoche looked incredulous, shocked. Private rooms? Where could they have heard such a story? Her establishment comprised this floor and the one beneath, but nothing above—but no, nothing whatever! However, if they would be pleased to enter, they would be shown an original and amusing entertainment. Unique—comprenez? They might also dance, order champagne, divert themselves in a variety of ways. In all Paris the most striking, the most exclusive—

Christopher stemmed the flow of eloquence. "Yes, yes, madame, but the point is, we ourselves are exclusive. We have no wish to mingle with a crowd. We, furthermore, know that this place exists, because one of our party—" he drew forward the shrinking Bilfilian—"has already visited it. We return to England to-morrow, therefore, if we can not have what we want now, why, we must seek elsewhere." He moved towards the landing.

"Tenez, monsieur!"

The business eyes of madame took stock of them singly out of a face which no longer smiled. The doorman followed suit, whistling between his teeth. Presently the two withdrew to whisper together, and when the proprietress returned a decision had been reached. Very well, then, since this was the gentlemen's last evening in Paris, they should have their desire—but the price must be paid down now. Twenty English pounds. It was not excessive.

Haggling ensued. Fifteen pounds, not a penny more. It was all they possessed. Impossible? Then, good-evening...

The offer was accepted, the notes counted and crammed into madame's tight bosom, and from the same hiding-place a Yale key produced and put into Christopher's hand. They would find the little hole under the rug beside the couch. There must be no disorder left, for the owner was very particular. What, no champagne, nothing to drink? Then *au revoir, et merci bien*.

The black eyes watched the little group mounting the remaining flight of stairs. Then Madame Hoche, still thoughtful, shrugged her plump shoulder and closed the door.

CHAPTER XXXIV

THAT they had been permitted to enter the rooms at all seemed crushing proof that they would find nothing there. Too late Christopher saw that the one sensible course would have been to lie in wait for Jethro and, if the latter went out, follow him; but it was useless to cry over spilled milk.

On the dark top landing a single door faced them. Into this Christopher fitted the Yale key, and an instant later found himself in a stuffy, ink-black passage filled with some subtle and cloying-sweet scent. Going forward he discovered a second door, which when opened pressed against folds of heavy material. An overlapped slit in this obstruction gave at his touch, but though he strained his eyes he could make out nothing in the dense, impenetrable gloom.

"Where's the switch?" whispered Rank in the rear. "Oh, I've got it. ... Suffering tomcats! Will you look?"

A subdued radiance, blossoming forth from sources unseen, shone on a low-pitched room fully thirty feet square and entirely devoid of visible outlet. From ceiling to deep-piled carpet hung tapestries—or no, not tapestries, but arras of wool velvet painted in a design portraying contorted human forms mingled with those of beasts, an effect beautiful, but vaguely perverse in its suggestion. On the floor cushions were heaped, but there was no article of furniture save one immense couch such as a Roman emperor might have used, and near it a four-sided bookcase, the low top of which held a crystal ash tray and a box of matches. Evenly spaced at some distance from the couch were several smooth, tall plinths of black Purbeck marble, each supporting an African sculptured head, rough-hewn, with thick-lipped, bestial figures and grotesque contours. A fireplace, but no fire—yet the air was warm, hinting at concealed hot-water pipes. The curtains hung flat to the wide mantelshelf, on which stood the leering figure of a bronze satyr.

"No one's here," declared Rank in a tone of flat disappointment.

"No one's been here either, for some time," added Coppinger contemptuously. "You can see by the dust."

It was true, dust lay thick on the debased negro heads, the ash trays, the bronze satyr. Still, this was probably not the only room the flat contained. Rank, like a terrier, ran noiselessly round, prodding the curtains, hauling them up to peer behind. Following his example Christopher came upon a set of bookshelves, flush with the wall and filled with leather-bound volumes which he was just stooping to examine when a cry from the boy announced the discovery of another door.

"It's a sliding one. How the hell does one get it open? Here, hold up this infernal curtain so I can tackle it."

In another second the door had run back into the thickness of the wall, light shone softly from a ceiling-globe, and the four men gazed in on a marble-floored interior the chief object of which was a sunken, malachite bath. Every inch of wall-space was covered in grossly suggestive paintings, spread without break over a row of cupboard doors, yet, as in the case of the arras, the obscene detail melted into a supremely rich and beautiful whole.

"What's in the cupboards? Are they locked?" muttered Rank, after a brief survey.

"Nothing's locked—and look, here's a remarkably classy garment hanging up," remarked Coppinger, taking from a peg a man's sumptuous dressing-gown of thinly-wadded satin striped in brown and green. "Is that what the bloke was wearing?" he demanded of Bilfilian.

The latter nodded. "And aren't those pyjamas folded up on the shelf?" He touched a pile of thick, soft silk, crumpled as though worn.

Christopher shook out the pyjamas, noticing that the maker's tags had been removed. The same was true of the dressing-gown, which exhaled an odour of the prevailing scent. In one pocket was a crushed Turkish cigarette of an expensive brand, but there was nothing to reveal the slightest clue to ownership. No other clothing was in sight, except a pair of green Morocco bedroom slippers, lying on the floor.

The second cupboard contained towels and a bathmat—luxurious ones. The third showed a row of glass shelves, on which were shaving materials, a few bottles, two ivory-backed brushes, a comb, and some pots and jars. Christopher sniffed at the bottles, and as he held the last one to his nostrils frowned in a puzzled manner.

"Spirit-gum—or smells like it. What's that for?"

"Don't waste time. Come on," cried Rank impatiently opening a door on the far side. "What-ho, a kitchen. Not used, apparently. No food in the larder...."

Christopher lingered behind, staring slowly over the sybaritic appointments of the bath. From a sunken recess he picked up a round cake of soap. Moist! That seemed odd, for the shaving-soap he had just inspected was bone dry and cracked. Someone must have washed in here—recently, too, for in this warm atmosphere water would soon evaporate. He pried into a painted receptacle in the corner and fished up a soiled towel. It also was damp—and it was covered with sooty-black marks. Yes, and the soap itself lay in a little pool of darkish sediment. For some obscure reason his skin began to prickle ominously.

Rank was calling to him. Crossing a small, dusty kitchen, he found his companions poking about in a long, dark, unsealed room which ran the length of the eaves.

"Found anything?" he inquired apprehensively.

"Only this big wooden crate. Can you make anything of it?"

It was a packing-case, empty, with not a single finger-print in the thick coating of grime on the boards. On the floor beside it lay a heap of straw, newspapers and rags, thrown out in careless confusion. To judge by appearances, the crate had not been touched for months, even years. By the flare of a match Coppinger was turning the rubbish over. He straightened up with a disgusted expression.

"That's all, I take it. Nothing we've overlooked? Well, I've enjoyed the run, but as far as finding this uncle of yours is concerned, we might as well have stayed in Oxford."

Christopher directed their attention to the soap, but not one of the three could see anything peculiar about it. Some individual from below had had occasion to come up here, got his hands black from the dirt—there was plenty of that—and washed them. If the stains on the towel had been red—but, no, they were unmistakably dark.

"Anyhow, you can see there's no possible hiding-place for a body to be put into," declared Coppinger. "Not a nook or cranny anywhere.

We'll run round those walls again, but I don't think we'll find an inch of concealed space."

He was right. They had seen all there was to see, except the hole in the floor, which did not interest them though Bilfilian pulled back the Persian rug and peered through the small orifice for a few fascinated moments. Christopher drew out one of the volumes from the square bookcase and glanced at the title—*Casanova*. It was one of a complete, handsomely-bound set—but what was this? A translation into German?

He stared hard, his thoughts straying back to the Teutonic professor, Emil Karl Klauber. Then he realised how absurd it was to suppose for one moment that these extravagant rooms could belong to a man resident as far away as Prague. He evidently had got Klauber on the brain. Glancing quickly through the volume and several of its fellows, he saw that in none of them was any name inscribed. Many passages had been underscored with red ink, but nothing whatever furnished the least idea as to the owner's identity. If it was Jethro who came here to indulge peculiar tastes, he had successfully covered up all revealing traces of his known personality. Indeed, it came over Christopher overwhelmingly that whoever this unknown person was, he could not be Jethro at all, nor even an Englishman.

Coppinger, prying into the other books behind the curtain, echoed these depressing reflections.

"Can't be our man," he murmured in a decided tone. "Every word's in Latin or German—mainly German. Classics and modern, all of a fairly putrid sort, to judge by the illustrations. Decadence, sadism . . . What a mind this chap must have! Some of these had book-plates, but they've been torn out. . . . No, Bilfilian," he concluded, dropping the hangings and dusting his hands. "You were boiled, old son, that's plain. You fancied you saw Jethro, but my sole wonder is you didn't think you saw the devil with horns."

Bilfilian looking injured, withdrew his eye from the hole.

"I couldn't have been mistaken. I still say it was Jethro I saw," he bleated obstinately. "I don't insist he owns this place, but—"

"Oh, we're dished," broke in Rank bitterly. "Let's pass it up and get away from here. The stink is making me sick. Still, I might have been right. You'll have to admit it was a spiffing idea." His strained eyes sought Christopher's. "Where do you suppose the poor old blighter's got to?" he asked despondently. "I wonder if we'll ever know the answer. . . ."

Christopher made no reply. He arranged the folds of material back in place to hide the bathroom door, and switching off the lights followed his friends out to the landing. As they arrived at Madame Hoche's door, he offered a half-hearted suggestion. Since Bilfilian's belief remained unshaken, why not try to worm out of the concierge a description of the top floor tenant? It was hardly probable that such inquiries would put them on Rostetter's trail, but it might help in the other directions if they could discover a secret, undesirable side to Jethro's life.

"Right," agreed Rank gloomily. "And hold on to the key, in case we want to use it again—though I don't imagine we shall."

In the garlic-smelling loge the concierge was dozing in his chair. Struggling up he shook a stubborn head and denied the existence of a tenant above the Hoche establishment. Who said there was one? The rooms up there belonged to Madame herself.

Christopher dug up a last hundred-franc note, which produced an instant alteration of tone. Well, yes, the attic they mentioned belonged to a German gentleman, who took it over some years ago and had it done up to suit his fancy.

"But he's very seldom here. Sometimes months go by and I don't see him. At the most he never stays more than a few days at a time, and once he's inside he sticks there, not even going out for meals. I should call him very eccentric. He put a lock of his own on the door, and I've no key to it. In the whole eight years I've not set foot inside the place, so I can't tell you what it's like; but if you're thinking of wanting the apartment, it's a waste of time to inquire. The doctor won't give it up."

"Doctor? What name does he go by?"

The concierge hesitated. "Schneider—Dr. Schneider. Yes, he's German, not the slightest doubt of it. Speaks French, but with a strong accent. Not that I've exchanged a dozen words with him, all told. He has no visitors and no letters."

"What does he look like? Young, old?"

"Middle-aged—maybe more. It's hard to say, but he has a grey beard, trimmed to a point, and wears thick glasses, like so many Germans. His clothes are on the shabby side. Very out of date, though I don't see how he can be poor, for all that."

It sounded suspiciously like Klauber. Christopher, allowing Rank to carry on with the questions, fell into deep cogitation. Spirit-gum—if it was spirit-gum—might be used for attaching a false beard. The man Bilfilian had seen was clean-shaven, otherwise he could never have been mistaken for Jethro. And then those shaving-materials.... A man with a genuine beard would hardly require them, but a hermit emerging from retirement might not care to exhibit himself in public with a three days' growth of hair on his chin, which in any case, would render it difficult to resume the disguising adornment.... Was it Schneider who had washed his hands in the bath during the past twenty to thirty hours? At this moment it was being said that the doctor had not appeared for fully six weeks, but the concierge might be lying about that.

The soap, moist, dingy round the edges ... marks on the towel, blacker than ordinary dust, more like—well, just possibly they could be accounted for by the thicker grime seen in the room under the eaves. On the crate, for instance ... and yet the objects in question showed no sign of having been disturbed.

The crate! In a flash of recollection Christopher saw before him another crate, very similar to this one. It had stood in the hall of the Bedford Square flat, waiting to be unpacked. A purely childish association of ideas. One case of this sort was extremely like another. All the same it suggested something he had not thought of before. There was an art-dealer's address plainly stencilled on the London one. Might there not be some distinguishing inscription on the crate upstairs, a bit of lettering they had overlooked? A dealer could turn up his accounts and tell to what customer a particular order had been delivered, even years ago. Without doubt in this instance it was the horrible African heads....

Christopher started to speak of this, but stopped, arrested by a question on the concierge's part. Why did the gentlemen want to find out all this about Dr. Schneider? Was it the rooms which took their eye, or the owner himself who interested them?

"Why do you ask?" parried Rank suspiciously.

"Because, monsieur, another Englishman was putting the same sort of questions about Dr. Schneider, only a fortnight ago. He was evidently anxious to make sure I'd kept nothing back, for he came again last week to go over the same ground."

"Tommy!" whispered Rank, his eyes blazing. "He has been here! Tell me," he fired eagerly, "was he about my height, slender, with black hair, eyes something like mine?"

The man shook his head positively. "Nothing at all like you, monsieur. He was a very heavy, big person, dark, slow-moving, and slow-speaking. I believe he is someone known to Madame Hoche, for he came here from her place, early in the morning—that is, the first time. On the second occasion it was soon after midnight. Who he was, I can't tell you."

Christopher's eyes narrowed and again he experienced that strange prickling of the skin. He wavered no longer, but muttering a word or two in Coppinger's ear slipped out and ran swiftly across the cobbled court to the building at the rear.

Afterwards it seemed to him that some invisible force had drawn him irresistibly back to the rooms which promised no clue to the owner's identity. Certainly he had small hope of obtaining any overlooked information, though he did have a burning desire to search, on his own, for possible laundry-marks, a book-seller's name, to examine inch by inch the packing-case, and if necessary, steal some toilet article which might be studied for finger-prints. At any rate, he must not let this chance slip away from him. Another time might be too late.

He bounded up the four flights of stairs, and out of breath inserted his key into the door. He pushed straight through the heavy curtains, and then, even as he fumbled for the switch, stiffened all over. Directly opposite, where ten minutes ago he himself had arranged the folds of thick material, he saw a thread of brilliant light outlining the whole bathroom door!

The key was in his possession—yet that someone had got in during the brief interval of their absence was apparent, not merely from the light and the pushed-back curtains, but from the faint sounds which reached his ears. Water was plashing into the bath. There was a noise of something being dragged across the marble floor.

He took in a tight grip the Colt automatic which was in his coat pocket, and with the bright gleam for a beacon stole cautiously forward.

He had gone but three paces when a startling thing occurred. As though by magic, the sliding door ran back to reveal a dazzling rectangle, livid green, enclosed in a frame of darkness. Against it was silhouetted the kneeling figure of a man, coatless, with shirt-sleeves rolled high—a man whose face could not be seen, but whose movements betrayed the fact that some task was being performed with rapid, busy absorption. Suddenly a bared arm shot out to hurl a mass of clothing on to the carpet. Trousers with braces attached, a waistcoat and shoes fell in a heap, to be swiftly followed by socks, shirt, undergarments.

Christopher's hair rose as he grasped with sickened understanding the nature of the toiler's occupation. This man, entirely unaware that he was watched, was engaged in stripping a helpless victim to the skin—and that victim was Rostetter. Those were his clothes.

For a second he could not move. With staring eyes he saw the stooped figure turn sideways to haul a white, inert body across in front of him, then thrust the head of it, with the short, black hair in full view, over the rim of the sunken bath. At the same moment he caught the flash of a lifted razor, and guessed the horrid intention behind it.

He cried out hoarsely, took a flying leap, and landed on the butcher just as the severed head rolled free to tumble, splashing, into the green water. For a single instant he beheld a bearded, unrecognised face on a level with him, and dodged as the razor, dripping with blood, made a sweep for his eyes. Almost simultaneously his assailant struck an upward blow with the other fist, and a sharp but not loud report coincided with the extinction of the light.

Particles of glass showered down upon him. In pitch darkness he closed with a being of demoniac strength.

CHAPTER XXXV

Crash!

Christopher slid on the wetness of the marble to plunge headlong into the bath, but not before the razor had gashed his scalp from temple to ear. With the stench of blood in his nostrils he floundered in cold water, while against his side sopped and bobbed the thing that was a head.

He found his footing, leaped to the floor-level, and with murder in his heart struck out wildly at empty blackness. He was alone.

Obviously the assassin was lurking somewhere in the gloom of the curtained room, with implacable determination to end the life of the intruder on his labours. He had no choice but to slay and dismember another body—two to destroy instead of one. He could have no idea that so short a time before these rooms had been visited, or else he would not have dared embark so soon on his undertaking. That meant he would not hesitate now.

The trickle of blood filling Christopher's eyes made it hard to think clearly. Not once did it occur to him to fire a random shot on the chance of summoning aid. Light was what he wanted. He located the switch, turned it, but as he had expected nothing happened. Then he remembered the kitchen and blundering over the decapitated corpse fumbled blindly at the other door, which refused to open. With the feeling that the unseen enemy was creeping cat-like upon him he groped his way back to the main room and stationed himself to listen for the first sound. In his hand he held the revolver, cocked in readiness, but as the thing was wet he felt no certainty of its functioning.

Minutes of dead silence ensued. The suspense became insupportable. He decided to venture forward, in hope of reaching the light switch opposite, but as he took his fourth muffled step the noise he had waited for came, surprisingly enough from the bathroom behind—a metallic tinkle on the marble floor. Instantly he wheeled to fire, and as he did so a violent blow hurled the weapon from his grasp.

Too late he realised the trick. A swish, and his knuckles were slashed to the bone. He lunged forward, only to receive another cut along chin and nose. Mad with rage, he cast himself bodily towards the region whence the attack had come, and felt the curtains swathed round him. Half-suffocated, he fought tigerishly, ripped the material from its rings, and with his legs still entangled aimed flail-like blows in all directions. Twice he hit the wall, once the corner of the mantelpiece, with agonising result to his damaged knuckles; but the fourth punch landed on what he took to be the point of a jaw. He followed it up, and this time succeeded in locking his arms round a panting, twisting body.

Together now they rocked and swayed, stumbling over cushions, colliding with the pedestals, and knocking the sculptured heads to the floor. It seemed incredible that in a space so empty, countless obstacles should crop up, and as it was impossible to see anything, there was no avoiding either these or the razor, which at every fresh turn swooped to inflict another wound. Once they encountered the couch, tripped and rolled upon it. For a second or two Christopher lay pinioned under the other's body, while fingers tore at his collar, and in the night above him he sensed the hovering steel, but by a fierce upheaval he threw off the encumbrance, planted a savage uppercut, and with triumph heard his adversary gasp. The next moment, however, the battle continued, and though he made repeated attempts to wrest the weapon from the elusive hand, luck was not with him.

Events became blurred. Although Christopher scarcely felt the injuries he received, the loss of blood must have been considerable, for he realised his strength was diminishing. If this continued, he was done for. In grim desperation he clung to a hazy idea of driving his opponent back in a straight line till they reached some obstruction, in which case he thought he might succeed either in getting possession of the razor or in fastening a strangle-hold on the throat which thus far had kept beyond his clutches. He pushed and shoved, not yielding an inch. Was he gaining ground? For all he knew, they were moving in circles. Four times his head had struck hard marble, but where the pedestal was he could not say. The last contact had left him dizzy. . . .

The curtains at last! Feeling them against his finger-tips, he summoned all his remaining force and drove one knee into the opposing stomach. The man fell back, but the arms which held him dragged him along, too, not against solidity, but into space and cool air. What was this? Through parted curtains he dimly perceived an opening, hitherto unsuspected—yes, it was a window, thrown wide, upon a fire escape. In the lesser gloom of outdoors details began to emerge, but before he could take them in a terrific kick sent him reeling.

He staggered upright to see, through a mist of blood, the bearded one leap upon the sill and reach the iron frame-work. Inhuman eyes blazed as he essayed to follow, and the razor cut a pale arc in the direction of his eyes. Then he sprang.

Under his heavy onslaught the other's spine bent back in a bow. His hands closed in a steel grip on the wind-pipe, he shut his eyes tightly to escape the tearing nails which made for them, and pressed, pressed, with consciousness ebbing, and but one idea in his clouded brain—to hold on, no matter what happened, till the creature responsible for that headless body in there was exterminated.

From afar off he heard a warning crack, but it meant nothing to him. Then with lightning swiftness the catastrophe occurred which flung him face downward, the upper half of him suspended over vacancy, while the figure he had leant upon slithered free to hurtle the full four stories to the ground below. A distant thud—then silence. Under a broken, rusted iron rod which had formed the insecure railing of the platform, he lay, straining his eyes stupidly into the black chasm. He had no desire to move.

Windows were flung up, footsteps clattered across the cobbles, voices cried out in staccato French. A lighted match made a little glow above something dark and huddled.

Christopher made an effort, and hauled himself back stiffly into the room, where he stood, clinging on the curtains to steady himself. He could not think why the hair he wiped back from his eyes should be sticky, dripping. All his clothing, too, was soaked. Perhaps it was sweat.

"I've killed him," he repeated to himself in a dull, uncomprehending way. "I've killed the man who killed Rostetter . . . but I wonder who it was?"

Frantic pounding on a door brought him slowly to himself. He became aware that voices were shouting his name. Of course, it was those English chaps. Funny, he'd forgotten about them. He groped his way to the door, turned the knob. A panting trio burst in, lights went up, and a horrified clamour broke forth at sight of him.

"Loughton! Good God, man, why you're hacked to ribbons! You're dripping blood like a sieve. Your face, your head—here, was it you who chucked that fellow out?"

Christopher did not register the words any more than he realised his own lamentable condition.

"I caught him at it," he explained dully. "He had the best of it for a time. The railing broke, and he fell."

"I should jolly well say he did. Neck's broken, eyes half out of his head, bits of beard sticking to his chin—took some recognising, but all the same—"

"Is he the German?"

Rank's mouth fell open. "German—my hat! You did him in, and you don't know it's Jethro? What sort of a scrap was this? But hold on—you say you caught him at it. Caught him at what?"

Christopher wet his lips. His gaze wandered painfully away.

"Cutting up the body. Rostetter's. In the bath. You'll see."

With faces suddenly ghastly, the three men fell across to the opposite door, but Christopher did not come with them. He sank heavily upon the sumptuous sofa, conscious only of the supreme misery of defeat. Even in this he had failed. Not entirely, for Dinah was safe, but the man she loved had been wantonly sacrificed. Perhaps if he had got here a little sooner . . .

Astonished cries roused him.

"What the blazes! This poor devil's not my uncle. Here, look for yourself."

Not . . . ? Christopher reached the kneeling group, and stared incredulously into the dead features which dripped with reddened water. Black hair, but not his friend's—a face never seen till now. He must be dreaming.

"Clothes," he muttered, waving a vague hand towards the wide-strewn garments. "Maybe . . . identification . . ."

Coppinger had seized on the waistcoat, and from the inner pocket dragged a wallet and a business-card.

"Jolivet? Alphonse Jolivet? Who the hell's he?"

"Hôtel manager. He was missing too."

"What hotel? What—how does he come into it?"

However, Christopher was incapable of dealing with the machine fire of questions. His spurt of hope had already perished as he realised that Rostetter must have met some similar fate. Seeing the look on his face Coppinger forced the neck of a brandy flask between his lips. The stimulant revived him a little, so that the chief point of the mystery found some answering response in the brain.

"How did he get in here? Through a window. Look. I'll show you. Probably open all the time, only we didn't know. He must have been on the roof the whole time. Yes, because there's a sort of ladder . . . then the marks on the towel. Soot from the tiles. . . ."

"Roof? God, what fools we were! Quick, Coppinger, before the police barge in on us! Throw some water over Fil. He's fainted, but no matter. No, you ass, you leave this to us! You've had your share."

The last was thrown at Christopher, who, hard on their heels, was staggering again on to the fire escape. He was half-way up the perpendicular iron ladder which led to the roof-top when the voices of his two companions reached him. They had found an old, disused tank, hidden from view by chimneys.

"Big enough to . . . to . . . strike a match, will you? There's something inside . . . oh! I knew it!" Rank's excitement waned to a sickened note of despair. "He's here all right. We've found him."

Christopher swayed against the rusted rungs.

"Dead?" he muttered.

There was no reply.

The scene swarmed with Frenchmen, shrugging, gesticulating. One, a doctor apparently, was prodding a motionless form laid out on the couch and emitting disparaging sounds. Christopher came to, struggled up, but Coppinger, who was bathing his head, pushed him firmly back. He must lie still. The ambulance would soon be here.

"Blast the ambulance! I want to know about *him*. Is he—?"

"Alive? Yes—but I'm afraid he won't last the journey. See those ropes? He was bound—and gagged with a towel. Skull's fractured. If he'd lain on top, instead of the other—but we'll not discuss that. Anyhow, it's you who saved the evidence. By morning the job would have been finished—but I dare say you know that, by the look of that map of yours. You'll want about a hundred stitches."

Beyond the first sentences Christopher heard nothing. The strange, teeming room whirled before him, and he fainted again.

CHAPTER XXXVI

"Has he the ghost of a chance?"

Christopher, a mass of gauze bandages, fired the question at the inspector who had come to secure his statement. While the horrified public, with storm-centres at Oxford and Paris, clamoured for details, this, to him, seemed the only point worth bothering about. He was curiously indifferent to the whys and wherefores which had led up to the crashing denouement. The paralysing discovery of the revered scholar's hidden personality left him cold, but the inspector's dubious headshake sent his temperature soaring.

To his intense annoyance he had been taken home, where the combined ministrations of his mother, a nurse, and solicitous friends drove him almost mad. Only when he saw that escape could be achieved by submission for a brief period did he cease to rebel, and long before he was judged fit to walk about he was haunting the nursing home where his friend dangled precariously between this world and the next. Dinah he had not seen, nor had he any expectation of encountering her. She was released—that was enough. With all his thoughts centred on Rostetter's fight for life, he thrust his own past out of sight, put the lid on the box, and sat on it.

Why Rostetter had not perished outright as his less fortunate companion had done seemed at first an insoluble mystery, but soon a possible explanation was offered. Medical opinion declared that both victims had been given enormous injections of morphia, which in one case had killed, in the other produced merely deep coma. Jolivet, it was discovered, suffered from a valvular heart weakness; the journalist's heart was in perfect working order—but that was not all. The morphia used, found in a secret hoard of drugs under the flooring of the wrecked room, showed on analysis a dilution to less than half-strength.

"*Et voilà, monsieur!*" was the inspector's significant comment. "A fact certainly unsuspected by the murderer, and one for which we have this Madame Hoche to thank."

"I see you've arrested her and the door-keeper. Does that mean it was those two who supplied Jethro with drugs?"

"And a vast number of other people as well, monsieur. Ah, yes, we are pleased over that part of it. It begins to look as though at last we had got our hands on the ring-leaders of the movement. But as for your friend, he was lucky in more ways than one. He lay underneath, you see, and it was a case of first come, first served."

The speaker shrugged grimly, and while Christopher sickened at the thought of what might have happened, went on to mention another piece of information. Together with the bottles of cocaine, morphia, hypodermic syringes and so on, they had dug up a document, very difficult to decipher, because it was partly illegible, and entirely in German. When it could be translated, it might supply answers to some of the questions now being propounded. It seemed to be a sort of random diary, kept at intervals over a period of years.

Christopher, listening with no great interest, learned that the woman, Hoche, denied all knowledge of the supposed doctor and his habits, beyond the fact that on his occasional sojourns he shut himself up for days at a time. She did, however, admit giving him food, which twice daily she herself carried up on a tray and placed just inside the door left ajar to receive it. One of these times must have coincided with Bilfilian's tour of exploration. It seemed certain that Jethro never suspected the rooms were entered in his absence. The windows were provided with barred shutters, the door with a special lock. Hoche had obtained her duplicate key by bribing the lock-maker when the alterations were made.

"So you see, monsieur, she not only exacted heavy payment from the tenant himself for the privilege of the private view into her domain, but she also raked in additional sums in the intervals of non-occupation. One shrewdly guesses, too, that she made a good thing out of blackmail, though that is not proved. She knew that this doctor, whatever his real position in the world, would not dare bring action against her. He had but one redress: vacate the premises; and this she had ample reason to know he would not do, simply because, rather than be evicted, he had made himself landlord of the entire premises."

"Landlord!" exclaimed Christopher, roused at last. "How did you get hold of that fact?"

"From the lawyer who handled the transaction, six years ago, in the name of Schneider. Yes, to prevent the buildings being torn down and rebuilt, our friend bought the freehold at an exorbitant figure, since which event Hoche, who probably got a fat commission on the purchase, had lived rent free. You may well stare, monsieur. We are viewing the conduct of a lunatic, who let himself be sucked dry rather than sacrifice pleasures which men like ourselves would not consider pleasures at all. What were they? Women, drink, gaiety, anything a normal being can understand? No, just solitude, with books, drugs, and a hole through which to look on at obscene orgies in which he had no desire to participate. Bah!"

A vast bourgeois contempt went into the expletive.

"His own money, I suppose, had vanished?" asked Christopher.

"Evaporated. A few hundred pounds in the bank, secured from rush sales of shares, is all we have been able to find. No doubt we shall come upon a whole history of wild efforts to recoup which hastened insolvency, but on the surface all his affairs were in order. No debt, no sign of retrenchment, nothing whatever to show the rottenness underneath. He could go on without any embarrassing questions being asked till his daughter's fortune passed into his possession, and but for some accidental slip would have continued to enjoy complete safety from interference. What that one slip was, we have yet to discover. If your friend dies, the truth may die with him."

Immediately after this conversation, a woman employed by Hoche was arrested, and the shabby suit-case taken from her, opened and examined. In it were some oddly-assorted garments—an ancient English greatcoat, an Austrian felt hat, on the inner band of which were the initials E.K.K., and a pair of new, black boots of French manufacture. The prisoner, swearing her ignorance of these articles, explained that just before the entry of the police into the Hoche establishment she was given the bag by Madame and bidden to dispose of it secretly. Hoche, for her part, declared that on October first she had received from Dr. Schneider a *petit bleu* containing a claim ticket and instructions to collect a suit-case from the Gare de l'Est and keep it hidden till the writer called for it.

Telegrams flew between Paris and Prague. A horrified professor of bio-chemistry furnished conclusive proof that he had not been in Paris since September 14th, while the night of the 30th he had spent in Cologne, at the Belgishcherhof. The hat, however, was his. It was an old one he had left behind after a short visit to Mr. Basil Jethro, whom he had held in high esteem since their student days in Berlin, and whose house in Oxford he had gone to see during a short stay in England. That there had been an undesirable side to his colleague's character shocked him profoundly. He could scarcely believe such a thing possible. As for the Hôtel Stanislas, he had never heard of it.

Christopher found this last statement hard to believe. That Jethro and Schneider were one was established beyond any doubt, but that Jethro had possessed no accomplice in the first instance was striking at the very root of his own preconceptions. For him, therefore, the mystery deepened instead of clearing, nor did the Jethro diary, issued in small doses to an amazed public, shed light on the actual commission of the original crime. It did, however, make plain a fact hitherto undreamed of by startled readers, the mere setting down of which at all must be attributed to that strange psychological urge, half vanity, half craving for expression, which so often impels the criminal to some form of self-revelation; but of that we shall speak presently.

One more provocative item marked these days of agonising suspense. The concierge in the Rue de la Tour d'Auvergne, on being shown various photographs, picked out Bannister Mowbray's as that of the Englishman who had cross-examined him about Schneider. Hoche, under pressure, admitted that Mowbray, some weeks before, had visited the rooms overhead with a party of friends, also that he returned unaccompanied the following week, and on the pretext of having left a cigarette-case behind went again to the top floor. More than this she refused to say, and though much was hoped from her impending trial, it was still uncertain as to what, if any, connection had existed between her nefarious schemes and the suicide which had given rise to such conflicting theories.

And then, with the betting on Rostetter's recovery firmly fixed at two to one against, the moment came when Christopher and Rank were allowed access to the scene of the valiant struggle. Eyelids they had never thought to see open again fluttered uncertainly, disclosing the bland, impudent blue orbs of the old unregenerate Tommy.

"Rank, you confounded whelp!" The murmur was distressingly weak. "What about that seven quid?"

"Oh, curse and blast you, you damned old miser!"

The patient frowned surprisedly at the drops trickling off the end of the snub nose, then shifting his gaze, perceived his other visitor.

"Loughton?" Realisation was creeping back, a tide filling the drained spaces. He tried to rise. "Here, tell me—is it true, is she all right?"

"Every single thing's all right—thanks to you."

"To me?" Tommy writhed as though stung. "Me, the world's prize booby? Wait, wait till you hear about it. Wait till you know how I walked like a sheep into a pen, like a—"

"I know this much," retorted Christopher huskily, "you'll have to hide if you don't want a medal pinned on you. Now get that through that thick skull of yours."

On the way back to the somewhat dreary lodgings he had chosen to occupy since his emergence from captivity, Christopher whistled a tune, but on waking to what tune it was became abruptly silent. He heard again his friend's eager question about Dinah, and at the same time thought of the note now reposing in his waistcoat pocket, the concluding portion of which ran thus:

"I asked you to find him. I didn't know that by doing it you'd get almost killed yourself. Only if you hadn't—but it will only bore you if I try to say all I'm feeling. Thank you, Chris."

What further assurance was needed to show him how the land lay? Those two, the only human beings he cared anything about, were booked for a happy journey together. Well, good luck to them. He would perish before he showed himself a dog-in-the-manger . . . but he whistled no more.

Some days after this, on entering the nursing home, he ran bolt into a statuesque but shattered young Apollo just coming away, and, turning to take a second look, recognised Ronald Cleeves.

Now what was he doing here?

CHAPTER XXXVII

"You saw Cleeves?"

Tommy, a pipe between his lips, laid aside the pair of brass knuckle-dusters he was examining, frowned deeply and decided to take Christopher into his confidence.

"Only you mustn't let it go farther. That poor blighter came because I sent for him. I bluffed out of him something he's tried frantically to keep dark—and I can't say I'm particularly proud of my achievement. Anyhow, this is it."

It seemed that shortly before the fatal dinner Mowbray piloted Cleeves and two other Englishmen to the rooms above the Hoche resort. Having been there before, he had often speculated about the mysterious owner's identity, and now, glancing through the set of *Casanova* he came upon a marginal note in handwriting which, though unfamiliar, struck him as unmistakably English. He showed it to Cleeves, and later questioned the concierge with the meagre results already known. Here the matter rested till, in Dorinda's apartment, he made a startling discovery—Basil Jethro's signature, in books presented to Lady Agatha. The writing appeared to be the same as the specimen which had recently roused his curiosity. He slipped one of the volumes in his pocket, meaning to compare the inscription with the supposed Schneider's hand. When the murder occurred and placed him in a precarious position, he wormed out of Benedetto certain suggestive facts regarding latch-keys and telephone calls, began, like Tommy, to draw tentative conclusions, and to look about for a motive. Following vague information obtained from

Cleeves, he put through a trunk-call to London, and was eagerly awaiting a report of Lady Agatha's will when Tommy interrupted his tête-à-tête.

"I see now," said Tommy, "precisely why Mowbray was so furious about my handing the drug over to the police. It was not merely the prospect of jail. It was the knowledge that a six months' incarceration would prevent his tracking Jethro down while the trail was warm. Still, thanks to the law's tactics of allowing him rope, he managed that same evening to revisit the Montmartre premises, and to find the famous journal, from which he tore out the final pages—undoubtedly those which dealt with the first and unsuccessful attempt on Dorinda's life. If you look at the original manuscript, you'll see that the latest entry breaks off just after the date September fifth—and that date immediately follows the author's first stay, in disguise, at the Hôtel Stanislas. In short, the pages Mowbray filched represented trump cards. He intended to use them, in fact, did use them—but said nothing to Cleeves, who was puzzled that his friend, after taking so much trouble, should suddenly announce his unwillingness to pursue the matter.

"It's significant that on learning of Mowbray's death by drowning, Cleeves should instantly have tumbled to the true facts. It shows, I think, that in spite of his worship he had a pretty strong line on the fellow's character. He's hysterical, and no doubt was overwhelmed by shock, but if he put his head in the gas-oven it was chiefly because he knew that once the correct interpretation was put on Mowbray's end no one would believe his own part in the plot had been an innocent one."

"But you think it was innocent?"

"I do, though it's evident his idea of this is just what mine was before I allowed dust to be thrown in my eyes. He pictured the arranged meeting, on a bridge, late at night; Mowbray producing his damning proofs, and Jethro, prepared, rounding on him like a flash with these delightful playthings."

Tommy picked up the knuckle-dusters and fondled them lovingly.

"Found on our philosopher," he explained. "And I, for one, take off my hat to his skill in using them, as well as the calm dignity with which he squashed my theories at the very moment when the alien-slip which would have proved them right reposed in my note-case. I can't get over the shame of it. The fact is, Strauss's wiring me about the real Klauber hadn't left me a leg to stand on. This partly authentic story coming on top of it—"

"How do you mean it was partly authentic?"

"Why, that old Renouff does translations of philosophical works, is afflicted with arthritis and lives in Montmartre. No, I never really twigged anything wrong till, in the gloom of that top-landing, something like a ton of bricks crashed down on my skull. The truth flared up in a rush of sky-rockets, one-eighth of a second too late."

"And so you intend to keep Cleeve's admission secret?" asked Christopher after a pause.

"Why broadcast what can do no one good and Cleeves a vast deal of harm? After all I took an unfair advantage of him by letting him think I knew more than I did. If he hadn't been terrified by those statements of Hoche and the concierge he'd have seen I was four-flushing."

Christopher, having mused over this new instance of the journalist's sporting spirit, brought up a point which still mystified him. It was clear why Jethro had deemed it necessary to exterminate Jolivet, who, if questioned by the police, would certainly have let fall some damaging item; but how had he got the manager into his power?

"My fault, that," answered Tommy sorrowfully. "It is fairly plain what happened. To make my fiction more acceptable, I'd told Jolivet I might require him to identify Klauber, promising him remuneration. In gassing to Jethro the poor chap must have mentioned this, little guessing he was providing the tip by means of which he would be enticed to his doom. Once I was disposed of, all Jethro had to do was to ring up Jolivet from a call-box, ask him to come immediately to an address where Klauber was being held, then go back to lie in wait for him. He may have imitated my voice; he may have pretended to be speaking for me. It didn't greatly matter which, the prospect of easy money being a good enough bait."

"I suppose any other method of killing wouldn't have served."

"No, because it would have been fatal to leave traces of either of us. His plan was to pack the dismembered bodies in the empty crate, ship the crate off to the south and collect it in person. At Cap Ferrat he had his own car, motor-boat and landing-stage. Given a dark night, he could have chugged out to sea and heaved the thing overboard. The butchering, however, was a lengthy job, which is why he had to leave it till the second night. There was my car to get rid of, disinfectant to buy, and no shops open till morning. That he parked us on the roof indicates a dim suspicion of the double game Hoche was playing. He wasn't taking undue chances."

"It strikes me he took great chances all along the line, though at that stage I dare say he was forced to do it."

"Were they so great? Except at the single moment when the attacks were made, what snag did he expect to encounter? He hadn't a notion you and I had been putting our heads together. There was, to be sure, a possibility of my disappearance being connected with Jolivet's, but if nothing could be proved he was safe. The risk of entering the building with me was negligible, since minus the beard he was a stranger, like myself. Neither of us was likely to attract attention in a large place like that, where chance comers pass unchallenged except after midnight. Actually we didn't meet the concierge, and I don't suppose Jolivet did. Even on the second evening, although Jethro took the precaution of wearing his familiar disguise, he seems to have got in unobserved."

"He had a strong predilection for Germans. Why was that, and why, having acted the part of Dr. Schneider for eight years, didn't he use the same role for the alibi?"

"My argument is this: since certain physical attributes were unalterable, his best device for disguise was a change of nationality. As it was impossible to get by as a Frenchman, he chose a German, that imitation being easy to him. You see, having spent his childhood in the Berlin schools, he spoke French, as a rule, with a German accent. That accounts for the Schneider personality, and for the choice of a German in the second instance. As for his hitting on a living model to copy, I think I can supply the answer to that, too. He had to pass muster in the same hotel as his normal self, therefore, was obliged to adopt a handwriting utterly dissimilar to his own. Now, if you've ever tried, you'll know how hard it is to invent a convincing handwriting. Your own characteristics will crop out; but any one with average ability can copy a hand which already exists. When old Klauber paid him a visit at the villa, he left behind a discarded hat which fitted. Probably that incident gave the plotter his cue. Why not let the hat form the nucleus of a new disguise? The professor's handwriting and mannerisms could be studied and reproduced. By using an old overcoat already in his possession, padding himself out with cardigans and mufflers, and keeping to his Schneider beard and spectacles he could step into a ready-made personality suitable for all purposes. All he had to buy was a pair of continental boots—I suspect because no footwear of his own was sufficiently unelegant."

"He could have adopted a non-existent name."

"Which would have necessitated the invention of a signature, and the signature was all-important as well as hardest to originate. No, I should say he chose the way easiest to the amateur. The imposture would never be discovered, either, for Klauber would not be in Paris at the same time as himself and when there meant to put up in a different locality. In these days passports don't figure, except at the frontiers, so that part presented no difficulty."

"If he tried to murder Dorinda early in September, then he must have known she would be in town at that time."

"He did know, from Helen, who travelled up with her, and who at his urgent request was going to stay with the girl. He planned that deliberately, in order to gain access to the apartment, for Dorinda alone would have viewed his overtures with distrust. Having failed to bring off his crime, he postponed further operations till later in the month, the second time elaborating his preparations by posting letters to Klauber from Marseilles as he passed through. What his scheme was then we shall never know. Certainly it went by the board when at Sophie Waldheim's he stumbled on the gorgeous opportunity offered by the dope-party, which allowed him to distribute potential guilt amongst a dozen defenceless persons. He set to work at once. On Friday morning he deposited five hundred pounds to Dorinda's account. In the afternoon he took his degree at the Sorbonne, and from there went to collect the disguise conveniently left at the apartment. He then concocted his tale about the latch-key—his one stupidity, to my thinking—and hurried off to the railway cloakroom to convert himself into the professor."

"Why," asked Christopher curiously, "did you still suspect him after assuring yourself his alibi was good?"

Tommy puffed thoughtfully at his pipe.

"It sounds silly," he admitted, "but I believe it was a feeling I had about his handwriting. If you'll give me that coat of mine from the wardrobe, I'll show you what I mean."

From the inside pocket of the blood-smeared garment he fished out a crumpled memorandum, smoothed it out, and pointed first to the irregular letters, then to the margin and the heavily-inked e's and o's.

"Here," he said, "are four outstanding characteristics—scientific bent, intense egotism, extravagance, and—sensuality. Two I'd expected, the third did not astonish me, but the fourth? The man's personality struck me as peculiarly frigid, in spite of his full, puckered lips, which in another subject might have suggested plenty of animal nature. Magnetism he had, but it was almost inhuman in quality. You couldn't get near him. Aside from his well-known reputation for clean-living, I myself had noticed his instinctive shrinking from human contacts. I had seen him draw away with a sort of distaste when Helen, warmly impulsive, laid her hand on his arm, yet Helen was his friend. It didn't go at all with those muddy, clogged loops."

"Well?"

"I worked it out like this: if the man is sensual, then he not only keeps the fact well hidden, but the sensuality itself is of some odd, introverted variety. It must be so; but since experience teaches that no dominant instinct is entirely suppressed, I said to myself, whatever it is, it's got an outlet somewhere. By a natural sequence of thought I turned back to what I had shoved aside as worthless testimony—the story my nephew told me about Jethro's having been seen in dubious surroundings. Without much hope that it would lead to anything pertinent, I started a letter to Rank, then as you happened along I entrusted the inquiry to you and got back to the alibi end of things. Your coming in was the biggest piece of luck I've ever experienced. But for that I shouldn't be talking about it now."

"About the *majun*—had Jethro any first-hand knowledge of its effects or was he merely guessing?"

"He knew exactly what it would do. Mowbray's practices were an old story to him, as you'll see by the details regarding various drugs set down in this journal, though the man himself he'd never met. Before settling down to cocaine he'd tried most of the familiar narcotics, saving them exclusively for the occasional orgies when brain and nerves were driven to breaking-point, and never letting them interfere with his everyday life. They provided relaxation, removed the tight check-rein, and allowed his salacious imagination to run riot. You saw his books, the hole in the floor? Something of the sort I ran across in the case of a celebrated London surgeon. There are individuals like that, you know, who derive no pleasure from direct relations with men and women. Jethro was one of them."

"Purely vicarious vice, I suppose."

"Yes, with doses of cocaine regulated with methodical nicety to obtain the maximum of rapture with the minimum of bad results. After each bout he emerged revitalised for further intellectual feats, and became once more the machine of ice and steel. Nothing left to hint at past debauchery except that strange, dead-pallor of the skin."

Christopher, still studying the scrap of handwriting, suddenly thought of the newest sensation. The police had discovered that a certain enormous consignment of cocaine and heroin seized by the port authorities a few months back had been backed financially by Dr. Heinrich Schneider, a fact elicited from Hoche's Egyptian confrère. With so much to talk over he had temporarily forgotten it, but he mentioned it now, with the remark that Jethro's business judgment must have touched upon madness.

"No," said Tommy, "he was not mad—merely one-sided. A spendthrift, a reckless gambler perhaps, but this particular venture, if it had come off as many similar ones have done, would have quadrupled his stake and stabilised his position. It was the total loss of his last few thousands which threw him back on Dorinda's fortune. No, I think I've put my finger on the basic factors in his make-up—inordinate craving for luxury, and fastidious shrinking from mankind. That mighty brain of his was an adjunct, superimposed. The combination's simple enough, once you've grasped it. You doubt my statement? Then cast your eye over this letter from my Reuter friend, Strauss, who was a fellow-student of Jethro's at the Berlin University. It furnishes some illuminating sidelights. Freud would revel in it."

While Christopher perused the typed sheets handed to him Tommy kept up a running comment.

"Poor and resentful of his poverty—a spoiled arrogant youngster, taking all his parents or others could offer him as his kingly due; making no friends except those who could further his ambition, held for a bit by the vicious life of Berlin, but soon withdrawing, either from insufficient funds or reluctance to let anything hinder his advancement. The pure narcissus type, demanding all and giving nothing—centred in self, every impulse turned in, colossally concentrated on work, attracting, yet holding at arm's length. That was the Jethro known to Strauss. Now let's look along the years and see what happens.

"Grubbing, grinding, but no remarkable headway in his career. Why? Simply because he is no Spinoza, cheerful to toil in a garret. He has the tastes of a sybarite. Sordidness stunts and hampers him, the life of a poorly-paid schoolmaster gives him no chance for expansion—and whether or not you accept my theory, he didn't for a long period, expand. All at once, when he is engaged in tutoring an earl's son for Oxford, he meets a rich widow who becomes romantically infatuated with him and marries him out of hand. What then? Rapid unfoldment. Under the warming influence of wealth, the butterfly spreads its wings and takes its place in the sun."

"Dorinda told me her mother made him," said Christopher slowly. "Perhaps she was right."

"Intuitively, yes, though her reasoning may have been wide of the mark. Certainly she sensed the unhappy situation which rose between those two who to the outward eye were congenially mated, saw how her mother's love was thrown back from a stone wall of unresponsiveness, how bewilderment, hurt pride and anger led to unavailing reproaches. She could hardly have realized though, that Jethro's peculiar temperament unfitted him for marital ties, that concrete woman and particularly a demonstrative one revolted his sensibilities. Superabundance of money he wanted, but he was unable to pay the price exacted. Read the record of his reactions, and see how he was nagged and exasperated till in sheer desperation he created the Montmartre retreat in which to hide and indulge his warped cravings. By allowing the discordant elements within him to crystallise into a Jekyll and Hyde duality, he obtained release while safeguarding his reputation. He couldn't have done this successfully without his wife's money. It was what he had needed all along."

"Did she suspect?"

"He was never sure, but eventually the domestic scenes grew too distracting for him to cope with. Then it was that he hit upon the really Machiavellian ruse of making her a victim to morphia. You know, of course, that he himself supplied her with the stuff?"

"It's true, then? I couldn't believe it, after what Bramson told you."

"Making Bramson his unwitting ally was a stroke of genius. He knew that confiding his secret suspicions would absolve him from any hint of complicity. He also knew that, like all morphia addicts, his wife would lie categorically to defend the source of her supply. Having snatched at the drug in the first place as a beneficent remedy against physical pain, she was now enslaved to its use, relying on it utterly, ready to fight like a tigress rather than give it up. In short, the diabolical scheme worked. The unfortunate woman, at once weak-willed and stubborn, retired bit by bit into an unreal world and left her husband in peace.

"What broke that state of things I can't quite say. Probably all the time some deep-seated sense of injury lurked in the drug-disordered brain, and at intervals the victim woke up sufficiently to realize she was in the man's power and to get a dim inkling of the motive behind it. What a situation! Loving and hating him at once and at the same instant; depending on him, storing up jealous resentment and finally evolving her plan of revenge. What did he want of her? Money—nothing but money. Well, he should not have it. She decided to reverse the will drawn up in the first moments of her enchantment, reduce him to poverty again. Perhaps, too, she contemplated a separation. Anyhow, she telephoned Macadam, and Jethro overheard what she said."

"He didn't see the letter she hid away in the book?"

"Apparently not, but the indiscreet taunts flung at him told him her intention. The prospect appalled him. Quick action was demanded. He contrived to treble the quantity of morphia she was preparing to inject, went quietly out, and returned to find her dead by her own hand. No suspicion ever attached to him. It wouldn't now, but for this smug recountal of his triumph. Men of his type, forced to live with women they loathe, can be fiendishly cruel. He was. In murdering his wife and later on her daughter he not only felt no compunction, he considered he had performed as natural, inevitable an action as treading on a cockroach. In just as callous a way he would have crushed Dinah. If he did not kill her at the moment when she rose and left the apartment, it was because, recognising her semi-somnambulistic state, he saw what a perfect scapegoat she would make for his crime."

"You think he did see her go out?"

"Personally I'm sure he did. The inspector tells me he saw Jethro's face change for one paralysed second when at the reconstruction she exploded her bombshell about having passed him as she went out the door. That was before she'd explained what door she meant."

"And the inspector kept that to himself?" burst out Christopher angrily. "He would. If you ask me, every blasted official from the bottom to the top, was hypnotised by the power of a name."

Tommy shrugged. "I warned you, didn't I, how useless it would be to bring a charge unless we could prove our case up to the hilt? That name of his would have gone on shielding him, even though an understanding of Dinah's actions might have suggested what is now perfectly plain—in other words that however freakish her response to the drug may have been, she was merely fulfilling a series of logical desires."

Plain now—but both men fell silent over the thought of how easy it had been to put a different construction on the affair. Christopher, stirring awkwardly in his chair, asked if Dinah was all right now. Tommy shot a covert glance at the battle-scarred face before replying.

"Oh, absolutely. She's a plucky one and no mistake. Every day she brings me violets," he quoted dreamily. "Sits here, puts up with my petulant humours and treats me as though I were made of wax and might crumble. And speaking of wax—what price that dastardly trick they played on her, substituting the figure of the corpse? My God, Loughton, my blood boils at the—hello, I knew the nurse couldn't leave us alone for long. Well, what is it now?" he demanded querulously of the sister who tiptoed in, beaming archly.

"A young lady to see you," burbled the disturber of peace.

"Shall I let her in or would you rather this gentleman went away first?"

Christopher sprang up guiltily.

"I'll clear off," he mumbled. "See you tomorrow."

Noting the homeless-dog look in his eyes, Tommy stretched out a detaining hand.

"No," he said. "Wait in the lounge till she's gone, then come back and chew a chop with me. It's beastly feeding in solitude. You will? Right."

Christopher entered the lounge. As the door closed behind him a light step along the corridor made him clench his hands and set his teeth. He moved mechanically and stood staring down at the withered chrysanthemums in the garden below, his heart as dry and dead as the prospect he viewed.

CHAPTER XXXVIII

DINAH, very intent on putting fresh violets into a pickle-bottle, shook a stubborn head. In every line of her trim-clad figure was armed defence, while her heightened colour masked for a moment the shadows beneath her eyes.

"Not a bit of use," she declared in a low voice. "I applaud your missionary zeal, but I can't arrange my feelings to please you."

Tommy gazed at her thoughtfully.

"Mine," he sighed with resignation, "is the fate of all reformers. I hadn't much hope; and yet I've been flattering myself on my cleverness at diagnosing situations. Shall I tell you what I've been thinking about yours?"

"I see you're going to. I suppose I can bear it."

"It always strikes me," he began, frowning into a smoke-cloud, "that in matters of—well, unfaithfulness, the whole point is this: we can trust ourselves, but we can't trust the other person. Is that so, or isn't it?"

"And what if it is?"

"Nothing, except that it ought to make us more generous in our judgments. Just assume, for argument's sake, the positions in this case had been reversed—that in Christopher's absence, feeling down, even perhaps despising yourself a little, you had in a weak moment succumbed to a passing attraction—one which meant nothing, but which boosted you up in your own esteem. Wouldn't you have known to a dead certainty that it left your basic attitude towards Christopher unaltered?"

She met his eyes squarely, bit her lip, and turned a deeper red.

"Maybe," she admitted reluctantly. "It's hard to say, because it would never have happened."

"What—are you so perfect? Do you mean to tell me that while you were lounging about the Lido you didn't indulge in a single mild flirtation? Think, girl, think! Moonlight nights, tangos playing, sunburnt youths bending over you to—"

"And if I did flirt a little?" she interrupted defiantly. "Why not? It did me good and I knew just how far I could go."

"Exactly!" he cried in triumph. "You were sure of yourself, but not of Christopher—which proves my contention. Even now you are afraid this flutter of his went deeper than your own harmless dalliances. More, you're green with jealousy lest another woman's charms were found superior to your own. Only you won't call it jealousy. No, like a child with its nose out of joint, you say to yourself, 'Well, then, I just won't play any more.' Once bit, twice shy. You daren't risk cheapening yourself. No, let me go on. Did you by chance inform Christopher of these innocent flirtations?"

"Certainly. I always told him that sort of thing."

"Well, don't look so confounded virtuous about it. Your motive's nothing to be proud of. You did it to enhance your value in his eyes, and would not have been sorry to make him as miserable as he made you. Be honest."

"Perhaps I felt justified," she answered after a pause.

"You wanted to punish him because he'd shown himself a trifle too subservient to his mother? Ah, you see I've got the right dope on it, haven't I? Maybe he didn't take a proper stand. Maybe for your own sake he was unwilling to subject you to hardship. No matter which it was, you considered him weak, and let him see it—a fatal error in tactics, let me tell you. A clever girl like you ought to know how dangerous it is to injure any man in his self-esteem. You were asking for trouble, and you got it. Yes, I mean it. I hold you responsible, *you*, not for Dorinda's death—that you couldn't have prevented—but for all the rest of this ghastly mess. You've not seen that former lover of yours, have you? You ought to. He looks like the hero of a dozen Heidelberg duels—all on your account. Now what have you got to say to that?"

Hoisting himself in bed, Tommy fixed her with a baleful glare.

"You," he thundered. "You, with your intolerance, your petty self-righteousness, your unequal standards of honour—you have done all this. You're one of those fine, good girls who ought to be thrashed. If I were feeling more fit, I'd volunteer for the job."

She had been staring at him with stunned amazement. Her eyes had begun to flash blue-green sparks, but now they clouded with tears.

"Don't, don't," she implored in a stricken voice. "As though I ever forgot for one moment the trouble I've caused! You, that poor Frenchman—Christopher, too . . . Oh, I can't bear it! And I dare say what you think of me is quite true. One doesn't see these things till it's too late."

She hid her face. Tommy's expression softened, but his voice retained its sternness.

"Well," he said briskly, "don't snivel. How about reparations?"

She grew very still, her shoulders stiffening.

"No," she whispered. "If it's Christopher you mean, I—I can't do anything. You just don't understand, that's all. Something broke in me. I can't mend it. I'm sorry."

"You couldn't, as you once said, paint another picture over the old canvas?"

"No."

"Not even if it's a very fine canvas?"

She shook her head. Tommy sighed again and carefully restoked his pipe.

"Then," he remarked philosophically, "that's that. To me you may seem hard—as hard as granite; but I may be wrong."

"I'm not hard! Oh, Tommy, I'm not, I'm not!"

"As you say—but I can't help feeling devilish sorry for Loughton. After all, he's saved my life at imminent risk of his own, chanced getting chucked out of a career, and cut loose from a comfortable home to pig it in rooms where the drains are probably bad. Point is, what does he get out of it? But there—we'll speak of something else."

However it seemed impossible to continue the conversation. In strained silence Dinah smoothed out her gloves, while the scarlet of her cheeks faded slowly. The clock ticked; and then, history repeating itself, the nurse came in to announce Helen Roderick.

"Poor old Helen," murmured Tommy, glancing from Dinah to the huge sheaf of pink tiger-lilies laid upon his bed. "Mustn't be hard on her. She'd poured out our story to Jethro before I ever cautioned her to hold her tongue. She meant no harm."

"I know," agreed Dinah shortly. "But I can't see her—yet."

She quickly dabbed powder on her nose, straightened her hat and prepared to slip away.

"Where are you off to?"

"To see some editors and try to land a few orders. I've still got my living to make, you know."

"Offices'll be closed now. Pop into the lounge till Helen's gone, then come back and have a bite with me."

"Sure you want me?" she asked uncertainly. "Well, then, I'll wait."

When she had gone the invalid drew meditatively on his pipe and bestowed a seraphic smile on Helen's floral offering. The latter had a penitential look. . . .

Dinah walked dispiritedly into the lounge. In the fading light she did not at first recognise the tall, rigid-backed figure stationed by the window, and when the head turned and two haggard brown eyes surveyed her out of a lean face criss-crossed with red her heart pounded to suffocation. Christopher! She half-retreated, then getting a grip on herself went forward to meet him. At the same time his distant manner confirmed the unconfessed conviction which all along had stood between her and capitulation. She said to herself that he was sorry, ashamed, anxious to atone, but that he no longer loved her. Still, sore and chastened from her recent scolding, she summoned all her courage to acquit herself creditably.

"I'm glad we've met," she said, holding out her hand with a show of spontaneousness. "I'd wanted to see you and to ask if—you're getting all right."

"Oh, quite, thanks." He touched the healing scars as though to remind himself of their existence. "I got off rather lightly, as it happened."

She swallowed, wishing her heart would stop behaving in so stupid a fashion.

"And about—other things," she began again. "Has this wretched business hurt your prospects very much?"

"I'm sorry, in a way, that it hasn't," he replied conventionally. "Although I'd have hated for you to think of that, one way or the other. It's too unimportant. Actually, it's meant a good break for me. They're sending me to Vienna."

"Vienna!" She caught her breath. "But that's what you were longing for, isn't it? How splendid! I am glad. After being so unhappy over dragging you into all this. . . ."

"Dragging me?" he echoed incredulously. "What about yourself? I'm nothing."

"I deserved all I got. The rest of you didn't. I can't get over that."

"What absolute rubbish! You'd better not let Rostetter hear you say anything of the kind."

"Tommy?" She laughed waveringly. "Oh, you don't know how he regards my conduct. I love him dearly, but he's got the lowest sort of opinion of me. He's told me so."

Christopher took in only part of this speech. Of course, she loved Rostetter. Why not? He braced himself, and the effort at control made his voice colder than before.

"I shouldn't lose any sleep over what he thinks of you. He's one in a thousand . . . but so are you, and he knows it. I'd like to wish you both happiness. From the bottom of my heart."

Her lips parted.

"Why, what on earth are you talking about? Tommy Rostetter and me—? You seriously suppose we—Oh, but it's too, too silly for words!"

She laughed again uncontrollably, and to her intense annoyance felt tears welling into her eyes.

"Good-bye," she said brusquely. "I'm in rather a hurry."

"Dinah!"

He caught her hand in a tight, awkward clasp. She tore it away, chagrined to discover that his touch could still send through her the almost frightening thrills she had experienced at their first meeting. The Embassy Ball . . . *Miss Virginia*, played on dulcet horns . . . she steeled herself. Let her get away quickly, before she was fooled into imagining the old rapture could be renewed. . . .

His hands pinioned her shoulders.

"You mean you're not going to marry him either?" he demanded in a low voice.

"Certainly not. The whole idea's ridiculous."

Her flippant tone quenched the flare within him, yet as he saw how small but how independent she looked in her little close-fitting blue frock, his arms ached to crush her to him.

"Dinah," he said roughly, "I shan't crawl to you again. Weeks ago I told you I'd never cared for any one but you. It was true then and it's true now. If you think me such a hopeless rotter you can't overlook what happened, just say so, and that'll finish it. Only as this may be our last meeting it's best to know at once and for all."

"I don't think you're a rotter at all, Chris. God knows I never did."

"Prove it, then. Prove it, by coming with me to Vienna. It'll be hard going, I promise you, because I'm not taking a penny from my mother, but if you're equal to that—"

"Equal to it! Was it ever money I wanted?"

"You'll have everything else."

She dared not raise her eyes to the scars for which she was answerable. In her ears sounded the words Tommy had spoken about the folly of damaging a man's self-esteem. Was Tommy a wizard? But this was sheer weakness! Chris didn't love her. How could he? Yet, if this lump of ice in her breast went on melting . . . She saw the buttons on his coat through a blurred mist, and when his arms, strong and hard, closed round her, she had no strength left to resist.

"Dinah?"

His lips were on hers. Her head swam and her trembling fingers found the back of his tawny head and stroked it. Too choked for speech, they clung blindly together, feeding the starvation of their souls. The room grew dark but they had no need of light.

Across the corridor, Tommy drew his watch from beneath his crumpled pillows, opened wide eyes at sight of the time and rang for the nurse.

"Lay for three," he ordered, and knocked the ashes from his pipe.

THE END